THE SLEEPLESS

LIAM BELL

First published September 2023 by Fly on the Wall Press
Published in the UK by
Fly on the Wall Press
56 High Lea Rd
New Mills
Derbyshire
SK22 3DP

www.flyonthewallpress.co.uk
ISBN: 9781915789105
Copyright Liam Bell © 2023

For my girls, with love.

PROLOGUE

The disciples stood facing the platform, with their faces upturned. Sweat glistened on their foreheads, the armpits of their white robes grew slick and pungent. They were waiting, as Liz was, for Swami Ravi to emerge.

She watched the dust swirl and settle. Liz had put sheets over the entrances and newspaper over the wire-mesh windows, but still it found a way inside. The room wasn't the sterile one Ravi asked for, but she hoped he would focus only on the stage beneath the spotlight – the taped-down plastic sheeting and sparkling instruments laid out on their tray.

He emerged from the shadows. As he strode onto the platform, heads flicked sideways to follow him and there was the sound of breath catching in multiple throats. Liz closed her eyes. It was her favourite noise in the world, the collective gasp at the very sight of Ravi.

"Dear ones," came his familiar voice. "We have sacrificed much these past days and weeks, our adherence to the methods has been strong and we have lived the life of the wakeful. You are to be congratulated."

Liz opened her eyes and murmured her thanks along with the others.

"But…it is not enough. We know this. This project is not to wrestle some sleep back, not to be content with saying that we have seen the error of that habit. Our teaching is not that we can survive on less sleep, friends. No, no. We are aiming for the life of the truly wakeful."

His dark, curled hair was slicked back from his face. Liz tried to have it trimmed every fortnight or so, but Ravi didn't like to sit still. Even now, he paced the platform as he spoke, his heel squeaking against the plastic sheet as he turned.

"In my conversations with the so-called experts," he said, "a common critique emerges of my methods, yes? I have told you this before. This is what they say — it'll mess you up, they say. And why? Because of these toxins. Even the chemistry of our bodies has grown reliant on sleep. Whilst we are unconscious our brain cleanses itself for the new day..."

He stopped, abruptly, and turned so that he was facing his audience. As always, Liz felt he was staring directly at her, talking to her and her only. A flush blossomed across her neck, quite separate from the prickling heat of the room.

"We lose seven or eight hours a night," he hissed slowly, "to a fucking clean-up operation. Think what we could do with that time. Think what we could achieve, friends, if we were able to drain those toxins. Like extracting pus from a wound, yes, and leaving only clean blood..."

He extended an arm out to the side of the stage. The Sleepless craned their necks forwards, peered into the shadows. Only a select few knew it would be Max. He was an unremarkable man with thinning blond hair and a tension at the shoulders like a permanent shrug. He'd been diligent in following the methods, though, and eager to volunteer.

Ravi welcomed him with an embrace. Then he took him by his hunched shoulders and positioned him right in the centre, facing out. Liz studied his face for signs of fear and doubt, but his mouth was slack and eyes glazed. They'd added something extra to his tea that morning.

Ravi fitted the long, silver drill-bit. It was the one Liz would have chosen: not thin enough to snap and with a small, sharp point at the end of it. She had been careful with cleaning that one.

Once it was secure, Ravi stepped forward. He laid a hand on the back of Max's head and, with the other, brought the drill up to rest on his forehead, between the eyes, an inch or so above the line of the eyebrows. Max's eyes swivelled up, but his arms remained by his side and he continued to breathe shallowly and steadily.

"You are the vanguard, dear one," Ravi said.

There was a pause. And then Ravi's finger moved down onto the trigger of the drill. He started slowly so the noise of it was like a murmuring. As he pressed it in, though, it raised in pitch and became a whine and then a squeal. Liz looked at Ravi's arms. The muscles were straining with the effort, the hand at the back of Max's head pushing forward towards the drill. She looked, then, at Max's face. It was contorted into a silent scream – eyes popping, mouth stretched, jawbone shuddering. And as the drill screeched, his voice rose to meet it with an unholy noise that was a mangled, garbled, cacophony of vowel sounds and curse words, reminiscent of wild animals fighting in the nighttime. The kind of sound that can be made in ecstasy. And then Ravi's arm jerked, seemed to punch forward slightly. The drill went silent and so did Max. He slumped forward into Ravi's arms. The drill was still lodged, at an angle, in his forehead. And the liquid that trailed from the tip was not the steady amber trickle of toxin that they had hoped for, but the familiar, knotted glistening of blood.

Liz clutched a fistful of her robe. Maybe if she stripped off and ran forward with it then she could stem the flow? Perhaps they could get him to a discreet doctor or leave him on a hospital concourse? But the bleeding was too much, it was already too late.

Ravi let Max fall to the plastic sheeting. He stood looking down, his back turned to the audience and his shoulders slumped. Liz knew how bitterly disappointed he would be.

To draw a breath in the thick, stagnant air of that room felt impossible, never mind to make a noise. And yet, from somewhere towards the back, came the faint gulping sound of sobbing. A single disciple indulging themselves.

Ravi's head snapped up. He turned, eyes blazing. Stepping over Max, he peered out into the dimness of the room.

"Don't *cry*," he snapped, "don't fucking cry. When we talk of this in the years to come, we won't focus on his failings, you understand? We will not note that he flinched as the procedure took place, or that he cheated and released the toxins with micro-sleeps and restful moments alone...

We will remember him as the one who paved the way for the next disciple. For the one who will be pure and follow my teachings to the letter. Somewhere – in this room or out there in the world – that disciple is watching what we have done today, is listening more precisely to what I have said, and is preparing themselves to follow in this unfortunate's footsteps.

Our task is clear, friends. We need to be patient and wait for them to show themselves..."

BOOK ONE

1

Five minutes before he was due on air, Grafton brewed tea in his favourite mug. The one his son had made with SAT NAV stencilled on the side. A wee joke; an affectionate nickname. He gulped from it while checking last-minute motorway snarl-ups and train cancellations for his traffic report.

He tipped the mug to get the dregs and felt the wet slap of the teabag against his lips. He'd forgotten to fish the bugger out. No matter, the extra caffeine would get him through drivetime. Friday rush-hour was always a busy one.

He put his headphones on and listened to the live feed from the studio:

"And where is the commune?"

The voice in the cans was Kathy, presenter of the afternoon talk show. There was silence for a moment, but with the soft static of breathing. Grafton checked his own mic, but he was definitely still muted.

"Ardnamurchan. As far west as you can go," the caller said to Kathy.

Grafton looked at the traffic map on his screen. There was never any congestion on the roads up there, although there was the odd accident. It was a good four or five hours from Glasgow, out on enough of a limb that even tourists rarely ventured there.

"Lovely part of the world," Kathy said. "Where in Ardnamurchan?"

"Can't be specific. Not yet."

"Oh. And you're trying to live a more frugal life, is that it?"

"You're not listening, Kathy."

The caller was a young woman, with an accent that was hard to place; somewhere way up north, maybe, or from out in the Hebrides. She spoke quietly, carefully. There was another pause.

"We believe," she said, "that society conditions us to sleep. It keeps us docile and prevents us from reaching our full potential. Humans need no more than two or three hours, beyond that we're only doping ourselves into...acqua-acque-acquiescence."

"I see," Kathy said. "Like Margaret Thatcher then?"

"Pardon?"

"She only slept four hours a night, didn't she?"

"You're trivialising it, Kathy. We follow the teachings of Swami Ravi, who tells us that there is tyranny in the alarm clock and that exhaustion comes not from a lack of sleep but from the absence of being fully awake."

Grafton reached forward and slid up the volume in his headset. He placed his hands against the headphones and listened intently. Again, there was the sound of the caller's breathing, with the slightest catch on the inhale.

"Well it sounds fascinating," Kathy said, "but we'll have to move on—"

"With the coming challenges," the caller said, "sleep will be a luxury we can't afford."

"Strong opinions—"

"It's up to each of us to break the stranglehold of mindless routine."

"—but it's about time to go across and get an update from the traffic and travel desk."

"Wakefulness is watchfulness."

"Traffic and travel."

Another pause. Grafton listened for the inhale-catch-exhale of the caller's breath, but it had gone.

"Grafton?" the producer's voice in his ear.

Shit. Dead air. He grabbed for his papers and stabbed at the mute button.

"Sorry Kathy," he said. "We'll start with the ferries, shall we?"

"Sounds like you nodded off yourself there...?" Kathy said. She tried to trill off a wee laugh, but he could tell she was needled.

"Just intrigued," Grafton said, with a chuckle. His levels were all off. He slid the volume down and leant in towards the microphone. "High winds have claimed a number of crossings from Oban..."

After his report, Grafton rose from the desk and made his way into the producer's booth. Danny didn't like interruptions mid-show, but Kathy was deep into a chat with some new synth-pop duo so Grafton decided to risk it.

"Sorry for that," he said. "Missed the link."

"Not like you." Danny kept his eyes on the console.

"Aye."

"Ach, we were early coming to you anyway. Shouldn't have let the nutjob on."

Grafton nodded, but didn't leave the booth. Danny was in his mid-thirties, a good two decades younger than Grafton, but he'd risen through the station hierarchy as quickly as he'd lost his hair. Only wisps and tufts of it remained, shaved short.

"Do we know anything else about that caller? The last one?"

"The nutjob?" Danny shrugged. "She called for the discussion on the climate crisis and some fucking idiot who should know better—" he pointed a thumb up at himself, "—let her on the air."

Grafton nodded. He knew Danny's attention would only remain on him for a short time. The segment was nearly at an end. It was now or never. This was the first lead he'd had for years.

"Could we do a follow-up?" he asked.

"On her?" Danny screwed up his face. "On that commune?"

"Aye, on both. Could we go up there and investigate for a feature, maybe, for Kathy's show or…"

"Ach, Grafton—"

"A podcast series, maybe, if you think it's better."

"And when you say we…?"

"I mean me, I guess. I have some experience in that area, you know."

He had no idea if Danny knew what had happened with Liz, his ex-wife, but it seemed likely that he'd have heard at least the echoes of gossip. He was less likely to know that Grafton had a folder on his laptop with files and links to news stories on Swami Ravi and his teachings.

"Sorry buddy." Danny rocked back in his seat. "We're tight enough running the usual show and you're…well…better to stick with things as they are."

Grafton nodded slowly, his teeth set together until it seemed he could feel every crown, every filling.

"Sorry, really I am."

"Just an idea, Danny, no worries."

Grafton turned to the door and Danny hooked his headphones back over his ears.

Once he was on the other side of the glass, Grafton stood and stared at the red light of the On Air sign. It hadn't been Liz's voice on the call, he was certain of that, but if that Ravi character was involved then she wouldn't be far behind. And, after eight years, Grafton reckoned he was entitled to answers. In that time, her only communication had been a yearly postcard to wish their son, Isaac, a happy birthday. The cards were postmarked Jaipur, Pune, Malta, and Zurich. She'd missed a year, then another two from Jaipur and one from Vienna. That had arrived only a few months ago. And now there was the possibility that she'd settled a few hours up the road without even letting them know that she was back in the country.

If his online research was anything to go by, there was a story in there too. He was sure he was right – in his gut – about that. And, in this day and age, you didn't need a radio station behind you, did you? His phone would do the trick for recording. He'd take a week of annual leave and travel out to Ardnamurchan for a busman's holiday. To hell with Danny. Journalism didn't have to be a young man's game, he still knew how to chase down a story. He'd get some answers from Liz and expose this Swami Ravi charlatan at the same time – two birds, one stone.

2

Friday night was pizza night. Grafton stopped off at the place on Clarence Drive. But when the guy behind the counter asked if he wanted his usual, Grafton found himself shaking his head. Instead, he ordered two baked potatoes with tuna and cheese.

With the plastic bag dangling from his fingers, he walked back to the flat. Isaac wouldn't be happy with the change in menu, but even he would have to admit that they were in a rut – in a mindless routine – with the steady succession of unhealthy takeaway food.

Isaac was nestled in the corner of the sofa, with the laptop open on his knees. The wrestling was on the muted telly. It had been a constant backdrop to their lives, especially through the lockdowns. Isaac had dug up recordings of old Wrestlemanias and half-watched them like other folk did with the news channels. A hell of a thing for a seventeen-year-old to be fixated on, Grafton thought, but Isaac argued that it was part of his artistic process. His sketches and clay moulds were spread out across the dining table behind the sofa.

"Evening Sat Nav," Isaac said. "Good day?"

"Hi son. Aye, fine."

"What's this?"

It hadn't taken him long to notice the absence of pizza. The Friday night tradition stretched back years. Since Liz left. In those early months, it had perhaps been the most consistent part of Grafton's parenting.

"Thought we should go healthier," Grafton said. "Baked potato."

"You know potatoes don't count as one of your five-a-day, right?"

"Cheeky git." Grafton threw the bag down onto his son's stomach, so that Isaac flinched and the laptop toppled to the cushions. Grafton pointed down at it. "Could I look something up, while you have that open?"

"Aye, what you after?"

Isaac passed the computer across and Grafton sat on the arm of the sofa. He typed in a search for the sleepless commune up in Ardnamurchan, then he braced himself; Isaac was an expert at sniffing out opportunities to be scathing.

"Young woman called Kathy's show today," Grafton said, "from some collective out on the west coast who don't believe in sleep."

Isaac had lifted one of the Styrofoam containers from the bag. He opened it, wrinkled his nose and shook his head. "If I say I don't believe in jacket potatoes, can I get a pizza?"

Grafton smiled, but didn't answer. He was looking at the laptop. There were one or two articles about the commune, mostly about the disruption they'd caused local residents. The followers themselves didn't seem to have any web presence. It was only at the bottom of a forum that Grafton found the address – a series of abandoned holiday chalets outside Kilchoan.

He turned to show Isaac and realised that his son was staring at the wrestling on the telly. He still hadn't touched his potato or, in fact, done anything except for twitching his face into a frown.

"Is this about Mum?" Isaac asked, quietly.

"What?"

"Is this something to do with her…?"

Jesus, nothing got past Isaac. Must have got his brains from the maternal side. All the same, he knew next to nothing about where his mum had ended up or the teachings she followed. Only what was in those postcards – the odd mention of Ravi, or just 'R', and the regular flitting back-and-forth between India and Southern Europe.

"Oh, buddy, no," Grafton said, deciding on denial. "It's a story. For the station."

"You're the travel guy."

"I used to do stories, Isaac, don't forget. It's not—" He cleared his throat. "There's a story there, I'm telling you."

"Would you be so interested if it wasn't for Mum, though?"

Grafton paused and thought about what to tell him. It was rare that they spoke about Liz. It was about routine, again. They'd made their peace, individually, with the fact that she'd left and there seemed little point in wasting their breath on the whys and wherefores. Sure, Grafton spent the occasional evening trawling through webpages in search of a breadcrumb trail that led back to her and Ravi, but he had always kept his son insulated from that.

It was different for Isaac. He'd find it difficult to remember a time when his mum was living with them, when communication from her was more than the occasional postcard. Grafton had seen Liz leaving as more of a drift, but for Isaac it had been an abrupt departure.

Grafton was near-forty when they met and her energy seemed to strip the years from him. She was impulsive, but endearingly so. She had these wide brown eyes that were always flickering from one side of a room to the other and when she smiled – or frowned – there wasn't a muscle in her face that wasn't involved.

Her desire for a child only seemed an extension of Grafton's run of luck. He'd resigned himself to the idea that the best he would manage was a puppy, so this younger, beautiful woman wanting to start a family with him was like a lottery win from a forgotten ticket.

The warning signs were there, though. He'd leave her painting her toenails on the sofa and return to find her up a ladder painting the living room walls. She'd suggest taking a long weekend away and come back from the travel agent's with brochures for round-the-world cruises.

The full radiance of Liz's attention shifted from Grafton to baby Isaac and they all muddled through. Liz was on maternity leave from her nursing role at the hospital, and Grafton was picking up enough commissions to get by. Sure, it itched at him that he had to pass up some opportunities because Liz needed her spells away, her solitary time, but staying at home with the baby was tiring and she needed to recharge. She was an introvert, she told him, even though all evidence pointed to the opposite.

It was when Isaac was six or seven that Liz started to go travelling abroad. Working on the wards, but willing to rearrange shifts and take annual leave so she could have a break in Paris or a weekend in Berlin. Her son was well settled in school, after all, and Grafton could do the pick-ups. She'd always wanted to see Sri Lanka, always wondered about Vietnam. Then, when Isaac was nine, she went to India for a week. Two months later they had received the first postcard.

"This is just a really good story," Grafton said, finally, smiling across to Isaac. "Promise."

"Is it a radio thing, then, or print?" Isaac asked.

Grafton shrugged. "I'm going to go up there for a few days to find out more."

"Jesus."

"I'll write it up as an article and as a programme idea and pitch it around. If it's what I think it is then someone'll be interested."

"Aye, get the Rolodex out, is it?"

Grafton swatted a hand at his son's knee, but Isaac jerked it away. On the telly, a wrestler jumped from the corner of the ring – from the top rope – twisted in the air and brought his opponent down to the canvas in a headlock. Grafton looked across at the table, to the sculpture Isaac was working on: a wrestler carved from the shoulders up, face contorted, as bulging, disembodied arms wrapped around his neck in a chokehold.

"You're taking me driving this weekend," Isaac said. "Don't forget. And it's my exhibition show at college next Friday afternoon."

Grafton felt a wince of irritation in his chest, but he was fairly certain he kept it off his face. He'd completely forgotten his promise to take Isaac out in the car. But he didn't mind, not really.

"I'll leave on Monday," he said. "Probably for the best – gives me time to prepare."

"And you'll be back for the exhibition?"

"Course I will, Hockney."

Isaac nodded and leant across to the coffee table. He lifted one of the potatoes, in its container, and handed it to Grafton.

"Now that you're done researching," he said, "you might want to take a sniff of that…"

Grafton lifted the lid. "Bloody hell!" He didn't need to put his nose to it, the smell was rancid even from a distance. "How did the lad in the shop not smell that?"

Isaac grinned. "No one gets tuna on a pizza, do they? It's probably been sitting out for weeks."

"Bloody hell."

Isaac took the Styrofoam container off him and walked through to the kitchen. Grafton heard the bin lid, then a drawer opening and closing. When Isaac came back through he had a handful of takeaway menus in his hand. He threw them down onto Grafton's chest.

"I'm not sure any of these places will do a quinoa salad," Grafton said, with a grin.

"Learn your lesson, old man."

3

Liz noted the brocade curtains at the bay windows, tied back with a royal blue sash, and the ornate cornicing around the ceiling. The carpet felt thick beneath the thin soles of her slip-on shoes, and soft orchestral music played from a radio in the corner. Ravi would have said something about opulence and ostentatious wealth, about possessions encouraging sloth.

On a mahogany side-table, beside a vase of white lilies, was a notepad and pen embossed with the British Embassy logo. Liz pocketed the pen but left the paper. Then she moved over to the standard lamp and flicked it off. Ravi would say it was decadent to have artificial light when enough sunlight was angling in.

There were four seats to choose from: an armchair large enough to serve as a carriage; two wingback chairs with tasselled trim; and a small sofa with plumped-up cushions. Liz considered each of them in turn. Maybe if she took the cushions off the sofa? Or sat upright in the armchair? No, none of them would do. She would sink in, she would be lost. Instead, she moved back over to the side-table and lifted off the notepad and vase. She set them carefully down on the carpet. Then she hoisted herself up to sit on the table. She drew her legs up, folded them into a basket like a child at school assembly, and rearranged the pleats of her skirt.

She didn't know if she'd come far enough. It had been a ten-hour drive, through Slovenia, but maybe she should have continued further than Budapest. Maybe Swami Ravi's name would still be greeted with suspicion here; those doctored arrest warrants would probably show up on their system. She didn't want to drive too far east though, because she'd be heading back west afterwards.

"Ms Whelan?"

The young man was as carefully crafted as the wingback chairs. His suit was tailored to the point that a good meal would strain the stitches and his smile was as polished as his shoes. He showed the smile for only a second, then he caught sight of her up on the side-table.

"Oh, um, that's not actually for sitting on."

"It was where I was most comfortable."

He considered this. A hand went up to his hair and swept it to the side. "Not to worry," he said, smiling again. "Won't you come with me?"

Liz followed him through double-doors and up a gently curving staircase. She avoided making eye-contact with the men in military uniforms who studied her from the portraits on the walls.

"You require an emergency travel document, I understand?" the young man said, as he ushered her into an office at the top of the stairs. His desk was also mahogany, sturdier-looking than the side-table, and he had another of the small cushioned sofas, along with more cornicing and brocade curtains.

"An emergency passport, yes," Liz said.

"Indeed. We don't refer to it as that, generally."

"Why not?"

"Well...erm..." He sat down and held out a hand to a wooden chair on the other side of the desk. "It isn't a replacement for a passport, strictly speaking, and it does need to be tied to concrete travel plans."

Liz nodded. She flashed him a smile of her own and moved over to the window. Natural light. There was a window seat and a potted plant beside it.

"What's this plant, do you know?" she asked.

"I'm not sure on that, sorry."

"It's not plastic, though?"

"If it is, it's been a mistake to have been watering it all these years."

His joke hung in the air for a moment. Liz had long ago given up worrying about laughing at the right times, following the right social cues. That type of anxiety, that fixation on niceties, led only to exhaustion. You need to channel your energy. There are more important things.

She closed her eyes, felt the sunlight through the window. Yes, this was the position. She opened her eyes and sat herself down on the window seat.

The man cleared his throat and wheeled his chair across a touch, out from behind the desk, so that he could see her around the long leaves of the plant.

"You're going back to Britain, are you, Ms Whelan?"

"Yes, I have a car."

"Ok, right you are. And you'd get the ferry or use the tunnel, would you?"

Liz turned to look out of the window. The gardens below had quite an exotic array of plants and trees; the British imperial project in miniature. Then there were high stone walls, with cameras facing outwards onto the grey streets of Budapest.

"I'll put that down," the man said, turning to his desk. "Do you have a form of identification?"

Liz sewed her own skirts. Long ones with plenty of pockets. She reached into a pocket now and drew out the sheet of folded paper Ravi had given her. He'd smiled and told her it was a key to be used to open doors.

She held the letter out to the consular official. He looked up from what he was writing and wheeled his chair across to take it from her. She watched his face as he unfolded it and read. There was a flicker there, yes, the slightest blanch. He was public-school, so he quickly smoothed it over, but he had recognised Swami Ravi's name. Liz felt a small satisfaction that his fame had travelled so far, but it was tempered by the knowledge that this man would only have been fed the official line.

"This letter doesn't actually tell us much," he said. "This gentleman doesn't have the authority to request that his adherents are given safe passage."

Liz smiled. In the coming years, a letter with an instruction from Swami Ravi would be more valuable than anything these people had left in their vaults.

"We'll have to make enquiries," the man said. "Verify your identity, you understand."

"Perfectly."

"The whole process will take two days." His forehead creased into a frown. "At least."

Liz nodded. She wasn't worried about time. That was only an imposed construct, used to train citizens into a day-week-month pattern of drudgery.

"I'll wait," she said, and drew her legs up onto the window seat. It really was just the right position, with the sunlight and the firm wooden seat and the potted plant to the side.

"You can't stay there, though." The young official swivelled in his chair, first one way then the other. He looked at the papers on his desk, then at the door.

"Don't worry, I won't bother you."

"No, but…" The man looked again at the door. "You can't sleep here."

Liz smiled. "I won't."

4

On Monday morning, Grafton packed up his little black hatchback. He didn't want to wake his son, so he left the last of his cash where he was sure Isaac would find it and made a mental note to text him the login to book a supermarket delivery. Then Grafton headed out of Glasgow on the road towards Loch Lomond. In his rucksack he'd opted for the bare minimum: two changes of underwear, a stick of deodorant, toothbrush, extra t-shirt and a woolly jumper.

As he drove the twisting, fast road beside the loch, Grafton thought over his cover story once again. He'd always found that the best lies held at least a nugget of truth within them. So, he was a single dad – no need to mention that Isaac was practically an adult – who was struggling to juggle parenthood and the pressures of work. That was where the fib came in, because he couldn't tell them about the radio station, so he'd decided to tell them he was a teacher. Of course, if Liz was there then the cover story would come unravelled within minutes, but it would surely be enough to get him over the threshold.

It had been a long time since he'd driven through Glencoe. No scenery more Scottish than these mountains, with the road carving through the middle of them. And the way the slabs of shadow moved across the steep rises on either side – sweeps of green and brown turning slate grey in an instant. The higher the road climbed the more persistent the drizzle became, but the mist didn't drift down from the summits.

There had been a summer, Grafton remembered, when Liz had taken a notion to go hill-walking, with Isaac in the baby-carrier. Grafton would have started with a hill out in Stirlingshire, but only a Munro would do for Liz, so they'd travelled all the way up to Glencoe. They made it to the first ridge, before stopping and opening the thermos of coffee. Grafton and Isaac had turned back for the car, but Liz had carried on towards the peak. It was dark by the time she returned.

On the other side of Glencoe was the Corran ferry, to take him across to the Ardnamurchan peninsula. Only a small boat, with a smell of diesel and a surly lad in a hi-vis taking the money. It gave Grafton a chance to get out of the stale air of the car, though, and stand in the stiffening wind; strong enough to water the eyes and catch at your breath. He watched the outline of the inn at Ardgour getting closer and closer, sharpening into whitewashed walls with black-framed windows.

As he drove off the ferry, he felt the first twist of nerves in his stomach. That beautiful hit of adrenaline which is half-fear and half-anticipation. He hadn't felt it – not really – in years. He flicked down the shade against the low sun and looked at the clipping he'd tucked in there the day before. His last by-line, from seven years ago: an investigation into a middle-aged publican playing at being Al Capone in a small Ayrshire town.

For years, Isaac had called his dad Sat Nav. He'd struggle to remember him as anything other than the travel guy on the radio, he'd never seen what his dad was truly capable of. Especially because the traffic beat through the pandemic had been trimmed down to little more than a call-in service for key workers. And Isaac taking his own art seriously and planning on taking up a place at Glasgow School of Art next year was like a wee nudge, a dig in the ribs, for Grafton. A reminder that he used to have his own ambitions.

The roads on the peninsula were single-track and punctuated by the kind of blind summits that made your stomach lurch. Grafton wound down the window and breathed in the smell of the pine forests.

At the very least, this trip would tell Grafton if he still had it in him to be a journalist, even if he didn't find Liz or get answers to those questions. That was worth a few days out west. Even if the commune itself was nothing more than kids getting excited about staying up late – midnight feasts and truth or dare – a proper journalist would be able to spin that out into a story. The important thing was to get yourself in the middle of it and let it all unfurl.

Kilchoan was spread out along a meandering road that traced the curve of a bay. There was a pebbled beach with a single white rowboat aslant on a patch of seaweed, but it was hard to see where the centre of the village was. Grafton reached a junction with the churning sea in front of him, and had to choose which way to turn. Car idling, he craned his neck to look. There was a concrete pier to his right, the end of it visible in the receding tide. To his left was a large grey farmhouse, set imposingly high in a sheep-dotted field. Then he caught sight of a small sign nailed to a fence post on the shore side of the road. It was white-painted wood, no larger than a sheet of paper, with black letters stencilled across it: SHOP & POST. The arrow beneath pointed right.

He didn't encounter any other cars on the road along and an inspection of the handful of whitewashed houses told him only that net curtains were popular out here and that the salt-strewn gardens grew little beyond battered lobster creels. An aroma of peat-smoke drifted in through the air-vents.

The Pier Shop was a long, low white building with a single petrol pump outside. It had a view of the moorings opposite and, beyond that, the silhouette of Mull. Grafton pulled up in the tight turning circle and went inside to ask for directions.

There was a young lad, no more than fourteen, stacking shelves beside the door. He looked up and then quickly away as Grafton entered. Just like Isaac had been at that age, as though his skin was a touch too tight.

"Afternoon," Grafton said. "Do you know how I'd find my way to the commune?"

The boy looked down at the tin of peas in his hand and sighed. Deeply, as if the peas had broken his heart.

"Gran," he called out. "Another one for Seattle."

Grafton turned. From behind the counter at the back of the shop came a woman with close-cropped grey hair and dangling earrings. She rose more steeply on her right side than on her left when she walked; either a hip replaced or in need of replacing. This hirple set the earrings swinging wildly.

"My advice," she said, "for what it's worth, is to turn back to wherever you came from. Or, better yet, there's a hotel further up the road with comfy beds."

"It's the commune I'm interested in."

He stopped short of explaining his interest. It sounded like the locals had some opinions on it that might be worth hearing first, starting with that nickname the boy had used.

"Do you call it Seattle after that Meg Ryan film?" he asked, looking to the gran and then to the boy.

"You're a sharp one," the boy muttered.

"Manners," the gran said.

Grafton smiled, to show there were no hard feelings. He stepped closer to the gran and left the boy to resume his shelf-stacking.

"What do you make of it?" he asked. "Their ideas, I mean."

"Ideas?" She shook her head, earrings clacking. "There's no sense that comes out of that lot. Bunch of spoiled wee bairns is all they are, playing at zombies up on that hill. Treat this place like some Neolithic visitor centre."

"What d'you mean?"

"Eh?"

"Why a visitor centre?"

"Ach, they think we're some pure rural past, maybe, or we're backward enough to buy their snake oil, I don't know." She peered up at Grafton. "We're not as daft as we look, and we're definitely not as daft as you, if you're on your way up to join them."

She kept her gaze on him. Grafton didn't look away.

"So how do I get there?" he asked.

"Straight along the shore road. They're in the wooden chalets, on the left, that stretch up the hill. If you reach the kirk with the phone box outside then you've gone too far."

"Thank you."

"Word of advice?"

"Please."

"Buy yourself an apple or an orange before you leave. They seem to live on nothing but dried pasta and rice. Poor sods are kept awake by rickets, more than likely."

Grafton nodded. "I'll take one of each. And some indigestion tablets, if you have them."

"Smarter than you look," the woman replied.

5

The entrance to the commune was a wide sweep of pebble-strewn tarmac, up a slight incline. On the left was a wooden chalet with a hand-painted sign that said 'Office'. After parking, Grafton walked to the turn in the road to look up the hill. There were five buildings he could see – four log cabins and an A-frame. All the wood was stained the same shade of brown and the grass and gravel paths between the buildings looked well-tended.

"New arrival?"

He spun around. A man had come out of the office and was standing on the top step. He was in his twenties, maybe, with hollowed-out eyes and hair that had been unevenly shaved. The robe he wore had once been white but had yellowed under the armpits and greyed at the hem. It failed to mask how painfully skinny he was.

"Yes." Grafton smiled and held his hand up in a half-wave. "I'm Grafton."

"Eddie," he said. "But, that's – Grafton can't be your first name."

"No one uses my first name. At this point, I'm not sure I can even remember it."

Grafton grinned, but Eddie's smile was more like a wince.

He turned back towards the office and Grafton stood for a moment, nonplussed. Was he supposed to follow or wait? Had this Eddie character decided that if he didn't give his first name then he was refused entry? He wasn't entirely certain why he hadn't given it – there was just something about folk using his first name that caused him to set his teeth together; it had echoes of an earlier time in his life, it felt like a separate identity.

As the door swung shut behind Eddie, Grafton decided to follow. He'd not been told otherwise, after all. Climbing the steps, Grafton took his phone from his jacket pocket and started the voice recorder.

Inside, the office was spacious but sparsely furnished. There was only a desk, a wooden chair, and a metal filing cabinet. There was an ancient-looking desktop computer, but no sign of any other technology. On the floor was a worn grey rug. The only colour on it came from a wet patch over beside the window. It looked like an infected wound, ringed with rust-red and oil-spill purple. It wasn't clear if the moisture was seeping up from below or dripping down from above.

Eddie sat in the chair and Grafton was left standing. "Age?" Eddie asked.

"Fifty-seven."

Eddie had a single-sheet form. He filled it in with his tongue poking out through his teeth, like a toddler with crayons. Grafton readied himself to tell his cover story – widower, single dad, teacher, untapped potential. He didn't need even a word of it, though.

Eddie looked up, staring. "You're ready now?"

"Sorry?"

"For the–" He snapped his fingers a few times, rapidly. "Like orientation, but – erm–"

"Initiation?" Grafton asked, with a wee flutter of anxiety about what that word might mean, about what tasks or rituals might go along with it.

Eddie closed his eyes, shook his head.

"Induction?"

"Yes!" Eddie snapped his fingers again, but now he looked delighted. His smile showed a row of teeth that had the same yellow tinge as his robe. One of his incisors was dead, dull grey in colour.

"Is it you who does it?" Grafton asked.

"I'll start you off." Eddie sniffed. "Just with the basics."

Eddie looked down at his sheet. He shook his head slightly and picked up his pen again, but he didn't change anything on the form. He turned it over to look at the back. It was blank.

"We start with three questions," he said, "but I've only got two here."

"Ok. Maybe the third will come to you?"

There was a pause. Grafton watched Eddie's hand holding the paper. There was a tremor, a very slight but definite shaking. This young lad was nervous, it seemed, of being trusted with the induction. Grafton stood a little straighter and sized Eddie up. He was confident that, if it came to it, he could out-muscle the younger man.

"What does the induction involve?" he asked. "Is it based on Swami Ravi's teachings?"

Eddie frowned. "You know his teachings?"

"Well, I have a friend...an old friend...who travelled to learn from him in India. Maybe you know her? Liz Whelan, she's called. Elizabeth."

Eddie shook his head. With the pen, he gouged some dirt out from underneath his fingernail. It fell to the sheet of paper on the desk. He sat staring at it for a couple of seconds, as if wondering how it got there.

"Swami Ravi has good ideas," he said, finally, "but our way is better."

Grafton nodded. "So, his teachings are the basis for what you do, is that right?"

Eddie gave no answer. Instead, he stood abruptly. He came around to Grafton's side of the desk and reached out his hand to grip Grafton's shoulder. There was some dig in his fingers, more strength than you would have anticipated from looking at him.

"I'll show you some methods," he said, "then we'll go to the others in the A-frame."

This raised more questions than it answered, but Grafton decided to stay with it for now. He'd come this far, after all, and he hadn't found out enough. It didn't sound like Liz was here, but it was possible that she hadn't crossed paths with Eddie yet. Or that she was going by another name.

"Two questions," Eddie said, looking him in the eye. "The first is – how long are you staying for?"

"Until Thursday, maybe. I'm a teacher and I need to get back for–"

"Fine," Eddie interrupted. "And are you a policeman or a journalist?"

Grafton gave a laugh, then realised that it was too loud and too short, more a bark than a chuckle.

"I'm a teacher," he said, smiling. "Like I say."

"It's one of the questions."

"And the third one?" Grafton asked.

"What?"

"Did you remember the third question?"

Eddie looked back at the desk and frowned. He let go of Grafton and lifted the sheet of paper. He turned it over to the blank side again. He gazed at it for a moment before blinking and looking back up.

"What's your contribution?" he said.

"Sorry?"

"Your contribution."

Eddie was staring at Grafton now.

"You mean…" Grafton paused. "Well, I could help with cleaning and maintenance or, maybe, if there are children, I could help with the lessons…"

"No." Eddie shook his head. "No. What is your contribution. We will feed and clothe you, right?"

"Ah, I see."

In some ways, this was reassuring. It was easier to understand if it was all a grift. There was a simplicity to the whole thing if everyone had to demonstrate their sincerity by paying their way in. Although the thought struck Grafton: what had Liz's

31

contribution been when she first travelled to India?

"I have no cash," Grafton said, "but maybe folk could use my car for the time I'm here?"

Eddie shook his head. He was more assured now, his face set in a scowl and his arms folded across his chest.

"You have online banking?" he asked.

"Yes."

"Use the computer. Log in."

Grafton looked over at the desktop. He thought of scams he only vaguely understood: skimming and identity fraud, hackers and credit card cloning. He wished Isaac was there.

"I'll do it on my phone," Grafton said, pulling it out of his pocket and quickly closing down the voice recorder app. He opened the banking one instead.

"Fine," Eddie said, "but then the phone goes away, ok? No phones allowed."

Grafton nodded. Now he was into the app, he had no idea how much to give. He had been intending to take Isaac up north that summer, to celebrate him finishing college. Maybe it would need to be a camping trip rather than an Airbnb.

As he stood there, undecided, Eddie moved across to the desk and lifted a sheet of paper. He scribbled down the six digits of a sort code and eight of an account number, then handed it over.

There was a story here, Grafton was sure of it. Even if it was only about a few gullible souls being cheated out of their savings. Or a more personal piece about searching for his ex-wife. He could shop it around the papers and make his money back that way.

"I'll send three hundred, ok?" Grafton said.

"Whatever you can contribute."

"Two-fifty, then?"

"Three," Eddie said. Then he stepped over to the far side of the room. There was a door. Eddie beckoned to Grafton and opened it. Behind was a cupboard with several shelves of neatly-folded white fabric. Eddie reached up to the top and pulled out a robe. It looked cleaner than the one he was wearing, at least.

"Get changed," Eddie said.

"Here?"

"Where else?"

Grafton stood for a moment, considering. He wasn't especially shy about his body, beyond a bit of a gut and the odd tuft of greying hair, but the robe didn't seem to have any pockets. He looked down at his phone, with the confirmation screen from the banking app still showing.

"What do I do with my valuables?" he asked.

"We can keep them safe for you, here in the office."

"I'd rather lock them in my car, I think."

Eddie bit at his lip. "Fine, fine."

Grafton took the robe and stepped back outside. He clambered into the driver's seat and started to get himself changed. Eddie had followed him, but stopped on the steps of the office. Grafton thought back to taking Isaac to play football on Saturday mornings: young lads getting changed into their kits in the back of the car, leaving the smell of boot polish and Deep Heat behind them. Grafton used to stand alongside, staring off into the distance to give the boys their privacy. He looked up now and, sure enough, Eddie was looking anywhere except the little black hatchback.

He folded his jacket, t-shirt and jeans and placed them on the backseat. His wallet and housekeys went in the glovebox, but he kept his car-keys and his phone. He pulled on the linen robe – tight around the middle, but comfortable enough – and was relieved to find that the cuffs were elasticated. He tucked his phone in one sleeve. Then, just to be safe, he pulled his Dictaphone out of the glovebox and slipped it in his other sleeve. He climbed out of the car.

"Socks and shoes," Eddie said.

"What?"

"You won't need socks and shoes. We'll give you sandals if necessary."

Grafton looked down at the black plimsolls on Eddie's own feet, like a child's gym-shoes. They looked too big for his twiggy ankles. Grafton shrugged and placed his shoes and socks on the driver's seat before locking the car door.

"Back inside then," Eddie said.

Grafton followed him back into the chalet. He was aware of holding his arms slightly unnaturally, with the weight of the phone in one sleeve and the Dictaphone in the other, so he clasped his hands in front of himself. Isaac would laugh if he could see him, ask him why the fuck he was dressed as Jesus with short hair.

"Give me your keys," Eddie said, holding out his hand.

Grafton looked down at his car keys. "I'll keep them."

"You don't have pockets."

Grafton shrugged, conceding the point. He didn't want to draw attention to the elasticated sleeves. "I'll hold them," he said, instead.

"Give them to me."

Reluctantly, Grafton held out the keys. Eddie took them and hung them on a spare hook attached to the wall behind the desk. There were dozens of sets of keys there – none of them were marked or labelled.

Eddie gestured for him to follow. They moved to the back of the room and another wooden door. Beyond it was a small, dark room. There was a black-out blind on the window, so the only light came from the doorway itself. Grafton was worried that Eddie would shut it and they'd be in darkness, but he left it open. There was little in the room besides two straight-backed chairs, facing each other, and a small stool. In the corner, on the floorboards, was a kettle and various mugs.

"Have a seat," Eddie said, pointing to a chair. Grafton did as he was told.

Eddie suddenly dropped to the floor. There was a pause, and then he started to do a series of vigorous press-ups. He grunted between each one. After ten, he switched to sit-ups. Then star-jumps. All the while, he didn't say a word. Grafton watched, certain now that he'd under-estimated the young lad's strength; this work-out routine didn't seem to be straining him in the slightest.

"Method one," Eddie said, when he was finally still. "Callisthenics."

Grafton could only nod.

"I'll show you three methods for now, but they're only introductory." Eddie breathed deeply. "There are more advanced methods we can show you if – well – once you're sure about joining."

"Stupid question," Grafton said, half-raising his hand before realising the absurdity. "Three methods for what?"

"For wakefulness," Eddie replied. He moved over to the kettle in the corner and crouched to set it boiling. Then he lifted a small jam jar. He carried it over and handed it to Grafton. "Take a sniff."

Grafton unscrewed the lid and smelled the contents of the jar. It looked and smelt like a spice mix: more Italian seasoning than Indian spicing, but with a hint of chilli or paprika in there. He handed the jar back to Eddie and raised his eyebrows. Eddie grinned.

"Gives you a wee jolt of energy," he said.

He moved back over to the kettle and spooned some of the mixture into two cups. Grafton wondered if there was anything in the jar other than tea and herbs, but he held back from asking. In the time it took for the kettle to boil, he had a choice to make: trust Eddie enough to drink this strange concoction; or turn tail and get out of there with the opening of a story about a cult that spent their nights doing push-ups and drinking the contents of the spice rack. Was this how Liz filled her days? Was it this odd mix of Eighties aerobics and pagan tea that had convinced her to leave her family?

"What's the third method?" Grafton asked Eddie.

Eddie poured the boiling water into the cups before answering. He stirred one of them and brought it over to Grafton. The steam rising off it smelt a little like masala chai but also a little like the mud and foliage experiments Isaac used to mix together in the park when he was a toddler. Something in it caught at the back of Grafton's throat and he had to gulp to stop himself from gagging.

"In every room," Eddie said, "is a music player and headphones. The volume is set as high as it can go. You listen to it in thirty second bursts."

"What's the music?"

Eddie sat down in the chair opposite, taking a drink from his own mug. "All sorts. You never know if you're going to get acid jazz or death metal."

"Right."

So far, harmless. Grafton was finding it hard not to be disappointed. The Sleepless were staying awake with exercise, loud music and a homemade tea-blend. Hardly a scandal. And hardly the illuminating, life-altering experience that might encourage you to abandon your child. As Grafton raised the mug to his lips, he was almost hoping that the tea was laced with some hallucinogenic class-A substance. He took a sip. It was rancid – he had to force it down – but it didn't cause more of a sting or a head-rush than a nip of that cheap, paint-stripper vodka. The stuff he used to drink.

"Any other questions?" Eddie asked.

He had tons, but Grafton shook his head and took another sip of his tea. Better to take things slowly, he thought. The tea, on second taste, was slightly more palatable – there was a touch of cinnamon in there, and maybe some cumin –

Brrr. Brrr. Brrr.

It was his phone vibrating. Grafton jerked his arm in against his body to try to muffle it, but Eddie had heard. He was staring and Grafton saw the real hardness, the violence, in the young man's eyes. Eddie was the type of lad you'd find in any number of housing schemes around Glasgow: one of those who'd never held a pool cue except as a weapon; never built a fire except to burn a row of derelict houses to the ground.

Brrr. Brrr. Brrr.

Grafton pulled the phone out from his sleeve. He glanced at the screen – Isaac.

"It's my son," he said. "You ok if I take it?"

"Give it," Eddie said, holding his hand out. Any trace of uncertainty in the young lad had gone. He was fully focused now, he'd caught a scent.

Brrr. Brrr. Brrr.

"I know you said no phones," Grafton said, "but I need to keep in contact with my son."

"Give it."

"Surely I can leave it here – in the office – and come back to check in with him?"

"Fucking give it or leave."

Eddie hadn't blinked in all the time the phone had been vibrating. It stopped now, but he still didn't look away. The shadows under his eyes were as dark as bruising. He continued to hold his hand out and finally, reluctantly, Grafton gave him the phone.

Grafton held his teeth together and let his breath leak in and out through them. He was no longer confident of being able to fight his way past this scrawny lad, no longer confident that he wouldn't leave some part of his own insides spread out across the floor of this log cabin. He thought again about the stain on the rug in the other room – could it be something other than damp?

Eddie held the phone in his hand, as if weighing it. He kept his eyes on Grafton. Then, with a grunt of effort, he hurled it across the room and against the wall on the far side. There was a definite crack and the phone fell to the floor in two pieces, split longways. The white wall now had a dent in it.

"No phones," Eddie said, softly. "If you're with us then you're present at all times, in the moment, paying attention and listening. No contact with the outside."

Grafton swallowed. "Until Thursday, right? That's when I'm leaving."

"Sure, Grafton, until Thursday."

6

"Bloody useless," Isaac said, hanging up the call. He was standing in front of the open door of the fridge. Inside was empty except for a twenty-pound note weighed down by a jar of mayonnaise. Isaac didn't know if that was his dad's idea of a joke or if he'd had every intention of filling the fridge and hadn't quite been able to follow through. And now the old skinflint wasn't even answering his phone.

Isaac made a quick mental calculation. He would probably need a taxi to college later in the week, to transport his sculpture, so it looked like he'd be shopping for value bags of pasta, tins of tomatoes, and anything with the yellow discount stickers. He was used to pulling meals together from odds-and-ends.

Moving through to the hall, he scrabbled in the pockets of all the hanging jackets to see if there was any loose change. No luck. He might still need some materials too. They were supposed to present two pieces and his sculpture — with the wrestler caught in the sleeper-hold — was the only one close to being finished. The other options might still require more clay and a couple of paints. Fabrics too. Fuck, he'd forgotten about the fabrics. He could always pilfer some art supplies from college, but he had no interest in seeing any of his classmates. Except for Shauna, who'd made it clear that she had no interest in seeing him.

Isaac wasn't angry that his dad had gone off chasing the story. Truth be told, it was better that he did. Most of the time, his dad was very much in the day-to-day routine, but there was the odd week here or there when he'd space out. Still present in body, but otherwise absent. You'd find him sitting on the sofa staring at the blank telly screen. Or you'd realise he'd been in the shower for a good forty minutes and it would take a knock and a shout before he emerged from the steam. Nothing major, but it had been noticeable when Isaac was still at school because those were the weeks when he got cream crackers spread with apricot jam for his packed lunch and when they drove past the pitch for Saturday morning football and ended up parked outside the supermarket instead.

At one point, when he was thirteen or fourteen, Isaac had tried to chart these wee spells of vacantness. To see if they tallied with something: the anniversary of his parents' marriage maybe; or the time of year when his mum left. He made a list of all the factors: weather, school calendar, financial pressures, what they'd been eating, who'd been calling. There was no pattern to be found.

Isaac decided to leave the trip to the shops until later. Perhaps hunger would be good for his artwork; give it a keen edge. He needed to concentrate on his second piece for the exhibition. Through in the living room, he flicked on the desk lamp and sat himself down at the table. He was trying to get a ripple, a flow, to a miniaturised clay cape. It needed to stand alone, but with a sense of movement – like it had been thrown off someone's shoulders. He wanted to get across the theatricality of it, that sense of show, but also the way wrestling was tied in with masculine identity. At least, that was the tale he'd spun in his essay.

He worked on the clay with a scalpel for fifteen minutes or so, but his cuts were too ragged and didn't have the fluidity he was looking for. So, he set the cape to the side and turned his attention to the other options. He had a half-finished version of Mankind's studded mask formed from the same hessian rope as went around the ring; a papier-mâché beer can with trailing chiffon foam coming from the top, as a homage to Stone Cold Steve Austin; and a wide-brimmed hat modelled on the Undertaker's, which was formed by layering up Nineties wrestling stickers.

All of them were too straightforward. They were copies of wrestling paraphernalia or gimmicks rather than something that nodded to anything more. When Isaac detailed his sculpture of the sleeper-hold he could add veins in the arms and crow's feet around the wrestler's eyes; he could show that even the performance of physicality takes effort and that the most practiced, mundane, everyday move has the potential to cause injury. He could show the strain of it all. But these other pieces said nothing.

Isaac flopped himself down on the sofa and pulled the laptop across. He and his dad shared it. There was a folder with Isaac's college work and another with his dad's preparations for travel reports. A couple of other folders had pictures from trips they'd taken together and there was a scattering of old school essays. And then there was a folder labelled 'Recipes'. That was his dad's idea of subterfuge. Even though he rarely cooked beyond opening a jar or piercing a film lid. Inside the 'Recipes' folder were the screenshots and documents his dad had pieced together in his search for Isaac's mum.

Opening it up, Isaac clicked on the most recent one. It was a news article Isaac hadn't seen before. The man who went by the name of Ravi was being investigated for manslaughter in Austria. That fitted with the pattern of the previous articles: the Swiss authorities wanting to talk to him about false imprisonment; the Canadians investigating the possibility of extraditing him to face charges of assault causing bodily harm. Attached to this new article was a photo of him in sunglasses and handcuffs, olive-skinned and sleek-haired. His real name was Steven Francis. He had abandoned it at the same time he took up spiritual healing.

As always, Isaac scanned the text for a mention of his mother. Other women had come forward, spoken out, but there was nothing from her. Young girls often made allegations about the things that Ravi had done, but Liz Whelan maintained her silence.

Isaac was better at following the trail than his dad was. Armed with the charges and the names of the accusers, Isaac found his way onto some German-language websites which detailed the court case and the eventual conviction of Swami Ravi. The translation wasn't perfect – he ran it through an online converter – but it was possible to get the basics. Ravi was in jail, his 'harem' scattered to the winds. Switching tabs, Isaac opened Facebook and found the public page for Ravi's followers. Sure enough, there were dozens of messages from well-wishers and a few condemnations with a long trail of angry comments beneath. Several of them linked to Youtube videos and webpages with Ravi's teachings.

When he emerged from his virtual rabbit-hole, Isaac lifted his head and realised that it was dark outside and the supermarket would be closed. Hunger gripped at his stomach like a clawhold. At that stage, he would have eaten the twenty-pound note itself, but instead he went rooting through the freezer and found a single potato waffle at the bottom of a box. Hallelujah. He popped it into the toaster. It took two goes before the waffle was soft and warm enough. Then he ate it, spread with mayo, standing at the kitchen counter.

As he chewed, he thought about what the jailing of Swami Ravi meant. Probably nothing. It seemed unlikely that it was tied to his dad going off on his mission up north. And, for his part, Isaac found it hard to dredge up any sense of hope or excitement. Perhaps it was more likely that his mum would come home now, all these years later, to find her son and try to reconnect. Maybe. But if she did come wafting through the door, in that swirl of fabric and rosewater he remembered, then he'd greet her with no more enthusiasm than the man who came to read the gas meter.

With something in his stomach, Isaac could go through, find the spot in the corner of the sofa where the cushion sagged and put the wrestling on the telly. Many times, through the odd timeless days of the pandemic, he'd fallen asleep in that exact position.

As he made his way through to the living room, he idly wondered what Ravi and his followers would think about sleeping the night through on the sofa under the soft flicker of the light from the TV. What would those at this new commune his dad had travelled to make of it? And, in an instant, Isaac had an idea for his second exhibition piece. He looked across at the sofa, those familiar angles and the way the light fell from the streetlight outside the window. He'd need to rewrite his essay, no doubt about that, but what if he was to play with the idea of *wrestling with sleep*? Wrestling as metaphor. Make a scale model of the sofa with the hessian rope of the ring around it and the Nineties wrestling stickers across the surface. It would be about all those late nights Isaac and his dad stayed awake to watch a match-up from a US timezone and all those days he'd dozed off with the commentators screeching in the background. More than that, though, it would give him the chance to incorporate some of Ravi's words and show that beneath the sheen and performance, beneath the effort and strain of wakefulness, you always inevitably ended up collapsed on the canvas, or on the cushions of the sofa, breathing soft and slow.

7

"Wait here."

Eddie had led Grafton up the path and they stood, now, in front of the A-frame building. The downstairs curtains were drawn and there was no sound or sign of life. The windows upstairs had newspaper plastered over the inside of them. Eddie went over to the door and disappeared inside, leaving Grafton standing on the gravel in his bare feet.

There was a thin drizzle. It beaded on Grafton's robe, then began to seep through. He shivered. The sky was overcast, but it was a mild enough May day. Grafton dreaded to think what wearing the robe would be like in the Winter, when both wind and rain were more insistent and the west coast was being re-chiselled by the weather.

Grafton turned away from the A-frame. Stretched out in front of him was the bay, with the Pier Shop and a huddle of houses over to the right and the ferry terminal and a longer string of houses over to the left. Between was one large farmhouse surrounded, on three sides, by fields of sheep and, in front, by the road and a seaweed-strewn stony beach. Closer to the entrance of the commune was a grey-stone kirk with a red phone box to the side of it.

At the mouth of the bay, the waves caught against and sprayed above the rocks of the breakwater. You could see the line in the water: white-fringed and chaotic on one side, rippling and reflective on the other. Inside the encircling arm of it were bobbing orange buoys to mark the moorings, but no yachts attached to them. As Grafton watched, a grey buoy surfaced. He narrowed his eyes and peered at it. Not a buoy but a seal, turning its head now.

Reaching into his sleeve, Grafton felt for the record button on his Dictaphone. He knew it by touch. This was the one he'd used for years – top of the line when he'd bought it, although he knew most of them wouldn't take tapes anymore. It had a clunk to the buttons but it was small and thin enough to be discreet. He was glad he'd thought to bring it as back-up.

How many years since he'd used the Dictaphone? It wasn't as cut-and-dried as being a journalist before Liz left and then seeking out a steady nine-to-five afterwards. There had been a few months of uncertainty about whether he was a single parent. Liz might have come back. It might have been another jaunt, a brief hiatus to give her fresh energy for motherhood. He'd known it wasn't, though, and, soon after, he'd known that the unsociable hours, the boozing, and the shadiness of chasing stories – the need for the brown envelope passed under the table – wasn't really compatible with the school run and the Saturday morning football.

Eddie appeared at the door. "We're ready for you."

Grafton nodded and covertly adjusted his sleeve. The negative of going back to analogue, he realised, was that he only had an hour of recording time. He'd need to click it on and off, as best he could, because he'd left his extra tapes in the car.

As Grafton squeezed past Eddie, in the doorway, he smelt that stale aroma that rises from clothes when they've been put away before they're dry. He remembered it well from his first weeks of washing Isaac's pyjamas and school uniform. The smell was coming from Eddie's robe, no doubt, but it was also stronger and more pervasive than that. It hung in the room that Grafton entered, a fug that settled across the men and women gathered inside. There were thirty or forty of them, all seated cross-legged on the floorboards. Not one of them turned to wave or smile a welcome.

Grafton scanned the side of their heads, the set of their shoulders, for a sign of Liz, but he couldn't see anyone who might be her. Truth be told, he couldn't imagine her sitting as silent and still in any case. Every single person in the room faced forwards, dust motes dancing around them in the light from the gaps in the curtains.

They were facing a makeshift wooden platform at the far-end of the room. It had once been a kitchenette, judging by the hanging pipework and jutting sink at the back of it. Any cabinets or worktops had been removed, with only the scars of them left against the plasterboard. Packing crates had been used to build up the floor into a stage. The main room, in front of it, was empty of furniture and had the feel of a small church hall, with all the devotees gathered there. It had once been separated into two rooms, Grafton would have guessed, because there were the remains of studwork and the sawn-end of what looked like a supporting beam jutting out halfway across the space.

Other than the white-robed Sleepless, the only other thing in the room was a small table, at the side. Grafton moved towards it, with Eddie watching from behind. On the table were a series of cards and small clay pots, a bouquet of flowers and an unlit candle. Child-like drawings were blu-tacked to the wall behind. They showed a brown-haired woman dressed in white, with her arms spread out like a deity. Scrawled letters spelt out 'Joan'.

At that moment, there was a collective murmur. Like the noise at a family party when one of the children comes in dressed in a frock or a miniature tuxedo. Grafton turned and looked in the same direction as the Sleepless. There was a set of wooden stairs to the left. A pair of bare feet were coming down them, belonging to a young woman with brown hair. She wasn't wearing white but a navy dress with multi-coloured flowers patterned across it. A summer dress. She kept her head lowered as she came down the stairs, then she looked up. She looked straight at Grafton. Grey eyes. There was a twitch of a smile.

"Sit down," Eddie hissed. "Joan's here."

Grafton looked down at Eddie, who was sitting cross-legged to the side of the shrine. He realised he was the only one standing. Feeling a flush spreading across his neck, Grafton fell to his knees. As he did, Joan began to slowly walk over towards the platform. For every step that she took, for every second that passed, Grafton ardently wished – prayed even – that she would turn, once more, and fix her gaze on him.

When she got to the platform, Joan sat, cross-legged like those in front of her. She didn't look up. With both hands, she began to smooth and gather her brown hair together, then she twisted it into a bun on the top of her head. She held it there with one hand, until someone from the front row passed her a biro pen. Smiling her thanks, she used the pen to fix her hair in place. Then, finally, she looked up to the back of the room.

"Good afternoon," she said, "and welcome."

Her voice was soft and slow. Each vowel held for a little longer, each pause a beat more than you'd expect. Everyone in the room sat there, silent, and waited for her next word.

"We have a new member." Joan looked, again, at Grafton. He felt the heat in his cheeks once more. "And you've arrived at an auspicious time, I must say."

She pronounced it as 'awe-spick-ish'. It had been Joan who had rung the radio station, Grafton was certain; these words had the same pauses and catches, the same careful articulation and missed pronunciation, as he'd heard in his headphones that afternoon.

"Today is day four. By day twelve, I will have remained awake for over two-hundred-and-fifty hours using nothing except our own methods. At that point, I will be ready to take the next step and become truly wakeful."

Those grey eyes were still staring steadily at Grafton across the sea of the Sleepless. He could feel the heat of the bodies, could tell that some of the heads in the room had turned to examine him now. He tried a nod.

"Stand, will you," Joan said.

Grafton stood.

"The weaning process, even for you, begins tonight. I'd like you to sleep for only four hours," she said. "We'll help you. Are you willing?"

Grafton considered. What could be the harm in that? It was one night with a little less sleep than he was used to, but not at a level which would do any lasting damage. Even if he kept it up for a few nights he'd emerge only blurry-eyed, not hallucinating and scratching at the walls. He nodded to Joan.

"You may sit."

As Grafton lowered himself back to the floor, Joan started to pick people out from the group and ask them how long they'd slept the night before – two hours, nearly three, only two bouts of twenty minutes. Each disciple stood to give this report and then sat down again. It didn't appear that anyone was taking notes of the times or passing any sort of judgement; it was a simple statement for each of the Sleepless.

The astonishing aspect was Joan herself. If this was day four, then she'd been awake for three nights and yet her attention didn't seem to drift even once, her gaze never faltered, her shoulders didn't sag. In the stuffy room, with the repeated mantra of hours slept, it was inevitable that your eyelids would get heavier, that your thoughts would begin to slide, but Joan sat upright and alert throughout. There was no trace of shadowing under her eyes or pinched skin at her cheeks; she had the healthy look of a yoga instructor, up there on the stage. Was this what Swami Ravi's teachings gave you?

"When I was a child–" she said, suddenly. The disciple who had been standing fell to the floor as quickly as they could. "When I was a child, wakefulness was frowned upon. My mother would find me reading under the covers, by torchlight, and she'd screech at me. My father saw me at the window, peering at the moon, and bricked over my window."

She took a deep breath. Grafton found that he was leaning forward slightly, crouched with his forearms on his knees.

"One-third of our life is spent in sleep," she said. "A third of our time is wasted. When we could be learning or sharing our love. One-third. That is a tragedy of our time, brought about only by habit and by sloth and indolence."

Again, she struggled with the pronunciation – 'in-doo-lens'.

"We need that time, friends," she said. "For the coming challenges. Food will be harder to come by, security and comfort will be harder to achieve. Our supply chains are breaking, our eco-systems are collapsing. We are at our weakest – our weakest – when we are asleep. We are unprotected."

Several heads in the room were nodding along. Grafton noticed that Eddie was watching him, so he gave a slight nod too. He recognised, within Joan's words, shards and snippets from the reports of Ravi's speeches: the talk of sloth and laziness, of the need to recapture energy and reframe what was meant by wakefulness.

"We've been told," Joan continued, "for many years, that sleep is a necessity. We've been biologically conditioned, socially conditioned. From birth. Sleep training, they call it. Just consider that. They actually call it sleep training…"

Joan stood, abruptly. The pen fell from her hair with a clatter. She pointed to the back of the room, directly at Grafton. She began to stride across the room towards him. The Sleepless parted to let her through, shuffling and scooting to either side.

"You're sceptical," she said, once she was in front of him.

Grafton flinched a little, he could feel it. "I've just arrived," he said.

"If you're full of doubts, Grafton, then you'll definitely fall asleep. Like that." She snapped her fingers. Grafton was jolted to hear his name from her lips. "Our brains tell our bodies to crave sleep, because we have been told, over and over, that sleep is what we must have."

Those grey eyes. Up close the irises were flecked with blue. The pupils, against the paleness, were the purest black. They seemed to dilate as Joan smiled.

She turned and Grafton thought that she was finished with him, but she was only signalling to a disciple over by the stage. He rose and scurried off up the stairs. For the minute or so he was gone, no one moved. Joan stood with her back to Grafton and the rest of the Sleepless stayed cross-legged, facing the front. There were no whispered conversations or even so much as a sniff or clearing of a throat.

When the white-robed disciple returned, he was carrying a small white dish with a blue floral pattern on it. In his other hand was a delicate paintbrush, the kind you might use for watercolours. He handed both over to Joan and then returned to his space on the floor.

"The first night can be difficult," Joan said, stirring the paintbrush in the dish. "There's adrenaline after your arrival and then it fades and you're left with no energy..."

Grafton watched the brush in the dish. Was this part of the initiation, perhaps, a ritualistic painting of his body with some identifying mark? He couldn't see ink or paint on the exposed skin of any of the others, so maybe he was going to have to undress in front of the whole room? The thought caused him to grip at the hem of his robe.

"All of our methods are simple," Joan said. "You've seen that already, yes? And this is no different. It is just chilli-oil made to our own recipe."

Grafton looked at the people either side of him. They both smiled at him encouragingly.

"Close your eyes, Grafton," Joan said. "I'm going to brush this on your eyelids."

She stood, waiting. The rest of the Sleepless sat, waiting. Perhaps only five seconds passed, but it felt longer. Grafton didn't particularly want to put chillies into his eyes, but he had to weigh up what refusal would mean: he would be asked to leave before he'd had the chance to have a proper look around.

And chillies were only going to sting, nothing more. It was something that happened to every home-cook, no worse than chopping onions. He nodded, closed his eyes.

He felt her breath first, on his cheek. It smelt of mint, but there was a sourness behind that too. Then came the oil on his eyelids, gently applied with the brush. Slick, at first, but quickly drying. There was a tingle of warmth. The brush was lifted and he opened his eyes, blinked. It was then that he felt the full surge of heat, the claw and bite of it against his eyeball. Screwing his eyes shut only seemed to make it worse, the watering of his eyes only intensified it. Like holding his eyes open over a burning flame, feeling the flicking touch of it and then bringing the flame closer until the blue-heat of it was right up against the white of the eyeball. Grafton let out a yelp.

"Everybody!" Grafton heard Joan's shout. He rubbed at his eyes, but he couldn't focus, couldn't open them fully. The floorboards started to shudder beneath him and the thought ran through his head that it hadn't been chilli-oil at all, that he'd been poisoned.

"Again! Again!" Joan called and Grafton realised that hers wasn't the only voice. There were shouts and screams from all around. Like cats in a cul-de-sac, the Sleepless were yowling and screeching. The shaking of the floor was from their stamping feet. Grafton opened one blurred eye and saw that not one of them was still sitting. They were jumping, swaying, leaning into one another.

"Wake up," Joan's voice was in his ear. Again, the feel of her breath. The sting of the chilli started to fade. "Wake up, Grafton!"

He opened his eyes.

8

The room Grafton was shown to was in a log cabin further up the hill. There were six beds in total, split across two bunk beds and two mattresses on the floor. Grafton was relieved to find that he was assigned a top-bunk, but less delighted by the shroud of spider's web that hung, like mosquito netting, across the far end. He swiped at it with his hand.

The walls themselves were exposed wood, rounded beams which were mostly smooth but which had cracked and splintered around the double doors. Those doors led out to a veranda, treated with thick brown wood-stain, that looked out over the bay. It was idyllic, in many ways, restful even. He listened to the quiet. There was a distant outboard motor and then the bleat of a sheep on the hillside behind, but both were shushed by the breeze. Grafton took a lungful of air and fancied he could taste the salt of the sea. There was a time when it would have given him a keen thirst.

He would sleep for only four hours tonight. Grafton tried to remember the last time he'd slept so little – probably one of those nights when he'd sat up with Isaac to watch SummerSlam or one of those other wrestling events. Once Isaac was a teenager, though, there'd been no need to do more than get him a bottle of Fanta and a plate of snacks and leave him to it.

It was in his days as a journalist that Grafton had regularly burned the candle at both ends. Back when he was searching for the thread of a story in the bottom of a bottle, trying to chase a deadline before the hangover struck. Those habits had been ingrained in him from his early days as a trainee reporter on the news desk of an Edinburgh daily: the wee nip to clear the head in the morning; the sharpener at lunch; the pint or two to loosen up a source in the afternoon. He'd been a cliché, a stereotype.

It was Liz who'd had the steady job. She worked as a Senior Charge Nurse. Nothing fancy and not well-paid, but well-suited to the no-nonsense manner she had in those early days. The new wing of the hospital was where they'd first met; Grafton travelling through on the train to do a story on the opening and Liz sidling up to him at the press event.

"The wine's like vinegar," she said to him, as he lifted a glass of red. He looked across at her. She wrinkled her nose to emphasise her point and her freckles were lost in the folds.

"I'll have had worse," he said. Not Grafton at that stage, but still going by Tom.

"Ah, I'd taken you for a connoisseur."

"Oh, aye? Is it my trainers or my hiking jacket that mark me out?"

"It's the notepad."

"Tool of the trade."

"You want a quote about the new building?"

"Sure, what you got?"

"Bastards have been hiding the bedpans from the photographers."

Grafton smiled, took a gulp of his wine. It was fine, but he made a face anyway. "Can I buy you a proper drink somewhere?" he asked.

"You can buy me a curry."

They'd dated for eighteen months or so before they started trying for a child. She fell pregnant quickly.

There'd been nights, in those early days of Isaac's life, when Grafton had been woken by the screaming of his son or by the shifting of Liz feeding him, but he'd mostly slept through. Dosed up with cheap whisky and pre-emptive paracetamol. In that way, he managed a good spell of sleep every night, even before he decided to give up the drink.

Stepping back in from the veranda, Grafton moved over to the chest of drawers. On top of them was the music player Eddie had mentioned. A clunky thing that would have been obsolete two decades ago. Grafton lifted the headphones and slipped them on, then pressed play. Drums and guitar thrashing, then the throaty voice of Chris Cornell. Soundgarden. Grafton remembered them well enough; he'd have been mid-twenties when they were around. He clicked it off.

The music player reminded him that he needed to fetch fresh tapes for his Dictaphone from the car. As long as Eddie was willing to hand back his keys. Although, now he had a set of headphones so perhaps he could listen back to the tape that was in there and decide what was vital and what could be jettisoned…

"Hi, howdy, hi there," said a voice from behind.

Grafton spun around. It was a lady, maybe in her sixties, with long hair trailing down over the shoulders of her white robe. Her hair still held threads of red, but it was mostly grey. She wore wire-rimmed glasses and a smile that flickered through the spectrum from slight curl to wide grin, and back again, in just a few seconds.

"Didn't mean to startle you," she said. "Apologies, if I did."

"Not at all, no." Grafton went mid-spectrum with his smile. "Off in my own wee world."

The woman giggled. It was an odd sound, almost coquettish. Like the smile, it was as if she'd scrolled through and hadn't quite been able to find the right laugh.

"Debbie," she said, stepping forward and extending her hand.

"Grafton."

They shook hands. Debbie's eyes slid away after a second, fixing somewhere over Grafton's shoulder. Grafton glanced back to see what she was looking at, but there was nothing but wooden wall.

"I guess we're roommates then," Debbie said.

"Really?" Grafton had presumed that he would be in an all-male dormitory. "I mean – sorry – how many other folk are in here with us?"

"You're the sixth. Worry not, though, most of them keep to themselves."

"I wasn't expecting it to be mixed."

Debbie flicked her hair from her shoulder. "It makes no difference – no, no. Joan knows she can trust us. Maybe not the younger ones, certainly, but…"

"Ah."

He'd been categorised along with the seniors then. No matter. He had to remember that he was three times the age of some of the Sleepless, at least twice the age of Joan. They would see him as somewhere in the mid-life crisis bracket, but that might allow him to fly under the radar.

He looked at Debbie again. Bare feet, but with a bunion plaster across the toes of her right foot, and with a varicose vein peeking out from the bottom of the robe. Her eyes were ringed with deep shadows, like poorly-applied kohl, and her skin was sallow on her cheeks. Maybe she wasn't older than him, perhaps it was just lack of sleep.

"Have you been here long?" Grafton asked.

"Here? Nearly a fortnight now."

"And you enjoy it?"

"Love it, Gaston, love it." She gave an uncertain smile. "It was what I needed, you see, what I – you don't want to hear about me…"

"Please."

"No, no."

"I'm fascinated, honestly, by what draws people to a place like this."

"Well, you're drawn here too, aren't you? It's for you to answer as much as for me. And there's Joan, of course, you've met her. She's a wonder, she is, and so brave to be taking that next step."

Grafton needed to be careful here. He didn't want to raise suspicion by launching in with a whole slate of questions, so he nodded and gave her another smile. Debbie walked over to one of the thin mattresses on the floor. She seemed to go down in stages: crouching, kneeling, then twisting her hips to lie down.

"Are you here because of Joan then?" Grafton asked. "Or Swami Ravi?"

Debbie looked up. "I knew Ravi," she said. "For a time." She paused. Her eyes were on the double-doors, on the sky beyond. "This is more my speed."

"And how do you pass the time?" Grafton asked.

"That's for you to decide. You can learn a new skill or reflect on what you've, eh, learned or found out about yourself."

"But what do *you* do with the extra hours?"

"Me? Well...I help with the veggie patch. And I'm on laundry duty for a few of the cabins. There are plenty of odd-jobs to keep us busy..."

Grafton nodded, but kept quiet.

"...there are mushrooms to pick in the woods," she said, her voice growing quieter, slower. "And it's not a method, but I think chewing wild garlic helps with wakefulness."

Debbie tipped her head back and closed her eyes. Her breathing grew shallower almost instantly. Grafton watched as her arm, held up at her side, slumped down to the mattress. Her fingers uncurled. She let out a small, grunting snore. Grafton wondered if this was allowed, if she would be angry with herself for having drifted off. Should he wake her? As he watched, though, she gave a second snore and then jerked awake. Her eyes flickered open, her head rocked forward, she pulled her hand back up from the mattress.

"Ask me more questions," she said, slurring slightly and shaking her head. "Otherwise I'll fall asleep."

He didn't like to point out that, to all appearances, she had just done exactly that. Instead, he decided to make the most of the opportunity.

"Do you know a woman by the name of Elizabeth Whelan?" He drew his breath in and held it.

Debbie's eyes opened wider and she gave her brightest smile yet. "You know Liz?"

"Eh, yes." Grafton found himself leaning forward, over the mattress. Then he realised that it might seem like he was looming over her. He stepped back. "I used to be her husband." He hesitated, wondered about his phrasing. "I mean, she was my wife."

"I didn't know she was married." Debbie's smile flickered into a frown. "It never came up."

"You know her well then?"

"We were close. At one stage."

Grafton paused, tried to take the edge off the urgency of what he said next; tried to make it sound casual. "Is she here?"

"No, no." Debbie shook her head. "She'd love it here, though. I know she would."

"She's never been here?"

"No, I knew her back in India, you see."

"Where is she now then, do you know?"

Debbie didn't get the chance to answer. There was a knock on the door and then a young lad appeared in the doorway. His head was hanging down, so far that you could see the swirl at the crown of his hair. Close to sleepwalking, but awake enough to lift his eyes to Grafton.

"You're to come and keep Joan company," he said, in a Glaswegian accent.

Debbie gasped from her mattress. "Lucky duck," she said.

9

There was a definite smell in the car now. Liz tended not to use underarm deodorant, preferring a quick spritz of rosewater and a sprig of sage in her blouse pocket, but she decided to purchase a stick of antiperspirant for the overnight drives. Particularly as she was wearing both a thick jumper and a woollen cardigan against the cold.

She'd made it through Austria and then taken the autobahn past Munich and on towards Stuttgart. As the sun came up, she flicked her headlights off. The road sign showed a turn-off for a service station, so she set her indicator clicking.

Inside, the strip light hummed above her. She screwed her eyes shut against it for a moment, then refocused on the shelf of toiletries. She wanted something unperfumed, something aluminium-free which wouldn't clog her pores. And none of the items on the shelf were natural. Except for a small bottle of tea-tree oil up in the corner. Could that go under her arms? No reason why not. It might be a handy thing to have in the car, anyway, for antiseptic use.

She lifted it down and carried on to the bakery section. There were pastries and buns set out in baskets, with plastic tongs, and loaves wrapped in clingfilm. Nothing appealed. To the side, though, were a few limp pieces of fruit. Liz selected an orange. She took her purchases up to the slumped girl at the cash register. The girl had a patch of eczema across her chin. She scratched at it before lifting the tea-tree oil to be scanned.

"*Ist das alles?*" she said, without looking up.

"And pump nine. *Neun.*"

The girl nodded. She pointed at the number on the till: 51.60.

Liz looked at the coffee machine over her shoulder. "Do you have herbal teas?"

"Yes. Peppermint. Hibiscus. Ginger and Lemon."

"One of each, *bitte*."

"You want three?"

"All in one cup." Liz nodded, handing over three twenty-Euro notes. "All of them together, yes."

The girl lifted her eyebrow, but it quickly sank back down and she turned to the machine. Liz looked across the tiled floor to the two round tables by the window. One was littered with empty takeaway cups and the other had a puddle of something brownish underneath. Off to the side was a small wooden booth with a computer. The kind you'd see in the library.

"Internet?" Liz asked the girl.

"*Ja*," the girl said, turning back with the tea. "Two Euro. Fifteen minutes."

Liz smiled her thanks and took the tea over to the booth. She pushed a two-Euro coin into the slot and jiggled the mouse until the screen came on. It had been a few weeks since she'd been online. During Ravi's trial she'd posted quite regularly – updates to his followers and the occasional request for funds to help with his costs – but she hadn't been on since the verdict.

She scrolled through the notifications, whilst peeling her orange. The profile was in his name – his photo – so there were plenty of messages, mostly small notes of support, but with the occasional journalist request too. Breaking the orange into segments, she clicked through to 'like' the supportive posts. In the private messages was one addressed to her from a couple of weeks ago. She chewed at the orange as she read:

Dearest Liz, on my way to a small collective out in Ardnamurchan. There is a girl there who follows Ravi's teaching. She's a marvel. The way she speaks is like it was with Ravi in those early days. You hear her and you remember exactly what that was like – that energy, that vitality. That sense of purpose. Hope all is well. Debbie xx

Liz read the message again, taking a sip of her tea. It was hot and sour and sweet. She reached up to tuck a strand of hair behind her ear. It had clumped and grown greasy. She should have bought a comb really. No matter, it had gone unwashed for longer than this in the past. Absent-mindedly, Liz picked up the orange peel and began to break it into pieces – placing each of them on her tongue and tasting the bitterness of the pith before swallowing them down.

Debbie had been there in the Jaipur days. Liz remembered her as an enthusiast but not a pragmatist. The kind who clapped her hands but never made a fist. Ravi had been quite taken with her flame-red hair, despite her being a fair bit older than his usual sweethearts. Older, even, than Liz. But she was pleasant enough – never a threat – and she'd slipped away quietly when Ravi's affection had run its course.

Liz put the final piece of peel on her tongue and washed it down with a swig from her tea. She looked over her shoulder. The girl at the till was watching her with her scabby chin nearly down on the counter. As if eating the skin of an orange was the most backward thing she'd ever encountered. If it was, then she was in for a shock once she'd seen a bit more of the world.

There was still ten minutes left on her browsing session, still a couple of gulps of tea in the bottom of her cup, but Liz wanted to be on her way. The road she was on would take her to the border. And now, with a tank full of petrol, she was certain that her destination was the right one. Once she was in France, she would turn north. On the drive, she'd decide whether to take the tunnel or the ferry. Either way, she was heading back to Scotland. Back home.

10

Off to the left of the path was a wooded area. It would have been a stretch to call it a forest, but there were trees and enough thick undergrowth to screen the log cabin behind. This cabin was in a worse state than the ones further down the hill: wood beneath the windows warped by rainwater, weeds growing from the cracks between the roof tiles, guttering hanging loose.

Grafton was led through the front door and into an open-plan living room. There were two worn-leather sofas and a coffee-table piled high with books. Off to one side was an ancient-looking treadmill and a mismatched set of weights. Clothes were strewn across the carpet. It looked like student digs, but with the addition of several squares of rough-cut cardboard pinned to the walls. They were scrawled, with colourful felt-tip, in capitals: WAKEFULNESS IS WATCHFULNESS; CONQUER SLEEP, COME ALIVE; RECLAIM THE WASTAGE; SLEEP IS HABIT; AWAKE!

The young lad didn't take more than two steps into the cabin. Silently, he pointed at a door at the back of the room. Then he turned and left.

Grafton stood for a second and considered. This was the perfect opportunity to look around, he realised, but Joan was presumably waiting for him on the other side of that door and he didn't want to get caught snooping on his very first evening. So, he settled for having a quick look at the spine of the books on the coffee table. There was a variety of textbooks: Chemistry, Physics, Philosophy. On top of those were a few gardening manuals and a couple of paperback novels. He didn't recognise the names of the authors.

He glanced longingly towards the corridor at the far-side of the room, but decided against investigating any further. Plenty of time for that. Instead, he stepped forward to the door and gently tapped his knuckles against the wood.

"Come."

The voice was male. As he entered, Grafton saw that it belonged to Eddie. He was sitting on a chair to the left of the doorway. Beside him was an avocado-coloured sink and a toilet with a seat that was slightly askew. Steam hung in the air. Joan lay in the bathtub, also avocado, with one arm draped out over the side. Her hair was pinned up again, but now held with a toothbrush rather than a pen.

"Grafton," she said. Her head was tipped back, eyes closed. "Join us."

He could see the full length of her slender neck and the curve of her clavicle. Below that was masked by the lip of the bath. But if he took even a single step forward...

He found he had to swallow before speaking. "I don't want to disturb."

"Nonsense." Joan opened her eyes, lifted herself and turned. Grafton caught a glimpse of her breasts, the gentle pendulous swing of them, before she crossed her arms over the side of the bath. "I need all of the Sleepless to help me in this effort, Grafton. It's a collective endeavour."

She pronounced it correctly, but there was a split-second hesitation in the middle of the word. Grafton looked over at the fogged mirror above the sink. It seemed safest to keep his eyes there.

"Take Eddie's seat," Joan said. "We'll take a break from reading."

Eddie rose. In his hands was a thick hardbound book with the title *Crop Cultivation for Smallholdings*. His finger was marking a place only a few pages in. Without a word, Eddie walked past and out of the door. Grafton was left alone with Joan.

He sat. Joan had slid back into the water. The tiles above the bath were white but decorated with tiny marble flecks that made them look like they'd been splattered with dirt. As if someone had given a dog a bath and it had shaken itself dry.

"You can top me up," Joan said.

"Pardon?"

"A burst from the hot tap, first, and then there's a bucket underneath the sink."

Grafton did what he was told. The taps were by Joan's feet. Her toes were above the water, toenails rounded and healthily pink. Grafton took a breath and tried to think, instead, of Debbie's feet with their blue bunion plaster. He turned on the hot tap. There were several leaves floating in the water – some sort of herb, perhaps. They came into view beneath the swirl of water, but he didn't want to look too closely because beyond them was the smooth slope of Joan's legs.

"Enough," she said. "Now the bucket."

He turned off the tap. The bucket beneath the sink was green plastic. It was filled with the same leaves that were floating in the bath: pea-green with slightly forked tips.

"All of them?" he asked.

"Just a handful."

Grafton reached in and gathered a handful. He felt the itch of it immediately, in the web between his fingers. Quickly, he dropped the leaves into the water by Joan's feet. He looked down at his hand rather than at her.

"What are these? Nettles?"

"Poison ivy."

He couldn't help looking then. She met his gaze levelly. Her shoulder had a long red strip, like a welt, that ran down onto the top of her arm and there was a raised rash across her stomach. Her legs looked like they'd been shaved imperfectly; red, puffy and with uneven pock-marks.

"Finally, you look at me," Joan said.

"Sorry." Grafton averted his eyes again.

"Not at all. Look. It's my body and I give you permission."

Grafton was getting used to doing what he was told. This

time he allowed himself to look at the pinkness of her nipples, below the surface of the water, and the seaweed-sway of her pubic hair, further below. He felt that familiar stirring.

There had been two women since Liz. Two in eight years. One had lasted for a month, the other for only two weeks. He'd slept with each of them four times. That seemed to be his limit. Otherwise it was him and his laptop; where girls in their twenties often lay in the bath, bodies slick with water, and asked older men to do their bidding. Not normally as old as Grafton, though, and never with the addition of poison ivy.

He cleared his throat. "Why poison ivy?"

"Itches like hell," Joan said. "No getting comfortable with poison ivy."

"So, it's another method?"

"Of course."

Grafton was aware, now, that the thin material of the robe had raised, had lifted, at his groin. He felt the quickening in his chest, the urgency of his erection. He turned to the side in an attempt to hide it, but that only set him in profile to Joan.

"Don't be embarrassed," she said. "That's why I wanted you to come here. Not to do anything, you understand, but to speak about it."

"Ok," was all Grafton could manage.

"We don't do anything about those things here at the commune. There can be no release, because that release is soporific."

She sounded out the first part of the word as 'soap'. That added another layer of detail to the scenes playing out in Grafton's head. He closed his eyes and took a breath.

"Even self-release," she said, "is forbidden."

"Ok."

"I brought you here so that you could understand that. There's often an agreement in principle with these things but then people start to live in close proximity and to co-mingle and

64

to grow bored and..."

"I understand."

Grafton heard the suck and slurp of water. He opened his eyes. Joan was sitting up in the bath now. A few stray strands of brown hair trailed down her back. A rivulet ran down the line of her spine.

"Rub some of those leaves on my back," she said.

"You're sure?"

Turning from her, he rolled up his sleeve, taking care to keep the Dictaphone lodged beneath the elastic. It wasn't recording because he hadn't yet had the opportunity to collect a new tape. He took a fistful of the leaves and tried to keep them between his fingers and her skin as he started to massage her shoulders. He felt the sting and itch of them against his knuckles. She showed no sign of flinching, no desire to scratch. She sat upright and breathed shallowly.

"Why are you here, Grafton?" she asked.

"At the commune?"

"Yes."

He cleared his throat, tried to will a redirect of blood from his groin to his brain. "I have a high-pressure job as a – as a teacher, and the workload is something that keeps me up in the evenings anyway and, erm–" He had to pause. "My son is a teenager and I'm a single dad, so..."

The thought of Isaac sharpened his guilt about his hand being on Joan's bare skin. His son was far closer in age to Joan than he was. There was something indecent about him touching Joan, even if she had stated that it wasn't sexual. He pulled his hand away, dropped the damp leaves into the bucket at his feet.

"...I've not had time for myself in years," he said, softly. "To pursue my own interests, my own ambitions. My own relationships, even. And I think of the time I wasted in my youth – the time I squandered – and it...well...it panics me."

Joan nodded. She tipped backwards and lay, full-length, in

the water again.

"Anything else?" she asked.

"That's about the size of it."

Grafton realised two things. Firstly, there was very little of what he'd just told Joan that wasn't the truth. And, secondly, his erection had gone. He sat down again.

"Good," Joan said. "Now let me tell you why I'm here…"

There was a long silence after that. Joan's eyes were closed and her breathing was soft and regular, but Grafton never thought that she was asleep or, indeed, that he should prompt her to continue. Instead, he sat there and listened to the gurgle of the water-tank, behind the wall, and the evenness of her breathing. He found that his inhale-exhale started to match hers and that his mind began to drift.

Liz had always had a higher sex drive than him. Not in a carnal way, he'd suggest, but in the sense of wanting to experiment and explore, to experience new pleasures. She would be the one to suggest relocating to the shower, or to the kitchen worktop. It had been her who'd bought those latex stockings, who'd asked if Grafton ever fantasised about having someone else in their bed. She'd always been more impulsive than him. It wasn't that she'd been bored, just that she wanted sex to be more than repetition.

That side of things hadn't been a factor in her leaving, though. Or, at least, not the biggest factor. There were other areas of their life which were in a deeper rut, Grafton saw that now, and she'd been the only one trying to dig them out. There were other reasons why she'd needed her freedom. Most folk did that by taking an evening class or buying themselves a new car, but she'd taken herself off to India instead.

"There's a practice called sleep training," Joan said, from the bath. "Have you heard of it?"

"With babies?" Grafton nodded. "You mentioned it earlier."

"Multi-million pound industry. Teaching you how to train

your child to sleep through the night, whether by coaxing them or by letting them cry or…" She gestured with her hand, flicking water over the side of the bath. "You get the idea. My parents didn't do sleep training, Grafton. Not like that, at least. They doped me. Right from the start, they made sure I slept by giving me doses of antihistamine or cold medicine.

Then, as I grew older, they upped the dose, added ground-up sleeping pills, and started to lock my bedroom door. My bedtime was the same when I was twelve years old as when I was six months. Past seven o'clock, they wanted me to be asleep so they packaged me away, with a plastic potty in the corner of my room. I was still using that plastic potty, at nighttime, as a teenager."

She opened her eyes and looked over at Grafton. He nodded to show that he was listening.

"They would go out. Not every night. Some nights they would sit through in the living room, drinking and listening to music. But, often, they would go out. To a restaurant or to the dancing. They'd leave me in my room and they'd lock the front door and off they'd go. If there'd been a fire, I'd have cooked. If I'd taken ill, I'd have died in my bed."

Her eyes were on him. There was no trace of tears or even the slightest glistening, she spoke as if reciting from one of the textbooks out on the coffee table. Those eyes, though. Grey is usually associated with dreich days or dirty dishwater. But not her eyes. They were gossamer.

"I started to fight against the medicine they gave me. Not in terms of taking it – I'd tried that struggle – but afterwards, fighting to stay awake. I dug my nails into my hands, I shone torchlight directly into my eyes, I pierced my thighs with pins. And, slowly, I won through. The sluggishness ebbed away, the alertness returned. Night after night, I managed to push back that tide so that I could sit cross-legged on the floor of my bedroom reading books or listening to the radio.

It was then I did my learning, not at school. There was focus in those hours. I found that I was staying awake right through until my parents came home at two or three in the morning, that I wasn't missing the sleep. I could survive without it. More than that, I could flourish."

Grafton thought of Isaac. Of the evenings when he would sit at the dining room table with his art materials scattered around him, fully immersed. He had always been a night owl. It was Grafton who needed to get up early in the morning and yet he would chide Isaac about the need to go to bed, to be fresh for college the next day. Then, through the lockdowns, it had been Grafton who'd kept the household running to his alarm clock, even though time had been formless and arbitrary. He guiltily thought back on the times he'd shouted at Isaac for dozing off on the sofa while watching the telly. There was a fair difference between nagging your child and giving them medicine they didn't need, mind you.

"I'm sorry you went through that," Grafton said.

"Sorry?" Joan smiled. Her eyes lit up. "Don't you see? My parents were right."

"How so?"

"You're focused on me. You're thinking about the way society wants us to treat sleep, as this thing to be cherished, this restorative. But my parents were the ones pushing against that. They were out until the early hours and they went into work the next morning as usual."

Grafton shook his head. "What did they do?"

"For jobs? Does it matter? He was a salesman – something to do with valves – and she worked shifts in a supermarket. They didn't need sleep, Grafton, they needed time to live."

It was at that moment that Grafton felt a rush of weariness. The heat of the room, the intensity of the conversation with Joan, all of it seemed to sag at his shoulders. He yawned. When he looked up, Joan was looking at him triumphantly, as if he'd provided all the evidence she needed.

"We didn't have internet in the house," she said, "but I could go online in the library. And I could print out page upon page. Hide them inside the textbooks I brought home to read at night. At first, I simply looked up ways to stay awake; things I could do to fight off the exhaustion. But then I came across the teachings of Swami Ravi. You've heard of him, Grafton?"

Grafton took a second, then nodded. "I've heard the name."

"In the teachings of Swami Ravi, sleep is a societally imposed construct. We are conditioned to sleep at the end of a day. We pull our every behaviour to that end. Sometimes we have to force it or we lie awake tormented by insomnia, rather than admit that we're simply not tired. That we haven't used up every last ounce of energy – emotional, spiritual, physical – through the day. You see why that would make sense for that young girl locked in her room night after night?"

"Yes." Grafton leant forward. "So, did you travel to India? To this Ravi?"

Joan shook her head. "No. His teaching was important to me, it was foundational, but I knew that travelling out to him would be a mistake."

"Why?"

That gaze again. Her eyes unblinking. "I was a young girl. And Swami Ravi has weaknesses."

She watched him for a moment, making sure that he understood. Then she sat up again, reaching a hand to the side of the bath to steady herself. She slid forwards, the water lapping against the far end, and leant her chin against the avocado edge.

"I don't blame him for that," she said. "None of us is infail-in*fall*-ible. And the rest of his teachings, Grafton, the rest of his teachings were everything. They were mother's milk to me, they were that first thick milk that comes through in the hours after the baby is born."

"Colostrum," Grafton said.

She blinked at him in surprise. "Is that the word?"

"My ex-wife was a nurse," he said, by way of explanation. The mention of Liz made him wonder if Joan knew her. She'd never been to India, but they might still have encountered one another. Before he could form the question, Joan continued with her story.

"You know what I did? At the age of fifteen, I told my parents that they were right. Not to lock me away or to dope me up — that was wrong — but to fight against the expectation that we sleep for seven or eight hours a night, that we are supposed to happily forgo a third of our lives. I told them that they were pioneers and visionaries. I showed them the printed pages of Swami Ravi's speeches.

"After that, there was no more medicine and no more locking of the doors. If they went out, I came along too. Although I'd always bring a book."

Grafton wished he'd been able to record this. All of it. Not to produce it wholesale in a radio documentary or to poke fun at it in a newspaper piece, but so that he could listen to it again — from first to last — and decide how he felt about it.

As he tried to digest everything she had said, he had a sudden, dreadful thought. A thought that seemed to drain all warmth from his body and jolt him back to full wakefulness.

"You're not still a teenager, are you?" he asked. "You're older than eighteen, I mean?"

Maybe he'd severely misjudged her age. It was possible, was it not. If she'd had her realisation at fifteen, then why would she wait to spread her message to the world?

Joan chuckled. "I'm flattered," she said. "But, no, I'm practically an antique — a heirloom — at this stage."

Higher-loom. Grafton realised that her mispronunciation of words must come from the fact that she'd only ever seen these longer words written down; that she'd learnt them from the pages of a book rather than from conversation or school.

"My parents were right," she said, "but they were also negligent. I couldn't let that go, Grafton, you can't let that go. They poisoned me, they imprisoned me. So, they had to pay for that and I'd read enough law texts to know that I was best to do it while I was still a minor. My research at the library wasn't only about the most effective ways to stay awake."

Grafton stared at her. Her gaze was as steady as ever. She gave the slightest nod and then pushed herself up from the edge of the bath. The disturbed water slapped against the end, flicked up over the taps. She stood there, naked and dripping. Her only imperfection, as far as Grafton could tell, was the intermittent rash from the poison ivy.

"Pass the towel," she said.

11

The hill behind the Seattle commune loomed over the chalets, green in patches of sunlight and brown in shade. It was scarred through with grey rock, ridges and overhangs. The bulk of it sheltered them from the worst of the wind, but the rain tended to settle in its shadows as well, so that you could be looking out to open, blue sky at sea and yet standing in the mizzling grey at the foot of the hill. Grafton would have dearly loved to set out to clamber his way to the top of it – to feel the strength of the wind, take a survey of the land out as far as Ardnamurchan Point, and add his stone to the cairn at the summit – but he had a feeling that his absence would be noted.

It was Debbie who advised him to volunteer for something early on. You wanted to be seen to be keen and you didn't want to be stuck with the jobs further down the list. So Grafton raised his hand for maintenance. He was placed in a group of four given the task of clearing a thicket of nettles down by the entrance to the commune.

They were given buckets but no shoes, gardening tools but no gloves. Barefooted, the four of them stepped gingerly onto the dewy grass at the verge and stabbed at the weeds until they came loose. The youngest lad, sandy-haired and with a wispy beard, waded in after a spell and started passing fistfuls out to the rest of them. No one followed him in. A watery-eyed woman whose name Grafton instantly forgot swung a hoe in the direction of the sandy-haired lad in an uncontrolled way that threatened his ankles more than the nettles.

The fourth member of the group was an older man named Jed. Grafton had met him the night before, after coming back from keeping Joan company. Along with Debbie, they'd sat up until one in the morning, drinking that tea concoction and playing cards.

Jed had told them his history in the pauses between hands. He was widowed. For forty-odd years, he'd worked in a lino factory in Fife and, after retiring, found that he couldn't scrub the smell of the place off his skin. Towards the end of the night, Debbie disappeared for a spell and Grafton was able to question him more directly.

"You seem a pragmatic man, Jed," Grafton said.

"Aye?"

"So, what do you make of–" Grafton paused. "There's a biological need for sleep, isn't there? Like, there's a fault-line in the reasoning behind this place, is there not?"

Jed thought that over, shuffling the deck of cards as he did.

"No one goes without sleep, Grafton," he said. "Only less sleep."

"Joan is going without, no?"

"Aye, she's doing that as inspiration, though. Like a boss might work deep into the night to show the workers they need to work harder, push further..."

"So, you're not expecting to find some cure, some panacea here then?"

Jed began dealing the cards. "Personally, I'm here to find some form of community, I'd say. I want to have folk around me, and to feel like I'm useful to them. It's nice to have a sense of purpose again."

"That makes sense."

"At my age," Jed said, "I can handle four hours sleep if it means I get company for the other twenty hours of the day, you know?"

Soon afterwards, they'd all gone off to bed and slept until five a.m., when Eddie woke them with a wooden spoon clattering off a saucepan lid. Truth be told, Grafton had probably managed less than his allotted four hours, by the time he'd twisted himself into a comfortable position on his top bunk.

He paused from his weed-clearing and tried to assess his level of tiredness. He felt it as a hollowness in his stomach. Like hunger, but with an edge of nausea. At home, he would have tried to quell it with crisps and sweets and chocolate. But here there was nothing but nettles and bracken. Until lunchtime, at least. There were no snacks and you visited the Pier Shop only with permission.

That morning, Grafton had been handed a small bowl of porridge. It was made with water instead of milk, seasoned with salt instead of sugar. He'd grimaced it down. Now, he thought of the orange and apple in his glovebox. He looked up to the office chalet at the top of the driveway. If he could nip in there unaccompanied, even for a few moments, then he could liberate his car keys from the hook behind the desk. Then he'd be able to replace the tape in his Dictaphone and fetch his notebook as well. Trouble was, Eddie and another man, Stevie, were inside.

They'd come out, twenty minutes or so ago, to take delivery of a couple of wooden pallets which had arrived in a white van. The pallets were covered in black plastic, like bin liners, and were heavy enough that it took both of them to lift them. One at a time. They took them to the side of the office building and stacked them there. Then they glanced down at the nettle-clearance operation and disappeared back inside.

A young boy, seven or eight years old, was coming along the road. He veered from one side to the other, kicking a crushed coke can and muttering away to himself. Probably commentating on an imaginary football match — Isaac used to do the same thing. Grafton stopped raking and watched the boy. He wore grey school trousers and a black puffer jacket. His backpack hung loosely off both shoulders, so that he had to keep shrugging it back on after each swinging kick of the can.

"Don't you grin at him."

The scolding voice came from behind the boy. It was a young woman, in a half-buttoned tweed jacket and with brown hair like an unravelling loom. She strode quickly towards them. At first, Grafton thought her shout was directed at the boy, but then he realised she was frowning at him. Grafton blinked, looked down at his white robe. Of course. He twitched the smile from his face.

"They should all be going as well, you know," the woman said. "You should be ashamed."

"Sorry?" Grafton frowned.

"You should be," she replied.

The watery-eyed woman stopped swinging her hoe. She held it out in front of herself, like a medieval pike, and turned to the young mother. The mother took a rocking step backwards onto her heel, but then pointed at them, one-by-one, with an extended finger.

"Don't you think I'm intimidated by you lot," she said. "My dad is a member of the Wee Free Church and I told him where to go, so I'll do the same with you lot and no mistake."

Grafton tried a softer smile and raised a hand to placate her. He'd have dearly loved to ask her some questions, but he was aware that the others were in earshot.

"Maybe I could walk you up the road a way—" he said.

"What are you – a pervert?"

"Eh, no. I just thought I could explain…"

"I can explain," the watery-eyed woman said. "Our children are home-schooled. They aren't forced to sleep, or wake, to fit with the school-bell. They learn, they play, they rest here with us."

"Brainwashing kids, is all you're doing."

The young boy with the can had stopped further down the road and was looking back now at his mum, chewing on his lip. Again, Grafton wished that he could have a quiet word – to say that the robe was only a disguise, that he was only gathering information. Then he could ask the young lad if he'd played with any of the commune kids, if he'd asked them what it was like living with the Sleepless.

Come to think of it, Grafton hadn't seen any children. Either that morning or the evening before. Were they all housed somewhere else? And did the Sleepless really expect them to survive on only a few hours a night, or were they allowed longer?

"Is there a schoolhouse in the commune?" Grafton asked the watery-eyed woman.

She sneered at him. "They learn from all of us."

"Bloody spaceman," the young mother muttered, "doesn't even know the shit that's happening right under his nose…"

"I've just arrived," Grafton said, turning back to her. "I'm trying to learn more—"

He felt a sharp dig in his ribs. His first thought was that he'd been attacked by the watery-eyed woman with the hoe but, when he twisted, he found Jed there. He'd only used his elbow. He jerked his head up towards the office chalet. Eddie and Stevie had both emerged. They skipped quickly down the steps and jogged down towards the group by the nettles.

The young lad scampered. Backpack swinging, side-to-side, he sprinted off down the road towards the kirk and the red phone-box on the corner.

"Jamie!" his mother shouted after him. He stopped and half-turned, but still stood poised to run.

"What's the issue, madam?" Eddie said, coming up to them.

"I'm telling this lot that your children should be on their way to school too."

Grafton admired the woman. The way she stood her ground as Eddie stepped closer, pushing his neck out until their faces were inches apart. She jutted her chin up and met his stare.

"Doesn't seem like that's any of your business," Eddie said.

"We were assured every child would be registered at the primary," she said. "So the teachers could keep an eye on them, at the very least."

"The school schedule doesn't suit our project."

"Fuck your project, what about the kids?"

Eddie nodded, then smiled. It struck Grafton as a dangerous smile — the curled kind that film gangsters wore when they thought of a new way of disposing of a body. Eddie turned to the four of them in the nettle-clearing crew.

"Back up to the office, all of you," he said. "We need to remind this lady of the benefits we've brought to the local community."

Jed, the watery-eyed woman, and the sandy-haired lad immediately turned and started to walk back up the driveway. The sandy-haired lad still carried a fistful of nettles, but he didn't seem to feel the sting and burn of them.

Grafton, for his part, wanted to stay. He wanted to make sure the young mother and her son were okay, of course, but he was also keen to hear what Eddie would say next. What was it he had to remind her of — a threat to the locals? A bribe, maybe?

"What're you waiting for?" Stevie hissed, leaning towards him.

And Grafton then realised something else: both Eddie and Stevie were down here on the road, so his car keys were hanging unattended. Here was his chance. The schoolboy, Jamie, was far enough away that he could make a sprint for it and what were they, realistically, going to do to the mother out in public, in broad daylight?

Grafton let his rake fall to the grass and set off after the other three. He lengthened his stride to close the distance and kept up the pace as he passed them. He needed to arrive ahead of them, even if only by a few seconds.

As he reached the steps to the office, he turned and looked back. The other three were only halfway up the drive, dragging their feet so that they could steal glances back at Eddie and Stevie. Those two were still down on the road, standing out in the centre of the tarmac. The young mother was hurrying away from them now, half-tripping in her haste. She waved at her son to walk on. There was no limp and she wasn't clutching at her face or crying. At worst, Eddie had put the frighteners on her.

Satisfied, Grafton jogged up the final few steps to the office.

12

Isaac had scrabbled through the communal recycling bins for pizza boxes. Not only the ones outside his flat, but all the way up and down the street. Like a fox in the nighttime, keeping to the shadows and nudging open bin lids. He came away with a haul of twelve boxes, but he had to discard one because the oily grease in the centre of it had soaked its way through. With eleven boxes, then, he sat on the living room floor and began to construct. His stomach grumbled about the smell of melted cheese and garlic.

As much as possible, he wanted the sculpture to be self-supporting and to mesh together without glue or tape. So, he used his scalpel to create slits which could join together to form the corner unit. Once he'd made the basic structure, he was going to cover it over with fabric and then with stickers and the painted slogans from Ravi's teachings. He still hadn't decided if he was going to include a figure on the sofa itself, but his first thought was that he'd position his sleeper-hold sculpture facing it – so that the arms holding the wrestler's head were forcing him to confront the sofa-ring, as if to invite him to decide between rest and action, between giving in and fighting back.

Isaac worked with jazz music playing from the laptop in the background. He'd turned off his phone, to concentrate on his work, but the notification chime from Messenger sounded out over Charlie Parker. Gritting his teeth, Isaac considered whether to check it or carry on. As soon as the thought had occurred, the spell was broken. He'd need to look. Besides, he could do with a pause. The model was already proving bigger than he'd intended, maybe even a quarter of the size of the original sofa behind it. Any smaller and the hessian rope would dominate, would look like the main focus of the piece, and there'd be no 'ring' to speak of in the centre. Bigger was the only option, but it did mean that he was going to need more cardboard.

Moving over to the laptop, Isaac clicked on the message. It was from Shauna: *Are you around college? Fancy some lunch? x*

Isaac tried not to fixate on the kiss at the end. It meant nothing. Over the past few months, Isaac and Shauna had made a habit of going to a campus café. Only a casual thing after class. Shauna would talk about her parents' divorce, back when she was a toddler, and how she couldn't really remember it but every so often her mum would needle her dad about the damage it had done to their kid. She'd say it all with a matter-of-fact tone and the slightest, tightest smile on her face. Then she'd look up at Isaac with brown eyes that matched the smell of roasting coffee and ask about his parents. And the first couple of times, he'd shrugged it off. But then, after five or six weeks, he'd taken a deep breath and found himself telling her not about his mum and dad, but about Swami Ravi. About this man who'd left a trail of allegations through Europe, North Africa and India. About his concern for what it meant for his mother and how far she might have trusted this chancer, who had been born and raised in Colchester and then set up as a self-styled guru. Shauna listened to the whole spiel, start to finish, and then folded him into a hug that smelt of vanilla syrup.

Pulling the laptop onto his knees, Isaac tapped out a reply to Shauna's message: *Working on pieces at home, sorry. Also no money for lunch.*

The reply came quickly: *I'll treat you if you come in x.*

Isaac paused. His stomach gurgled again. He could get the bus into college and take Shauna up on her offer, but then he'd lose the afternoon working on his sofa-sculpture. Better to go down the street to the pizzeria and get himself a margherita. He'd only bought a breakfast roll, teabags, and some milk from the twenty quid, so far, so he had enough. And maybe they'd sell him a wee bundle of unused pizza boxes if he explained it was for a college project.

He started to type out his reply: *Just going to work here, thanks* – but then his eye drifted back to Shauna's message and that phrase 'treat you'. Was there subtext beneath that? Could it mean that she'd reconsidered what she said the other week?

It had been back in the same café and they'd sat in the corner table by the toilets. There was a sour smell of bleach fighting with the richness of coffee beans, but it was a busy day on campus so those were the only free seats. Isaac had been rehearsing how to ask her out, in his head, for days. Perhaps it was the way that he shifted and fidgeted in his seat that made it awkward or maybe it was all that he'd revealed about his mum and the ways she was mixed up with Swami Ravi.

"I realised…" Shauna broke the silence, stirring her coffee. "During the first lockdown, this is, I realised that I might be asexual."

"Oh." Isaac couldn't get out more than that syllable. Her conversational opener was so unexpected that none of the hundreds of rehearsals he'd undergone had taken him even close to it. "Oh?" he repeated, managing to turn it into a question.

"Not that I couldn't have a friendship with a man, you know, or a relationship even, but that finding that first connection wasn't necessarily going to be…well…physical." Her eyes moved up to meet his. There was a perfect flick of eyeliner on either side. "You know what I mean?"

And, suddenly, Isaac did know exactly what she meant. She was letting him down gently, telling him that he'd misread the signals and that nothing could ever happen between them. She was pre-emptively cutting him off before he asked her out. It was a warning not to ruin their friendship, not to take the step that he'd been steeling himself for all week long.

"I think I know, yes," Isaac managed.

"All that time alone, or just chatting online, and you realise that we're told to look for that connection first, maybe, when actually it's a stronger foundation to get to know someone first and—"

"Does that make you asexual, though?" Isaac interrupted.

"Yeah." Shauna shrugged, raised her cup to her lips. "Dunno."

Thinking back on it, with the cursor blinking on Messenger and his words to Shauna left unsent, Isaac remembered Ravi's material that he'd read the night before. It spoke about the wasted energy that we expend on frustrated romantic love and how it could be better used in pursuit of higher goals. Sexual exhaustion, in his teachings, was a useful tool, but the fretting and agonising over whether feelings were requited or dating in the conventional sense were only distractions.

Isaac could lose the afternoon by taking the trip into college, but he could equally easily squander the time by having a back-and-forth with Shauna online. Better to take a wander to the pizzeria to get himself some food and, hopefully, the material to complete his sofa-sculpture.

He held the backspace key until his message to Shauna disappeared. Then he closed over the laptop and reached over to the dining table to scoop up the tenner and scattering of loose change that he'd left there that morning.

13

The minibus hurtled along the single-track road. Through the open window, Grafton caught sight of signs telling him that deer were likely to cross and rocks likely to fall. Eddie was driving, though, and Eddie wasn't stopping or slowing for man nor beast. If anything was coming the other way, then it would be the one swerving to the side of the road, whether into a passing place or the ditch.

There were a dozen of the Sleepless squeezed inside. Seats and seatbelts were largely notional, you just took any spare inches of space and were thankful to be wedged against your neighbour as Eddie flung the minibus around the corners. It was a battered old thing, each hubcap different and the white paintwork still bearing the lettered scars of the Church group that had owned it previously, but Eddie seemed proud of it and keen that all except those undertaking essential duties at the commune take the trip out to the beach at Sanna.

They'd been allowed to bring a jacket with them, to cover their robes, because they'd feel the chill off the sea. Eddie had relayed this information with a scowl that indicated that he wasn't necessarily in favour of the concession. Either way, it meant that Grafton had a pocket to hide his Dictaphone in. It had a new tape inside, with the full one left in the car boot, tucked up against the wheel jack. He'd already eaten his apple, but the orange was in his other pocket. His notebook and pen were tucked in underneath his mattress back at the cabin.

All of the Sleepless had taken their coats off at different stages of the drive. Grafton was one of the fortunate ones pressed up against the open window. The countryside was a blur of purple heather, with the interruption of grey rocks and sheep-shorn grass. Grafton found himself wondering about the wire fencing – miles of it with only three thin strands strung from post to post. Who maintained it? And was it honestly supposed to keep any animal contained?

Most of the landscape on either side was flat, windswept and treeless, but there was the occasional sweep upwards. It was from here that they were to expect landslides. As he peered up, Grafton saw a large stone with JESUS SAVES scrawled on it in white paint. There was no doubt that this was the right kind of setting for a cult – isolated, dramatic, eerily quiet – it was easy to imagine a Jim Jones or David Koresh style compound out in this bog and scrubland. That tag didn't seem to fit the group going off on their trip to the beach, though. They were full of chatter and, somewhere towards the back, Debbie was starting a wee sing-along of 'You Cannae Shove Your Granny Off the Bus'.

Grafton had to admit that he also felt pretty chipper on four hours sleep. He was aware that if he'd slept for such a short spell in the normal course of things – if he'd been forced to get up early for a flight, say, or stay up late for some bloody social event at work – he'd spend the next day yawning in a way that threatened to dislocate his jaw and with irritation bubbling in his chest like heartburn. So far, though, there'd been none of that at the commune. If one of the Sleepless saw you stifling a yawn, they'd tap a finger against their temple to remind you that it was all in your head.

All the same, Grafton couldn't help feeling that the mood was dependent on Joan. In some ways, she was preaching to the wrong folk. If she dressed herself up in a suit, hooked up a radio mic, and took to the stage in Edinburgh and London then surely it would be CEOs and business owners who'd be converted to her cause, adopting her words in the name of efficiency, synergy and holistic growth.

The minibus careened into the car park at Sanna. To the side was a dilapidated brown barn, with bales of hay positioned underneath the patches where the corrugated iron roof was still intact. On the side of the barn, facing the car park, was a message daubed in blue paint: INDYREF 2 NOW!

The Sleepless all trailed off the bus, stretching and taking deep, cleansing breaths. An oystercatcher, off to the right, peeped angrily at the group. Grafton tucked his hands into his jacket pockets and started to follow Eddie and some of the others towards the path. He wasn't used to walking with bare feet, so he trod slowly and carefully – keeping an eye out for broken glass and thistles – but he was also thinking that if he lagged then he would have the opportunity to be on his own for a spell.

The sand on the dunes was beautifully fine and held a little warmth if you dug your toes in. It slid off his skin as easily as water and, when he looked behind, he saw that he'd left no footsteps. The wind swirled through it and caused little eddies and flurries. He was glad, for a couple of minutes, that he'd been forced to give up his shoes, but then they came to some coarse grass that jagged at his heels and poked at his ankles. There was sheep shit everywhere. He was so busy thinking about where he was putting his feet that he didn't notice that Debbie had stopped to wait for him.

"Look at that," she said.

Grafton raised his head. The bay was laid out before him in a horseshoe. Sand as white as spilt salt was flattened, spread and rippled by the wind until it looked like a second sea – purer and calmer – beside the churning grey of the water. At the edges, the grass was trying to claw its way in and there were slatted rocks punctuating the beach like groynes. The waves kicked up against these, but the dominant sound was the fall and drag of the water on the main stretch of sand – the shushing of a patient mother comforting a newborn.

"Muck and egg, I think," Debbie said.

"What?"

He looked at her and saw that she was pointing out to a couple of islands on the horizon. Of course: Muck and Eigg.

Low-hanging clouds clung to the top of them. It looked like there might be rain out there, but it hadn't come inland yet.

"The others have walked on," Debbie said, reaching out and linking her arm in with Grafton's at the elbow. She wore an orange puffer jacket, like some oversized flotation device. Grafton longed to shake her off, but he knew that wasn't in the spirit of the group. They began walking, arm-in-arm.

"Did you come here because of Liz, then?" Debbie asked.

Grafton paused for a moment before answering. How honest did he want to be? How likely was she to tell the others? "I guess," he said carefully, "I came because I wanted to understand her."

Debbie made a noise in her throat, but didn't look up from her toes trailing in the sand.

"Do you know where she is?" Grafton asked. "Now, I mean."

"Your guess is as good as mine, I'd say."

"We only get the occasional postcard."

"We?" She looked up at Grafton. Strands of grey-red hair whipped across her face. She pulled them away from her lips. "Who's we?"

"Me and the boy."

Debbie sighed, an echo of the wind.

There was a shallow rivulet of water running in front of them, down towards the sea, with stones strewn along the side of it. Placing careful feet in it was like an endurance test, the chill of the water as exquisitely painful as hot coals.

"You didn't know she had a son?" Grafton asked, when they were on the other side.

"No. She never said. Not a word."

It only took a few steps on dry sand for the sharpness of the cold to ease in Grafton's feet. It was replaced by a numbness that made his footsteps heavy and clumsy.

"Mind you," Debbie continued, "we didn't talk much of life beyond the commune."

Grafton nodded. "Was it the same as this place?"

"In India, you mean?" Debbie considered. She turned her head away, towards the water. They were on an open stretch of the bay, where the white-fringed waves came in long sweeps that reached far up towards the tideline and left glistening sand in their wake. "That's a complicated one to answer," she said, finally. "It was the same but not the same."

"How d'you mean?"

"Well, the setting was very different for a start. Swami Ravi lived in one cramped apartment, above a market, and the rest of us lived in small flats scattered throughout the city. We'd often stay with him – or some of us would – but we'd also rent out halls and take journeys out to wasteland where we could set up a makeshift stage. Even those spaces, though, were nothing like this…"

She waved a hand towards the sea. Far in front, the rest of the Sleepless had fragmented off into smaller groups and were hunched and huddled over, searching the rocks like kids looking for crabs.

"And Ravi?" Grafton prompted. "Was he as…as persuasive as Joan?"

Debbie turned to him again. Her smile flickered to full beam. "Oh, heavens, yes."

Grafton nodded.

"Again, though," Debbie said, "it was different. He was full of brilliance and enthusiasm and, my word, you were *stirred* by what he said. You came out of his presence and you had your own pulsing energy field, you know." She shook her head. "It was hard to find ways to direct all that, though. He found it hard to utilise all of his own energy, never mind that of his followers."

"He was wired, you mean? Like a kid on candy floss?"

Debbie laughed. The wind whipped it away. "Yes," she said, "I suppose so. It's a good analogy, maybe, because he's also very impulsive."

"And Joan isn't?"

87

"No. No, Joan has focus. She never wavers."

For a spell, they walked in silence. There were tendrils of seaweed running through the sand, brown and with bubble-like capsules along the length of them. Grafton had to step around a 7-Up can – rusted at the base, the design faded to grey – and he caught sight of the ragged edge of a lobster creel, but mostly the beach was pristine.

"I'd lost touch with my daughter," Debbie said. Grafton turned to her, but the wind flicked her hair towards him so he looked ahead instead. "That's why I went to Ravi," she continued. "Four years ago. Which means wee Elsie is six now."

"Your granddaughter?"

She nodded. "Wee Elsie."

Grafton sensed that he was supposed to ask what had happened, that the thread had been left dangling on purpose, but he didn't. He had a feeling that hearing about the fault-lines in her family history might mean reciprocating and telling her about Liz leaving.

"I looked after her..." Debbie was going to tell him anyway. "Monday through to Friday, I looked after wee Elsie. Whilst her mum was at work, you know. Her dad wasn't on the scene and I thought it was the gran's role to step-in. So, we had this lovely little creche from when her mum set off until she returned at dinner time.

"It was exhausting, mind you. I knew I was blessed but it was tiring and my daughter knew it too. She was knackered as well, of course, and so she blamed what happened on the exhaustion. If she knew I was here, if she knew what Joan was teaching, then she'd only think it proved her point, only think she was right all along..."

Grafton stayed silent. Debbie sniffed a couple of times, but that could have been the cold.

"Truth be told, though," she continued, "I still don't see why there was all the hoo-ha. There was nothing wrong with–"

She took a breath. "I'm not explaining it well. It was a Tuesday morning. I left wee Elsie in her crib in the living room, a few toys around her, and went out back to water the plants. I thought nothing of it, honestly. But in the time I was away, the postie had arrived and heard a call or a cry from Elsie – can't have been much, mind you, or I'd have heard it myself. Anyway, he comes in and he thinks I've abandoned the baby. So, he calls the police and they call my daughter. By the time I come back inside, the full cavalry is on the way…"

They had reached the rocks. The rest of the Sleepless had carried on, so Grafton and Debbie hopped from rock to rock to follow them to the next bay. Grafton stretched his bare feet from one to the other, but he could feel nothing beneath his ankles. His toes curled, as if automatically, to grip at the stone. He wondered if he'd have chilblains or frostbite later.

"I explained myself," Debbie said, softly, "by telling my daughter that I'd often leave wee Elsie on her own for a spell. Just to run the hoover upstairs or nip out to the postbox, you know. And, honestly, you'd think I'd admitted to lifting the bairn by the leg and swinging her against the wall. I have more love for that wee one than anything or anyone else on this earth…"

Debbie stopped. Grafton carried on to the next stone, but then felt the drag at his elbow. He had to stop too, had to turn. Her hair continued to flail in the wind, the colours of it the same as the rusted 7-Up can, and she tried to catch at it and tame it with her spare hand.

"I've not seen wee Elsie in four years," she said. "Four bloody years."

Grafton knew that this was the gap he was supposed to fill with his own life story, that Debbie had shared her heartache with that expectation. The thought even crossed his mind that Debbie might have been asked – by Eddie, by Joan – to probe the new recruit a little.

What could he tell her? Liz had abandoned her son and her husband and flitted off to India. For a break, the note had said. A break from what, Debbie would ask, and Grafton would have to either bite back the truth or tell her about the drinking. That there was a spell in his life when he'd sit with his laptop and a bottle of blended whisky, of an evening, and set to writing. At first there would be more key-taps than sips but that quickly switched, until the sips were constant and the key-taps intermittent.

Debbie would be the type to ask follow-up questions too. The first would be why Liz didn't take Isaac along with her, especially if Grafton's drinking was out of control. Although he was in control. When Isaac was awake, he was only ever hungover. It's as easy to hide high-functioning alcoholism from a child as it is to hide it from yourself. All the same, if he was honest, he had to admit that he'd never quite worked out the answer to that question: why Liz hadn't come back for her son.

"That's tough," Grafton finally said, looking across at Debbie. "About Elsie."

Debbie shrugged. "I'm lucky, I've found family here."

Grafton wanted to ask her if she really thought that was the same thing, if she'd honestly rather be on this beach than at home with her granddaughter. Instead he reached into his pocket and lifted out the orange. He dug a nail in under the skin and the zesty smell rose and then faded. He carefully peeled the skin off in one piece – an elephant trunk and ears – like he used to do for Isaac.

"What d'you get from all this in the end, though?" he asked, offering half of the orange to Debbie.

"How do you mean?" She took the half-orange.

"Like, is the idea that you become the perfect babysitter – never needing a rest?"

"Maybe that was the idea at first. But then I realised I was gaining time." Debbie began chewing. "And once I had that, I got greedy and wanted more of it. I lost that sense of panic that time was slipping away."

"Simple as that?"

"Joan sometimes likens it to those projects where they reclaim land from the sea. You know, man-made islands or peninsulas in the Middle East. Reclaiming time from sleep."

Grafton considered this. In that pause, that silence, he realised that his teeth were chattering between eating each segment of orange. He wrapped his arms around himself, pulling the jacket closer. The cold wasn't only coming from the spittle-spray of the sea; it was spreading upwards through his body, like an anaesthetic, from his feet.

"The others," Debbie said, nodding her head to the bay beyond and jamming the final two pieces of orange into her mouth. She pointed at the remainder of Grafton's orange, so he followed suit, chewing and swallowing quickly.

When he turned, he saw several of the Sleepless coming towards them. Eddie was at the front of the group, holding up a clear plastic bag. It took a minute before he was close enough for Grafton to see what was inside: cans and bottles and crisp packets and wire and driftwood and rusted hinges and a frayed shuttlecock.

"Give that here," Debbie said, taking the orange peel from his hand. "It's just some rubbish we found on the shoreline, ok?"

14

Grafton watched Morven open a dozen cans of condensed milk and empty them into a big saucepan. The flame was turned up high but the milk showed no sign of boiling. She turned to him, eyes wide and pleading. He could only shrug his shoulders.

"Do I just keep stirring then?" she asked, holding up a wooden spoon.

Morven was a youngster – maybe only a year or so older than Isaac – with bitten down nails and a tattoo on her forearm. It was meant to be waves and a tiny drifting boat, but it looked like a child's scribble. Her eyebrows were also drawn on, but the left was thicker than the right. Her black hair was tied up in a yellow scarf.

"I've always worked off ready-meals and takeaway," Grafton said. "Sorry."

It was Debbie who'd assigned the cooking of the dessert to the two of them. He knew from the start that she'd chosen poorly, but she was adamant that the recipe was easy – boil the condensed milk until it turned to a light brown caramel and then smear it across digestive biscuits. Nothing could be simpler, she said.

Mealtimes were communal. Each cabin was given a dish to prepare and then the whole lot was brought to the A-frame. Meals were basic, true, but it wasn't quite as grim as the woman in the Pier Shop had made out. It only required a bit of improvisation and imagination; like the cheapskate version of millionaire shortbread they were making.

"Keep at it," Grafton told Morven, "you don't want it to stick to the bottom."

She looked up, panicked. "Where are you going?"
"Toilet."

Once he was out of the kitchen, he moved quickly past the

bathroom to the bedroom. Other than the two of them, the cabin was empty. He needed to make use of these opportunities.

He reached in underneath his mattress, pulling out his notebook and pen. Then he moved back across and closed the door. He sat with his back against it, to buy himself a few seconds if anyone tried to come in. Turning to a blank page, he began to write:

Joan. Antihistamine. Plastic potty. Parents abandoned her nightly. Father a postman. Sleep training – look into it. Revenge on parents? Time in prison? Age? Jed here for companionship, really, and community. Debbie similar, but to replace family. And Morven? Young and uncertain. Maybe running from something?

His thoughts were slippy. Like when you forget a word and start a game of mental charades with yourself in search of it. There had been more to it than that, Joan had said more of substance. But tiredness was starting to drag at him now, mixed with a worry that someone would try to push their way into the room and find him scribbling. For the first time in years, he craved a dram of whisky, to settle his nerves and sharpen his thoughts.

The notes he had would have to be enough. For now, it would have to be enough. He'd get Joan on tape next time so there was no need to fret about not having perfect recall. He pushed the notebook back under the mattress. Then he paused. He closed his eyes. It was Debbie who had talked about the postman, wasn't it? Had Joan mentioned her dad's job at all?

Grafton pulled the notebook out again. He carefully scored out the line about her father. It meant he had even less to go on, but he needed to be patient – it was only his second evening in the commune, after all.

The curtains were drawn in the A-frame, not against sunlight but against the blotchy grey sky and the insistent drizzle of rain. Grafton wondered if he could hear thunder, from somewhere far off, but it could just as easily have been farm machinery or the evening ferry grinding its ramp against the slipway.

All of the Sleepless sat, cross-legged, on the floor of the central room. On their knees was a paper plate with fusilli cooked in a tomato and courgette sauce. Grafton scooped the pasta into his mouth quickly, the sea-air and exercise had left him with a keen hunger. He wondered what Isaac would be having – he had visions of donner kebab or fish and chips.

"You don't need to stop eating," Eddie called. He was up on the raised platform, arms out. "But listen up for a minute, ok."

Behind him was Joan, flanked by an older woman in a white robe. Joan was eating on her own, but the other woman had been tasked with napkin-dabbing and spot-cleaning duties. Joan's head was sagged, her chewing slow. She wore wide sunglasses.

"Guard duties for tonight," Eddie announced, "are as follows: Stevie and Whippet on patrol, myself and John in the office."

Grafton looked across to Whippet. It was an ironic nickname, because the man was the size of a gable-end. In his younger days, he might have been a prop forward but he would never have been fast. There was more hair on the back of his huge hands than remained on his head.

As Grafton looked away, he caught sight of a movement over by the shrine. Underneath the table was a bundled robe, maybe, or a pile of bedding. It shifted again and Grafton saw that it had a face and tufted brown hair. A young boy, maybe ten years old, was crouched in underneath the table looking out at the adults in the room. His roving eyes moved across and met Grafton's stare. Unblinkingly, they held each other's gaze for a few seconds. And then the boy lifted a finger to his lips.

Up on the platform, Eddie looked over his shoulder at Joan. He took a wee step forwards and then a step to the side, like he was rehearsing for a ceilidh. There was a pause. Grafton watched Eddie's hand, which clenched and unclenched at his side. Then Joan put down her plate and held a hand out to the woman beside her. She was helped to her feet. Eddie stepped to the side as she shuffled to the front.

"Friends," she said, in a voice that was softer than usual. The Sleepless leant forward, as one, to catch her words. "We are in the midst of a great experiment which will, I'm certain, alter things. And...and...there will be challenges along the way which I want, which I wish, to talk to you about."

She drew in a breath. Her voice was growing stronger, but the glasses stayed on.

"They won't like their hypocrisy being exposed. There will be push-back and we will have to be prepared for that. Sleep is sedation, remember, sleep is sedation. But it is not their only method – they distract us with work and with gossip and with technology and with forms to fill in and meetings to attend."

Her hand went up to her temple and rested there for a moment. Grafton thought he could see a slight tremble to the fingers.

Grafton looked across to the young boy underneath the table. He was focused on the platform, drinking in Joan's words. He wasn't supposed to be here, wasn't supposed to hear this. The simplest solution, Grafton knew, was to draw someone's attention to it, but something prevented him from raising his hand or beckoning to Eddie. What was it? Was it simply that the boy wanted him to keep it quiet? Or was it that he didn't trust in Eddie's judgement of a suitable punishment for a child caught sneaking in where he wasn't supposed to be?

"They are content for us to forgo sleep if it suits their ends, yes?" Joan continued. "Those of you who have engaged in the relentless grubby pursuit of money can attest to that, I'm sure, and those of you who served in the forces..." She gestured behind herself, to where Eddie was standing. "They keep you awake, keep you wired, for those short spells but they never speak about how we can make use of those hours not for destruction, not for killing or for profit, but for self-improvement, for finding a way to better deal with the coming challenges.

"Use those hours that they controlled not in sedation or in thrall to their agenda, dear ones, but instead to wrestle yourself free. Sleep is sedation, but you are all awake."

Another pause. There was no doubt, though, that she was gaining in strength. The last line was delivered in something close to a shout and her nostrils were flaring. Grafton realised, belatedly, that he should be recording. He reached out to his sleeve, but stopped short when Joan reached up to remove her sunglasses. She was staring right at him. Her right eye was flooded with blood, all of the white now obscured by red. Red against the grey of the iris.

Grafton kept his focus firmly forward, not daring to break eye-contact with Joan. Even a darting glance at the shrine, he felt, could expose the boy's hiding place. He thought of playing hide-and-seek when Isaac was a toddler, that deliberate performance of searching elsewhere even though he'd immediately seen where his son was.

"Animals are fattened before slaughter," Joan began again. "We know that. And they're caged and they're clipped and they're corralled." She didn't get close to the correct pronunciation, but it didn't matter. "They don't need to sedate the poor beasts before slaughter, friends, because those animals are so acclimatised, so indoctrinated, so docile that they inch forwards to the knife without even a growl or a cry of protest. That is achieved not by sleep deprivation, you understand, but by limiting the time they have when they can actually be awake.

"Every day millions of people in this country – across the world, even – will wake up and gulp down a coffee. It will be the first of many and it will come from a franchise worth billions and be drunk from a plastic cup that will pollute our seas. Then those same people will go to their offices and move numbers around a spreadsheet until the bottom line matches the number they're been told to aim for, yes? And then they'll go home and they'll put the television on for their children and they'll drink a glass of wine or two. The children will go to bed and, if they stir or they lie awake, they'll be firmly told to get back under the covers. Downstairs, the adults will yawn and tell each other how tired they are, how important it is that they get a good night's sleep. And all the while, outside those walls, the seas are poisoned and the natural resources are pillaged. The climate teeters on the brink of collapse, dear ones, whilst we are lost in sleep.

"We push ourselves, friends, through these eleven nights because then – on the twelfth day – I will show you how to remove the last barrier to being truly wakeful. We have been quiet, but we will be loud. We have kept to the shadows, but we will come to the light. We have gone unnoticed, but they will take heed."

Joan drew in another breath. As she did so, she stumbled forward a step. Like a gymnast balancing after a dismount. Both Eddie and the woman with the napkin moved towards her.

The distraction allowed Grafton to look over, again, at the shrine table. The boy was sitting upright now, his legs crossed and his hands clasped together. All his attention was on Joan.

Up at the front, Joan was waving Eddie and the woman away. She looked again at the Sleepless, on the floor in front of her. No one was eating now. Half-empty plates of pasta were discarded to the side or lay ignored on laps.

"They won't like that next step." Joan moved her head slowly around the room, scanning the faces. "It gives us an advantage. We're ahead of the others. When food is short, they will have to leave their spreadsheets and go foraging. We will already be in the forests. They will have to let their television babysit the kids and go fishing. We will already be at the river. They will, finally, have to abandon their sleep and go out to the fields. We will already be harvesting.

"And I'm warning you all – it is my message to you all – that they won't like that. They won't accept that we saw this coming, that we wrestled ourselves free, that we saw we were being controlled. They will be angry, you mark my words, and they will blame us for their own ignorance. They are insidious and mendacious and they will come for us.

They will offer you creature comforts, yes, but they will be all the sedatives you have already turned your back on, you have already learned to live without. They will offer you processed food, they will offer you entertainment, they will offer you money and lifestyle. And you will say: I have learned how to live the life of the truly wakeful, I have seen the twelfth day.

But they will return. Believe me. They will come back with court orders and with policemen and with stretchers and ambulances and pills and stretchers and canisters of sleeping gas. They will try to sedate you by force, dear ones, and, when they do, you must resist."

Joan closed her eyes. She held her arms out to the side. Her head tipped back. The applause started off to Grafton's right. It travelled in a rippling wave, and he found himself caught up in it. Lifted by it, to his feet along with the others. Paper plates fell to the ground, robes were splattered with tomato and courgette sauce. The clapping became rhythmic, a steady beat.

Grafton remembered about the boy. He ducked through a couple of bodies, found himself an angle where he had a sight of the shrine. There was the young lad, still sitting underneath the table with his legs crossed. He had a beatific smile across his face and he was clapping along with everyone else. Even if he was found, they'd soon realise that he was only here to see Joan preach, to join the rest of the Sleepless in savouring each and every word which came out of her mouth.

From somewhere up in front came some music. Electronic music replaced the hand-clapping with a throb across the fusilli-strewn floorboards. And Grafton, along with everyone else, raised his hands and began to dance.

15

It was one of those chain hotels with an abstract painting of a flower on the wall and a branded purple counterpane across the bottom of the bed. Liz set down her bag and moved across to the wooden shelf beside the TV. There was a procedure to be followed. She took the mini-kettle to the bathroom sink and filled it from the tap. Carrying the water through, she emptied it over the pillows. She went back to fill it again and, this time, poured it over the rest of the sheets. After two more trips, the mattress was sodden.

She'd performed this ritual at countless budget hotels over the years. As they moved from one city to the next. It was unlikely that she or Ravi would succumb to the temptation of a soft bed, but they often had greener, weaker followers with them. Youngsters who might trail a hand over a pillow and remember Sunday morning lie-ins; decide they were chilly as an excuse to wrap themselves in the duvet; then smell the freshly laundered linen and find their eyelids drooping.

Ravi taught that sleep comes unbidden after spiritual or emotional exhaustion. You don't lie in comfort and call sleep to you, you resist it and push yourself as far as you can. If the body succumbs and you sprawl on the cold floor, then so be it, but you should wake with a crick in your neck or a spasm in the muscles of your back so that, next time, you stay awake longer, go further, experience more.

Liz wheeled the bed to the side of the room, exposing a patch of carpet where the sun hadn't faded the striped-green pattern. It was commendably clean, only dust and a few copper coins. In other hotels, she'd found chocolate bar wrappers, folds of toilet roll splattered with blood, used condoms, once even a hypodermic needle. All the tools of human frailty, as Ravi would say.

Liz returned to the wooden shelf and gathered up the teabags and sachets of coffee, sugar and sweetener. She carried them over to the window. It was on a catch to stop it opening more than a crack. Still, she could stuff them through, one at a time, and send them fluttering down to the streets of Glasgow: a twirling confetti of Kenco and Twinings, Silver Spoon and Canderel.

She stood there for a moment, looking down on the familiar sight of the M8 cutting through the city centre, the dome of the Mitchell Library on the other side and then, beyond that, the streets stretching along to the leafiness of the West End. Had she missed this place? Maybe. She was Glaswegian born and raised, after all. And she'd not had a bad childhood: her and her mother living out in Maryhill in a top-floor flat with a view not dissimilar to this one. When her mum had been working late in her cleaning job, an elderly woman from across the hall, Mrs McKenzie, would come to sit with her. Liz remembered her as a miasma of cigarette smoke and gameshow theme tunes.

This wasn't the way to conduct self-critique. You don't reminisce about the past, you access it properly. You don't stare out of the window, dewy-eyed; you place yourself in a space and isolate your own experience from the societal pressures and expectations which surround it.

Liz moved across to the square of carpet where the pattern was sharper. She shed her clothes. First her skirt, then her blouse. She pulled the bobble out of her hair. Unclipping her bra and peeling off her pants, she kicked the bundle of fabric to the side and stood naked. She closed her eyes and raised her hands, moving them through the empty space. Then she sat, cross-legged, on the carpet.

After such a long journey, Ravi would have argued for pursuing physical exhaustion – following the path she was already on – but Liz knew that only an emotional examination was possible in this particular moment. She'd come back to Glasgow, so she needed to think about Isaac. About her boy.

He had been in Primary Four at school when she'd left. She remembered him as a waif of a child with hair that started the day in a side-parting and ended it as a bird's nest. He wore a red school jumper and she had a memory of him in grey, knee-length shorts. But that wasn't right. He hadn't worn shorts, he had worn trousers, scuffed at the knees.

Abandoning your child, Liz knew, ran counter to the common conception of motherhood. It was verboten. Yet, it had been clear that Isaac was becoming more-and-more self-sufficient. He woke himself, dressed himself, fetched his own breakfast. He was at school and, when he came home, he would be drawing or watching wrestling clips online. Increasingly, she felt that she needed to be present only because there needed to be a living-breathing adult in attendance. She was Mrs McKenzie, minus the cigarette smoke and the gameshows.

And then she would take herself away for a long-weekend or for a few days and find such richness and fulfilment. Yoga workshops and cultural tours, residential courses, and silent retreats. To come back from those to the emptiness of her life in Glasgow – with her nursing bound up with red tape and her home-life conducted in the snapshots of attention her husband and son paid her – meant that she felt like she was sleep-walking through her days.

She thought, sitting there on the hotel carpet with her eyes closed, of her own mother. A working woman who hadn't had a passport until her fifties. Who'd taken another decade to work up the courage to step on-board a cruise ship and then decided it wasn't for her and disembarked when it stopped off at Southampton. Nothing wrong with that, necessarily, but couldn't she have done more? Or, maybe the better question, when did it become impossible for her to do more?

Ravi didn't talk of children as anchors. That wasn't part of his teaching. But he did talk of the need to attend to the potential of the present moment and of the danger of building a routine based on the needs of others. Relying on that dependency was itself a crutch, used to mask the injury done to the self.

Liz remembered hearing that in an audio clip from one of Ravi's speeches. And looking, with her headphones on, at her young son drawing over on the dining room table, her chest had ached with grief. She felt it as a contraction of her ribcage. Because she knew, in that moment, that what she'd miss about him wasn't the relationship they had, but the intimacy that they had shared in the past. That tug of him breast-feeding; those sticky hands clawing at her shoulder at meal-times; those calls in the night to find his teddy or turn his nightlight to face him. That feeling of being needed.

And she hadn't intended on separating from him entirely. Her original plan, eight years before, had been to travel to join Ravi and lay the groundwork. Then, when the time was right, to bring Isaac out to live with them all.

Her eyes flickered open. Her gaze moved across to the mirror, to the side of the wooden shelf which she'd stripped of its amenities. She caught her own eye.

"And I did come back for him," she said, aloud, to the empty room. "I did try."

16

Truth be told, the main challenge in the commune was staving off boredom. There was tea to be drunk, music to be blasted and exercises to be done, but there was a limit to how often the minibus could take them out to Sanna or the chore rota extended with busy work. Kilchoan itself had little to offer by way of entertainment; the Sleepless had been barred from the pub because they only ordered tap water and the elderly woman in the Pier Shop was known to throw a tin of peas at your head if you went in to browse her magazines.

Twice daily, though, the children of the commune took a walk along the coast road. Grafton found out about it by accident. After a long morning of clearing rain-sodden moss from the tiled side of the A-frame, he was returning tools to the office and saw a wee clutch of half-a-dozen white-robed kids milling about. Two older teenage girls stood beside them, gently corralling them away from the empty road. Stevie was coming out of the office as Grafton climbed the steps. He was, in many respects, a carbon copy of Eddie, but with ears that jutted out a touch more and a paunch-belly that stretched out the fabric of his robe.

"Busy?" he barked at Grafton.

"Just putting these back." Grafton held out his trowel and a bucket.

"Grab some plimsolls and come with us."

"Where are we going?"

"The youngsters like to watch the ferry coming in."

As he collected his shoes, Grafton also stopped by the car. It was hidden from the group, down at the road, by the pile of wooden pallets at the side of the office. The pile had grown – there were now a total of seven pallets stacked there, all wrapped in black plastic. They formed a perfect barrier to shield him as he took the keys from the tyre, in underneath the wheel-arch. Opening the passenger door, he dipped into his wallet in the glovebox and found some loose change.

"You try on all the shoes in the shop, aye?" Stevie asked, as he walked up.

Grafton returned his smile. "Needed to find a pair to match my outfit."

"Ha," Stevie said the word, rather than actually laughing. "Do you know Gillian and Becky?"

He gestured to the two girls. One had straw-coloured hair and the other mousy-brown. Grafton nodded at them both, without knowing which was which.

They set off. Grafton scanned the group of kids, looking for the young lad who had been in the main hall the evening before. The children ranged in age from perhaps four or five to fifteen or sixteen. Grafton looked for signs of exhaustion but, if anything, they seemed to have less of the slump and sigh kids usually have. There were no yawns or dark bags underneath their eyes. And there was the boy, right at the back. Dark hair and a drag to his feet as he walked.

One of the minders, the one with straw-coloured hair, dropped off from the back of the group and fell into step alongside Grafton.

"I'm Becky," she said, with a small smile.

"Grafton. Nice to meet you."

As they walked, she stretched out an arm and pointed up to the hillside behind Seattle. There was a thin fog, spreading out in tendrils. You could still feel the looming presence of the hill, but only a small strip of it was visible.

"They'll not see much today," she said, softly.

"What's that?"

"The ones up in the hills."

Grafton shook his head, still none the wiser.

"The government spies," Becky said, smiling. "They'll not see much today."

And, with that, she skipped forwards to catch up with the children and left Grafton a pace or two behind. Grafton watched her go. Did she really think there were government spies in the hills? Was that an idea straight from Joan or had she cooked it up herself? Paranoid fantasies of agents of some internal agency or police force sitting up there in the bracken and heather, sipping from a flask of coffee and watching them all through binoculars.

The small band of the Sleepless turned left and followed the hook in the road. The kirk and the phone box was to the side, but Grafton knew better than to peel off immediately. He needed to wait until the others were lost in muttered conversation or in their own thoughts.

The morning's rain had left the verges of the road lush and heavy with thick-bladed grass and all manner of wildflowers slobbered with cuckoo spit. Sticky willow reached out to pluck at his robe. The air had a faint sour smell – like that left by a sick toddler – but Grafton wasn't sure if it came from the dripping plants or from the seaweed down at the shore.

As they passed the play-park, the group paused to read a laminated sign attached to the gate. Grafton came level with it a minute or so later. LOCAL CHILDREN ONLY, it said in typed letters. The ink was smeared by rainwater.

Stevie, Gillian and Becky had bunched up, walking on and whispering together about the sign on the play-park gate. Grafton saw his chance. He took a few paces back and then ducked down behind a bin. The curve of the road took the group out of sight. As soon as they disappeared, he hurried back through the ankle-high grass, stepping carefully to avoid thistles and thorns. Within seconds, his shoes were saturated and the hem of his robe hung heavy. He glanced over his shoulder and then moved out onto the road. His toes squelched as he started to jog back towards the phone box.

He was breathing heavily and holding a hand to the stitch at the side of his stomach. Those callisthenics up at the commune didn't seem to be doing him much good. He lifted the receiver and fumbled some coins into the slot. Isaac's mobile number was, of course, programmed into his destroyed phone, but he could remember the landline number. Finally, a benefit of being from the analogue generation.

He dialled and listened to the ringing. Come on, Isaac. Come on. Pick up. It rang out, switched over to the automated BT answerphone. A message would have to do, he decided. Isaac might well be out at college, or wherever, and Grafton didn't know when he'd make it to the phone box again.

"Isaac," he said, after the beep. "Mobile's broken, so just a quick call to let you know that all is well. There's definitely a story here, kiddo, definitely. I just need a bit more material. I'll try tonight and will leave…well…the latest I'd be would be Friday morning. So, I'll be back for your exhibition. Promise. In the meantime, order yourself a supermarket delivery. The password for the login is WrestlemaniaX7, with a capital W and X, and then use the saved card details. Ok, buddy." He paused, considered. "Love you," he said, before placing the receiver back in its cradle.

As Grafton strode back along the coast road he tried to think when the last time he'd told his son that he loved him was. It became a given once he was a teenager. There was no need for that nighttime tucking in, that whispered 'sleep tight'. All the same, he wished he'd said it more, over the years, instead of shouting along the hallway for Isaac to switch his bedroom light off and then settling down in front of the nightly telly routine.

It was like Joan said, for years he'd been living like he was sedated.

17

The ferry was beginning to manoeuvre around to meet the slipway as Grafton turned the corner by the Coastguard Station. That was the first thing he saw: the black and white hull of the boat churning up spray, the red and yellow emblem on the funnel. The second thing he saw was Stevie. He was striding towards Grafton, something held upright in his hands. For one absurd second, Grafton thought that it was a baguette. Then he realised that it was a wooden fence post, soil still clinging to the base of it.

The children, with Becky and Gillian, stood further up the road, beside the queue of waiting cars. They weren't looking at the ferry, ramp starting to ease down towards the concrete, but at Stevie coming along the road to meet Grafton. Those on the passenger deck of the ferry were looking too, seagulls wheeling above them and screeching out in alarm.

Run, Grafton thought. *Turn the fuck around and run.*

His feet didn't move, though. It was too unreal, this angry young man in a white robe and black plimsolls pacing towards him wielding a fence post. And, surely, he was protected – wasn't he – by the sheer number of witnesses, by the presence of the kids. Even so, as Stevie stepped closer, Grafton could make out a twist of something grey and spiky at the top of the fence post. A curl of barbed wire.

Run, run.

This time he did move. He spun on his heel and set off, but his foot caught – on the uneven tarmac, on the sodden hem of his robe, on god-knows-what – and down he went, hands splayed out in front to break his fall.

Stevie was up to him in a moment. Grafton flinched, tensed for the blow. It never came. Instead, he felt a hand on his shoulder. He looked up. The anger that had contorted Stevie's face was fading, to be replaced by concern. The fence post was propped up against his leg, held in place by his other hand.

"Did they get you?" he asked.

"Eh?"

Behind them, the ferry ramp clanged down onto the concrete.

"Who stopped you? Was it someone from the houses or the police or...?" Stevie had a firm grip of his shoulder. "Did they ask about the children?"

Grafton closed his eyes, tried to compose himself. He wasn't under suspicion. Or, at least, not for going off to make a phone call. Stevie was worried that the locals had been interrogating him.

"Not that, not that," he stammered, opening his eyes. "Nothing like that."

"What then? Where were you?"

The growl of a car engine behind them bought him a few seconds. The ferry was beginning to unload. They stepped off the road, onto the grass at the side. Stevie heaved the fence post over as well. It fell with a wet slap, sent up a spatter of mud. As the first car passed, Grafton caught sight of a woman staring at them open-mouthed from the passenger-side window.

"I felt faint," Grafton said. His palms stung from the fall. "My head was...I was light-headed and I couldn't keep up. You were too far ahead."

"And no one asked you questions?"

Grafton shook his head. "I sat down at the side of the road."

He took a fistful of his robe, from down past his knee and held it up for inspection. It was soaking wet and grass-stained.

Stevie was still frowning. He held Grafton's gaze for a few more seconds and then his eyebrows lifted.

"Fuck," he said, smiling. "I thought you'd been snatched."

"No, not me."

"But you're just a bloody lightweight, is that it?"

"Must be – still getting used to it all." Grafton tried a smile.

"Ha. You fought through it though, right?"

"Right."

Stevie put his hand back on Grafton's shoulder. He squeezed it and hooked the rest of his arm over too. It was uncomfortably close to a headlock, but Grafton didn't protest – he was just relieved that the fence post had been discarded. Stevie kept him in the rough cuddle for a few seconds and then released him.

"Let's go join the others," he said, "watch the ferry loading up again."

They waited for the last of the cars to pass and then walked up the road to the others. Becky insisted on having a look at his grazed hands. There was a scrape of skin taken from each hand, but nothing more. She wiped at them carefully with a damp dock-leaf and asked if it eased the pain. Grafton didn't have the heart to tell her that dock leaves were for nettle stings, so he nodded his head and turned to the slipway.

The foot passengers were disembarking now. Several of them waved to the children. Gillian encouraged the younger kids to wave back, nudging at those who didn't. Stevie only stared, with his hands at his sides. There was no attempt to engage the incoming folk in conversation, no sign of a flyer of their teachings being handed out or a call for tourists to come and see the commune for themselves.

As the first waiting car, with caravan attached to the back, moved up the metal ramp onto the ferry – clank, clank – Grafton took a breath. It was the first breath he was conscious of taking since he'd caught sight of that fence post. And with it came a tremor. Starting from the base of his spine. A shaking that trembled through the centre of him and spread right out to his fingertips. His stomach churned and gurgled.

Then, as the final pulse of adrenaline faded, Grafton felt his knees buckle. And then all he could think, over and over, was why that word? Why not unbuckle? Why buckle instead of unbuckle? Buckle-buckle-buckle. He felt his body sway, his centre of gravity pitching like those seconds before sleep when you sometimes skydive while lying motionless in bed. He jerked himself upright, then pulled his arms across his stomach and squeezed. All the same, he knew that if he didn't sit down then he'd simply keel over.

Checking the grass behind, Grafton lurched back and sat on a stone that jutted out from the grass verge. It wasn't dry, but neither was he.

The small, dark-haired boy took a step back from the main group. A subtle movement, but enough to leave him beside Grafton. He looked down and smiled. His teeth were cluttered in the middle and full of gaps at the edges. An orthodontist's dream. Grafton hadn't noticed that the night before.

"I'm Zack," he whispered.

Grafton nodded. He didn't trust himself to speak. It would have come out as a stutter or a morse-code of chattering teeth.

"I thought he was going to hit you with the wood," Zack whispered.

"Me too," Grafton hissed. He couldn't help grinning back at the kid.

"Glad he didn't."

"Thanks." Grafton paused. "I'm Tom."

Zack held out his right hand for a handshake. Grafton unfolded his arms and reached out. The youngster's grip was firm and he gave no sign of noticing the tremble to Grafton's fingers. He held on. As the seconds passed, the grip didn't loosen. The ferry ramp started to creak upwards, with the last of the passengers safely on the boat.

Grafton was in awe of the simplicity of the gesture from Zack. He'd seen Grafton was rattled and he'd stepped back to hold his hand. His mind wandered to the countless times he'd held Isaac's hand on the walk to school. That curious step-skip walk that Isaac had done to keep up, his schoolbag swinging loosely from his shoulders. And the nattering that he'd always kept up – the questions about why the men were digging up the road, and how the birds knew to fly up from the trees as a group, and whether the house with the boarded-over windows would be fixed up again. When had that stopped? The hand-holding, yes, but also the questions that presumed Grafton to be a fount of knowledge? It had faded away in Isaac's teenage years – if not before – and suddenly his son was not questioning the world around him but the wisdom of his father: How did he know anyway? What made him the expert?

Sitting there, with Zack's hand in his own, Grafton had another thought. For years he'd judged Liz for not taking Isaac with her. Not because he wanted her to, but because he couldn't understand how she could have abandoned her son. But here was a young lad having to offer support to a middle-aged man threatened with a fence post. So, maybe Liz had left Isaac not out of selfishness – or not entirely because of selfishness – maybe she hadn't taken him because there were things in these communes that she didn't want to expose him to.

"Have you been?" Zack asked, finally letting go of his hand.

"What's that?"

"To Tobermory. Have you been?" He pointed at the ferry.

"Long time ago. With my son."

"The houses are painted different colours, I've heard."

"That's right, aye."

"Maybe you could take me?" Zack asked.

"We could ask your mum. Or your dad."

"Maybe." Zack squinted out at the ferry, beginning its turn out into the Sound of Mull. "Better to ask Joan. Or Eddie."

18

Isaac had black paint smeared up to his elbows when the phone rang. He would have left it anyway, most likely, because no one ever called him on the landline. It was only ever sales calls and wrong numbers. So, he paused in his work and listened to the ringing until it cut out, then he got back to it.

He was putting the finishing touches to the sofa-ring sculpture by painting the cardboard legs. The main structure was covered with a rough weave fabric, in purple, and on it were patches of wrestling stickers and scrawled slogans, in yellow, lifted from Ravi's speeches: *Awake! Wakefulness is watchfulness! We cleanse ourselves for the new day.* Around the structure were three hessian ropes, looped around turnbuckles made from painted cardboard tubes. There were four of them, in the corners of the sofa-ring, and on each Isaac had carefully inscribed one of the words of wrestler Brock Lesnar's catchphrase: Eat, Sleep, Conquer, Repeat.

Isaac picked up his phone. He hadn't had so much as a text from his dad since Monday. Two days ago. Maybe there wasn't much by way of reception up there. Either that or his dad was choosing to ignore the plea for extra funds he'd sent via text, Facebook, and Twitter. At this stage, he'd be willing to try carrier pigeon if it got the message through. After the pizza, Isaac had spent the rest of his money on a few art materials and a half-loaf of bread. He was down to the heels now.

His dad would be back by tomorrow, wouldn't he? Even if it was late in the day. And he'd bring some sort of food with him or, at least, a credit card. Isaac would have carted his pieces across to college by then, cleared the dining room and – with a final slice of dry toast – officially finished every last morsel of food in the house.

He turned back to the sofa-ring sculpture. It was sitting on spread-out newspaper in front of the actual sofa and, now that he stepped back from it, Isaac could see how big it had become. As wide and bulky as a small chest freezer, it would have made a comfortable seat for a toddler or a decent-sized dog. And it was awkwardly shaped too, with the back rising higher than the front and the turnbuckles fragile and liable to snap from the corners.

Still, he was proud of it. It was partly from pride then, and partly from a fear that he might never get it out of the door, that he opened the camera app on his phone and took a few snaps. At least if it broke apart then he'd have some evidence to show the examiners. He moved across to the sleeper-hold sculpture and took a couple of photos of it too. Then he had another thought.

He sat down in front of the laptop on the table. Syncing his phone with it, he opened the photographs he'd taken, cropped and tidied them a little and saved them to the desktop. Then he clicked onto Facebook and again found the Swami Ravi public page. He uploaded a photo of each of his two sculptures and a brief line of information about the exhibition. What was it he wanted? Did he expect Swami Ravi himself to comment? Or his mum to find the photos and realise the error of her ways? No, it was simpler than that. He wanted an acknowledgement that what he'd created was good, that it said something and spoke to something larger than himself. As he clicked 'post', he breathed out and, only in that moment, realised he'd been holding his breath, behind clenched teeth.

As he waited for the paint to dry on his sculpture, Isaac again opened the bookmarked online grocery page on the laptop and attempted a password. He'd tried until he was locked out the night before. His dad wasn't a complicated man, it shouldn't have been difficult to guess the password, but try as he might, Isaac couldn't get in.

It was into the evening before the paint was dry and Isaac was ready to make his journey to college. In the meantime, he finished off his half-loaf of bread and also gulped down a tin of peaches that he found at the back of the cupboard behind the reusable shopping bags. They were a year or so out of date, but they tasted fine.

He had the sleeper-hold sculpture in one of the shopping bags, encased in bubble-wrap, and he would have to carry the sofa-ring in an awkward embrace for the walk to the bus stop. He had his pass, but he was mindful that he might have to convince the bus driver that a coffin-sized artwork was something that could be safely brought on-board.

Isaac grappled the sofa-ring through the front door, bumping it forward with his leg, and then swung the canvas shopping bag around. It was heavy, with the clay sculpture inside. It was difficult to get the cardboard feet of the sofa-ring clear of the door. He scraped them against the frame – shit, shit – but the paint didn't seem to be scuffed. He set it next to the shopping bag on the landing, then checked that he had his keys before he clicked the door closed.

Right. Stairs next. Then the walk to the bus stop. Not walk, perhaps, but series of shuffles and scuttles.

"Hiya Isaac." It was Rachel, from the flat next door. "Moving out...?"

She grinned, pointing at the sofa-ring. Isaac gave a wee grunt of a laugh. There was an opening there, because Rachel was a nurse and she'd be driving in for the start of her night shift. She was in a sky-blue tunic with a navy trim, underneath her jacket. He could beg a lift, surely, and they could put the back seats down to fit in the sofa-ring sculpture. Or he could ask to borrow money for a black cab if she was in too much of a hurry.

The moment passed. She gave a little wave and padded off down the stairs. Even then, Isaac could have called after her. He should have. But he did nothing, and the outside door creaked open and slammed shut.

Nothing for it, but to get back to Plan A. Isaac decided to do the sofa-ring first. He hitched it up onto his hip and pinned it to himself with his left arm. His right arm was for the banister. Slowly, slowly, peering around the heft of the thing and feeling each new step with the toe of his trainers. It took him a fucking age to reach the first-floor landing and then he had to stop to let the cramp in his leg fade, take a breath and resist the urge to fling the bloody thing down the rest of the stairs.

Deep breath in. There was an aroma of spices from the flat on the right. Some sort of curry – cardamom and chilli and garlic. It smelt divine. His hollow stomach let out a groan. You couldn't go knocking on doors asking for something to eat, though, tempting as it might be.

Even the thought of the food revived him. He got the sofa-ring down to the ground floor and then went back up for the sculpture in the canvas bag. That should have been the easy one, but the heavy bag swung from his hand so erratically that it cracked against his knee and then caught at his heel. He paused again on the first-floor landing. Onions were frying as well. Dear god.

Holding his breath, for the sake of his overworked saliva glands, Isaac cradled his sleeper-hold sculpture like a baby and carried it down the rest of the stairs. He knew that holding it like that would be impossible when he had the sofa-ring to contend with too, but maybe he'd have to accept that he needed to make two trips.

When he reached the ground floor though, carrying the bag, he found that the sofa-ring had slumped forward onto the floor. One of the front turnbuckles was bent, with the weight of the rest of the sculpture pressing it down to the concrete. Shit, shit. The carefully inscribed words on the side had a scuff and a scrape to them too.

"Fuck you," Isaac hissed, to the empty hallway. "Fuck you."

He closed his eyes, considered. The overwhelming urge was to tear the thing apart — cardboard and fabric strewn across the floor, flecks of yellow paint on purple fabric — but he knew he didn't actually want that. He wanted to fix it, he needed the grade for his conditional offer to Art School.

Isaac pulled out his phone. He typed out a message to Shauna: *Don't suppose you could give me a hand lifting my pieces across to college?* He slid his phone back into his pocket and lifted the canvas bag. He'd take the sculptures back to the flat for now and regroup. If Shauna couldn't help out, then Isaac could always wait for his dad to come back. It would give him bugger-all time to set up, but as long as he was in time for the exhibition then all would be well.

He'd carried the sleeper-hold sculpture back to the door of the flat and made it halfway back up the stairs with the sofa-ring by the time his phone pinged. He heaved the sculpture onto the landing, with his knee, and then went to his pocket for his phone. A reply from Shauna: *Of course buddy, can run you across in the car tomorrow morning xx.*

Isaac stared at it. He sank down to the top step, still holding the phone in his hand. The smell of tikka masala was all around him: sweet and spicy. He closed his eyes, imagined dipping a piece of naan into the rich, tomato sauce. With the taste of it on his tongue, he lent his head against the cool tiles at the side of the stairway. And he wept.

19

At first, Grafton thought it was a foghorn out beyond Ardnamurchan Point. There was evening sunshine, though, not even a wisp of mist. Grafton was with Jed, picking brambles from the thorny bushes at the back of the cabin. They looked at each other and set down the plastic tubs they'd been filling. Jed walked with a slight limp, so Grafton strode ahead.

Eddie stood out at the front of the A-frame with an air horn in his hand. He sounded it again and then shouted, to all the Sleepless emerging from the cabins: "Meeting! Now!"

Grafton turned and offered an arm to Jed. He wanted to walk slow now, to give himself time to think. What if some of the ferry group had told Eddie that he'd gone missing for a spell? What if someone had seen him in the phone box?

The two teenage girls who looked after the children were ushering their flock away from the A-frame, but the rest of the Sleepless were streaming towards it. As they reached the door, Eddie gave them a curt nod. There was a vein bulging up near his temple and he had his jaw set tight.

Grafton helped Jed to ease down to the floor at the back of the room, then took a seat next to him. Ideally, he would have liked to have been closer to the door, but there were two of Eddie's crew there now anyway. Grafton looked to the window behind the shrine. It would only take a few steps and a jump. There would be lacerations, yes, but there was no fall on the other side so he should be ok to make a run for it from there.

That was all ridiculous. Even if they had seen him use the phone, it could be easily explained away with the truth – he was calling his son. What was the worst they could do? Eddie might be angry, but he wasn't going to take it any further, was he? There could well be a bit of shouting involved, but that wasn't any reason to go jumping through windows.

All the same, Grafton reached into his sleeve and set the Dictaphone recording. He gave a wee cough to cover over the sound of the *click*. No one looked over at him.

Once everyone settled, Joan came down the stairs and walked over to the stage. Her movements were more confident than the night before, her posture more upright. She wore a yellow dress, with a sash around the waist. The sunglasses were in place again and she itched at her hair several times before turning to her audience.

"It gives me great pain to announce this..." she said. Her head dropped down to her chest. Grafton had the fleeting thought that she might be about to admit to falling asleep. "We have a traitor in our midst."

The noise from the gathered Sleepless was more a growl than a gasp. Immediately, the disciples started to look around at their neighbours. Grafton felt her words in his chest, like a jolt from a defibrillator paddle. He tried to keep his features neutral and to meet the gaze of those around him as they looked from face to face. All he could think, though, was how quickly the whole room could turn on him.

"We don't ask for much," Joan continued, "but there are rules to this process and the rules are there for a reason. No television, no sexual intimacy, no stimulants, no communication with outside."

Her head swivelled from side to side, but the sunglasses made it impossible to tell if her gaze was resting on him. Grafton let his breath leak in and out. His heart was a jackhammer.

"We have to be pure," Joan said. "That is not easy, I know, but we have to be. Otherwise they will criticise our methods, our great experiment. And our next step will fail. We have to be unpeachable."

For the first time, the word was wrong, not just the pronunciation. No one corrected her. All of the Sleepless were tensed, taut, ready. Joan paused and gathered her hair up into a loose bun. She looked to those in the front row, but nobody made a move. She let the hair fall to her shoulders again.

"The methods can't be faulted, dear ones, they can't be tainted. We must run this experiment with the precision of a scientific laboratory. Yes? There is no room, within our ranks, for those who seek to bend the rules or cut corners. Does anyone disagree?"

Silence. Grafton looked, again, to the window, again to the door. The heavies were still there and the jump through shattering glass still seemed a risk. Better to take the dressing down, surely, and trust Joan to control it. She wouldn't let it escalate.

"Friends," Joan said, "we pluck out the weed because otherwise it will infest the garden, you understand. We don't want the whole barrel to be rotten."

Grafton closed his eyes, concentrated on the faint whirr of the Dictaphone tape. That was his safety net – he'd record it for posterity. Although, fuck, they'd be even angrier if they found that secreted up his sleeve.

"Bring her out," Joan said.

Grafton opened his eyes.

"Bring her up here."

He spun around, to the door. Whippet was coming through, leading a figure that Grafton instantly recognised from the red-threaded grey of her hair. Debbie. She was sobbing softly, with Whippet's huge hands guiding her by the shoulders.

She stepped onto the stage, beside Joan, with her head bowed.

"Tell them what you've done, Debbie," Joan demanded.

Debbie shook her head, slowly.

"You've betrayed them, Debbie. You owe them an explanation."

Grafton's mind stumble-slipped around: was she the one who told on him and she was being forced to out him to the group? Or was all this because they'd shared an orange? Or was he actually in the clear and...? What else could Debbie have done?

Joan took her sunglasses off. The bloodshot eye had cleared a little – there was white showing – but now there was purple bruising beneath. And a cluster of spots on the opposite side, as angry as a teenager's acne. She pushed the sunglasses up onto her head.

"The methods haven't been enough for Debbie," Joan said. "We haven't been enough for her. She has sought out alternatives. She has weakened our great experiment."

Debbie murmured something.

"What? Speak up."

"I couldn't keep up," Debbie said.

"She couldn't keep up. And rather than ask us to wait for her or for us to..." Joan waved an arm. "Rather than that, she went and sought out medical aid."

She spat out the word 'medical' like it was a particularly virulent disease which had wiped out a civilisation or two. With her face in a grimace, she made a dry clacking noise with her tongue. Eddie, from the back of the room, strode forward. He handed her a bottle of water and a small white tub.

Joan took a drink. Then she held up the tub, showing it to the room with an arcing sweep of her hand. Grafton, along with the others, peered at it, but he couldn't make out the words on the label. He felt his left eye twitch, in at the tear-duct. He held a finger there to still it.

"Pep pills," Joan said, "like a common trucker."

Debbie gave a moan and her body shook with sobs.

"She went to the shop and she bought caffeine pills. As if we wouldn't find out, Debbie, eh? As if we wouldn't keep an eye on the only shop for miles. As if we'd let you poison us all with crushed-up pills in our food. Was that the plan, yes?"

"No, no." Debbie looked up, wild-eyed. "They were only ever for me."

"There's enough here for a battalion, Debbie."

"That was the only size and...you young ones all have energy. I couldn't keep up."

Joan half-turned towards her, staring. Debbie couldn't meet her gaze. She slowly sank to her knees, up there on the platform.

"Forgive me, Joan. I just wanted to follow you, I just wanted to be able to..."

There was a moment when Joan and Debbie's breathing seemed to slow in sync, one subsiding from sobs and the other from rage. Grafton was suddenly aware of everyone else in the room again, of all the tightly-held breath. Anything seemed possible in that instant: the Sleepless could as easily storm the stage or burst into hysterical laughter. No one moved, everyone waited for Joan.

"You have a choice then," Joan said. She was measuring her words. "Either you are banished from the commune, Debbie, or you accept a punishment of our choosing."

"Punishment?"

"Our methods haven't been enough, that much is evident, so we will have to extend to a more advanced method."

Debbie considered this. She was on her knees, yes, but she looked a lot calmer now. There was a path laid out for her – an escape – and Joan could use the word 'banishment' all she liked, as long as Debbie was able to walk away unharmed. At least, that was the way Grafton saw it. He lifted the finger away from his eye, but the twitching started again instantly. He pressed at it again.

"I'll take the punishment," Debbie said, softly.

"Very well," Joan said. She smiled, with only her lips. "Very well then."

She again gathered her hair into a bun. This time she pinned it up with the arm of her sunglasses. The lenses swung loose.

No one spoke, but Eddie had stepped forwards again – waiting for instruction. Debbie kept her head bowed to the rough wood of the platform.

What did Joan mean by a more advanced method? Grafton thought of waterboarding, but he only had the vaguest concept of what that was – an image of a head in a sack with water being trickled slowly down. Clearer in his mind was the punishments they used to inflict in Northern Ireland. He'd done a feature once on a Belfast surgeon who'd become the world expert on repairing knee and elbow joints because of the punishment shootings. He'd seen the scars.

Joan beckoned to Eddie. He leant in and she whispered something. Grafton watched the young man's face, the way the eyes widened and the curl at the side of his lip deepened. He gave a nod and then hurried away.

"We have no desire for cruelty," Joan said. "The aim here is not to shame or to humiliate Debbie. The aim, friends, is to refocus her mind on the task at hand. She was offered the choice between leaving or renewing her commitment to us and she chose to stay, so we have a duty to help her in that... erm..."

Joan looked down at the white tub of pills, still clutched in her hands. She shook her head at them and gave a little sniff. Grafton wondered if she was crying. Certainly, a second or two later, she wiped at her eyes with her thumb and forefinger.

"Take these things away," she said to Whippet. "Burn them."

Whippet came forward and took the white tub of pills.

Joan took a breath. "We could inflict any number of punishments on Debbie. But most punishments are about spectacle and this one needs to be about process, about improving her ability to stay awake. Yes? This was a plea for help. She wants to keep up. So, we don't want to give her a general ache which could be numbed by sleep, we want to give her a single point of focus."

Eddie came back into the A-frame. He was carrying a hammer. Just an ordinary hammer, which had probably been used for all manner of repairs around the commune – fixing the cabin roofs, hanging pictures, cobbling together the platform at the front of the room. And now it would be used on Debbie's soft, yielding flesh. Grafton lifted his finger away from his eye, no longer caring about his facial convulsions.

Here it was, the moment when he had to decide. Should he stand up and speak out, stop this from happening? There was nothing Eddie could do with that hammer that wouldn't be an outrage, so it was up to Grafton to stop him. Didn't matter how. The story couldn't take priority over a middle-aged woman whose only crime was wanting to fit in, who'd already lost her daughter and granddaughter and was now willing to endure some form of hammer-horror so that she wasn't cast adrift again.

Grafton felt the certainty that he was going to intervene as a squeeze, a twist, in his stomach. He tasted the nausea of it in his throat. It was worse than when he'd contemplated crashing through the window earlier, because he knew that – whatever he did – he'd find himself dragged up onto the stage beside Debbie.

He felt a push on his shoulder. It was Jed, beside him. The old man was leaning all his weight against Grafton, using him as a lever to creak himself to his feet. As he straightened, all eyes in the room turned to him. Even Eddie stopped mid-stride.

Jed cleared his throat. "I won't allow this," he said. "She's done nothing wrong – not really – and you should be ashamed."

"Please, Jed, please," Debbie said.

"I won't allow this."

"It's my choice, Jed. It is. I want to stay, I want to do better."

Joan had watched this exchange, along with the rest of the Sleepless. She gestured, now, for Eddie to hurry up. He stepped towards the stage. Joan moved across to place a hand on Debbie's head.

"We are a family," she said. "Not in terms of hierarchy, but the closeness of our bond. Your concern for Debbie does you credit, Jed, but it is a freely-made choice. Stay or leave. It doesn't matter. The punishment has been decided anyway. Debbie made a misstep and we will correct it."

Eddie was up on the stage now. Jed remained standing, but he didn't say anything further. Grafton, slowly, got to his feet too. The corner of his eye was twitching furiously. Joan watched him. There was a pause – a gap – where he could have spoken out, but he stayed silent. Standing beside Jed was a small, symbolic act, but at least it was something.

"Set your hand on the wood," Eddie said, crouching down beside Debbie.

Debbie leant forwards, placing both of her hands in front of herself so that she was on all-fours. Her hair hung over her face as a shroud. Joan's hand remained on top of her head, moving gently back and forth. She was making soft shushing sounds, like an owner preparing their pet for the vet's needle.

"Spread your fingers," Eddie said.

He didn't hesitate. Up and down. Debbie didn't snatch her hand away either. One decisive blow – *crack* – on the index finger of her right hand. A moment. And then the howl, the screech, from Debbie. No one had the time to flinch away from the first sound, but everyone winced away from this second noise. Looking across the room, Grafton could see one or two Sleepless break down in tears and someone began rocking back-and-forth with their knees hugged up to their chest.

The cries went on, a pause between each one so that they became like a bark. Grafton looked up at the platform. Joan had fallen to her knees and was embracing Debbie, holding her tightly. Debbie was trying to push her away with her undamaged hand, was trying to look at her finger, but Joan wouldn't let her. Eddie, for his part, took a final look and then walked away. He held the hammer by its head, the wooden handle swinging gently.

Grafton reached up to his sleeve and, through the material, clicked the Dictaphone off. It served no purpose to record Debbie's pain; it seemed an intrusion. As he pressed the button, however, Grafton realised that what he had on the tape was no longer material for a story, it was evidence. He squeezed his eyes shut against the room, feeling the pulsing spasm at the corner of his eye. Tomorrow, he told himself, tomorrow he'd get himself out of there.

20

It had been many years since Grafton watched a sunset from gloaming through to starlight. That night, he carried a blanket out to the veranda and sat in the wooden chair beside Debbie's. She was curled up underneath her own blanket, cradling her damaged finger with her other hand. For a long time, they didn't speak.

The water in the bay shifted from pale grey to deep purple as the sun dipped below the horizon. The sky was a dark terracotta for a spell, banding through orange and pure red. If you'd told Grafton, in that moment, that there was an oil spill alight out at sea or a wildfire spreading across the whole of Mull, then he would have believed you. Above the red was a rippling of clouds seamed with yellow and then back to grey. And it was from here that the stars slid across in a parabola like the slickest of planetarium shows.

The spasming in his eye had eased. After returning to the cabin, he'd taken himself through to the bathroom and slumped down on the toilet seat. It was the only alone-time they were allowed. And if you did it right – if you repeated *ten minutes, ten minutes, ten minutes* – then you could steal a micro-nap that wouldn't raise suspicion.

All was still, all was silent. Would a single breath, let out up there on the hillside, travel all the way down to rustle the sails of the yachts in the bay? Certainly a shout would carry that far, or a cry of pain.

Debbie sat with her head lowered, looking at that index finger. It was hidden from Grafton's view by the curl of her left hand, but he imagined it going through a similar colour-shift to the sky: rash-red first as it swelled; then blotchy with purple, and with a dent from the hammer-blow that was turning yellow. More than that as it worsened: the whitish-green of pus

126

beneath the surface of the skin; blackening, deadening to a stick of brittle charcoal. The bone inside, shattered, would crumble and the sinew would snap, leaving it dangling there attached only by a nerve, which would need to be cut through to save the rest of the hand – the body even – from the gangrenous, rotting stump which used to be her finger.

"You should have some ice," Grafton said. His voice sounded so gruff and unnatural that he had to listen to the echoes of it to make sure that the words made sense, that they were ordered and sounded out as more than a clearing of the throat.

Debbie looked across, shook her head. "The pain is the whole point."

Grafton considered that. Of course, Joan would frown on pills or injections to mask the pain, but he didn't think that she'd object to a cube of ice or a bag of frozen peas. All the same, he didn't know if the box freezer above the fridge in the cabin even had anything in it.

"I'm sorry that happened," Grafton said. "When Jed stood up, I…well…"

"Don't," Debbie said. "I'm not sorry or angry. It's a reminder, isn't it, that staying awake isn't some chemical or drug-driven craze, it's a process to be followed and a journey to be undertaken…"

"Still, it's a hell of a thing to happen."

"I'm thankful, Grafton. Rest assured."

Grafton paused, thinking about how to word his next question. "Would Ravi have done something like that?" he asked, slowly.

Debbie let out a small laugh. A squeak almost. "Ravi would have brought out the whole toolbox," she said, in something close to a whisper.

They lapsed back to silence. Grafton looked across. The pain had sucked Debbie's cheeks inwards and her skin had the colour and clamminess of cold porridge. Her eyelids were at half-mast but flickered open every few seconds as she drew air in through her clenched teeth. In the space of a couple of hours, she'd transitioned from looking like a freshly-minted retiree to a care home occupant who wasn't expected to see out the year.

"Tell me about yourself," Debbie said. "Distract me."

"Not much to tell."

"That can't be true."

Grafton tipped his head back to look at the stars. No one had ever taught him to identify the patterns in them, the shapes. His only reference point was the shard of the moon. The rest was just a shimmering, more plentiful than any night-sky he'd seen above Glasgow.

"I'm a single dad," he said. "My son is seventeen. It's been eight years since Liz left us and it's passed so quick, Debbie, honestly..."

She nodded, but didn't speak.

"...for the first spell, I tried to carry on as normal. But the normal was fuelled by alcohol, you see, and so it couldn't continue. I sometimes wonder if Liz knew that. Maybe the whole thing was a test to see if I could straighten myself out, you know, to force me to the edge of something.

"I don't think so, though. That's saying that she saw some innate goodness in me, and I think it was the opposite. I think it was that she didn't see how I was going to sort myself out. Even for my son's sake. So, she took off and left him with me, even though that meant she was condemning him to live with a waster, a drunk. For years, I told myself that I didn't blame her for leaving. And I don't. Not for leaving me. But Isaac...?"

Grafton winced. He hadn't meant to mention Isaac's name. It was out now, though. From somewhere, further inland, a sheep bleated. It was answered by a dog barking at one of the houses down by the shore.

"It took me a few months to take responsibility. We had a few months of chaos and then I got my sister to come down and look after Isaac for a fortnight. I checked into a clinic for CBT and I dried myself out. They talked to me about Liz, of course they did, but I knew it wasn't all about her. It was my job as much as anything, the hours of it and the pressures I was putting on myself, so I knew I needed something steadier and something where I wasn't so emotionally invested."

Fuck. He was right on the cliff-edge of telling her he had been a journalist, wasn't he? Fucking stupid thing to do. He was a teacher, not a journalist. Grafton, not Tom. Chalkboards and textbooks, gym shoes and timetables, packed lunches and mock exams. He closed his eyes – teacher, teacher, teacher – and tried to channel one of his old schoolmasters. That had been so many years ago. What about Isaac's form teacher last year? What had her name been? Miss Rutherford. Dyed blonde hair and a slight squint to her brown eyes. He'd had a bit of a thing for her for a spell –

"You ok, love?" Debbie prompted him. "The clinic?"

"Aye." He was lucky she'd focused on that part of the story. "So, I spent my fortnight there and got myself on an even keel, you see. It was a nice place – converted castle – and I was thinking, the whole time, that I would show Liz. The sobering up wasn't motivated by looking after my boy, not really, it was motivated by saying fuck-you to her.

"I wanted her to come back from wherever she was, see how I'd sorted myself out and then beg me to take her back. And I'd look her in the eye and say 'screw you'. Except I probably wouldn't. I'd probably have been grateful."

"I wonder if that's what drew you here, then."

"Looking for Liz, you mean?"

"No. Your experience at the clinic."

Debbie smiled across at him. Grafton opened his mouth to ask what she meant, but he realised that he didn't need to. She was right. There was the appeal of the routine, the process to be followed. And the comradery of dozens of people all pulling towards the same goal. More than that, there was the welcome relief of having someone telling him what to do. For those first months of solo parenting, conducted with a permanent hangover, the greatest challenge had been dealing with the decisions. Constant decisions: what to have for dinner; when to rush out to the shops; how to clean the black mould in the bathroom; what to do with Isaac at the weekend; where to hide the half-bottle for easy access through the day.

Grafton tried a smile. "You mean I like being around folk who look like extras from *The Walking Dead*?" he said.

"The cheek of it." Debbie brought her good hand to her chest in faux shock. It allowed Grafton a glimpse of her finger. It was swollen to the size of a butcher's sausage. She brought her hand back down to wrap loosely around it.

"Not you, Debbie. I'm talking about wee junkie rats like Eddie."

He wasn't sure where that had come from. He'd spat it out. Just residual anger about Debbie's punishment, maybe. It was true that he'd seen young men like Eddie at the clinic. Normally with multiple addictions. They were vulnerable and watery-eyed when asked to talk in the group therapy, but then swaggered through in the evening like they owned the joint. They gathered their petty grudges with every glance around the room. And you'd watch them around the cutlery and the gardening tools. You'd certainly keep them well clear of the hammers.

"Don't, don't," Debbie said, shaking her head. "He's close to Joan."

"I know, I wasn't saying—"

"I don't need protecting."

Grafton nodded.

"We're all here looking for better versions of ourselves," Debbie said quietly, into the night. "That's the truth of it. We're all trying to be better."

21

It was five months after leaving that Liz returned home for her son. In those months, she'd carefully laid the foundation for Isaac to join her in Jaipur. Swami Ravi wasn't keen on the idea of kids under his feet, so she set up a room for them in the apartment furthest from the basement-hall Ravi was renting and she wrote out a chain of commune women who could take over Isaac's care and schooling if she was called away at short notice. As she so often was.

She chose her moment carefully. Ravi was under a lot of pressure, carrying the burden of their collective expectation on his shoulders. He would give four or five speeches a day, in that sweaty basement, to satisfy the demands of those curious souls who'd travelled for hundreds of miles to hear him.

"Lizzy." His smile was bleary, his eyes glassy. "Did I do well, Lizzy?"

"You were transcendent, my love."

His smile widened, his head lolled back in the chair. Liz had timed it well, had found that short window of time when he'd be receptive to the idea. She smoothed his slick-black hair away from his ear.

"Listen, Ravi," she said, softly. "I need to go back for my son."

He jerked upright, grabbed at the sleeve of her robe.

"Just for the weekend," she soothed.

"The auth-authorities won't—" He spun a finger in the air, inviting her to finish the sentence.

"I'm his mother, Ravi. As long as they have my consent, then they won't come knocking." She paused, considered how far to push him. "And think of what we might learn from disciples who haven't yet had the habits of sleep fully ingrained in them, whose brains aren't yet awash with toxins…"

Ravi nodded. His cheeks were paunchy, his skin grey.

"Only a select few, as a trial," she said. "Think of the influence you could have on young minds…"

He let go of her sleeve and nodded again. His chin was dipping steadily closer to his chest. Before he slid too far from reason, Liz reached into her sleeve and brought out the smartphone he used for social media. She usually tried to keep it from him when he was in this state, but it would be useful if there was a post or two to remind him, when he woke, that children were to be welcomed.

With his say-so, then, Liz had flown back for the weekend. She wore a simple kaftan, in light yellow fabric, that every gust of Glaswegian wind found a way through. She'd never felt cold like it, just as, five months before, she'd never felt heat like her first step onto Indian soil. Getting the taxi to drop her off on Byres Road, she stopped at a charity shop and bought a woolly jumper. Then, still shivering, she doubled back on herself and picked up a beanie hat as well. All around her, the milling students were going about their Friday in shirt-sleeves and sunglasses.

She walked up Highburgh Road, marvelling at how red the buildings on either side were. Why had she never noticed that before – the red of the sandstone? And the chatter of the people she passed was in an accent that she knew, in her gut, but which seemed to have deepened in the time she was away. She would have scoffed at it, in a film, for being over-done.

Turning off to her left, she followed the street up towards the flat. There was no anxiety that they might have moved – her husband was unlikely to have even run the hoover – but she did worry about the reception she might get. Of course she did. She remembered the time, a year or so before, when she'd come back from Cambodia. The signs that Isaac had made for every door in the house – every cupboard and closet even – with a red 'No Entry' symbol on them. And, when she took them down, he silently and diligently replaced them with the yellow-and-black 'Danger of Death' triangle with the man being struck with a lightning bolt. And she'd only been in Cambodia for three weeks, not five months.

Pressing the buzzer, Liz felt a tremble in her hand that wasn't from the cold. She folded her arms across her chest and waited. There was no answer. She tried again. What was the time? Coming up for five, so maybe he hadn't yet been picked up from after-school club. She decided to wait.

Crossing the street, she sat on the low concrete wall in front of the tenement opposite and looked up at their window. There was nothing to be gleaned from examining it – no symbols blue-tacked to the glass or signs of chaos and destitution beyond the curtains. In fact, the only thing she could see was a clothes-horse with Isaac's red school jumper and grey trousers draped over it.

She didn't have to wait long. They came up the hill on the other side of the road, Isaac skipping along the pavement in front of his father. Tom was carrying two pizza boxes, held flat on an upturned hand. He was smiling at his son, laughing. And Isaac leapt forward and jutted an elbow at some invisible foe, then turned and grasped at the thin-air above his shoulder, jerking his hands downwards. He was demonstrating some wrestling move, no doubt. Nothing had changed.

Except, *something* had changed. Tom's hair was neatly-cut and his stubble shaved. He wasn't hunched over or dragging his feet. When he laughed, it didn't deteriorate into a coughing fit. Even from this distance, he looked *well*. No grey pallor to his skin, no puffiness around the eyes.

They were only a few doorways away when a car pulled up. The door opened and Liz recognised Mrs Petrie from the next-door tenement. A prim middle-aged woman. She'd told Liz once, years ago, that the blanket on Isaac's buggy was no substitute for a raincover.

Isaac stopped his wrestling moves and slid back towards his dad. He huddled in close to his leg and looked up at Mrs Petrie. He nodded shyly as she said something. And there, again, was Tom's laughter, followed by a nod of the head and a patient smile. Liz could imagine what was being said. That smile was neatly-judged in response to some comment from Mrs Petrie about the demands of solo-parenting. The old crone was surely conferring sainthood on long-suffering Tom Grafton.

Liz pushed herself up from the wall and crept, on her haunches, to the parked car in front. A moment before, she'd been looking forward to the moment when Isaac looked up and caught sight of her but now – suddenly and desperately – she didn't want to be seen.

She stayed there, hidden behind the car, for several minutes. Then she peeked around the side. The pavement was empty. No Tom and Isaac, no Mrs Petrie. She looked up at the window again. The clothes-horse was still there, but nothing else. Quickly, Liz stepped away from the car, pulled her beanie hat down over her ears and strode away.

She didn't know how long she walked for. Long enough that the clouds in the sky began to darken with the spilt-ink of night and the streetlights started to flicker on. She did lengths of those streets she knew so well. Until, after looping around in a full circle, she found herself standing at the top of Gardner Street, looking down the steep slope towards Partick. The last of the light formed an orange seam around the shadowed buildings at the bottom.

Maybe it was easy, in the years that followed, to look back on it as some kind of serendipity or fate that drew her to Isaac's Primary School. It was possible to retrofit the idea that she intended to go snooping through the playgrounds – break into the buildings even – looking for a carved IG on a desk or a report card left behind in his tray at the side of the classroom.

In that moment, though, she had only been following the route she knew best. They'd walked together down this hill, his hand in hers, on his first day of school. Him in a red jumper with turned-up sleeves. Months later, he'd tripped on the concrete when chasing a friend down towards the gates, and she'd felt the lurch of panic for the next few nights when she woke – sitting upright – calling for him as he tumbled out towards the road.

Some of the windows in the school buildings were still lit up. The cleaners were in. Liz circled around to the back, where Isaac's classroom was. She cupped her hands up to the glass of the window and looked in. The main striplights weren't on, but enough light was angling in from the hallway. The classroom was empty.

Up on the wall, to the right hand side, was a display with red crepe paper and yellow cut-cardboard lettering. 'My Hero' it said. She scanned along it, looking for Isaac's. It was immediately obvious which was his: the figure was perfectly in proportion, the features delicately drawn and expressive. The man he'd drawn stood in a wrestling ring, clad in a blue-and-gold costume with a mask and billowing cape. On an upturned hand, he held two pizza boxes. Even without that, even with just the smile and the neat haircut, Liz would have known it was a drawing of his dad.

Pressing her forehead against the cold glass, Liz felt the tears trailing down her cheeks. She knew Isaac couldn't give all of this up – his routine, his father, his friends – for a tiny flat in the stifling heat of Jaipur with a succession of strangers home-schooling him. It would be selfish of her to ask him; far more selfish than her original decision to leave.

She choked back a sob, standing there in his school playground with her face pressed up against the window. He would be back in that classroom on Monday, she knew that. Maybe she'd always known that, really. And she would be on the way back to India with an empty seat beside her on the plane.

22

It was a second-hand spotlight with a blue bulb. The task was to install it in the back room of the office chalet, to allow the disciples to have sessions being 'washed' by the blue light. It should have been a ten-minute job, but Grafton's partner was a young lad called Ally who insisted that he wanted to strip the plug and connect the thing directly to the mains. He'd been an apprentice electrician, back before the acne on his neck had scarred over.

They'd missed lunch, so Morven brought them across a slice of toast each, spread with the thick, congealed remnants of yesterday's lentil soup. She stayed to watch them work. Ally explained everything to her in minute detail – pointing out a non-existent filament in the LED bulb and fiddling with the stand so much that it needed a length of tape to stay fully extended.

Grafton tuned him out. The raised, red bumps across his ankle were more worthy of attention. He scratched at them with a screwdriver and wondered if they were midge bites from sitting out last night or if he had a flea in his bed. It couldn't be one of the new methods, could it? Fleas in the sheets, to keep them itching through the night. Surely not. Joan had decided on the blue light and there were plans afoot for an ice-bath somewhere within the Seattle compound, once they could find a suitable space, but she wouldn't infest the commune with fleas, would she? Or did lice leave marks? And it was ticks, was it not, which caused Lyme Disease, but you normally saw them still attached—

Mid-scratch, Grafton suddenly realised the opportunity he had. Here he was in the office with the filing cabinet that held all the commune records only a few steps away. Ally and Morven were too engrossed in one another to notice. Ally was telling her that the yellow of the scarf in her hair was the exact same shade as the stripe on the earth wire. She giggled at that – god knows why.

They were so distracted that Grafton could probably even sneak outside and have a look at the wooden pallets. More of them had arrived. Ten in total now. And, again, they'd needed two men to lift them from the lorry to the side of the office. What was that heavy? Was it soil for the vegetable patch or building materials for the commune? Or was he right to worry that it might be something far more alarming?

Setting down the screwdriver, Grafton took a long sliding step towards the cabinet. He kept himself side-on to it so that he could see the door. Then he eased the drawer out. The records of the disciples were crammed inside, some of them dog-eared, folded, or torn. Grafton flicked his fingers through them, until he got to G. There was his form, but nothing for Liz. He went to the back and worked his way forwards to W. Still no Liz. Unless she was going by a different name, then she hadn't been here.

He didn't really know what else he was looking for, but the second drawer down had a peeling label with 'Next Step' written on it. Easing the drawer open, Grafton found another thick wedge of disordered papers. He pulled them out and started to rifle through. Some of it looked like mathematical calculations or the like; equations and sums scribbled in black ink. A few sheets in was a printed diagram of a human head. It had been sub-divided by dotted lines and labelled with the different sections of the skull. Each area had been shaded a different colour. To the side of the diagram was a handwritten note, again in black pen: *significant build-up of toxin required before incision*. The word 'significant' was underlined twice. Grafton frowned at the sheet and turned to the next–

There was a screeching of tyres from outside. An engine rumbled on for a moment, then cut out. Two voices, shouting. You couldn't make out the words, but you could hear the edge to it – like a brawl stirring in the pub. Grafton had seen enough of those. Quickly pushing the papers back into the drawer, he stepped through the main office and outside.

The minibus was pulled up, askew, on the gravel in front of the chalet. The doors had been flung open. Eddie was standing, nose-to-nose, with Jed. To the side stood Whippet, a good foot taller than both of them. He showed no sign of intervening.

"Fucking think you're better than me," Eddie was saying. "Don't you Jed?"

"Not that, Eddie," Jed said. "Not at all."

"Well, what was all that then, eh?"

They were glaring at each other, their mouths as close as lovers.

"Why are you even here, old man?" Eddie hissed. "Why the fuck are you even here?"

"You're not in charge, Eddie," Jed said. "Never have been."

"And you don't fucking *listen*."

Eddie tapped a finger on his own ear, then reached across to tap at the side of Jed's head. As Jed pushed him away, Eddie took a swing. It was a short jab, but it connected somewhere to the side of the eye. Jed gave a shout and jumped at Eddie. He buckled and the two of them fell to the floor, with Jed on top. He got a couple of punches in, but Eddie was kicking himself upright and clawing at Jed's robe. It ripped away from his shoulder.

Ally and Morven came out from the office and stood silently behind Grafton, watching. There was blood coming from Eddie's nose now, and Jed was hunched over, winded. They ran into one another again, but it was more like a rest hold from a wrestling match. Jed hooked his arm up to snare Eddie in a loose headlock and Eddie had both arms around Jed's midriff.

Morven let out a small, strangled cry. Grafton followed the direction of her gaze and saw a clutch of the Sleepless making their way down the path from the A-frame. At the front was Joan, striding along with her long hair streaming behind and her dress billowing. She looked biblical.

"Boys," Grafton called out, "Joan's coming down."

Instantly, the two of them released their holds. Eddie straightened up and Jed, with difficulty, raised himself to his feet. They didn't look at one another or at the path up to the A-frame. Jed studied the gravel, while Eddie lifted a hand to his nose and examined the smear of blood it left across his fingers.

Joan reached them. The bruising around her eye had deepened, although there was now only a single tendril of blood in her right eye. On the opposite side, the clutch of spots had been scratched until the skin sloughed away. The open graze was as shiny and angry as a boil.

She didn't say anything. Her eyes flicked from one to the other, glaring. Neither Eddie nor Jed met her gaze.

"He was about to do something stupid," Jed said, "but I stopped him."

Eddie snorted, shook his head.

"What?" Jed looked across at him. "That's what happened, no? Tell Joan, then, tell Joan everything."

Eddie gave Joan a sideways glance. Grafton was also watching Joan, of course, also looking at her aslant. As Jed spoke, she'd itched at her head and her hand had come away with a few strands of brown hair. She let her hand fall to her side and opened her fingers to allow the hair to drift away on the breeze.

"You." Joan pointed at Whippet. "You tell me."

Whippet shifted his weight from one foot to the other. His voice, when it came, was not as deep as Grafton would have expected.

"We were down at the Pier Shop," he said, "getting supplies and Eddie said something to the old lady in there about selling the caffeine pills. Said she shouldn't, you know, and that she should take them off her shelves. She said she wouldn't. Quite matter-of-fact about it."

"That's not the important bit, Whippet—" Jed began.

"Quiet!" Joan rounded on him, eyes wide. There was a vein showing in her forehead, redder even than the skin around it. "I asked him to tell it."

Whippet cleared his throat. "So, once we were outside, Eddie went over to the shore and lifted this big stone – this rock – and carried it back over. And he was going to throw it through the window, like, to teach the old lady a lesson. But Jed stopped him and then they were arguing and that…"

He ended with a shrug. Eddie had a wee grin on him now, obviously feeling he'd been vindicated by Whippet's version of events. Jed looked thoroughly miserable, wincing as he held a hand to his hip.

"Why?" Joan said, softly.

"They sold medical aids to one of our own," Eddie piped up. "It fucked – it corrupted – the process."

"Not you. Him." Joan pointed to Jed.

"Well…" Jed blinked. "You said we needed to be on friendly terms with our neighbours – the litter-picking and the clean up after the storm a few weeks back. Even beyond that, though, if we throw a stone through their window then they call the police, no?"

Joan nodded, with the ghost of a smile.

"But they weakened our experiment," Eddie spat across at him. "They need to be taught a lesson for that. Like Joan said, we pick out the weeds otherwise they take over the garden…"

Joan stepped forward, until she was only inches from him. She only came up to his chest. Grafton was fairly certain he could see a quiver and a sway to Eddie, though. *Crack.* The slap was a quick jerk of her arm, an open palm against his cheek. He lifted a hand to it.

"Don't dare use my own words against me like that," Joan said.

Eddie kept his hand at his cheek. "But, they sold Debbie those pills…"

"Don't you understand?" Joan hissed. "Nothing can be allowed to distract us from the next step. I'm close, Eddie, I'm so close. I've done the calculations, I've been patient in the way that Ravi never was and..."

"I'm sorry, Joan," Eddie stuttered.

"Just five more nights and then you can do what you want with them, yes?" Joan said, turning and walking back up the gravel path. "Until then – focus."

23

Grafton waited until quarter-past midnight. The majority of the Sleepless had gone to bed on the stroke of twelve, with only those on guard duties – and Joan, of course – staying awake. This was the window, then, when the commune would be at its quietest and he was least likely to be caught.

Eddie and his crew would be in two groups of two. The patrol circled around the A-frame, but Grafton should be able to time it right and get inside. He would love to have another look around inside the office too, but that seemed unlikely. He'd have to settle for a glimpse at the contents of the pallets stacked outside.

Lying awake while the others went to sleep had left him with a dull ache, almost a numbness, beneath his eyes and down the sides of his nose. It felt familiar, but he struggled to place it for a moment. Then he remembered: it was like those mornings – hundreds of them – when he'd not yet been sober. When he'd woken with the choice of sharpening up with a nip of something or surrendering to the hangover. Shaking the thought away, Grafton stepped outside.

The night was still and bitterly cold. The gravel path against his bare feet was enough to raise chilblains and wearing the robe outside felt like Scott of the Antarctic being kitted out with a nightie. Moving fast, Grafton skipped over to the copse of bushes at the side of his cabin. He listened to the silence. Not even an owl hoot. If you listened intently, though, then the sea started to murmur. And enough of a breeze stirred to carry the smell of seaweed.

The moon was three-quarters full; a delicate bite taken from it. Grafton used the light it cast to step around the small thickets of nettles at the back of the cabin. He wanted to skirt around the edges. The A-frame itself made for an easy target, because it cut such an imposing silhouette against the greyscale sea and the clouds which hung low over the water.

He ran downhill to the back of the next cabin along. There was a faint whirring sound coming from inside. He paused, wondering what it could be, but decided that it must be the electrics or a storage heater. The moment of listening allowed him to pick up another sound, from further away: a throaty chuckle. He waited. Sure enough, appearing around the side of the A-frame was Whippet and Eddie. They walked slowly, spoke softly. Grafton waited until they turned, following the curve of the path, and then he trip-skipped down to the next cabin.

He was at the side of it, exposed to anyone looking down the hill. The back, though, was shadowed by trees, by the edge of a small woodland. Grafton inched around, keeping his eyes on the open stretch of grass. There was a gasp, a grunt. He turned quickly. Two people were in the shadows, one crouched down in front of the other. The white robe of the one standing was bunched up and held at his stomach. As he tipped his head back, the acne scars caught the moonlight. Ally. And the figure kneeling in front of him was sure to be Morven, for once without the yellow scarf tied in her black hair.

"Fuck sake," Grafton hissed at them.

Morven looked up, trying to get both a cock and a yelp of surprise out of her mouth. Grafton raised a finger to his lips. Ally let his robe fall. He didn't seem surprised about getting caught. He turned to Grafton, gave a sigh and let his shoulders slump.

"They're only a hundred yards away," Grafton whispered. "What if they saw you?"

"We were quiet," Morven said. "Least until you jumped out."

"Yeah," Ally said. "What are you doing creeping around back here?"

"Never mind that."

Morven was getting to her feet. "It is a bit creepy."

"None of that." Grafton shook his head. "I'm saving you from yourself. If Eddie found you back here, he'd –" He stopped short. What would Eddie do? It wouldn't be the hammer again, but he had the impression that it might be something worse; something more inventive. "Get back inside," he finished, "before you lose your dick to frostbite."

"Fucking perv," Ally said, but he was already on his way.

"You won't tell on us, will you?" Morven's drawn-on eyebrows lifted.

Grafton shook his head, waved her on. He was alone now in the shadows behind the cabin. He waited for the thudding in his chest to ease, taking deep breaths to settle himself again. At least the adrenaline lifted the weariness, cleared the fuzziness from his head.

He went to the other end of the cabin and peered out. The next building down was the A-frame. There was the possibility that Morven's wee strangled cry had alerted Eddie and Whippet but, no, they were still strolling.

Hopefully, for their sake, Morven and Ally had heeded his advice and gone back to their cabins. If they were questioned, in the morning, then Grafton had little doubt that Ally would be quick to tell the story of the other disciple sneaking about in the moonlight. But Grafton would be halfway down the road to Glasgow by then.

As soon as Eddie and Whippet disappeared around the next corner, Grafton ran out and down the slope. It was only a short distance, but he felt horribly exposed; like an infantryman stumbling across no-mans-land. There were no shouts, no mortar shells. He reached the A-frame and grasped onto the wooden cladding. There were no lights on inside and the curtains were drawn.

Stepping forward on his toes, he moved over to the door. The handle gave with the slightest click. He swung it open a couple of inches. Again: no shouts or whistles or zipping bullets.

He opened it enough to dip his head inside. It was darker than the outside, the curtains keeping out most of the moonlight. His eyes took a moment to adjust. The open-plan room beyond was empty. It had that chill and quiet of the kitchen when you pad through in the middle of the night to get a glass of water.

He slid inside and clicked the door shut behind himself. He'd look around, quickly, and then he'd hightail it out of there.

Reaching into his sleeve, Grafton clicked his Dictaphone on. It was a fresh tape. He lifted his wrist to his mouth and whispered into the fabric. He felt like a secret agent but knew he actually looked like a loon. Good thing there was nobody there to see him.

"The main hall," he said, "used to be two or three rooms. Three. Looks-sh like a main living room and then a bedroom off to the side, but the adjoining wall's been knocked down and there's only s-studwork." He could hear the slur to his words, could feel his tongue as thick and unresponsive.

It was strange to stride into the empty space, to step up onto the platform that, to this point, he'd only ever seen from the back of the room. It was certainly cobbled together – old crates and plasterboard, sanded down and painted white. Grafton stepped off again.

"Perhaps the most interesting part of the downstairs," he said to his sleeve, "is a wee table at the side which is made up as a kind of shrine to Joan..."

He moved across to it. There was more on it than the day he arrived. Mostly it was hand-drawn cards with childish drawings of landscapes and of Joan herself. Was this what young Zack and the others spent their days doing? Was there a cabin further up the hill where they sat with Becky and Gillian and learnt the methods by rote? If they fell asleep with their head on the desk, were they prodded awake, told to sit straight? Threatened with worse punishments if they succumbed again? The thought of it made Grafton bone-weary, made him want to curl up under the shrine-table, where he'd seen Zack two nights before, and weep himself to sleep.

He certainly didn't relish the prospect of driving. He knew that he'd need cocktail sticks propping his eyes open if he wanted to make it more than a few miles. But he'd keep the windows down and have the radio blasting. He'd be able to put enough distance, between himself and the commune, before he stopped for a sleep.

"The shrine," Grafton said into his sleeve, "shows that the, erm, regard they hold for Joan isn't forced. The esteem, I guess, is organic. No images of Swami Ravi or mention of his name on the cards or drawings or knick-knacks..."

He grimaced. This was what he remembered most of all from his years as a journalist: the immediate second-guessing of what he'd written, the search for a more precise phrasing. The whisky had been his tool for quietening that voice, for dialling down its insistence. There'd been a sweet-spot, when he'd been lucid enough to form the sentences, but the alcohol glow had grown enough to leave the backspace key untouched. Back then it had been a fight against encroaching drunkenness rather than exhaustion.

Letting his arm drop, Grafton walked over to the stairs. He had to pause, breathe out, at the bottom. This had the feeling of crossing a threshold, breaching a trust.

The third stair up creaked. He paused and listened, but no sound answered it. He moved slowly and his eyes came level with the floor above. A sheet hung over the glass door to the balcony. And there, from the doorway on the right, was a faint glow of light.

He waited, listened. No matter how hard he strained, though, there was no sound. Not even the distant sea. He kept his own breath shallow, told himself that the sound of his heart was only internal and couldn't be heard by anyone else. And was there even anyone up there?

Grafton eased onto the next step. And the next — gently. Then he tipped forward, slowly, onto his hands and knees. Crawling up the final few steps, feeling the dust on the floorboards beneath his fingers, the knots and whorls in the wood. Just a crane of the neck away from the doorway now. He held his breath, leant forward.

The light was coming from a standard lamp in the far corner. The rest of the room was kitted out as a functional bedroom: single-bed with purple and blue patterned sheets; a side table with a few books stacked on it; a dressing table with an overflowing make-up bag and a kettle. On the floor was a coarse grey carpet. And sitting there, right in the centre of it, was Joan.

She had her eyes closed and headphones on. Whatever she was listening to was quiet enough that the sound didn't carry. Side-on, she looked like a teenager: cross-legged in the middle of her bedroom floor, in a navy nightdress, listening to music. She was biting and chewing at her lips, the movement so pronounced that Grafton wondered, for a moment, if she was mouthing along to lyrics. In her hands was a cup of tea, cradled between her fingers.

This felt like more of an intrusion, more of an illicit viewing of an intimate moment, than that first evening with the poison ivy bath. He'd been invited that night, but now he was spying. He should draw back, he knew that, but if this was to be his last sight of Joan then he wanted to inscribe every detail of her into his memory: her long brown hair, thinning at the scalp, and that seashell-smooth skin which was now puffed and grazed.

More than anything, Grafton wanted to see those grey eyes of hers; to feel their gaze meeting his and see the slight, gentle smile that told him that she understood his troubles, that she'd always understood.

Her eyes flickered open. Grafton rocked back, away from the doorway. Had she seen? There was no shout, no cry of anger.

Instead, he heard the floorboards groaning. He kept his breath in his chest and waited. If she came out of the room then she'd find him, on all fours, peering around the doorway.

He peeked into the room again. She was at the dressing table, looking into the mirror. It was angled away from the doorway. She picked at her lips with her fingernails, pulled at them to examine her teeth and gums. Even from a distance, the gums looked redder than they should; inflamed. She sighed. As Grafton had seen her do so often, she gathered her hair together and held it on top of her head in a loose bun. Then she let it fall. She reached into her make-up bag and took out a tiny plastic sachet, small enough to fit in the palm of a hand. It had white powder inside. She dipped her index finger into the powder and then brought a wee mound of it up to her nostril. She sniffed. Her shoulders twitched and she shut her eyes. Then she brought the same index finger up, again, to pull at her lips and rub at her gums.

Grafton felt a flare of anger. It burnt at his tear-ducts. Tears rising. He tried to squeeze them away, tried to think. There was the hypocrisy of it, after Debbie, but he had to be dispassionate, be a journalist. When the time came, he could write about it, but he couldn't take it personally, couldn't feel it as a betrayal.

Letting his breath out, Grafton clambered to his feet. He would be quiet on the way out, of course, but there was no need for the full cat-burglar bit. Joan was wearing headphones and, more to the point, she was high. Grafton could set fire to the A-frame and, likely as not, she'd just dance among the flames.

He longed to take a final look into the room — maybe the powder was some herbal extract, perhaps some sort of remedy for her teeth and gums — but he knew he shouldn't. It was time to go back to Glasgow, back to Isaac, and type up the story. The ending of which, he realised, had been decided for him.

Shaking his head, he turned and—

A hand over his mouth, twisting his neck back the way it had come. Holding him there, absorbing the shout he gave. Grafton squinted down at the hand. It was big enough to cover his nose and mouth, to squeeze at his cheekbones on either side. It was bristling with wiry, black hairs – the pores at the base of each of them raised and puckered. Grafton tried to swing his arms up to clutch at the hand and realised that another hand was gripping into his left bicep, that an arm had him across the chest and was pinning him back against a great, heaving hulk of a man. Whippet.

24

When explorers are lost in the jungle, they lick at lichen and suck at moss to get some kind of sustenance into their body. Isaac lay in the dark, fantasising about rolling up a dust bunny with tiny flakes and molecules of dinners from months ago, about scouring his tongue across all the plates in the cupboard for anything that had survived the dishwasher cycle. Before he went to bed, he'd stirred two spoonfuls of sugar into a cup of black tea and drunk that down. It hadn't even dulled the edge of his hunger.

He'd slept well for a spell, but now it was the middle of the night and his stomach was sounding out with the insistence of an alarm clock. From the table beside his bed, his phone periodically lit-up. He'd muted notifications the night before, because the constant chiming had grown annoying. The comments on his Facebook post and pictures of his sculptures were hugely gratifying, at first, but the sheer volume of them was overwhelming. And the majority of them were a parroting of Ravi's teachings or a rant, sometimes paragraphs long, about his wrongful imprisonment.

There was still no sign of his dad. Shauna had given Isaac a lift across to college, so his artwork was at least in place for the exhibition, but he knew that he needed to have something to eat before then. He couldn't survive the day otherwise, not without collapsing. He had planned to ask Shauna if he could borrow some money, but then she sent a text before picking him up: *Don't worry about petrol money, you can owe me a coffee xx.*

With an empty stomach through the night, then, Isaac was pinning his hopes on the exhibition itself. Surely there would be nibbles. Seven or eight hours was a long time to wait for stale crisps and maybe a sausage roll or two, but it was likely to be his next meal. In the meantime, he'd have to make do with another cup of black tea or with wetting a finger and running it along the shelves in the fridge or to the very back of the empty cupboards beside the hob.

Unless—

Rachel next door didn't come back from her night shift until about eight. He sometimes crossed paths with her out in the hallway; her on the way back from the hospital, him on the way out to college. It was always later than half-seven, Isaac was fairly certain. And there was a spare key to her flat hanging from a hook by the door. Isaac's dad had asked her to take a spare and she'd reciprocated, probably only from politeness.

He wouldn't take anything she'd miss. That would be his rule. Only things that there were lots of: a handful of cereal from a packet or grapes from a punnet, but not a banana that was lying alone in the fruit bowl or a bread roll that might have been earmarked for lunch. He didn't want his visit to be noticed, didn't want to freak her out.

It should have been a crisis of conscience. He should have been lying in his bed working out the pros and cons, twisting back-and-forth, drooling on the pillow while imagining the food, then swallowing down the idea of the invasion of privacy. But, as it was, he'd swung his legs from the mattress even as the thought occurred to him.

In t-shirt and jogging bottoms, Isaac padded out to the hallway and left his own door ajar. He crossed the landing. The concrete was ice-cold against his soles. He felt it across the length and breadth of each careful footstep. He listened. The building was silent enough that the act of listening took up a pulse which seemed to echo up the stairwell. He eased the key into the Yale lock of Rachel's door. It gave a small click. He paused before turning it, then swung the door open.

The layout of the flat was identical to the one Isaac and his dad shared next door. Isaac craned his head in at the open door of the master bedroom to check that it was empty. He was right, she was on night shift. If this were a film, he knew, the next thing he'd hear would be a key in the door. She'd be home early or he'd have miscalculated and he'd find himself needing to hide. He listened for it. Ludicrously, illogically, he stood in her hallway and listened for it. No sound, though.

He carried on through to the kitchen. Her flat smelt different to theirs. Fresher, yes, but with a chemical note to it too. Pine in the hallway, moving to vanilla as he passed the bathroom. The kitchen was stainless steel wiped with anti-bacterial spray, slate tiles mopped with bleach. Everything was spotless. Isaac was going to have to be careful not to leave even a crumb on the counter.

There was a wooden bread bin beside the kettle. He eased the lid off. Inside was a sliced loaf, open but with only about a quarter gone. Perfect – a couple of slices wouldn't be missed. He pulled them free. It was a seeded loaf, brown bread. Placing the slices on the counter, he folded the loaf bag closed again and replaced the lid of the bread bin. Then he moved over to the fridge. It whirred into light as he pulled the door open. He did a quick survey of the contents – milk and orange juice, margarine and veg, a few ready-meals – but decided against taking anything. He didn't want to swig from her cartons or leave a knife mark in her margarine. Come to that, he didn't want to have to wash a knife.

He opened a low cupboard – plates and bowls – and the one above – glasses and mugs. Next to it was one with sauces and flour and spices and gravy granules. At the top was a bag of raisins, also opened. That would do. As he lifted them down, the sticky re-seal strip came undone and he flinched and juggled and raisins went scattering. Across the hob, round the back of the bread bin, down onto the floor. *Fuck, fuck.*

Isaac closed the bag up again, smoothing a finger across the seal, and replaced it in the cupboard. Then he went on a raisin hunt. One-by-one he picked them up and piled them up on his bread. On his hands and knees, he scoured every inch of the floor. He swept a hand back and forth across the grey-black tiles to feel for any he'd missed. In the pit of his stomach, down where the hunger was, he knew he was likely to have missed one but he was desperate, now, to get out of there. He could look for raisins for the next hour, but then he really was in danger of Rachel catching him in the act.

Picking up his slices of bread, with the small mound of raisins on top, Isaac had a final check and turned to leave. Now, he knew, was the second moment in a film when a key might be heard in the lock. He moved out to the hall and listened for it again. Nothing.

He had stopped at the doorway to one of the bedrooms. It was as tidy as the kitchen: hairbrush and make-up lined up on the dresser, rug squared with the side of the bed, hospital corners on the sheets and duvet neatly turned back. There was one thing out of place, though. Hanging on the wooden frame of the bed was a pair of panties. Red with a white-lace trim. As if they'd been thrown there.

Isaac took a half-step sideways, towards the bedroom. What was it he wanted to do? Maybe he just wanted to find the underwear drawer and put them away – as Rachel had surely meant to – so that everything was tidy for when she came home. He didn't want anything out of place. But he knew that wasn't what he actually wanted to do. If his half-step turned into a step, and then another, then it would be to lift the red panties with the lace trim. It would be to press the fabric of them against his cheek and then bring them round to sniff at them and draw in the scent of them – natural, chemical. And then he might intend to return them to the bedframe, but he'd struggle to get them exactly as askew, with precisely that fold of white lace over red fabric. So, he'd have to take them, have to stuff them into the pocket of his jogging bottoms. He'd have to.

He rocked back, recovered his half-step. Bread and raisins were one thing, but that was entirely another. One was forgivable, the other was not. Isaac knew that. He drew in his breath, took a half-step in the right direction – and another and another – and left her flat.

25

The pillowcase was sucked in towards his mouth with every inhale. Grafton tried to breathe shallowly, tried to think sensibly. They could hurt him, yes, but they surely wouldn't kill him.

He'd been brought downstairs and tied to a chair on the platform. Even with the fabric over his face, even with precious little light coming through the fibres, he was aware that the room was filling up. The noise of the door opening, hushed voices, footsteps across the floorboards — he could hear the Sleepless entering the room and he could feel their eyes on him, hooded on the stage.

He was tied by the wrists to the arms of the chair and by the ankles to the wooden legs. He flexed his fingers, both to assure himself that he could and because he had the dread that Eddie's hammer might be coming out again. He was trying not to think beyond that, to what else they might do.

In the dim fug of the pillowcase, Grafton suddenly felt overwhelmingly exhausted. As if energy had been siphoned from every muscle, any remaining alertness drained. He kept catching his head as it dropped towards his neck. How long had he been sitting there — an hour, perhaps two? He had no doubt that he'd fallen prey to at least a couple of microsleeps, but he was determined to grunt and jerk himself back from the brink. He knew they were watching.

There was a change in the atmosphere of the room: whispered conversations ceased, someone tried to swallow a cough. Grafton tensed, listened to the silence. Then came the creak of the third stair. A moment later, someone brushed past him on the platform. It was Joan. He'd not realised, until that moment, that she had her own aroma but there it was — musky and subtly sour, somewhere between spilt beer and a jacket that's hung too long in the one place.

"They call us paranoid," she began. There was no weakness to her voice, her words were clear and with a throaty edge of anger to them. "They say that our lack of sleep leaves us prone to conspiracy theories and hifalutin fantasies."

She pronounced 'hifalutin' like it was a prescription medicine. As she paused, Grafton listened to the heaving in-out of her breaths. And there, beneath that, was a smaller, softer sound. Was it the grinding of teeth?

"But we've always been open to new disciples, welcoming of those who want to improve themselves, yes? Because, after all, we all know what's coming down the track — we all know — and if someone wants to save themselves, save their family, then who are we to say no? We have the tools, we have the key — we have the methods — so we will teach them to anyone who is open to it, anyone who is honest with us. Yes? Yes?

"But we will not tolerate, we will not allow, subterfuge and spying. We will not allow them to infiltrate and try to undermine us. We will not. Dear ones, there can be no viper in the family nest. And this man on the stage — this vermin — is the viper."

From the room in front of him, Grafton could hear the hiss. It rose like a wave, sweeping towards the stage and only breaking as the pillowcase was snatched clear of his head. He screwed his eyes shut against the light and kept his head bowed. He breathed in and out and tried to quell the thumping in his chest.

"This man is not who he says he is," Joan spat. "This man is a journalist."

The noise from the room wasn't a hiss, but a growl.

"This man was sneaking around while you were asleep, looking for information which might bring us down. He was grubbing around looking for falsehoods and chinks in our armour."

Joan paused, brought a hand up to wipe at her mouth. The

Sleepless were silent and expectant.

"I stay awake," Joan said, "for precisely this reason, yes? Because even the short hours that you allow yourselves — even that small weakness — can be exploited by them. And we can look out for each other — we can patrol the commune, we can watch for snakes in the grass — but the only true way to be alert — to be ready — is for all of us to be truly wakeful. Wakefulness is watchfulness."

Joan turned, then, to Eddie at the side of the stage and gave him a nod. He handed something to her. She gave Grafton a contemptuous look — those grey eyes cold as granite — and held up the Dictaphone.

"He has a recording device," she said, "which looks like something the Stasi would have used. And he's been taking measurements of the room, sizing it up. For what purpose, Grafton? Are you going to storm the place, pass on the details to the powers-that-be so that they can raid us? So that they can dismantle our buildings and break apart our community before our next step? So that they can pull the plug on our long-awaited twelfth day?"

Grafton decided that attack was the best form of defence. He had that nugget of information about the white powder, and all he needed was for one or two of the Sleepless to side with him. All he needed was for them to start asking questions.

"I've just seen —" His voice cracked. He cleared his throat and tried again. "I've just seen Joan snorting something. Upstairs. Up in that room at the top of the stairs. A white powder — maybe cocaine, or amphetamine. It's—"

"Conniving piece of shit!" Joan hissed. The force of this seemed to shock even her, seemed to cause a collective intake of breath among the Sleepless. She drew in a deep breath, pulled her shoulders back, and settled herself. "Your lack of faith astonishes me. Those were sleeping pills. I grind them up and I snort them, so that I can test myself, so that I can fight against something…"

"Bullshit," Grafton muttered, shaking his head. But there was no groundswell of dissent from the hall, no echoes of his accusation or calls for Joan to tell them more. They all stayed silent, looking up adoringly at Joan.

"This man has committed a heinous crime against us all," Joan said. "Nonetheless, we offered our last transgressor a choice, yes, so we'll afford this viper the same courtesy…"

Another nod to Eddie. This time he turned and made his way back up the stairs. Joan stood and waited. Grafton noticed that she was twitching slightly. You would only notice from up close, but there were flickers to her fingers, convulsions up the length of her arm. The sight of her trembling only served to shred Grafton's nerves further; the shaking in his arms caused the rope to chafe at his wrists.

Eddie came back down holding a white plastic tub. A large margarine container, it looked like, but with any lettering or label on the outside scrubbed away. He carried it carefully, in two hands, like a small child entrusted with a tea-tray. He handed the tub to Joan.

Grafton swallowed. "What's in the tub?" His voice sounded like there was a layering of rust in his throat.

"Hmm. If I tell you then that removes the trust from the exercise, no?"

"But—"

"I'll show you." Joan raised an eyebrow. "To allow you to assess your options…"

Grafton shook his head. "No," he said, "I'll leave, I'll walk away."

"Patience, patience."

Not a breath stirred the dust in the hall, there was no fiddling movements or shifting of backsides on the floor. Everyone was waiting to see what was in the tub. Grafton tried to crane his neck, tried to peer inside, but he knew it was useless – maybe it was some kind of venomous spider or snake that he would have to hold, perhaps a homemade concoction that he'd be forced to eat. It had to be something, didn't it, that would keep him awake? And that was a fact to cling to because it meant that whatever was in the tub wasn't intended to kill him.

Joan stepped forward. She reached into the tub. Propped against the side, at an angle, was a thin paintbrush with a red handle. She lifted it and held it up to the audience. Then she dipped it. Was she going to paint him? Was it a simple repeat of the chilli-oil from his first evening?

The paintbrush came down and she ran the bristles along his right forearm. At first, it was cool. Like being brushed with water. But then –

"Arrrrrghhhh – Jesus! Fuck!"

Napalm, was his first thought. A concentrated blowtorch. Not only on the surface, but with teeth or claws or fucking hooks that dug down into his flesh and scooped upwards, that tried to lift the meat from the bone.

"Shit, shit, shit. What the hell – !"

His left hand took on a life of its own, kicking and bucking at the rope in an attempt to get free and reach across to his right arm. The chair rocked, the chair tipped. Eddie ran over and braced it. Grafton peered up at him, eyes streaming, and saw that thin weasel face looking down at him with a grin.

"You wee dick, Eddie, you wee arsehole…"

"Now, now," Joan's voice was soothing. "He's done nothing wrong."

"What is that stuff?"

Joan knelt down in front of Grafton. He was thrashing his head from one side to the other. His whole body wanted to move, to squirm and lift and tear his forearm free, leave it behind. Joan took his chin in her hand and held it steady. Her grip was firm.

"Battery acid," she said. "Nothing more than battery acid."

"Fuck," Grafton whispered. And then he started weeping.

The pain in his arm was still like the shifting of tectonic plates, like lava bubbling free, but now with just the lightest salve of relief – he knew what it was, at least, he knew what it was. Small mercy, but something. "Ok," he said, "I've had my punishment, you can untie me."

"No, no," Joan said. "That was just to show you what was in the tub, yes? That was the demonstration, so that you know the choice you're going to make."

"You *cruel bitch*!" Grafton spat.

Another growl from the room, from the Sleepless. Animalistic now. The noise of it travelled up Grafton's spine as a chill. He slumped back in his chair, squeezed his eyes shut. It felt like a paring knife was being run, repeatedly, up and down his forearm.

"The choice," Joan said, "is banishment or..." She paused for effect. "I take this acid and brush it on your eyelids, so that you might truly open your eyes. You've transgressed, yes, but it isn't too late to show that you understand the error of your – "

"Listen!" Grafton pushed forward in the chair, leant out as far as he could towards the Sleepless in the hall. "Your leader – this girl – is threatening torture. That's what this is – that's what this amounts to. Fucking torture, and you're all complicit. Make no mistake, you're all complicit, unless you do something to stop it."

He scanned frantically from face to face. Some avoided his eye, others gazed back with the kind of blank impassivity of a cinema audience. Ally and Morven were sitting side-by-side. Ally was smirking, Morven was looking away. Grafton looked to Jed. The skin around his eye was swollen and purple. He sat with his hand held over his mouth, but he showed no sign of standing up or of speaking out. And Debbie, a few folk further along, met Grafton's gaze and gave him a small smile. Then she held both her hands up, palms out, as though she was in church. There was a lumpy bandage on her index finger, twice the size of any of the other fingers.

"Every one of you is complicit," Grafton said, through his teeth.

"You're finished with your traitor's tricks?" Joan asked.

"Fucking hell." Grafton sighed and, again, he felt like sobbing. "I thought you had something, Joan, I thought you were on to something here."

"We are. We are, Grafton. And that's why we don't turn our backs on you. Fair's fair – we're offering you the opportunity to prove yourself."

"I can't. It's torture. It's years of pain."

"No, it's peeling back your eyelids so you can finally see…"

Grafton shook his head. The tears were properly flowing now, were trailing down his cheeks, because he had no doubt that they were going to do it anyway. They had offered him the opportunity to repent, as they saw it, and he'd turned it down. But they weren't just going to shrug their shoulders, were they. And would they stop there…?

"You can show people the path…" Joan said. She hesitated. "…you can lead them to water, yes, but you can't make them drink. It is beyond me – it baffles me, dear ones – that anyone can live amongst us as this man has and not see that…erm… can't see the path forward–"

And it struck Grafton, suddenly, that Joan couldn't see her own way out. She had expected Grafton to accept his punishment, maybe, or to be able to take it to the point of paintbrush nearly touching his eyelid and then offer him a reprieve. He'd left her scuppered. Because she didn't want to take it so far that it would damage her cause, her message, her teachings, did she?

"Throw it on him," came a voice from the room. Not a shout, but a suggestion.

"No, no, banish him."

"Break his fingers instead."

"Quiet," Joan said, in a whisper.

"Shop him to the police for spying."

"Nah, he needs to learn his lesson."

"Quiet."

"Do the acid somewhere it won't show."

"Quiet."

"Take him out back and —"

"Shut the fuck up!" Eddie stepped forward, snarling. His neck was pushed forward, as though straining at a leash. "Shut the fuck up and listen."

The Sleepless did as they were told. Joan took a moment. She set the tub down on the platform and gathered her hair up into a bun. She used the thin paintbrush to hold it in place and Grafton silently, fervently wished that a drop of the acid — just a drop — would fall down onto her neck.

"We are at a crucial juncture, friends," she said. "We are at a critical... we are being tested. And we will be tested many times in the days to come, yes. As we approach our twelfth day. This is our first hurdle, maybe. This is the movement — the very ideas — being stretched and strained by outsiders, by them.

"Our first response, dear ones, can't be to play into their hands. We are on the verge, on the brink, of something truly revolutionary here, yes, and we can't allow it..." She drew in a breath. "We have to let him go, because otherwise we lose our purity. We have to hold our anger, because otherwise we lose our patience and our opportunity for that next step; for becoming a beacon to those who seek to follow in our footsteps. We have to bear these slings and arrows, friends."

She brought a hand up to her eyes, then, and covered them over. Her shoulders heaved. When she lifted her hand, there were tears glistening in her eyes. She looked directly at Grafton.

"You stupid man," she said, "we could have fixed everything for you."

And, with that, she moved to the back of the stage and picked up the Dictaphone again. She placed it in the white tub and swirled it gently from side to side. From beside Grafton, Eddie gave a wee snorting chuckle. Grafton would gladly sacrifice that recording, though, if he could get out of this room alive. He still had the other tapes in his car, after all, and the bloody wound on his forearm as proof.

"Let him go," Joan said, turning back to the stairs.

"Do we go back to bed?" someone asked, from the front row.

"No," she said, over her shoulder. "No more sleep."

26

As he was being untied, Grafton looked across at Debbie. He wanted to catch her eye, wanted her to understand that if the hammer hadn't been a step too far then the acid certainly was. She held his gaze for only a split second, before spinning around so that her back was turned to him. The disciple next to her followed suit. Then another and another. In a matter of seconds, Grafton was faced with a roomful of white-robed backs.

"Come on." Eddie grabbed him by the arm and lifted him from the chair. He grimaced and set his teeth together, but didn't give Eddie the satisfaction of crying out. With Eddie on one side and Whippet on the other, Grafton was marched out of the A-frame.

He found it hard to stay on his feet as they dragged him down the hill. His ankle caught on the gravel and he felt the warmth and wetness of blood. It was as nothing, though, compared with the acid burn on his arm. Eddie's grip stopped short of the wound itself, but he tugged and twisted at the skin around it like a masseuse trying to unknot a muscle.

It took all he had not to scream, not to whimper. But he couldn't stop the noise that came from deep in his throat as they rounded the corner. There was a thick cloud of black smoke. Beneath that, orange flames licked through the windows and rose from the bonnet of his little hatchback. The smell of burning petrol scoured at his nostrils.

He screwed his neck back to peer at Eddie. The wee bastard looked delighted. With firelight glinting in his eyes, he gave a cackle of laughter and winked across at Whippet.

Accusations and insults flew through Grafton's mind. He managed to hold them back. Whatever he threw at Eddie, the answer would be all wide-eyed innocence and protestations that he'd been with Grafton the entire time.

Grafton looked across to the stacked wooden pallets. Ten of them, with black plastic wrapping. They couldn't contain anything flammable then, surely, or Eddie would have thought to move them further away. Or would he? A wonderful, revenge-fuelled thought of the entire commune being blown to kingdom-come lifted Grafton's spirits for a moment. It was more likely that the crates contained acid, though. Gallons of it, enough to offer each and every member of the Sleepless the choice that Grafton had faced...

"Here," Eddie said, letting go of his arm and stepping towards the burning car. He hocked phlegm up in his throat and sent a huge globule of spit arcing over towards the flames. He turned back, arms spread out. "I tried."

Grafton brought his right arm in close to his body, to cradle it there. His car held not only the tapes but, more crucially, his wallet and house keys. How was he supposed to get back with no money and no car? How was he supposed to get home to Isaac?

Eddie circled around. He gave Grafton a shove in the small of his back. He stumbled out onto the road.

"Best get walking, old man," Eddie said. With that, he gestured to Whippet and the two of them turned back to the commune.

Out at sea, light was bleeding up from the horizon and lightening the grey clouds. There was nothing stirring on the shore road, nothing moving except for Grafton. He trudged along, bare feet against tarmac, and tried to keep his injured arm covered by a fold of white fabric without letting the hem of his robe ride up too high. The chill air swirled in, but he didn't know if it was that or the sudden sharp drop in adrenaline that left him shivering.

Halfway along the road was the farmhouse, set back beyond a field of sheep. He paused at the driveway, considering. He could go and ring the doorbell, throw himself on the mercy of the owner, but he feared the reaction. Plenty of folk around here would keep a shotgun handy, especially since the Sleepless came to the village.

No, Grafton decided he'd go along to the Pier Shop and wait for daylight. The old woman in there was gruff but at least she might remember him and take pity.

No sooner had he made the decision than the rain came. Heavy droplets that brought with them a rush of sound, as the rain swept along the road. Grafton held his forearm out, hoping that the rainwater might cool and wash the burn. Then he realised how thirsty he was. He tipped his head back and opened his mouth.

His robe was clinging tightly to his chest by the time he made it along to the white buildings of the Pier Shop. Rain ran in rivulets down the hairs on his legs and each footstep gave a slight squelch, but Grafton felt something close to elation. He was out and he'd survived. The sky was getting lighter and lighter, the line of the horizon now clearly defined as the darkness of the sea against the pastel yellow and orange of the sky.

On the other side of the road from the shop was a patch of grass shoreline. Sheep had grazed it down to a fuzz. A few discarded orange buoys lay scattered and, over towards the pier, there was a wooden rowboat. The green paint was warped and flaking, but there was a tarpaulin over the top of it.

Grafton made his way over to the boat and peeled the blue tarpaulin back. He grimaced as he pulled himself up, feeling the effort as a shooting pain in his damaged arm. It only lasted a second and then he was inside the cocoon of the boat. The wood was splintery and there was a sharp smell of paraffin. Most importantly, though, he was under cover.

Taking care to lift the fabric away from his arm, he pulled off the robe and pushed it away into the darkness. It wouldn't dry, but at least he was free from it for a spell. In only his underwear, he curled up into the foetal position. He felt the roughness of wood beneath his cheek, listened to the sound of the rain on the tarpaulin, breathed deep at the paraffin smell. He smiled. And he slept.

27

Conventional surveillance isn't ideal, because people are more attuned to their surroundings than we realise. That's what Ravi always told Liz. People know if someone is watching them in the same way they know that rain is coming or their bodies are about to succumb to sickness. Some of it is sensory, of course, but there's also an element which is instinctual. You know someone is watching you because the energy around you changes.

For that reason, Ravi rarely instructed her to follow someone. There were times when they needed to intercept a person who'd proven themselves an enemy – a judge, a journalist, a juror – but they tended not to tail them or set up a stakeout outside their offices. Instead, they trusted that the moment they turned up would be the right one, that serendipity would place them in the optimal situation without the need for meticulous notes or floorplans or listening devices.

With that lesson in mind, Liz didn't haunt the street outside her ex-husband's flat. She didn't stand on the opposite pavement, looking up at the tenement window and hoping to catch a glimpse of her son. Instead, she sat on the carpeted floor of her hotel room and twisted thin-gauge steel wire around her toes in figure-of-eight movements. Tight enough to bite into the skin. She had a sheet underneath in case she drew blood, but her feet were mostly toughened by scar tissue anyway. This was a technique she'd used on many occasions. The first time had been in Pune when she'd wanted to go to Ravi, but was uncertain if she should wait for a summons. One of the other women had the wire for jewellery making, so Liz had idly wrapped it around her big toe. After a moment, she'd felt a tug. And when she went to Ravi, he was pleased to see her. So, she used it again. And again.

That magnetic pull had served her well. Not only with Ravi, but with all manner of assignments she'd been given over the years. So, she sat patiently in her hotel room, twisting and untwisting the wire. Three times on Wednesday and twice on Thursday, it told her to set out. She strode off towards the West End, hobbling slightly until the slick blood turned crusty. When she reached their street, she strolled along as if she was on her way to the shops on Dumbarton Road or making her way home after a lunch meeting. She was no more conspicuous than the pigeons on the guttering, than the postie making his way from door-to-door.

Each time, she saw no sign of Tom or Isaac. Their window was empty – not even a clothes horse there now. On Thursday afternoon, though, she saw a light on in the living room and by the evening it was off. Someone must be home.

On the way back, Liz stopped off at Hillhead Library to check the social media feeds for Swami Ravi. Only a quick scan through to see if there was anything of interest. And there was her moment of serendipity, her magnetic pull, her sign from on-high. A post from Isaac. Without even realising that she was in the same city, he was reaching out to her. He wanted to know more.

When she got back to the hotel, the girl behind the front desk scuttled off into a back room at the sight of her. Liz strode quickly along the corridor, trying to make it to her room so she could clunk the lock shut behind her. But she could hear footsteps behind her. Hurrying footsteps.

"Ms Whelan?" It was the manager's voice. A middle-aged woman with a sour face. "Ms Whelan?"

Liz made it to the door, but she swiped her keycard too fast. The wee light blinked red. She tried again, but the manager was right behind her now. Liz only got the door half-open.

"Ms Whelan?"

"Yes?" Liz turned around, tried a smile.

"Ms Whelan, we're going to have to ask you to leave the premises, please."

"No, thank you."

"We've been inside your room, Ms Whelan."

Liz let the door go. It shuddered as it slammed. "On whose fucking authority?" she hissed. "I had a Do Not Disturb sign up, did I not?"

The manager only looked taken aback for a second. "There was blood across the carpet in the hallway," she said, crisply. "It led back to your room. We have authority to use the master key. And – I might add – the presence of blood gave some sort of moral authority too."

"You would rise quickly in a fascist government, wouldn't you?"

"I beg your pardon?"

"I said—"

"I heard." The manager lifted a wagging finger, but then lowered it again. "The state of that room, Ms Whelan. The sheer state of it. In twenty years, I don't think I've seen anything like it."

Liz nodded. "Twenty years. You really made the most of your potential, eh?"

"Gather your things and go."

"A life well spent."

The manager folded her arms. "We won't charge you for damages, as long as you leave now. But if you don't then we'll be forced to phone the police."

Liz swept into the room and lifted her few possessions. With head held high, she pushed past the manager in the hallway and out to the car park. Clambering into the driver's seat, she deposited her belongings on the backseat and then sat there staring into the grey of the Glasgow night.

She didn't need the wire around her toes. Not anymore. Sitting there, with the rain starting to spatter the windscreen, she knew that tomorrow would be the day she'd reconnect with Isaac. There was a time and a place. It would be in a public setting and with that came an air of unpredictability, a lack of control, that Ravi would not have approved of. She would have to keep her wits about her, take precautions and be wary of those around her. All being well, though, the next day she would speak with her son.

28

Grafton woke to the grumble of an engine, the sigh of brakes. Daylight bled in at the edges of the tarpaulin. He shivered. The cold was down in the marrow of his bones. He looked across the wooden rowboat to the slumped, sodden robe. Pulling that on again was out of the question. Beyond the blade of an oar, however, in the bottom of the boat, was an old dust sheet. Grafton crawled across and lifted it. His hand shook. The material was rough and crisp, in places, with dried varnish, but it was dry.

He wore the sheet like a toga, tied over the shoulder. The driver of the lorry was starting to unload newspapers and bread rolls from the back. He turned to watch Grafton walk across the grass towards the Pier Shop. He was chewing at a piece of gum, which gave him the air of a cow with cud.

"Morning," Grafton called.

The man gave him the slightest of nods; guarded, watchful.

"Is the woman who runs the shop around?"

A shake of the head. "Not open yet."

"Open for deliveries, though."

The driver conceded the point with another nod.

Grafton looked along the road, to where it rose gently and curved out towards the headland. The hills there weren't as large as the one behind the commune, but they still cast a deep shadow. There was a scattering of houses further along, but the first field had only a caravan at its edge. It was streaked with rust and sat at a lopsided angle, like a boat cresting a wave.

"So where would the woman be?" Grafton asked the delivery man.

"Moira."

"Moira, yes."

"She'll be round the back, in the stock room."

Grafton gave a smile of thanks. He folded his arms across his chest and stepped from the road to the gravel that surrounded the Pier Shop. At the far end of the building was a passageway, with bins at the end. Grafton edged past them and carefully negotiated the cracked paving stones with his bare feet. The doorway was a siren's call of heat and light. A radio sent out faint chatter, then laughter over the start of a pop song.

"Moira?" Grafton called, as he reached the door. The stock room was simply set out – whitewashed and windowless – with shelves of tinned goods and cartons of long-life milk. High in the corner of the room, attached by a bracket, was a barred electric heater which buzzed and whirred and gave off a pool of warmth that Grafton could immerse himself in. As he moved towards it, the woman he now knew as Moira stuck her head out from an open doorway at the back of the room.

"How do you know my name?" she snapped.

"You remember me?" Grafton held out his hands, palms up in surrender. "From, erm, from the start of the week...of last week..." He thought a moment. "Of this week."

She pursed her lips. "You're one of the nutters."

"Not really, not really. I'm a journalist, you see, I'm a... it's..."

Her frown softened and she set her head on one side. "A journalist? Goodness me, you're writing about that rabble then?"

He shrugged. "Honestly, I don't know anymore."

"And what are you wanting from me?"

"Could I use your phone, maybe? Please."

She brought a hand up to her cropped grey hair, scratched at it. "You've still not answered. How do you know my name? Do they talk about me, up at that compound? Are they scheming?"

Grafton shook his head, pointed. "The delivery man. It was him that told me."

She nodded. "And what happened to your arm?"

"That was them, aye."

He looked down at the acid burn. In the light, in the glow from the heater, it looked even angrier. The skin was as bubbled and warped as melted plastic, still with the sheen of blood but also with a clear liquid that was frothing at the edges.

"We should get you cleaned up," Moira said, "and into some proper clothes."

"I'd appreciate it. And the phone call?"

"Ach, I think we could stretch to a phone call."

It was Moira's grandson who brought him a change of clothes and the phone handset. The clothes were obviously his own, teenage in both sizing and design. The jogging bottoms only reached to the top of Grafton's shins and the grey hoody was tight around the middle and, for some reason, had the word FRESH across it in black, capital letters. Still, Grafton was grateful. Especially because the young lad took away the dust sheet and left him with some privacy to make his phone call.

He sat on a cardboard box, filled with bags of flour, and dialled the landline in the flat. It rang and rang. The answering machine clicked in. Grafton hung up, tried again. No answer.

"Fuck!" Grafton spat the word at the handset, stared at the numbers on the keypad.

"Have you someone else you can try?" Moira's voice came from the doorway. She was standing there watching. He had no idea how long she'd been waiting there. She'd maybe been planning on eavesdropping on his call. You couldn't blame her.

"I'm trying my son." Grafton held up the phone. "I'll try again in a bit."

Moira nodded, stepped into the room. She let out a grunting noise as she swung her hip up and around. As she reached Grafton, she turned the grunts into a hummed half-tune, as if that was what she'd been doing all along. She was carrying a first aid kit and a glass bottle.

"What's that?" Grafton asked.

"We're cleaning the wound, remember?"

"Yes, but what's in the bottle?"

"Vodka." She held up the half-bottle, so he could see the red label.

He shook his head. "I can't have that near me, sorry, it's... no–"

"Those rules from the commune don't apply here."

"It's not the rules. It's the drink." Grafton closed his eyes. "I've a past with it."

"Aye, this is for cleaning, not for drinking."

"Still–"

"This is the way I've always cleaned wounds, the way my mother did it. You can take it or leave it."

Grafton met her stare. It was level and determined. There might have been half a pharmacy worth of burn ointments and antiseptic lotions through in the main shop, but Moira had always doused her cuts in alcohol – her grandson's cuts – so that was what was on offer. Grafton bowed his head into a nod.

Moira pulled another cardboard box over and sat down heavily. She poured the vodka onto a piece of cotton wool. The sharp smell rose and caught at the back of Grafton's throat. He closed his eyes and swallowed it down, thinking of ice and lemon. The cotton wool was dabbed on the burn and the exquisite pain ran up the length of his arm, through his clenched neck and then sang in his gritted teeth. He breathed out, opened his eyes.

Moira did have antiseptic ointment, as it happened, and she smoothed some of that at the edges of the wound. Then she covered it over with a piece of gauze and a bandage. It was all done quickly, with nimble fingers.

"That should hold you," she said, giving out a groan as she rose from her cardboard box. "I'd get it seen to properly, mind; it's a nasty one."

"I will. Thank you."

She nodded. "You'll have a cup of tea, I'd say. And a wee scone or something."

Grafton tried to answer, but found that only a whimper came from his throat. Tears gathered in his eyes. He raised a hand, but the tears spilt down onto his cheeks before he could rub them away. He looked at Moira and managed a half-nod.

"Try your son again," Moira said, "I'll be right back."

He took a moment to compose himself. A few seconds to breathe and to draw the hood of his FRESH jumper up over his head. Then he looked around for the phone. It wasn't the first thing he saw. There was the half-bottle of vodka – only a neck's worth taken from it – propped up beside the boxes. It was a reflex, it was muscle-memory, which saw him reach out. He lifted the bottle and pushed it into the front pocket of his hoody, then he sat back and felt the weight of it against his stomach.

The phone was on the shelf behind. He twisted around for it and dialled the landline in the flat again. It rang and rang. No answer.

Grafton stared at the keypad. All those numbers and, without his mobile, he didn't know a single combination that would get him through to someone useful. There was always '999', but that felt like the nuclear option, particularly if he wanted to break the story of the commune to an unsuspecting world.

He sat looking at the phone. And then he realised that he did know another number. He knew it by heart, with a wee jingle to match. The call-in number for his radio station, which played through his cans every morning. He didn't even pause to consider before dialling.

"Good morning, you're through to—"

"Danny, it's Grafton."

"Grafton, hi. You're not due back in 'til Monday."

"Aye, aye. Listen, I need your help."

Silence. Static. "With what?"

"I'm stranded, mate. In Ardnamurchan. Wee village called Kilchoan."

"Not much I can do about that, Grafton, we've got a show to run."

"I know." Grafton screwed his eyes shut, pinched at his nose. "I'm not asking you to drive up…"

"What then?"

"I don't know. Send a taxi, maybe."

"Bloody hell. That would cost an arm and a leg, would it not?"

"Who gives a shit. Take it out my wages."

Danny went quiet again. Grafton could hear him breathing, though, so the line hadn't gone dead. He needed some convincing, that was all.

"Listen, Danny," Grafton hissed, "that story – the story – is really something, right? I've got it. I've been there and I've got the scars to prove it, mate. Literally. Get me back there and I'll give you the whole thing, the whole situation—"

Danny sighed. "Is this the cult, Grafton?"

"The very same, Danny, the very same."

"You told me you were taking a week's holiday."

"Aye, wee white lie."

Danny sighed again. The fucker should have been using the cough button if he was going to sigh that much. Grafton let out a laugh at that thought, just a wee snorted chuckle. It seemed to stir Danny, at least.

"Right," he said, "I'll look into getting you a taxi. But it's coming out of your wages, yes? And it'll be a few hours, I'd say."

"All the time in the world, Danny boy, all the time in the world. The pipes, the pipes are calling—"

He didn't know why he said that last part. He snipped himself off. Danny wasn't likely to withdraw the offer because of a slip into song lyrics, was he? There were others who'd have hung up on him long before now, but Danny was a decent sort.

"Where are you then?" Danny asked. "Where exactly?"

"The Pier Shop. Kilchoan. They'll find me here."

"Sit tight, then."

Grafton smiled. "I'll hang tight. Thanks Danny."

He said the last part to the disconnected tone. Not to worry, he'd thank him properly later. And, in spite of everything, he'd offer them first refusal on the story of Seattle. There'd be something poetic, something neat and poignant, about going from traffic and travel to guest reporter. Fuck me, the listeners would realise, that lad isn't talking about a snarl-up on the motorway anymore, isn't boring everyone to tears with delays at Glasgow Queen Street. No, he's talking about a commune out on the west coast where none of the disciples sleep, about punishments given out with hammers and acid burns, about a young woman staying awake for eleven nights. And, just like that, he would be known as the journalist who first broke the story, first spread the word, about Joan.

29

For the first spell of the taxi ride, Grafton was happy enough. He'd asked Moira for a pad of paper and a pen and she'd given him a couple of used envelopes and the stub of a pencil. It was enough. He spent the first half-hour of the journey scribbling away in the back seat, putting down everything he could remember from the past few days. Three days, was it? Four?

He was keen to get down all that happened on the final night, of course, but there was more to it than that. He wanted to get down the essence of Joan too. Try to capture the main points he'd had in his notebook. The way she could hold your attention absolutely, could pause for five seconds – for ten, fifteen – in the middle of a sentence and you'd stay sharp, listening, because you knew the next thing out of her mouth would be worth hearing. Hell, you knew the next thing she said might change your life.

The radio was on in the taxi. Not Grafton's station, it was out of range. The voices were talking about the weekend's football matches: the Edinburgh derby the next day. And it was only with that, only with their chatter, that Grafton realised that it was Friday. The day of Isaac's exhibition. He stopped scribbling and looked at the wee clock on the dashboard: 11.51.

The driver was about the same age as Grafton, with salt-and-pepper hair and a slight cast to his left eye. Heavy chap, with a bottle of Diet Pepsi in his cup holder. Grafton eyed him in the rear-view mirror, considering how to make the request.

"So, buddy…" Grafton cleared his throat, leant forward. "How would you feel about driving me all the way to Glasgow?"

The driver looked up to the mirror. Or his right eye did. Grafton knew he was a hell of a sight: the grey hoody with FRESH on it, the jogging trousers that barely reached beyond his knees when he was sitting down, his filthy bare feet and the second skin of grime across his face.

"Fort William station, I was told," the driver said. "Buy you a ticket, leave you to it."

"Come on. You can't do that to me."

"I absolutely can, mate."

"Look at the state I'm in..."

"Those were my instructions. Drive you to the train station, buy you a ticket."

"I'll level with you." Grafton shifted further forward in his seat, close enough to touch the driver's shoulder. "My boy has his final exhibition for his college course today. It starts in — what — eight minutes, but it runs until five. If you kept driving, then I might have a chance of making the end...?"

The driver went quiet. Maybe he had kids too — maybe there was a wee tug on his heartstrings about the thought of a dad missing out on his son's big day. Perhaps he didn't have many fares out in the sticks and the prospect of a sizeable whack on a radio station's expense account was tempting...

"How much is the train ticket?" Grafton said. "Thirty, forty quid? Take me as far as that pays for."

"It wouldn't take you far, not really. Certainly not to Glasgow."

"As far as you can, though. I'll hitch the rest of the way."

The driver sniffed. "Nope," he said, "I'll do as I said."

"Well, fuck you then."

"Aye, seems I made the right call, sure enough."

Grafton slammed his hand against the back of the passenger seat. Not hard, though, not really. He wanted to make it as far as the station, at least. Out of the window was a steady streak of trees and sloping hillside, often with loose stone and shingle reaching down to the edge of the road. If he was kicked out here, on the road to Fort William, then he was stranded.

"There'll be a train along mid-afternoon, anyway," the driver said. "Get you there just as fast."

"Aye? And what do I tell my son?"

"Not my issue, pal."

"Danny screwed me over."

"Not my issue."

Grafton slumped back against the seat. The bottle in the front pouch of his hoody gave him a gentle dig in the gut. Just reminding him of its presence. Grafton lifted the envelope he'd been writing on and carefully tore it in half, then again. He knew he needed to write the whole thing through, from start to finish, like he used to.

"I'll make you a deal," Grafton said to the driver.

"What's that?"

"I'll be a church mouse for the rest of the drive, ok, if you give me your receipt book…?"

The driver glanced up to the rear-view mirror again. It was hard to tell if he was looking at Grafton or at the road behind. Then he reached down and lifted the pad of receipts from the well beside the gear stick. He handed it back to Grafton.

"Much obliged," Grafton said.

He turned the receipt book over and flicked through – pages and pages of blank white space. He would spend the whole train journey back down filling it. Aye, he'd miss Isaac's exhibition, but at least he'd have the full story done. Ready to be typed up. Isaac would understand, once he read it in the Sunday papers or heard it on the six o'clock news.

Reaching into the pocket of his hoody, Grafton lifted out the half-bottle of vodka. The cap made a slight cracking noise as it opened. And the smell of it, Jesus, filling the nostrils like chlorine at the swimming pool. The driver was looking at him in the mirror, so he raised the bottle to toast him and then took his first grimacing swallow.

The driver shook his head and wound down the window, but he didn't say a word.

30

Isaac was in an out-of-the-way corner, tucked underneath the stairs. The loop of Wrestlemania clips he had playing on the screen behind made him feel like a subscription TV salesman rather than an artist.

Folk were milling around out on the college concourse, which was doubling as a gallery space for the exhibition. There was a cluster around Shauna's line drawings, over beside the toilets, and Isaac sometimes caught sight of her working the room. She wore a black pinafore over a flowery shirt and, for some reason, a bowler hat. Whenever someone new came up to her, she would doff the hat like a Victorian gent. The hat was never waved in Isaac's direction.

At the entrance was a tableclothed trestle table with wine, juice, and nibbles. Isaac had already made a half-dozen trips across to lift handfuls of dry-roasted peanuts.

There was still no sign of his dad, and no answer from the mobile either. Isaac sipped at his glass of orange juice. In a patch of sunlight, a toddler rolled across the polished floor and squealed delightedly. A younger brother or nephew of one of the students, probably. His whole family were watching him, grinning away, with their backs to the artwork on the walls.

It was only this morning, while putting the finishing touches to his set-up, that it had occurred to Isaac that he should maybe be worried about his dad. It wasn't unheard of, certainly, for him to get distracted, but it was unusual for him to leave his phone off. Back when he'd been fixated on tracing the financial records of the Indian commune, there'd been a spell of Isaac having to eat breakfast cereal without milk, but his dad had still picked him up from after-school club. And when he'd gone away for that radio production course, over a week in the summer, Isaac had been shunted off to a residential drama camp that he'd hated, but his dad had at least given him a call every evening to check in.

"These are yours?"

The question came from a grey-haired lady with a flash of purple across her fringe. It was hard to judge whether she was someone's grandma or one of the external examiners. She wore a red dress with yellow vines twisting across it. The external examiners weren't the only ones who decided the grades – the tutors had an input – but their opinion would certainly hold sway. And the rumour was that one of the examiners was a lecturer from the Art School.

"It's wrestling," she said. "Is that right?"

"Yes." Isaac forced a smile. "But it's also playing with the metaphor of wrestling with sleep, those fights we have between the impulse to sink back into a comfortable sleep and the knowledge that we have to get up and face the day…"

The woman pursed her lips, tipped her head tn the side. Isaac took it as a sign to continue.

"The pandemic saw lots of people struggle," he said, "with insomnia and with the break in routine, but I wanted to also take it back to that childhood feeling of staying up for the wrestling or any show really – desperately wanting to stay awake – and yet having the inevitability of your eyelids getting heavier. And there's this…erm…thinker or guru called Swami Ravi who–"

"They got confused with the pandas, did they not?" the woman interrupted.

"Pardon?"

"The wrestlers. The initialism, what is it, got mixed up with the wildlife federation?"

"Initialism?"

"Yes, like an acronym."

"Ah, WWF. They changed it to WWE."

"So, the pandas won, I guess." She raised a glass of wine to her lips and took a delicate sip, with her eyes on Isaac's sleeper-hold sculpture. "Very good," she said.

"Thank you."

"There's character and energy to it. I like it."

Isaac wanted to have another go at explaining it to her, at articulating why his work spoke to more than just wrestling. He needed to let her know that it was also about frustration, being pinned to the sofa with that feeling that time was ebbing away. The contradiction that we often lie deep in the cushions and watch athletes on the screen performing acts of great exertion and physicality.

He wanted to say more but at that moment, over the woman's shoulder, he caught sight of someone familiar at the refreshments table. She had a shawl streaming from her neck, skirt trailing on the floor. Her hair was matted and greasy, but she raised a hand as if to pat it into shape.

"Excuse me for a minute," Isaac said.

He made his way across the room, narrowing his eyes. Her hair was shorter than before, was thinning along the parting maybe, but it was definitely her. Older than in the photographs, less graceful than in his memories, but unmistakeably her.

"Mum?"

As he approached, she looked up and gave him a half-wave. Then she looked down at the table with the wine and juice on it.

"Alcohol is bottled compliance," she said to the server. "You know that, right?"

The server blinked at her. Then gave an uncertain smile.

"And the juice is, what? Orange?"

"Yes."

Isaac drew level with her, tugged on the sleeve of her blouse. "Mum?" he said.

"Isaac." She turned to him, giving him a flicker of a smile.

"I didn't know…"

Isaac shook his head. He had spent the past couple of hours waiting for his dad to arrive and here instead was his mum, who he hadn't seen for all these years. When was the last time he'd even heard from her? He'd had that postcard a fortnight after his birthday, but nothing since. And then she decided to breeze into his exhibition and act like they'd only parted ways at breakfast. Had it been that Facebook post? Was a scream into the void of social media all that had been needed all along?

"Where's Dad?" Isaac asked.

"How would I know, Isaac?"

She began lifting the glasses of orange juice and setting them further forward on the table, in front of the wine. The server stared, open-mouthed, but didn't intervene.

"So, do you want to come across and see it?" Isaac asked.

"See what?"

"My work for the exhibition."

"Yes, of course, in a moment."

Isaac nodded. He watched his mother. She set the last glass of orange juice down and tipped her head to the side, considering. There were bowls of green olives and crisps, along with the peanuts. She took one from each dish and licked them, one at a time, with the very tip of her tongue. Then she folded the single olive, crisp, and peanut into a napkin.

"Your father isn't here?" she asked, frowning.

"No, like I say…" Isaac sighed. "He went to do a story on some commune."

Her frown lifted. "Oh?"

"Some place in Ardrossan or—"

"Ardnamurchan?"

"That's the one."

"Is that where he is now?"

Isaac shrugged. "I haven't heard from him since Monday."

Any other mother, Isaac knew, might react to this news with concern. Was Isaac managing to look after himself? Getting enough to eat? Remembering to brush his teeth at night?

Liz began pulling the bowls of olives to the front of the trestle table, relegating the peanuts and crisps to the back. After a moment, she looked across at Isaac.

"Did you miss me, Isaac?" she asked, matter-of-factly.

How was he supposed to answer that? His first instinct was to laugh. He wanted to spit out some laughter, maybe hiss a swear-word at her. He found that he could only manage a strangled cough. He sniffed, nodded, and felt tears springing to his eyes. Where have you been? He wanted to ask. Are you coming home? Why now?

"Are you..." Isaac managed. "Are you back for long?"

"Passing through, passing through," she said. She looked at him and then away again. "You're a young adult now. Fully grown." She waved an arm at the concourse. "Exhibiting."

Again, Isaac had too many responses. He couldn't think how to select only one. It's been eight years, Mum, of course I've fucking grown. And, yes, I'm exhibiting at college, which just so happens to be the most important day in my young adult life, and yet you've chosen this moment to reappear. Not because you wanted to see the work and mark the achievement – oh no – but because you're passing through.

"Yes," Isaac said finally, lamely.

"I'm on my way north too, as it happens," his mum said. "To where your dad is. Quite the coincidence."

"*Fuck sake,*" Isaac breathed. He didn't know if she heard him. She showed no sign of it.

"Although what your dad is doing up there, I can't quite—"

"Are you back for me, Mum, or for the commune?" Isaac interrupted. It was best to be direct. Get your questions in quickly, because it might be another eight years before you get the chance to ask them again.

"It can be both, can't it?"

"It shouldn't be." Best to be direct with the answers too.

She nodded thoughtfully. "I'll visit with you, Isaac, and I'll have a quick visit to this project too, yes? It's not your father – the young girl there sounds like she has some fascinating interpretations of Ravi's teachings."

Isaac smiled tightly. It didn't surprise him that there was a grapevine for all the latest communes. The troubling thing, he supposed, was the idea that his dad might have had a sip of the Kool-Aid. He was usually clear-sighted about these things. Although, come to that, Isaac couldn't deny that Ravi's teachings had been useful for his exhibition pieces. He had no interest in shaving his head and screeching at the moon – or whatever they were doing up there – but it couldn't hurt to find out more about the ideas underneath it all.

Isaac considered. "I'm coming with you," he said.

"Pardon?"

"To the commune, I'm coming along."

His mother shook her head. She looked down at the napkin in her hand, as if noticing it for the first time, and handed it to the server.

"Isaac," she said, "you don't want to come all that way."

"They'll have food there, won't they?"

She frowned. "They should do, yes."

"Then I'm coming. I've not eaten properly all week."

"Come on, don't be dramatic."

Isaac took a breath, held himself back from reacting. He had his line in the sand and he was determined to hold it. He'd travel up with his mother and find his dad, then he'd find out a little more about Swami Ravi's teachings. For research, to give him material for his art. And, in the process, he'd make sure that one of his parents looked after him, that he was fed and given enough money to survive the summer.

"What about college?" his mum said. "What about this exhibition here?"

187

"This is the final thing on the course. After this, there's nothing."

"Still, you'll want to stay near your friends."

"I'm coming with you."

He took her firmly by the hand, intending to take her over to his exhibit. She tensed and Isaac thought she would snatch her hand away, but then she seemed to reconsider. Isaac led her out into the centre of the room. Shauna ran up to them.

"Isaac," she said, in a stage whisper, "you spoke to her, what was she like?"

"Who? My mum?"

Shauna shook her head, looked at Liz. Was it Isaac's imagination or was she careful to keep her expression neutral, careful not to widen her eyes or let her jaw drop. "Is this your mum? Nice to meet you, Mrs Grafton, I'm Shauna." She gave a tip of her bowler hat.

"Not Mrs Grafton, please." Isaac's mum grimaced. "Call me Liz. Call me Ms Whelan. Call me by my given name or my maiden name."

"Sorry —"

"And don't apologise."

This time Shauna did react. Her cheeks drained of colour, but there was a flush of red, in blotches, on her neck. She opened her mouth then closed it again. She looked, for all the world, like a toddler deciding exactly which form her tantrum should take.

"Who are you talking about then?" Isaac interrupted, hoping to distract her.

"What?"

"You asked who I was speaking to…"

"The examiner," Shauna hissed, "the one from the Art School. She's the lady with the purple flash in her hair — so cool — and she's been round all the exhibits, but you're the only one she spoke to, for some reason. And she's so *stern*, and did she mention my drawings…?"

"Ah," Isaac said. "No, we talked about pandas."

"Seriously?" Shauna rolled her eyes. "You're useless."

She span away, over towards the clutch of tutors at the far side by the fire escape. Isaac watched her go with only a sliver of regret. She was certainly pretty, but there was no doubt that she was self-centred. There had always been something pretentious about her – as if she was performing the role of artist – and then, as if to underline it, she'd turned up for her exhibition in a fucking bowler hat.

Isaac tried to pull his mum on, by the hand, over to his sculptures. She held his arm, though, and twisted him back towards her. Like a mangled dance step. Her eyes were wide and shone beneath the strip lighting.

"You see, Isaac," she said, "you need to stay here. With your work and your girlfriend."

"That's not my girlfriend, Mum. She's a friend. Barely even that."

Isaac tugged at his mum's arm again and, this time, she moved. They made it over to his exhibit: the clay head, with face grimacing and eyes popping, held by veined arms; the cardboard sofa, with its yellow lettering against purple fabric and its roped turnbuckles. They looked good, Isaac realised. There against the white wall, facing each other, with Wrestlemania playing silently behind, they looked professional. He turned and grinned up at his mum. She was looking the other way.

"Mum?"

"Yes, Isaac?"

"What do you think?"

She turned back, her eyes flicking over the pieces and then back to Isaac. She smiled, but it slid away seconds later.

"I think we'll need to get on the road soon," she said, "if we want to make it before dark."

"What about the exhibit, though?"

"Yes, where is that examiner the girl was talking about – can we ask her for your mark?"

"That's not how it works, Mum. They don't just tell you here and now."

"Well, why not?"

"There's a whole meeting, I think, and a discussion and–"

"Let's ask her. They'll make an exception."

It was Isaac's turn to hold her back. He gripped at her arm with both of his hands and held on. She absolutely could not go up to the examiner and demand a mark. Fucking embarrassing, the whole thing. If she made a scene and then Shauna, with a hand clutched to her chest, explained to everyone why they needed to take the circumstances into account, why they couldn't judge Liz Whelan without knowing the full story behind Swami Ravi and what he'd put her through...

Isaac's dad wouldn't have behaved like this. He'd have wandered around, like you were supposed to, grinning politely. And he'd have stood for a bit longer in front of Isaac's sculptures. Then, without being asked, he'd have reached forward to put a hand on Isaac's shoulder and say that he was proud and that Isaac should be too. Just that. Just the normal response to your kid's art show.

"Ok, we can leave, Mum," Isaac said, "but can we go get some food first, please?"

She sighed. "Fine. We'll get something on the road."

BOOK TWO

1

Grafton started out quietly, knuckles against wood and a soft call. But as he grew more frustrated, he began slapping at the door – until it rattled in the frame – and shouting out his son's name. He knew there was a slur to it, he could hear it, but Grafton could explain all that, if only he could get inside the flat. Isaac should be home from the exhibition by now, shouldn't he?

Grafton had finished the bottle on the train ride and he'd filled the receipt book with everything he could remember. And now he needed inside his flat, his own fucking flat, so that he could have a shower and a coffee, something to eat and a change of clothes. He could do with a bit of a freshening up, he knew that – the empty seats next to him on the train had told him – but after a wash and a shave he could get into the guts of this story.

Still no answer. Isaac should have been back a couple of hours ago. Was he huffing, maybe, or sleeping? Grafton heard an echo of Joan's voice – *napping through the day is the ultimate indulgence* – but he shook it out of his head and knocked again. Did Isaac know that his dad had taken a leap off the wagon and rolled around in the dirt? How could you tell that from a knock at the door? Besides, Isaac hadn't even been aware of the worst of his drinking in the old days; not really.

Grafton's mind drifted. There'd been that night, back when Isaac was a toddler, when he'd come back with a skin-full. And he tried his key in the lock, but couldn't get it in. He squinted, he stabbed, he pushed until the wood creaked. Then he realised – Liz must have changed the locks. Out he'd gone to have one or two to celebrate meeting his deadline and that bitch of a woman had switched the locks on him.

So, he'd gone back to the bar, first and foremost, and then on to a B&B. The money from the article was spent – even before the invoice had been paid – and the next morning he'd had to agree to Liz's latest jaunt before she would even open the front door –

"Is that you, Mr Grafton? You need your spare key?"

Grafton looked up. He realised his cheeks were wet with tears. It seemed like he'd summoned up the spectre of young Liz. In her nurse's uniform, coming out of the flat opposite. Except the uniform was a lighter blue than the one Liz used to wear. Her hair was the wrong colour and cut too. And Grafton snapped back to the present.

"Rachel," he said, "I'm a little – erm – I'm a little worse for wear, sorry."

She smiled tightly. "No need to apologise."

"Ach, it's mostly tiredness but –" He was definitely slurring his words. He stopped.

"You want your key then?"

He nodded. "I'm locked out."

"Aye. Hang on, then, and I'll get it."

"You're an angel, you are."

She disappeared for a minute or so. Pretty girl, Rachel was, although – here was a depressing thought – probably closer in age to Isaac than Grafton. She would be about the age Liz had been when they'd first met and in the same profession too. Hopefully she was better suited to nursing than Liz had been. Was that unkind? After all that Grafton had put her through, could he really blame Liz for the way her caring nature seemed to fray? For the unravelling of that sense of responsibility?

"Here you are." Rachel handed the key across. He respected her for that. Plenty of folk would have placed it on the concrete floor and slid it across with a toe or thrown it over to him like a coin flicked towards a rough sleeper.

"Lifesaver," Grafton said, his mouth dry and the words thick. "You're a lifesaver."

As her door clicked closed, Grafton pulled himself to his feet. He used more shoulder than he needed to, in opening the door, and entered the flat with his arms doing windmills.

Grafton made his way through to the bedroom, peeling off his ill-fitting clothes. He took a shower, but was too impatient to stand beneath the stream of it for more than a few seconds. Towelling himself dry, he sprayed a cloud of deodorant over himself and took a gulp of mouthwash. It barely took the first layer of fuzz from his teeth. He pulled out a fresh t-shirt and a pair of shorts.

Through to the living room. Isaac's things were across the table. Grafton cleared them to the side with a straightened forearm. Then he got the laptop out. He opened a blank document and watched the cursor blinking. And – what?

There were several ways to start the story. Write it through, using the notes from the train, as a first-hand account from his arrival through to his banishment. Or he could begin by outlining the structure of the commune itself: Joan as the figurehead, with Eddie beneath that and then an inner circle of acolytes who spent the evenings with her as she aimed for her eleven-night target. Maybe that was the way into the article: the promised next step and the unknown contents of the stacked wooden pallets at the side of the office; the Sleepless counting down to the twelfth day like Mayans predicting the end of the world.

Grafton passed a hand over his chin. His stubble was softening into a beard. It might serve him better to shave first, or to set out to make sure Isaac wasn't in a gutter somewhere. He looked out of the window at the darkening streets of Glasgow, the streetlights flickering on and the rain turning from grey to silver. Isaac would be out at a bar somewhere – you don't miss your dad for long when you're seventeen.

Coffee. That's what he needed. A cup of coffee would be rocket-fuel after a week without caffeine. No amount of callisthenics or spiced tea could make up for it. His mind made up, Grafton strode through to the kitchen and flicked the kettle on. There was only a dusting of coffee in the jar, though. Grafton felt the irritation of that like a spasm, through his chest and down his arms. And suddenly his thirst wasn't for caffeine, his urgency wasn't to get back to his laptop – he was tearing through the cupboards looking for some wee nip or dram that he'd overlooked from years before or that Isaac had snuck in without him noticing. A slosh of brandy left to garnish a Christmas pudding, a beer hidden away behind the expired mustard and gravy granules, some cooking sherry that he could grimace down. It didn't take him long to come up empty-handed.

Over to the fridge. Isaac had left it empty too. Or close enough. Only a jar of mayonnaise on the middle shelf, scraped nearly clean. Something beneath that too. An edge of lined paper. Grafton lifted the jar and slid out the note. Torn from a jotter, it looked like, with the writing across and outside the lines. In capital letters: GONE TO COMMUNE WITH MUM.

Grafton blinked at it for a moment. Then, with a deep-throated yell, he hurled the mayonnaise jar down against the tiles of the kitchen floor.

2

For the past seven or eight months, Isaac had been learning to drive on the residential streets of Glasgow, but he quickly found that navigating the single-track roads of the peninsula was a different proposition. It was getting dark as well and, in the absence of learner plates, Liz had improvised a biro-scrawled capital L on a burger wrapper and stuck it to the inside of the windscreen with ketchup.

It wasn't the twists and turns of the road that were the problem, or the occasional sheer drop to the side, so much as the impending dread, at every hairpin bend and blind summit, that he'd meet something coming the other way. Then he'd have to emergency brake and do a reversing manoeuvre trickier than anything in the driving test itself.

There was also the constant distraction of his mother. Because he was concentrating on driving, he kept forgetting her presence – for a split-second – and then remembering and stealing a sideways glance at her. There she was in the flesh, after all these years, smelling as ripe as a compost bin and with every second breath formed as a sigh. What was he meant to say to her? He had questions, of course he did, but each and every one of them seemed too much – too abrupt, too confrontational, too emotional – to break the silence with.

Liz had driven up until the loop around Fort William but then she'd protested a migraine brought on by the veggie burger they'd bought at the services. Isaac had taken over. Her car was an old estate, with a foreign number-plate. It was easier on the clutch control than his dad's wee hatchback, but difficult to fling around the tight corners as they got closer to the coast.

In the end, it was Liz who spoke. Her head was tipped back and the shawl, which had been around her neck, was now folded over her eyes.

"Quite the hypocrite," she breathed, "to take off like that."

Isaac didn't need to ask who she was talking about. "He did tell me he was going," he said, aware that his teeth were set tight together.

"To a follower of Ravi, no less."

"He left me some money for food too."

Only twenty quid. Still, it was true that he had left something and Isaac was damned if he was going to let his mum claim some sort of equivalence or – god forbid – moral high-ground over the fact that his dad had abandoned him for a week.

"It's true," Liz was saying, "that the thing we fixate on, obsess over and criticise others for is actually the flaw that's most prevalent, most present, in ourselves."

Isaac was silent. If she asked, he'd say he was concentrating on the road.

"He was always searching for something, your father. Some form of validation. The journalism was never about the stories for him – never – it was always about people acknowledging his genius, his unique perspective and insight on the world. That's what he wanted from it."

"He's not been a journalist for years. Not really."

She reached up and resettled the shawl. "There's always been that sense of him working the angle. Everything he does, he looks for a way to claim credit or martyrdom. He's always weighing it up and seeing what the upside is for—"

"Jesus!"

A motorbike zipped past, coming the other way, close enough that the leather-clad man clipped the wing mirror. Isaac braked and swerved, a moment too late, and the engine stalled and conked out. He watched in the rearview mirror as the motorbike slowed and rebalanced. The man on it didn't look back, but instead revved and carried on. In seconds, he was out of sight.

The shawl came off his mum's eyes. "Is it too difficult?" she asked.

Isaac drew in a breath, then another. "All of this is pot and kettle. You've got to be able to see that, no? You're analysing the man who's brought me up for the past eight years – because you fucked off, I might add – and accusing him of being selfish."

"I don't dispute any of that, Isaac..."

"And where have you been anyway? One postcard a year is keeping in touch, is it?"

She reached out to place her hand on his shoulder. "Anger can be a useful emotion. But hostility will only close you off from accessing your true feelings."

"But...Jesus..." He shook her off. "I was worried about you too. I read about that man and what he'd done, about all the women who came forward. I was looking for your name on some list, Mum. A list of victims – women he'd mistreated, women he'd killed and left boarded up behind a wall..."

"You've read those lies then." She nodded, withdrew her hand. "He's not a monster, Isaac. He was weak at times, but I could handle that. And his teachings – his words – persist and continue to instruct, even if they have caged him."

"And...?"

She pointed to the steering wheel. "And you want me to drive again?"

He sagged his head into a nod.

They switched places: she circled the front of the car, he went around the back. In the passenger seat, Isaac turned to the window and watched the passing countryside. His mum crunched up through the gears and took the corners at a speed that would have killed the motorcyclist.

Isaac thought back to his childhood. He didn't remember his parents arguing. Not really. Instead, all his memories of childhood were tied to one or the other: ice skating with his mum, Stirling Castle with his dad, art classes with Mum, watching late night wrestling with Dad. He struggled to think of anything they'd done as a family.

"Your dad's always told you that I left for India, yes?" Liz said, eventually. She looked across at him, even as the road turned and dipped sharply to the right.

Isaac nodded. "For a collective in India."

"And that's the truth." Her hands, on the wheel, lifted and flexed. "But it's also true that India wasn't my first trip. It wasn't a flitting from the nest so much as a confirmation that I could fly or...well...I left for India, but only once I was certain that you would be cared for."

"I don't want some tangled explanation."

"You won't get it. No, no. Just some context."

Isaac shifted his shoulders back against the seat, turning away from the window. The ice in the bottom of his takeaway coke had melted. He sucked the water up through the straw until it made that grating noise. He watched his mum's face for irritation.

"I suppose you remember those trips," she said. "I suppose you were old enough to remember them. You were never too happy when I left, that's for certain. Never exactly delighted when I came back either—"

"Can you fucking blame me?" The words snapped out.

"You're an adult now. Can we discuss this as adults...?"

She didn't look across at him. Her tone hadn't been scolding, the words were flat and emotionless. Isaac listened to his own breathing for a few seconds – the heave and hiss of it – and then bowed his head into a nod.

"So," Liz said, "you'll remember most of those spells away, but you won't remember the first of them. The very first. It was when you were eighteen months old. I'd booked this single room for a long weekend up at Crieff Hydro. And the plan was to send your father off and give him this ultimatum – stay dry for the whole weekend or stay away permanently. I guess it was meant to be some cross between an intervention and rehab, although I didn't have those words for it…"

Her hands had settled. Both of them were now gripping the wheel. And she was staring straight ahead out of the windscreen, although Isaac wasn't a hundred percent sure she was focused on the road.

"…and it got closer to the time when he was due to go up there and I still hadn't mentioned it to him. Then I got to thinking: why should he get to have the spell away? And how many bars are there at a spa hotel anyway? Probably a good half-dozen. You can have a champagne breakfast, if you choose, or a cocktail by the pool. Besides, the only time the bastard was sober was when he was looking after you, right, so why was I packaging him off into a situation where he was at a loose end all day and had none of the responsibility of fatherhood?"

Isaac was watching her properly now. She was calm and still.

"So, I reversed the ultimatum. I was going to leave for the weekend and he could look after you and dry himself out. If he failed then he'd have to ship out, yes, and if all went well then we'd have some kind of functioning parental unit for you."

"I was a guinea pig, then?" Isaac muttered.

"He wouldn't have harmed a hair on your head, Isaac. And, even if he drank, what harm could he do? He was never violent with it, just blundering and blustering and…well…you slept a lot as a child…"

Isaac shook his head. He'd never heard this part of the story before, but he didn't feel like it changed anything – his mother had still left her son, regardless. In fact, at the time, she'd left a toddler with a drunk. He was wary of the tale being spun any other way.

"Anyway," she said, "I came back from that weekend and the two of you were as happy as clams. You'd been down to the Kelvingrove in your pram and you'd smeared takeaway food all over your highchair. And your dad, Isaac. Your dad was so proud. You could see it. He was stopping old grannies in the street and telling them he was solo parenting. And they'd tut their tongues and he'd give them the suffering smile of the put-upon husband. He was loving it."

Isaac cleared his throat. "Aye, you saw all of that from up in Crieff did you?"

She smiled, looked sideways at him. "You're right. I filled in the gaps."

Isaac bit back his reply. It was going to be bitter and sarcastic. He was going to point out that one happy weekend with his dad didn't mean that he had no more use for a mother, that seeing them enjoying their time together should have made her want to join in, not run away.

"Fuck sake, Mum," he said, instead.

"What?"

"There's a difference, isn't there, between a long weekend and a month? Then between a month and eight years away? Full calendar years without seeing you."

She nodded. "I know. But it was the solution that saved all three of us – from drinking, from insanity, from insecurity. You know?"

"You think it saved me, do you?"

"No, you were the superhero doing the saving."

"I was *nine*."

"Every kid has those powers." She smiled, but it quickly faded when she saw his face. "We joke, but it's looking after you that's given your dad a sense of purpose these last years, isn't it, and a sense that folk are admiring the sacrifice he's made."

"You're a shit psychoanalyst. Shit."

She ignored him. "And now, when he's about to be faced with an empty nest, he's fallen back on old habits."

Was there something in that, Isaac wondered? He had been curious about why his dad chose to pursue the story. Was it the material, the commune, or was there something deeper there?

Over the years, he'd occasionally tinker with some ideas over the course of an evening or email off a pitch over a weekend. Once or twice, Isaac had found him leafing through a scrapbook of his cuttings. But this was the first article he'd properly committed to, the first he'd taken time off work to pursue.

"And you?" Isaac asked, cutting off that train of thought.

"Pardon?"

"What is it that you're hoping to find out here at this commune? What does this one offer that the years with Ravi didn't?"

Liz brought a hand up to her head and smoothed her hair back behind her ear. She smiled, with the edges of her mouth, and then her lips twisted into a frown.

"They're not entirely wrong about Ravi," she said.

"What d'you mean?"

"He's a genius, but he's also impulsive and impatient. In spite of everything he knows, his years of teaching, he hasn't found someone to successfully take that next step. He could never find a disciple dedicated enough. And now he's been forced to pause his search…"

Isaac looked across at his mum. Her eyes were firmly fixed on the road. The headlights were at full-beam on the road in front. Out to either side was a blackness that wasn't interrupted by even the reflection of a distant light.

"So," she said, "you could say that I'm here as a talent-scout."

3

Liz squinted into the torchlight. The beam swung across to Isaac, standing on the steps beside her, who held out a hand to shield his eyes.

"We aren't accepting new members."

The lad who stood barring their way was only in his twenties. He had a rash of scarred-over spots across his neck. As he spoke, he smoothed a hand over the redness of it. Liz could see immediately that the wee runt didn't have what it took. He wouldn't have been allowed within ten feet of Swami Ravi.

"We've driven a long way," Liz said. "Let us talk to whoever's in charge."

"What makes you think I'm not in charge?"

"Because it's not a fucking tuck shop."

Redneck sneered, but Liz could see that she'd wounded him. He blinked and let the torchlight fall to their shoes. He had bare feet, against the concrete of the steps up to the office, and the beam lingered for a few seconds on Isaac's trainers.

Liz tried to hold the irritation down. If this had been Jaipur, or the abandoned industrial lot in Malta, then she'd have been the one doing the greeting. She'd often welcomed hopefuls at the threshold. She would reach out and clutch them by the chin, squeezing her fingers and looking into their eyes. To see how they reacted. To see if their eyes watered or they flinched away.

She looked back down the road. There was a deep quiet – no distant animals or engines, shouts or sirens. The moon shimmered off the sea and the reflection of it gave shape to the hills enclosing the bay and drew the line of the horizon between the star-flecked sky and the black-grey of the water.

"We know some people in the commune," Liz said, "we've not just come off the street."

Redneck swung the torch back up to her face. "Who d'you know then?"

"My dad," Isaac said. "Tom Grafton."

Liz shot him a disapproving look. She had been going to mention Debbie's name. All the same, it was interesting to note Redneck's reaction. He pursed his lips and a faint whistle sounded as he exhaled. The torchlight moved across to Isaac.

"Eddie will want to hear about this," Redneck said. "He's on his way up and, mark my words, he'll want to hear about this. *Tom* Grafton, you said—"

He was interrupted by the sound of footsteps on the gravel behind them. Redneck immediately straightened. He lifted the torch to shine out towards the footsteps. Liz turned to watch as another man in a white robe strode up towards the office.

This was Eddie then. Liz assessed him through narrowed eyes. He was small and ratty, shaven-headed and in need of a dentist. He walked straight up to Redneck, without a glance at Liz and Isaac, and lifted a finger to hover in at the scarred-over throat. It was as if he'd raised a machete. Redneck squinted down at the finger and tried to inch himself away from it.

"Did you not tell them?" Eddie said. "Did you not tell them, Ally?"

"I did, boss. They know someone, though. You'll want to hear about it…"

"They're persistent fuckers, eh?"

Eddie turned away from Redneck and lowered the finger. Liz watched Redneck gulping in air. She knew, then, that her first impression of him had been spot-on. But what about Eddie? The fear he inspired could be a useful tool, if cultivated in the right way. He was the kind of disciple Ravi would show an interest in, she was sure, as long as the leash was kept short.

"Go on, then," Eddie said. "Who do you know?"

"We're looking for my dad." Isaac hesitated. "Grafton."

"Ha." A short, mirthless laugh from Eddie. "You've some fucking cheek. Did he send you?"

"Is he here?"

"He's not welcome here."

Liz noted the way Eddie eyeballed Isaac, the way he seemed to sway, ever so slightly, as if considering launching himself into attack. Ravi always said that the most useful recruits were feral animals, that they could be tamed and made loyal.

"It's not him we're here for," Liz called out, "I've no interest in him."

"Oh yeah?" Eddie circled round to her, his mouth cracking open into a grin. "And what's your interest then?"

"I'm here to offer my experience," she said, "and maybe to learn too. Who knows."

"Your experience? What the fuck does that mean?"

Liz held his gaze for a moment. Then she reached down into the pocket of her skirt. She saw Eddie's eyebrows furrow, but he didn't spring forward or make any attempt to stop her as she pulled out the folded square of paper. It was the letter from Swami Ravi; the key to unlock doors.

She passed it across to Eddie and he gestured impatiently for Redneck – for Ally – to bring the torchlight closer. As they read, Liz glanced across at Isaac. He was looking at her with widened eyes.

"I'll show it to Joan," Eddie said, folding the letter, "but we've had to grow cautious this past while. We've had to put our barriers up – even to friends – because of this one's dad."

"Is he ok?" Isaac asked. "Did you hurt him?"

"He hurt us," Eddie said, his lip curling, "but we did fuck all to him."

"He's not still here then?"

Eddie ignored the question. He leant closer to Liz. "What's Grafton to you, then?"

"My ex-husband. Estranged."

"Big word."

"It means—"

"I know what it fucking means," Eddie said, sharply.

Liz wasn't used to being spoken to like this. Ordinarily she wouldn't have allowed it. But — for the time being — she decided to let it go. She wanted to see inside the commune. She needed to meet Joan, most importantly, so that she could report back to Ravi.

"You can ask Debbie McVeigh about me as well," Liz said, looking Eddie in the eye.

Eddie nodded. "Ally, go and fetch Joan. Then go and find me Debbie and someone from the children's cabin."

Ally darted past them down the steps. As his torchlight moved off up the path, Eddie pushed at the door to the office. He beckoned them on. Liz stepped forwards but paused when she saw that Isaac was uncertain. He stood there, on the top step, shifting from one foot to the other.

Liz looked out to the sea again. Was that the sweeping beam of a lighthouse? There would be islands out there, no doubt, but they were distant. This was a remote spot, with tens of miles to the nearest large town and perhaps only a couple of local bobbies on the beat. It was the kind of situation which had always suited Ravi perfectly — where temptations were few and far between or, at least, containable and easy to keep quiet.

"I don't want to go inside, Mum," Isaac said, quietly.

"We can't drive back tonight," she said. "Not in the dark."

"I don't think Dad's even here, though."

"In the morning, Isaac, you can take my car and drive back."

"I only have a provisional licence, though, I need someone else in the car, I need—"

"Well, stay then."

Bloody hell, he was a whiny wee thing. She didn't remember him being like that, even when he was in nappies. Years with his dad had obviously melted away his backbone. She threw him a shrug and turned to walk into the office. As the door swung shut behind her, it was caught by his outstretched hand.

"Good boy," she said, over her shoulder.

Eddie ushered them through. "You can register and come to gatherings and meals," he said, "but you'll have a minder. For a spell, at least. At the end of that – if all has gone well – there'll be an initiation to prove you're serious."

So maybe arrivals and departures weren't Joan's decision after all. Liz looked again at Eddie, sitting now behind a desk in the corner. She knew well that the smooth running of a commune often fell to those who preferred to operate in the background.

"What kind of initiation?" Isaac asked, over the top of her thoughts.

"A small thing," Eddie said, "like a tattoo."

"What does like a tattoo mean?" Isaac asked.

"Quiet," Liz hissed across at him. She should never have agreed to bring him.

"Right, phones and wallets," Eddie said. "Or phones and purses, whatever."

"What?" Isaac said.

Liz sighed. His silence hadn't lasted long. "To immerse yourself," she said, "you need to let go of your anchors."

"Aye," Eddie said, looking from one to the other. "If you're staying, then no phones allowed."

Isaac had taken his phone out of his pocket, but he showed no sign of handing it over. Liz strode across and snatched it from him. He held on for a moment, but she was stronger than he was. Or more determined. She passed the phone to Eddie and then reached into her skirt pocket for a fold of Euro notes. There was a thicker wad stitched into the waistband, but she decided to keep that to herself for now.

Eddie also took her car keys. He reached up to a small key on a chain, hanging from his neck, and unlocked a drawer in the desk. Everything went inside. Liz took the opportunity to look around the room: the desk was piled high with a chaotic landslide of papers, with another unsteady stack on the metal filing cabinet behind; the blind at the window was open, but the gathered slats hung at a crooked angle.

There was a knock at the outside door and it creaked open. Ally put his head in. "Joan's on her way," he said, "and I've got Debbie and young Zack here."

"Zack?" Eddie frowned. "Why did you bring him?"

"You said to fetch someone from the children's cabin."

Eddie lifted a hand to his head. "I meant one of the minders…"

"Ah, fuck. You want me to go back?"

"No, just wait a minute."

"Outside? It's started raining."

"Get wet then."

Ally ducked back out. Eddie looked down at the clutter on the desk in front of him and lifted a stubby pencil and a sheet of paper. He started to write, with his tongue jutting out between his teeth.

"Tell me," Liz said. "Why are you here, Eddie?"

He sniffed, in that deep way that draws all the phlegm from your throat. He didn't look up, but gave a tight shake of his head.

"Please, so I can tell Swami Ravi about you."

Eddie stopped writing. He frowned down at the sheet of paper.

"You want to know what the commune has given me?" he said. "What Joan has given me?"

"Yes."

"I'm ex-army. And that has its issues." Eddie paused. "There have been spells when I've slept rough. I'd pace through the streets and shiver myself to sleep in some doorway. Everything was focused on finding that one place to rest. Then, during the pandemic, I was caged in a grim council flat scrabbling to find something – anything – to bring each day to an end. And that

207

was all a waste of energy, that was all a misuse of my potential. Joan's shown me that."

"Joan's shown you that?" Liz repeated carefully. There had been no mention of Ravi in what he'd said, no mention of the root that gathers water to keep the stem strong and the flowers fresh.

He nodded slowly.

"She sounds remarkable," Liz said, trying to keep her voice neutral. "Joan does."

"I'd die for her."

Liz was careful not to react to that either. She knew plenty of disciples who said they'd die for Ravi, but relatively few who said it with the same conviction as Eddie just had.

This time Ally didn't knock. He swung the door open and held it. His head was bowed, his chin tucked in over that red neck. There was a moment's pause and then a young woman appeared in the doorway. She wore a white dress with red polka-dots across it. The fabric was slick, at the shoulders, with rainwater and she had strands of grass across her bare feet. She looked up. Her face was drawn and haggard, with skin peeling from the ridges of her cheekbones and clusters of acne across her chin. Her hair seemed thinner on the left side than the right, as wispy and liable to drift away as sheep's wool caught on a fence.

"You're very welcome," she said, in a voice barely above a whisper.

"Thank you," Liz said. "I'm intrigued to meet you."

"You've been with Swami Ravi, is that right?" Joan's gaze was steady.

"For many years, yes."

Joan reached out a hand. The fingers were long and graceful, purple veins showed under the skin. She placed the hand on Liz's shoulder. Closing her eyes, Liz drew in a breath. She wanted to feel what she did when Ravi laid hands on her — that tingle at the point of contact, that spreading sense of warmth and calm, that sense that she was being connected to the very earth.

"I owe Swami Ravi everything," Joan said, softly.

Liz opened her eyes. Joan was smiling at her and leaning forward.

"I want you to know that," Joan continued. "But you must also understand that this isn't his. What is around you here isn't his. It's ours. Much of it is formed on the bedrock that he gave us, but we have built the structures and we have decorated them to suit ourselves and our tastes, yes?"

Joan was peering at her with widened eyes. Eyes with a light grey iris that also held a hint of blue. And, in that moment, Liz felt it: like the lightest touch travelling up the length of her spine and coming to a rest beneath the hand on her shoulder.

"I understand," she breathed.

Joan held her gaze for another moment and then her eyes moved across to Isaac.

"And you," Joan said, releasing her grip on Liz's shoulder. "Your father told me about you."

Isaac blinked. "He did?"

Eddie rose from his seat, then, and leaned forward across the desk. He was obviously trying to catch Joan's attention, but her stare never wavered from Isaac. She stepped towards him and lifted a hand. It didn't fall on his shoulder, but instead cupped his cheek.

"Joan," Eddie called, "can we risk having him here? He's his son."

Joan didn't turn. "All the more reason, Eddie, all the more reason."

"He'll need to go in with the children then, yes?"

Joan's hand moved slowly across Isaac's cheek. "We can't be judged by the actions of our fathers, can we? Everyone who arrives must be given the opportunity to prove themselves."

Liz turned to look out of the window again. She didn't focus on the moon or the stars flickering in the sky, the lights in the houses along the shore or the sweeping light out in the bay. Instead, she found an angle where all she could see was black. Here, at this commune, it was possible to find the absence of noise and the absence of light. And, within that, it was possible to push the limits of Ravi's teaching. There was great potential to that. But Joan was too soft-hearted. That much was apparent even from the first meeting. She was too trusting and too open and too ready to look for the good in others. Too naïve. She needed help if she was going to continue down this path. Eddie was already providing some of that, no doubt, but Liz saw how she herself could be useful. Debbie was right to suggest that she came.

4

"Any buses for Ardnamurchan tonight?" Grafton's words came out as gasps. On the other side of the ticket window, the seller screwed up his face. "Ard-na-mur-chan," Grafton repeated — slower and louder, like a Brit abroad.

"Never heard of it, pal."

"West of Fort William."

"You'll not get that far north tonight."

"Where's the furthest I could go?"

"Perth, maybe."

Grafton let out a bark. That was the word for it — neither a shout or a laugh, but some combination of the two. Perth was barely an hour away, in the wrong direction. But he couldn't be surprised that there were no buses to the arse-end-of-nowhere on a Friday night.

"Are you wanting the ticket then, pal?" the seller asked.

"No, not to Perth." Grafton turned away from the counter, but then turned back. "One more question...?"

"Aye?"

"Do you take cheques?"

"For payment, you mean? No."

"Why not?"

"Cause it's not the nineteen-eighties."

Grafton put his head in his hands, scratching at the hair above his ears. Scratching at the beginnings of a headache. He needed to think. The chequebook was all he'd been able to find, on his quick tear through the flat looking for cash. He hadn't held out much hope for it being accepted on the buses, but he couldn't think how else to get himself back to Seattle.

Isaac was a smart lad. He'd see that they were all nutters, he'd twig that his mum wasn't to be relied on. As he always had done, he would look out for himself and either get himself out of there or wait for his dad to collect him.

All the same, Grafton couldn't keep from thinking about those wooden crates. The ten pallets and the twelfth day. If there were guns in those boxes then maybe they'd be unpacked early so that the disciples could be trained. Or if the crates were full of acid – the wound on his arm twanged with pain – and they worked out that Isaac was related to Grafton and decided that...

"Arghhh..." Grafton cried out.

Buchanan Street Station was clustered with groups of teenagers waiting for buses back to the suburbs. None of them looked over at Grafton. They were all swigging and screeching, chasing each other between the metal benches. He'd kill for a gulp from their bottles of cheap cider. It might sort the pain at his temple, the haziness at the edge of his vision.

He sat and tipped to the side, lying across a few benches, bringing his feet up underneath him. If he could have a rest here – let the hangover loosen – then he could think again in the morning. Maybe there'd be a shop willing to cash a cheque. Back in the day, he'd known any amount of slightly shifty bar owners who'd take as little as an IOU on a bar mat, but those days were gone.

"You can't stop here, mate."

Grafton looked up. The voice belonged to a young security guard, with neatly braided plaits pinned to her head and a yellow reflective armband across the sleeve of her jacket. She was chewing gum and carefully staring at the space an inch or so above Grafton's head.

"I'm not homeless," Grafton said. "I'm waiting for a bus."

"Aye. Where to?"

"Well...Oban, maybe."

The guard shook her head. "Nothing until the morning."

"I was thinking I could wait here, though."

"Think again, buddy, think again."

The guard waited while Grafton dragged himself to his feet. Then she followed a step or two behind until she'd seen him off the premises. Grafton stood outside the bus station, looking across to the gigantic multi-storey cinema on the opposite corner – the lights blurring – and listening to the shrieks and laughter of the nightlife further into town.

There was nothing for it, he'd have to go home and regroup. Liz would look after Isaac in the meantime, surely. Or Isaac would look after himself. There were still four nights until the twelfth day. If Grafton waited – even just overnight – then it would give him an opportunity to get properly prepared, to work out a way to get his son out of there and to make sure that no one else was harmed.

What he needed was evidence, something concrete. Not only for his story, but also so that the police could shut Seattle down for good. And he wouldn't get that by charging back in there screaming and shouting. He needed to plan, to think of a way of exposing the reality of the commune to the world.

To do that, he had to rest and think it all through. He had to take his time. It was possible that he'd only have one chance to free Isaac from their clutches. Pausing and taking stock was vital. Christ knows, it would also give him a chance to catch up on sleep.

5

Joan led Isaac to a log cabin further up the hill. As she eased the door open, she turned and raised a finger to her lips. She let out a giggle, like they were kids sneaking downstairs at nighttime to pinch the last slice of chocolate cake. Or into a neighbours' flat to steal bread and raisins.

They tip-toed through to the darkness of the kitchen and Joan pulled the door closed behind them. She turned on the light, but it took a moment for the strip-bulb to flicker into life. It revealed Joan staring intently at him with the trace of a smile. She had a cold sore on her top lip. She raised a hand and cupped his cheek again. Her fingers were dry and soft.

"Don't worry," she whispered. "Debbie will look after your mum. We can have this time alone."

Isaac nodded gently, not wanting to dislodge the hand on his cheek. "Ok."

"We should be quiet, though, there are people asleep in the bedrooms."

"What are we going to do?"

Her smile deepened. And there was a flood of possibilities, in that moment.

"You look hungry," she said. "We're going to make sure you're fed."

Even that could be taken as a nudge-nudge for something else. No one ever quite said what they were thinking when it came to these things, there was a kind of code to it. And maybe Isaac was finally going to be let in on the secret. He dared to hope so, at least. Until he saw Joan reaching up for a saucepan, going to the fridge and lifting out margarine and milk.

"You do the cooking," Joan said. "I need to conserve my energy."

"Ok."

"I'll tell you what to do, if you're not certain. I'll be your cookbook."

She held out the saucepan and Isaac took it from her. He walked over to the hob and put it on one of the rings, but he was scuppered beyond that. He looked around at Joan. She was watching him. Her jaw was set now and there was a faint sound, like tyres against gravel. It took Isaac a moment to realise it was her teeth grinding together.

"You need water in that pan," she said, "and then another pan to make the sauce."

"What are we making?"

"A quick version of veggie curry."

Isaac ran the tap and filled the saucepan. He placed a second saucepan on the hob too and then looked over to Joan. She was nodding and trailing her hand through her hair. He noticed that several strands had come loose, that they were floating down to the floor.

"Now," she said, "the idea is to make a béchamel and then add curry powder. So, do you know how to make a roux?"

Isaac considered. "I understood about half of those words," he said.

Joan grinned. It transformed her. The shadows beneath her eyes were lost in laughter lines, the peeling skin disappeared into dimples. Her whole face was animated. Then, the next second, the grin faded. Isaac felt the loss of it as an ache through the centre of his body.

"You melt butter and add flour and then milk," she said.

Isaac lifted the margarine. "Why didn't you say so, then? You have your own language here, is that it?"

"It's basic French cuisine."

"I thought we were making a curry?"

He was trying to get her to grin again, but he only got the smaller, softer smile. It was enough to sharpen the ache, to give his need a keener edge.

"Zou make ze rooks." He waved a wooden spoon in the air. "And then zee bee-she-male."

Joan laughed. And, suddenly, the journey was worth it. The week of hunger. If a sheet of paper was set in front of him, in that instant, he'd sign up for any length of time, for unlimited liability. He'd let them keep the keys to his mum's car and he'd tear up his offer letter from the Art School.

"Your water's boiling," Joan said, "so here's some rice. And put your butter in the other pan."

Isaac poured in the rice and turned on the heat under the pan with the margarine. Then, under Joan's instruction, he added flour and stirred. Then milk. From the freezer box above the fridge, Joan passed him some frozen peas and sweetcorn. He added them to the boiling water. The sauce thickened. She handed him curry powder and he tipped some into the sauce.

"You're not convinced," Joan said, as he drained the rice and vegetables. "Are you?"

"About the curry?"

"About the project."

Isaac waited for the steam to dissipate. Joan handed him two bowls and he divided the rice and vegetables between them. Then poured over the sauce.

"Why do you think that?" he said, slowly.

"I can see it. Your dad was the same."

"Yeah?"

She nodded and handed him a fork. "Go sit down. It needs seasoning."

There was a small bench in the corner of the room. Isaac walked over and sat down. Joan busied herself sprinkling some salt and pepper over the two bowls. Then she came across and sat opposite him.

"There's a difference," she said, blowing on a forkful, "between you and your dad."

"What's that?"

"Your dad was cynical. At the moment, you're just sceptical. If you tip over into cynicism then you're lost to me. You know what I mean?"

Isaac dug his fork in. "You're speaking a different language again."

She grinned. "I'm not. You understand, I know you do."

The curry was good. There was no depth of flavour to it and not much by way of texture, but it was warming and there was a lot of it. If Isaac ever went through a week of hunger again, he knew he'd be fantasising about this curry, this moment.

"This is my calling," Joan said, chewing slowly. "People think of sleepwalking as this thing small children sometimes do where they wander through the house and have a tumble down the stairs or a pee in the fireplace, but if you look around on a commute through town or an evening out, how many folk are actually just sleepwalking? We're slaves to sleep. All of us. And no one thinks to wake us up."

"Except you?"

She lifted a forkful to her mouth and nodded. "But it was never meant to be about me. That's evolved because people need a figurehead, need to be shown the way, yes?

"This is my eighth night of wakefulness. But the point is to do more than demonstrate the principle, you know? It's to take the next step into the life of the truly wakeful. We have too much to learn, too much to do: the world is dying and we're asleep, there isn't enough food and we're asleep, our families are fracturing and we're asleep, our governments are embezzling and we're asleep."

Isaac realised that he was holding his fork in the mid-air between the bowl and his mouth. He set it down. Joan was leaning across the bench towards him. Her hands were out, as if to grasp at his shoulders. Her polka-dot dress hung open, ever so slightly, at the chest. Enough to give a shadow, but nothing more.

"You've heard of Randy Gardner?" she asked.

Isaac shook his head.

"He stayed awake for eleven days back in the Sixties. So we know the limits of what is possible – we can perhaps even inch beyond those limits with our methods – but Swami Ravi has long hypothesised that to go further still will require a leap of faith, a next step…"

Joan sat back. The fabric of the dress settled against her skin. There was still dampness at her shoulders, Isaac noticed. A small shiver ran through her. Isaac looked around for something to offer her – a blanket, a cardigan. He was still wearing his blue pinstripe shirt from the exhibition, but he'd left his jacket in the car.

"I tell you all this upfront," Joan said, "because your scepticism can't linger long. If you want to stay then you need to believe – or be open to believing – that what you see next Tuesday will shift the world on its axis."

She stood, then, and took the two bowls over to the sink. She ran the water to soak them, but left them there.

"And where is my dad now?" Isaac asked, staring at her back. Was there a tremble to her shoulders before she turned?

"We sent him away," Joan said. "When we found out what he was doing, we asked him to leave."

"And what was he doing?"

"He was trying to reduce this movement – this social awakening – to a headline."

"He's not hurt, though, is he?" Isaac asked.

Joan shook her head. "He's fine," she said.

"So, is he back in Glasgow or – ?"

"Zack will show you to your cabin," she said, softly, "and we can speak again tomorrow, yes? I can see you're tired, so we won't ask you to limit your sleep on this first night."

From the doorway, behind Isaac, came the sound of a throat being cleared. Isaac swivelled and saw a young boy. He grinned at Isaac through his fringe. His brown hair hung lank over the collar of his robe, you could see where the fabric was beginning to stain yellow with the grease of it.

"Come on," he said, "the others are playing torch-tag outside…"

6

Debbie was a second shadow. Ever since she'd been entrusted with the task of chaperoning Liz, she followed a half-pace behind with a simpering smile. If Liz turned, she would shrink back but then, next moment, she would be close enough to trip at Liz's heels.

In the night, she slept on the bunk below. They had been allotted two hours, but Liz knew she could do without. After ten minutes, Debbie started snoring softly, so Liz swung her feet clear of the mattress and jumped down to the floor. She padded towards the door. She wanted to have a look around, that was all, but when she looked back at the bottom bunk there was a pair of eyes shining in the dimness of the room.

"Where you going?" Debbie hissed.

"Bathroom," Liz hissed back. "You want to hold the toilet roll?"

It was an outrage, really. Debbie had always been fidgety and over-chatty, but that was easily dealt with when they were in India; Liz would foist her off on one of the other women or send her on an errand to a different part of the city. Here, her fussiness and friendliness had been given a formal sanction from Eddie and you could tell that Debbie relished it.

Liz was expecting an invitation to come to see Joan after breakfast on the Saturday morning, but there was no word. Still, Liz was never one to stand idly by. She could see that there were things to fix at Seattle – even if the rest of them couldn't – and she wasn't going to waste time. And if she was to be lumbered with Debbie, she might as well make use of her.

They stopped off at the office to collect a clipboard, some paper and a pencil. The man in there started stammering about needing to ask permission but Liz had already lifted what she needed before his first word was formed. Handing the clipboard to Debbie, she strode over the gravel to the stack of wooden pallets at the side of the building. There were twelve of them, covered in black plastic. She peeled it back and looked inside.

"Interesting," she said, more to herself than to Debbie. "I'll need to ask Eddie about that."

"Shall I make a note?" Debbie asked.

Liz shook her head. "Write that we need a spotlight here," she said, "and a barrier between the chalet and the field on the other side. The farmer's fence is electric, which helps, but it wouldn't keep out anything smarter than livestock."

"What are we doing, sorry?" Debbie asked, blinking at the blank sheet of paper.

"Note it down."

"The spotlight?"

"The spotlight, the barrier." Liz looked over to what Debbie was writing and sighed. "And draw in where the office is."

"So, it's like a map is it?"

"Gold star for Miss McVeigh."

They made their way across the front of the entrance and then looped up the side, with Debbie scribbling notes all the way. There was no doubt it was a big expanse to cover, so it was only feasible to have fencing and a gate between the office and the wall on the far side, but there could be spotlights behind that as well. And the most important thing was the patrol. They needed to be a visual deterrent and, for that, they'd need to be armed with more than torches and chewing gum.

Liz climbed onto a dry-stone wall and lifted a hand to shield her eyes. There wasn't glare from the sun, exactly, but the clouds were back-lit in a way that threw the landscape around them into stark relief. The hill behind was dark with shadow but in front was the green-brown of seaweed-strewn grass leading down to white-flecked rocks and the calm sea. A yacht, with its sail down, motored across the bay. A red car sped along towards the clutch of buildings over to the right, slowing to arc around a solitary walker. Yes, Liz thought, the setup here was perfect. Or it would be, with a few tweaks.

She looked off to the left, leaning forward to see along the road out of the village. There was a curve of road and then a grey-stone church with a few scattered graves in front. Beside a red phone box was a small clutch of people – maybe a dozen or so – and the blue, yellow and white markings of a police car. Liz shuffled forwards, on top of the wall, to get a better look.

"Well, well," she said, "not such a quiet backwater after all."

Debbie was on tip-toe, trying to peer past her. "Shall I go back for Joan?"

"Not Joan." Liz shook her head. "Fetch Eddie."

As Debbie bustled back towards the office, Liz paced out onto the main road. Maybe her instinct was wrong. Perhaps the villagers were meeting there for a Saturday ramble or to sell tickets for the village fête.

As she got closer, Liz could make out a trestle table covered with pieces of card and pots of paint. An elderly woman with short grey hair and dangling earrings sat behind it. She was passing a cardboard placard to a young boy, who stood beside a woman in a yellow hi-vis. KIDS BELONG IN SCHOOL, the sign said. The boy grinned as he bounced it up and down on its stick. Off to the side was a minister in a dog-collar tunic and thin rain-jacket. He also had a placard, propped against his legs. JOHN 11:12, it proclaimed in black letters. LORD, IF HE SLEEPS, HE WILL GET BETTER.

The door of the police car opened. The officer was young enough that the uniform looked like a dress-up costume, even as he drew himself up to full height and placed his hat firmly on his head.

"We're going to protest peacefully," the minister called. His voice had that deep timbre that Liz remembered from the men of god she'd encountered as a teenager. "I can assure you that it is all entirely legal."

Liz felt a shiver of revulsion travel across her shoulders. She didn't answer.

"We... erm..." the minister spoke again. "We have legitimate concerns about what is happening within your... erm... camp."

Liz pulled herself up onto the wall that encircled the church yard. She sat there, swinging her legs, looking over to the villagers. They stared back. After a moment, the minister stepped sideways and began a hushed discussion with the policeman. His hand went up to worry at his widow's peak.

Liz looked beyond them, out to sea. The ferry was moving away from the shore, churning up white surf as it began to turn. Just shy of the horizon, a tanker was inching slowly along. Sighing, Liz closed one eye and aimed a finger-pistol at first the ferry and then the tanker: *bang-bang.*

Why was it that every decision had to be referred back to Joan? Any time someone arrived or something unusual was stirring, it seemed that she was called for. There needed to be more resilience, the disciples needed to be more self-sufficient. Joan couldn't sort their petty squabbles – blow their runny noses – at the same time as preparing for the next step, could she?

The last time Liz had seen Ravi before his sentencing, he'd spoken of that. It was in a breezeblock visiting room. They weren't allowed to hold hands, but their knees touched beneath the small table. Behind Ravi, the vending machine was filled with European chocolate bars: Cailler, Ritter Sport, Milka. His hair had grown shaggy, grey at the temples, and he looked more exhausted than she had ever seen him before, with his cheeks sunken inwards and his eyes rimmed red.

"Those first days, Lizzy, those first days." He smiled, shook his head. "When everything was new and exciting and we were *energised* enough to take on the world, yes? It was like being an inventor or a...or a...skilled chef. Mixing ingredients, introducing people to tastes they've never known. But, then, more people arrive, hungry, to the restaurant. And they want the dishes you've served before, but they also want new recipes. They want you to keep accounts, they want you to train more chefs. Where is the health certificate, they say? And have you considered where you source your meat from? And suddenly…" He lifted a fist in the air and released it, let his fingers splay out. "You've forgotten the simple pleasure of feeding people, Lizzy, and of nourishing yourself."

She'd thought of that often in the months since. She had failed him. He had needed the headspace to think, to plan for the next chosen disciple. His time was constantly encroached upon, the moments of calm constantly chipped away by the demands of those in the commune. And it had been Liz's job to protect him from that. Because, without that shielding, his only release had been through his indulgences, his own human frailties…

"Fucking neighbourhood watch, eh?"

It was Eddie's voice. Liz blinked herself back to the present. He was striding quickly along the road, staring hard at the villagers and speaking loudly enough for them to hear. Debbie walked behind him, half-skipping in her attempts to keep up.

The minister stepped forward, but the policeman caught at his sleeve. Liz did the same to Eddie. She jumped down from the wall and pulled Eddie closer to her. She could feel his tensed muscles under the thin fabric of the robe, could hear the way his breath seemed to come out as a growl.

"Think about what you want to do, Eddie," she whispered, into his ear.

Eddie looked over to her. "You know what I want to do."

"Is that the best thing, though?"

Debbie poked her head forward, but Liz gave her a glare that caused her to step back again. In the field, on the other side of the road, a brown cow with a yellow tag in its ear came sauntering over to the fence and gazed at them with lazy eyes.

The minister was in front of his flock now. He cleared his throat. "*Close thine eyes and sleep secure,*" he sang, "*Thy soul is safe, thy body sure*". It was a slow hymn, sung in a deep baritone. Several villagers looked at one another, but they didn't seem to know the words.

"What do you want to do, Eddie?" Liz repeated.

Eddie looked confused now. His breathing had slowed. He was twisted, his head turned towards Liz but his feet still facing the crowd by the phone box. Liz wanted him to stop and think. He had a vital role in the commune, a key part to play, and he couldn't always react. He needed to be shrewd.

"I should go and let Joan know," Eddie said, softly.

"No." Liz squeezed her eyes shut. "No, Eddie."

Eddie had a frown as deep as a student given the wrong exam paper. The minister's singing had stopped. At the fence, the cow swung her head to look from one group to the other.

"They're not doing any harm," Eddie said, with his eyes on Liz's face.

She nodded. "And there's a policeman there."

"Aye."

"And they'll have camera-phones too."

Eddie bit at his lip. He obviously understood what she was saying, but it was difficult for him to go against what he was used to. As he considered, the young mother moved forward. "Let them sleep!" she chanted, lifting a fist in the air. "Let them sleep! Let them sleep!" Those around her found this easier to pick up and, within seconds, they'd joined in.

"What do we do, then?" Eddie asked.

"We wait," Liz said. "We take note of who's here and we act when the time is right. Yes?" She paused. "Most of all, though, we do all that. We don't bother Joan with it. The queen bee doesn't need a list of every flower visited, right?"

Eddie smiled at that. He nodded and turned to Debbie, who was still clutching her clipboard. Reaching out a finger he tapped at it, as though it had been his idea to take notes. Then he threw a final glance over his shoulder at the villagers and began walking back up the road.

"Oh, and Eddie...?" Liz called. She reached over and detached the top sheet of paper. It was the plans of the commune, with the details of where to put spotlights and fences and gates. Liz handed it across to Eddie. "It's your job to protect her," she said, softly.

"Joan's not keen..." Eddie frowned at the paper. "She says she doesn't want fortifications..."

"It's your job," Liz repeated.

Eddie nodded.

"So, maybe it's time to make plans for what you have in those pallets too, yes?"

With that, Liz turned back to the villagers. She plucked the pencil from Debbie's fingers and began scribbling down descriptions of those in front of her. As she looked up, she caught the eye of the minister. She paused in her writing and smiled. Then, slowly and deliberately, she raised the pencil into the air and performed the sign of the cross.

7

There was a slick of sweat across the side of his face, from where his cheek had been lying against the table, but also something stuck there, up at his temple. Groggily, Grafton raised his head and lifted a hand to it: a piece of paper, dog-eared and damp along one edge. It was what he'd been sketching out the night before, when it was pitch black outside the window and he was wired with adrenaline. How long had he slept for? How much time had he lost?

Scrabbling the laptop towards him, he opened it. The wee clock in the bottom right was showing 16:34. Half four? Half four on *Saturday*? He'd managed to pass out and sleep through most of the day when he needed to be alert and getting everything in place to rescue Isaac.

Fucking hell, his head was throbbing. He stumbled through to the kitchen and nearly went arse-over-tit on the pool of mayonnaise in the centre of the floor. It was starting to congeal and turn transparent. Stepping around it, and the glass shards of the jar, he ran himself a tumbler of water from the tap. He gulped it down. Then another. He remembered these days all too well: the desire to curl into a foetal position on the cold tiles of the floor, the need to cringe away from the daylight at the sides of the curtains. The temptation, as well, to settle for the simplest cure. He didn't have any alcohol in the house, though. That was a blessing in disguise. He'd have to fight through it the hard way.

Grafton made his way down the hallway, a hand on the wall for support. He'd have a shower and a shave. It took him a good five minutes to get his socks off and he was just gathering his strength to pull his t-shirt over his head when the front-door buzzer sounded.

He got to the bedroom door and then launched himself, headlong, down the hallway. It was more by luck than judgement that he ended up by the intercom.

"Hello?" he said, into the handset.

"Grocery delivery," said the voice at the other end.

"Aye?"

"Aye."

Grafton frowned and pressed the buzzer. His first thought was that the delivery must be for someone else – Rachel next door or the Rajendran family downstairs – but then a vague memory swirled in. He'd done an online shop last night, using his saved card. Past Grafton – drunk Grafton – had finally done something that present Grafton could be thankful for. There would be food in that shop – frozen pizza and crisps, chocolate biscuits and the odd piece of fruit – but, more than that, there would be coffee. He would make a vat-full of the stuff, strong and thick enough for a spoon to stand upright in it.

The delivery driver was in his early-twenties. He had a bright, toothy smile and it was to his credit that he kept it fixed in place when Grafton opened the door.

"You want these through in the kitchen?" he asked.

"Erm, no. Here is fine."

There were two crates. Grafton lifted things out quickly. He wasn't bothered about the eggs and the milk – not just now – or the bread, cheese, and bananas. He was frantically looking for the glint of silver packaging that was the ground coffee. And there it was, right at the bottom.

He grinned but felt it fading as the delivery driver lifted away the top crate. In the second crate were two bottles of vodka, a bottle of blended whisky, and a six-pack of beer. Of course that was what drunk Grafton – past Grafton – had been thinking of. It was a miracle, truth be told, that there was anything else in the shopping.

"We had everything you asked for then, sir," the delivery driver was saying, "no substitutes."

Grafton shook his head.

"Everything ok?"

He shook his head again. He knew that if even one bottle made it out of the crate then he'd convince himself that a wee dram could be added to his coffee, that a small glassful would help him with his planning, that the rest of the bottle would ensure a good night's sleep. He knew that he would lift all three bottles, and the beers, and that Isaac would be forgotten. He wouldn't be driving north and he wouldn't be saving his son.

"Take it back," Grafton said.

"What's that?"

"All the alcohol, all of it. Take it back."

"Is there a problem with it?"

"You can charge me for it." Grafton squeezed his eyes shut. His voice was hoarse. "You can take it yourself, mate. I don't care. Just please – please – take it away."

He heard the crates clanking back together. Still he didn't open his eyes. Instead he grasped for the door, began to push it closed. He knew he was forcing the delivery driver out, that the young lad would be hustled and harried by it, but he didn't care. He got the door closed and opened his eyes.

He turned back towards the kitchen, clutching his silver-foil packet of coffee. He needed to forget about the contents of that second crate, focus instead on those basics: coffee and plan. The shower and shave could wait.

Coffee made, Grafton crawled in underneath the dining table and began rifling through Isaac's art materials. There, right at the back, was a thick plastic bag with a heavy rectangle of grey clay inside. He hauled it out and emptied it onto the wooden table with a thud. He sat down and considered. There were supposed to be tools, weren't there? He ran a hand through the tray of pencils, pastels, and paintbrushes. There was a small red scalpel, with a plastic guard on the top, and a semi-circular scraper that had dried clay along the edge of it.

Right. He had a vague notion that potters also had a wheel, but he'd never seen Isaac using one. Not at home anyway. Instead, he slapped and shaped with his hands. Grafton lifted his right hand and gave the clay a hit. It felt solid. He tried again. Then he pushed his thumb into the side of it, but it barely made a dent. He lifted the clay scalpel and took off the guard. When he dragged it along the top of the clay it lifted a curl.

For a spell, he sat and shaved the block; half-inch twists of clay falling to the carpet. He was trying to form it into an oval, but it was slow work. He stopped and took a gulp of coffee. Then, he lifted a hand and gave the clay another slap. There was the slightest give to it. Another mouthful of coffee. He remembered, then, that Isaac usually had a bowl of water beside him, to dip his fingers into as he moulded. So, Grafton went through to the kitchen to fetch himself one.

He stepped around the spilled mayonnaise on the floor. The cupboard with the Pyrex bowl in it was below the cutlery drawer. He opened that and considered the knives. Maybe the bread knife would be quicker than the scalpel, or he could even use the potato peeler? He took both, and the bowl filled with warm water, back through.

Sitting down, he drained his coffee mug. Then he dipped his hand into the water. That pulsing at the corner of his eye was back again. A twitch, twitch, twitch. He pressed a wet finger to it, but it didn't stop. Twitch, twitch. So, he squeezed his eye shut and held it closed. Twitch. It started to travel, that pulse, down through his cheek and it settled in the nerve of a back tooth. He opened his eye, assessed the pain. It was a dull ache, but it was sharpening. He pressed his teeth together and then eased them apart. His jaw sang with the pain. And then it was on the move again, down the side of his neck and into his chest. Not a pulse, but a thump-thump-thump. Picking up pace, racing away. Thum-thum-thum. He put his whole hand flat against it and pushed down hard. Thu-thu-thu. Was this how it ended? Would his heart short-circuit and the pain shoot down his arm? Th-th-th. He gasped in a breath. Waited. But, no, his heartbeat was slowing. Th-thu-thum. A moment of nothing, and then the pulsing came back in the corner of his eye.

His skin felt tender, as though blossoming with bruises. As if someone had been gouging out his eye sockets and scraping a scalpel along his jawline, squeezing his temples into shape and flattening his forehead with some blunt object. And his mouth — as if he'd been eating great fistfuls of mixed clay and coffee grounds, coating his tongue and teeth with it.

He'd have to live with it. Wetting his hand again, he pushed and prodded at the clay. With the bread knife, he sawed off the top of the oval and started hollowing it out with the potato peeler. The additional tools were helping and the clay was getting easier to work with. Besides, the sculpture didn't have to be perfect. It only had to look enough like a head — like a bust down to the shoulders — that it could sit on the shrine table in the A-frame without attracting attention.

8

There was a wooden stile over the fence that separated the road from the fields beyond. Joan reached out for Isaac's arm to raise herself up onto the first rung and Isaac felt the thrill of her touch, of her fingers, through the linen of his robe.

They walked through thick, heather-laden grass, deeper into the hills. For the first time since arriving, Isaac was wearing shoes; black plimsolls that Joan had excavated from a heaped pile back at the commune. She was wearing a matching pair.

After a spell, Joan had to stop to catch her breath. Eyes closed, head tipped back to the clouded sky. When they set off again, she slid her hand in at the crook of his arm and pulled down on him, ever so slightly, with each step. Isaac didn't mind, not one bit.

At the end of a sheep trail of flattened grass, there was a dried-up riverbed. From the bracken at the side came the steady birr of crickets and Isaac caught sight of a small, black-specked frog. The dry river turned suddenly, sharply, to the right and dipped down. Across its path was another river, in full spate. There were boulders across it, placed there as stepping-stones.

He went first, stretching his leg from one to the next. Then he shuffled as far over as he could and reached out a hand to help Joan across. There were six stepping-stones and each time, as he pulled her on, she pressed in towards him and made a gasping noise in her throat, like a hiccup. Close up, her skin was a pasty grey, but there was also a sheen of sweat across her forehead.

On the opposite bank, they paused and Joan pointed upriver. There was a small waterfall there, the water cascading down into a brown pool with a swirl of foam at the edges. The smooth rocks on either side were freckled with moss. They walked towards it.

"When the weather is warm," Joan said, over the noise of the water, "I swim here."

It was the first time either of them had spoken, Isaac realised, since they'd set out. He nodded, imagining the scene: turning away as she let the robe fall, but still catching sight of her pale skin; her body slipping under the brown water and surfacing, with her hair streaming water.

"What I really want to show you, though," Joan said, "is beyond that rise."

Isaac swallowed. "Right," he said, "lead the way."

There was a spattering of rain, the grey clouds sweeping in over the hills and darkening the small valley they were in. It wasn't yet enough to soak through the robes, but Isaac was aware that neither of them had a jacket.

"Shall we turn back?" he asked Joan.

She shook her head. "The rain arrives when the tide comes in."

"Pardon?"

"You notice it when you live by the sea: when the tide turns, so does the weather."

She carried on up the mud path. It took Isaac a moment or two to catch up with her. When he did, he looked up and saw the ruined houses. A whole village – maybe a dozen buildings – scattered across the flat, treeless land between the hills. All of the houses were roofless, with walls made of intricately jigsawed stone. This giant game of *Tetris* was more complete in some places than others; there were slumps and landslides, partially framed windows and collapsed fireplaces.

"You can almost hear their voices, can't you?" Joan said, softly.

"Whose?" Isaac asked.

"The villagers. Those who lived here years ago."

Isaac listened. The wind was picking up. The rush of it maybe changed slightly as it found the gaps in the stone walls,

233

but it was a stretch to think of it as voices.

"What happened to them?" Isaac asked.

She shrugged. "This way of life wasn't sustainable anymore. This simple existence, with only a few crops to tend to and a small herd of animals. That riverbed we came along would be ok for a horse but there isn't a four-wheel drive in the world that could make it."

The rain was getting heavier now. They were close to the first of the houses. It was a single room, with a fireplace at the far end. The inside of the chimney was exposed. On the grass floor were scatterings of sheep droppings and a scorched, charcoal-strewn patch that looked like the remnants of a much more recent fire.

"People from the outside," Joan began, "people like your father, think that the commune is all about wakefulness, yes? But it's only the first stage, Isaac. We're programmed to desire sleep, to structure our every day to that end, and the project is to have the disciples realise that and wrench back control. Once we are truly wakeful, though, we can return to this simpler form of society, without the want and the striving and the ceaseless grind. A self-sustaining community – with crops and some hens for eggs, goats for milk. Society was on the cusp of realising it, wasn't it? During the pandemic, there was a stirring of unease, a short moment we all could have grasped. But routine took over again, habit reasserted itself."

Isaac turned to look out across the valley, trying to picture it. Simple structures – wooden bothies with corrugated iron roofs, perhaps – sitting alongside the ruined village, making use of the remaining stone walls to create pens for the livestock and windbreaks for the allotments. And there, in the middle of it, could be a studio – with a window at an angle that let in the early light – where Isaac could work on his sculptures and welcome Joan back from her morning swim at the waterfall. A simple, uncluttered life, with time and space to concentrate without needing to think of grades or tuition fees or deadlines.

He thought, suddenly, of Shauna. With her eyeliner flicks and the tipping of her bowler hat. The way she performed. She would never be content out here, with only the sheep to admire her. Whereas Joan, away from the cares of the commune, was animated and joyous. The exhaustion had lifted from her features and the sluggishness had disappeared from her movements. She was in her element.

The rain was blowing into Isaac's face now, he could feel it settling into a slick on the front of his robe. He stepped across to the ruined house, huddled underneath the lintel stone above the doorway. Joan stayed out in the open.

"That's the difference between me and Ravi," she called. "He wants to drain the toxins to show it can be done. I want to wash those away first and then move on to *all* the toxins which limit us…"

"What toxins?" Isaac called back.

"That's how we take the next step, Isaac. It'll take patience and it needs a leap of faith from all of us, bravery and trust in the process. But I've done my calculations, I've seen where Ravi went wrong…"

The rain was thundering down. Joan's hair hung in lank ropes around her face and the white robe was transparent where it pressed against her skin. Isaac could see the shadows of her nipples, the darkness of her crotch.

"Then we'll clear this whole valley," Joan shouted, gesturing out to the fields. "Disciples will come from all over the world and we will have prepared the ground for them…"

"What do you mean by toxins?" Isaac called, again.

But she didn't hear. With arms held outstretched, she was spinning with her head tipped back and her mouth open to the downpour.

"Come join me, Isaac!" she called.

And Isaac went to her. To dance with her in the rain and admire the way the fabric of the robe clung to her wet, goose-flesh skin.

9

Eddie was helping Liz set the stage. They'd spent the majority of their Sunday on it. A wooden chair in the centre, draped in thick plastic sheeting like it had been wrapped for removal men, and a black-and-gold patterned sheet pinned behind. To the side was a steel bucket and, beside that, a shallow bowl filled with sterilising fluid. Debbie was gathering all the clean towels she could.

"We have some numbing gel," Eddie said, "and it'll be Whippet with the pliers so it should be fast."

"No," Liz said, "no numbing gel."

"Really?"

"The pain is the point. You can hold them down if you need to."

This was the problem with Seattle: too many concessions. If the Sleepless were serious about being there, about following Ravi's teachings, then it was high time they embraced the experience. No more half-measures, no more allowing Joan to shoulder the burden.

Eddie was taping black bin-liners down under the chair and up to the edge of the A-frame stage. He pulled out a length of gaffer tape and held it there, scissors poised.

"I thought the point was to leave a gap," Eddie said, "for the tongue to find."

"The gap is there as the reminder of the pain. It's the memory that keeps you from sleep."

Eddie snipped the scissors.

"We must all test our limitations now," Liz said. "The time has come."

She was doing this for Joan, really. The young girl was impressive, certainly, but leadership was about more than setting a shining example. Liz needed to make sure everyone else was ready to go along with her, that everyone was strong enough for that journey. It would be Joan taking the next step, but the others needed to be ready to bear witness.

Eddie smoothed down the last length of tape and raised himself up onto his haunches to survey his handiwork. He nodded to himself, seemingly satisfied, but then looked across to Liz. She was pleased to see that. She gave him a smile and a nod.

"And is it only the pliers we need?" Eddie asked, standing.

Liz paused. "Is there a difference between a normal drill and the one a dentist uses?"

She knew the answer, of course, but she wanted to gauge Eddie's reaction. Was that a small shiver across his shoulders? If it was, it passed quickly.

"Pliers are fine," Liz said, as he opened his mouth to answer. "Only pliers for now."

With that, she turned and stepped out of the A-frame. The bell would be rung for dinner at any moment. The Sleepless would come streaming out of the cabins expecting their evening meal, but they would have to wait. This test came first, this surprise for Joan.

Liz lifted her face to the sky. The clouds had rolled out, taking the low-hanging grey far out to sea and leaving sunshine in the bay. Liz felt the warmth of it against her cheeks.

From down at the office came the ringing. It was an old-fashioned brass hand-bell, the kind that a Victorian teacher would have used. *Clang, clang, clang.* Liz wondered if the villagers listened out for it every night, if they speculated about what it meant, what it signalled. She could imagine the minister writing the times neatly in a ruled notebook.

Liz stepped back up onto the wooden porch and held the door open for the disciples as they began to arrive. She greeted each of them with a smile. They would be hungry, she knew. That was why she had chosen this time. She could use their frustration, use their hunger, to drive away any reluctance.

At the edge of the trees, a snaking line of children emerged, led by Becky. Towards the back, towering over the others, was Isaac. His head was constantly swivelling, watching the Sleepless as they converged on the A-frame. He was intrigued by it all, Liz could tell, but she was certain that he wasn't ready to fully commit. Not yet.

The test in the A-frame, that Sunday evening, was not for him. It was for the disciples who'd been in the commune for weeks now without being asked to prove themselves. For those who'd grown too comfortable. It would sort the wheat from the chaff. And Liz dearly hoped that Isaac would, one day, be in a position to join them, but it couldn't be forced and it couldn't be rushed.

Liz moved forward and placed a hand on Isaac's shoulder. He looked up but didn't smile. Liz gestured with her other hand and pulled him out of line, leading him towards the side of the building.

Once they were out of sight, Liz reached into the neckline of her robe and tore the extra fold of fabric she had added. She had hand-stitched the second roll of Euros in on the night of their arrival. She didn't know how much there was, exactly, but at least a few hundred.

"Here," she said, holding them out to Isaac. "Take it and go back home."

Isaac frowned.

"What?" she said. "Take it and go back to your dad."

"Are those Euros?"

She nodded.

"And what am I supposed to do with them?"

"Take them. Get the bus back."

"It's *Sunday*, Mum, and those are *Euros*. Where d'you think we are? Paris? Rome?"

He gestured around. On the hillside were a few dozen sheep. One of them bleated on cue, as if to add her voice to

Isaac's argument. High above, a buzzard swooped over towards the trees.

"Ok," Liz said, her teeth together. "So, you want the car?"

"I can't drive back alone. It'll be dark soon."

"Well…what do you want?"

"I want to stay."

Liz closed her eyes. She breathed in and out. *Patience.* Yes, he was being unreasonable and naïve, but it was understandable given the indulgence Joan had shown him. He thought of the commune as some kind of holiday camp, rather than as a movement with a serious purpose. One way of showing him the reality would be to allow him into the A-frame, Liz knew, but he hadn't even begun limiting his sleep yet, hadn't taken even the first step on the journey to wakefulness. Liz couldn't show favouritism.

She pushed the notes towards Isaac again. "Take it," she repeated. "There is plenty of time for you to learn more, for you to return here, but for now you need to go back to your dad. He'll be worried about you."

"Fine." Isaac scowled, reaching for the cash. "I'll maybe see if the shop can exchange it for me tomorrow, see if there's a bus going south."

He tucked the money into his sleeve and turned back towards the A-frame.

"Adults only this evening," Liz called after him. "Tell Becky to take the children – *all* the children – back to your cabin and you can have your dinner there."

Isaac didn't break stride. "Aye, god forbid we spend any time together, eh?"

"It's not that—"

"Save it. We can speak before I go tomorrow. Or in another eight years."

And, with that, he disappeared around the side of the building.

Liz took a moment – deep breath in, deep breath out – to settle herself. She concentrated on the sounds around her: the cry of a lamb from a distant field, the growl of a diesel engine either from the road or the bay, a murmur of excited conversation from inside the A-frame itself. She was making the right choice with Isaac. She wanted nothing more than for him to join her on this adventure, for him to witness Joan taking the next step, but he needed time to process the teachings and immerse himself in the practices. He couldn't skip the queue.

With that resolved, Liz took another deep breath and then walked around to join the rest of the Sleepless in the A-frame.

Up on the stage, Morven sat on the wooden chair. Whippet stood beside her, with his hands clasped behind his back. Liz knew what he held, of course, but she wondered if the rest of the disciples did. Would there be a protest? Would a dissenting voice or two call out from the crowd?

Liz looked around for Eddie. He was on the stairs to the side, staring out over the room with a scowl on his face. The Sleepless all sat patiently: cross-legged, waiting.

"Friends," Liz said, stepping onto the stage, "we have been weak. In allowing Joan to shoulder the burden of the wakefulness we have been weak. It is not enough to simply applaud from the sidelines, it is not enough to say that we will follow Joan in taking the next step..."

She paused. This wasn't her strong suit, she knew that. She wasn't an orator like Ravi, wasn't inspiring like Joan. But she was good at identifying weaknesses in the structure, at pinpointing possible issues before they arose.

"Distraction is our friend in this struggle," she continued, channelling Ravi. "If we sit and think of sleep, then sleep will come. If we grow used to a routine, then sleep will come. Even our methods, friends, can become routine. We follow them and there is a comfort to them. That comfort lends itself to relaxation and that relaxation to sleep."

Liz moved across to the chair at centre-stage and laid a hand on the yellow scarf tied through Morven's hair. Morven looked up at her and smiled.

"We are all familiar," Liz said, "with what I will call the *weight* of sleep. That feeling that every limb is getting heavier, that the very marrow of your bones is thickening. Imagine walking through some woods. Your legs are becoming more difficult to lift and your arms are dragging your shoulders down. Your body dips, your head bows towards the earth and, suddenly, everything around you is a pillow. That tree stump, that lichen-streaked rock, that patch of thistles. All of it is a pillow to your tired mind. And so you topple, dear ones, and your heavy bones give in to gravity. You smile in anticipation of sinking into that pillow..."

She paused, her eyes roving around the room. She had heard this analogy many times from Ravi, delivered at great length and with the list of possible pillows tailored to his different audiences, and it never failed in its effectiveness.

"...except – *crack*!" She clapped her hands together and was pleased to see some of the disciples in the front row flinch. "Your head does not meet a pillow. It glances off a root, it thuds against a jutting rock. Blood pulses hotly from the wound. And where is the weight of sleep then...? Where?"

Again, she looked around the room. No one answered, everyone waited.

"It is chased away by *pain*."

A second's pause and then applause rang around the room. Hands and feet thumped against the bare wooden floorboards. Liz stepped down from the stage and gave a small nod to Eddie, over by the stairs.

Eddie took the steps two at a time and disappeared into the room at the top. Liz wondered how much Joan had heard from upstairs. Eddie had been told to tell her that there was a surprise waiting for her, that the disciples had decided to mark her tenth night of wakefulness with a reaffirmation of their support, a re-dedication to accompany her into her eleventh day.

A moment or two passed, then Eddie re-emerged from the room with Joan behind. He held his arm out for her, to support her as she climbed down the steps. She wore a yellow dress, belted so tightly around the middle that it looked like she'd been threaded through the eye of a needle.

From the bottom step, Joan looked up at Liz. Her eyes were bruised, underneath, but still remarkably clear-sighted. There was a furrow to her eyebrows, a confusion about what was happening. Liz tried to reassure, by placing both hands together and dipping down on her knees in a half-curtsey. It was a gesture she'd used often with Ravi.

Eddie guided Joan into the crowd. There were excited murmurs from those in the front row as they shuffled sideways to make room for her. She sat, cross-legged, among the disciples.

It was time for the test to begin. Liz knew that she might need to explain it to Joan later, that there might be questions to be answered, but she'd made sure to rehearse things with Morven, so that she knew what to say before the act itself.

"Your strength—" Morven began, but she faltered. "Your strength is an inspiration, Joan."

Morven looked scared but determined. Her skin was so pale that you could see a thin blue vein beneath, up by her temple. She looked at Whippet and nodded. Her lips, set as nothing more than a narrow line, opened and she swallowed. Raising her chin, she looked out at the audience and opened her mouth as wide as it would go.

Liz thought of taking Isaac on his first visits to the dentist: the call to say 'ahh'; the bright light; the blue face-mask; the tinny pop music from the radio; the promise of a superhero sticker afterwards. All of those slight comforts were stripped away here. It was only Whippet and his pliers.

He reached in and his hand clenched as he took a grip of the tooth. One tug and then a second. Morven closed her eyes, a silent tear squeezing out and running down her cheek. Whippet leant back slightly, rocked away from her and then forwards. The chair moved with them. She whimpered, but kept her mouth open. His foot went up on the chair, then, to brace himself. He pulled and her whole body seemed to lift, juddered with the movement of him. A strangled call from her throat now and a noise like the scraping of rusty metal – bone against bone – as Whippet twisted the pliers. A final wrench away and a short, sharp scream from Morven. Then the tooth was out.

The cheers started from the centre of the room. Great shouts of joy. Arms were thrown in the air and folk began to whistle and call Morven's name. Liz clapped along, but she was carefully watching for Joan's reaction.

Her grey eyes were fixed on the stage. She hadn't moved, hadn't joined in the cheering. And her hand had come up to caress at her own cheek. Maybe Liz had misjudged. Ravi loved a sense of spectacle, a demonstration of love, but perhaps all Joan needed to encourage her towards the next step was solitude and quiet...

Eddie stepped onto the stage. He had a metal bucket in one hand and a piece of white gauze in the other. He knelt down in front of Morven, carefully avoiding the pool of blood. Thick globules of it trailed from her mouth to the plastic beneath. Eddie placed the gauze in her mouth. Her jaw tensed as she bit down on it.

The room had quietened. The rest of the Sleepless were waiting to see what Morven would do next. Eddie whispered softly to her. If you didn't know him, you could almost imagine there was tenderness to his words.

Morven nodded, sniffed. She raised her right hand to the gauze in her mouth and readjusted it. She lifted her head. The yellow scarf had shifted and her black hair now hung in curtains on either side of her face. From behind it, she looked up and out at Joan. And, after a second, she punched her left fist up in the air.

All eyes turned to Joan. There was a moment's pause. Then, Joan lifted her hand from her cheek and, slowly, raised her own fist up to mirror Morven's.

There was bedlam. The cheering and thumping on the floor was twice as loud as before. Chants of 'Morven, Morven' shortened to 'Morv, Morv' and then to a guttural grunting noise. It all continued for a minute or so, as Debbie stepped onto the stage and helped Morven up from the chair.

Eddie held a hand up, asking for quiet. He scanned the room. Gradually, the disciples settled towards silence.

He lifted the bucket and held it out towards Whippet. The makeshift dentist, with blood spattered across his white robe, moved across with the tooth still gripped in his pliers. He let the tooth fall. A faint ting sounded out as it struck the bottom.

"Right," Eddie called, "who's next?"

10

Grafton strapped the sculpture into the passenger seat. A bust of a head and shoulders, unpainted and fired in a pottery studio he'd found off Byres Road. Long flowing hair and staring eyes, with a scalp that lifted off to show the hollow inside. There was the trace of a smile on her lips. It simultaneously looked like every woman under the age of forty and like none of them. A mother would be flattered to receive it, but a girlfriend would be furious. It would have to do.

Finding the pottery studio and collecting the hire car had taken a chunk of his Sunday. Then he'd had to pay a visit to A&E as well. The dressing on his arm had yellowed from the seepage at the edges of the wound. It stung in the shower and even the gentlest dab from a flannel was agony. After a three hour wait, the nurse had given it a clean and bandaged it up tight. Better yet, she hadn't asked any questions.

Those errands had cost him time already, but he had one more to run before he could head north. He drove through the Monday morning traffic towards the station. Kathy spoke to him through the radio, telling him the latest about the climate crisis: flooding in Myanmar, drought in Mozambique.

Grafton had forgotten his pass, but it didn't matter, Danny came straight out of the booth when he saw him and pushed the door release.

"You're late," he said. "What happened to your arm?"

"Late?" Grafton was puzzled for a moment. Then he realised that Danny thought that this was him returning to work. "No, no," he said, "I'll need another few days."

He strode past Danny. The producer reached out a hand and tugged at Grafton's jacket, catching him at the elbow, but then seemed to think better of it. He let go and followed Grafton instead.

"Who's going to do the travel?" he called.

"You do it. Have Kathy do it. Get an intern." Grafton shrugged. "It's an easy job."

Danny opened his mouth and closed it again. He was wearing a flat-cap, in muted tartan. He sometimes opted for that, even though it looked ridiculous indoors. It normally came out when they had a special guest in for an interview, particularly someone young with luxuriant hair.

"You took a week's leave," he shouted, as Grafton walked on towards the storage cupboard. "One week, at short notice. And you owe me a small fortune for a taxi too…"

"I need a few more days." Grafton had the cupboard open and was poking through the stationery and printer cartridges inside. *Back off Danny,* he wanted to say. "It's a family matter this time," he said, instead.

"Yes? Can you tell me what?"

"It's private." *One more night and then god-knows what happens up at that commune…*

Grafton crouched. On the bottom shelf were a lot of random electronics – a spare mouse, some keyboards, even an old calculator. He followed a jumble of cables to its source, but it was only a USB desk fan.

"Well," Danny said, "unless you can tell me the reason, then you can't have the extra days, ok? Sorry, but I'm not having it."

Grafton turned. "Do we have a camcorder or something like that?"

"What? Did you not hear me?"

Loud and fucking clear, Danny, but I need to save my son.

Grafton stood and did a quick scan of the office. There were five desks in total, including his own. And there, on a filing cabinet to the side, was a pile of microphones and webcams and, right at the front, a small digital camera.

He stepped over quickly and lifted it. Again, Danny followed. His face had flushed across the cheeks. With that tea cosy on his head he'd be simmering away for hours.

"If you leave now, then you leave for good," Danny said. "I'm warning you."

"Understood," Grafton said. He curled his hand around the camera and walked past Danny towards the door. "Oh." He turned back. "Will you take a cheque for this? And for the taxi?"

Danny went back to opening and closing his mouth. Grafton wouldn't have been surprised to hear him whistling like a kettle coming to the boil. Reaching into his pocket, Grafton pulled out his cheque book. It was bundled up with the paper part of his driver's licence. The car hire company had been reluctant to accept it, but Grafton had pointed them to the section of their website where it was listed as an acceptable form of ID.

"I'll leave the amount blank, shall I?" Grafton said. "You can fill it in later. There's a calculator in that cupboard there if you need it."

He tore out the cheque and held it towards Danny.

"This is a hell of a way to go out," Danny said, taking it.

Grafton shrugged. "I'm only a glorified Sat Nav here, like Isaac always said."

"It's a good job, though, it's a wage."

"Aye, Danny. That's the issue – I always felt like it should be more than that, you know, if I'm going to spend every waking hour at it."

He turned back and pressed the door release, but then stood there holding it open. This was an opportunity to let Danny know what he really thought of him: that he was skilled but spineless, wasting any talent he had on pushing paper. There were stories they could be doing on the show – proper public interest stories that might make some impact – if Danny were willing to push for them. This was Grafton's chance to tell him that, to at least nudge him towards the truth of it.

"Danny," he said, instead, "that hat does you no favours, buddy."

11

Isaac discovered the ruined church by accident. He'd been walking, keen to have some time alone. Everyone at the commune had spent the morning giving each other toothy smiles and grimaces – like schoolkids after the tooth fairy has been. Morven had tied her yellow scarf under her chin, like a Hollywood starlet, and was loudly reminding everyone that she'd been the first in the chair.

Those who hadn't felt the pinch of Whippet's pliers walked about with their mouths tightly closed, avoiding eye contact. There was a sense of shame to it – like not having the right trainers or hairstyle – and Isaac found himself wondering if he would have stepped forward if he'd been allowed inside the A-frame. Would the agony have been worth it? For that sense of belonging, that sense of approval. That smile from Joan.

The grass of the graveyard was uneven, with gravestones jutting at odd angles, all arranged higgledy-piggledy rather than in straight rows. The lumpy ground – in some places as hard as gristle and in others soft and yielding – made it possible to think that you were walking directly over the dead, pressing their limbs back down with the sole of your foot.

The graves were centuries old and the church was little more than crumbling wall at this stage. There were droppings in against the stonework, where sheep had sought shelter from the wind, but the locals wouldn't have used this building since the kirk down on the road was built.

As soon as he'd had his walk, he was going to take his Euros down to the shop and ask them about getting out of there. He'd secure his place on a bus out of the village and then have a final heart-to-heart with Joan. For a brief second, he wondered if he could convince her to come with him, but he knew that was fanciful. She would stay here – of course she would – and he would leave.

"Isaac!" The call came from the other side of the graveyard, from beside a small stone mausoleum that had sunk lopsidedly into the earth. "Wait up."

It was Eddie. He jogged over. There was a grin on his face – none of his teeth missing – and he slung an arm across Isaac's shoulders. Isaac resisted the urge to squirm away.

"Where you off to, grasshopper?" Eddie asked.

"Just a walk."

Eddie nodded, kept the grin in place. He must have followed Isaac, there was no other reason for him to be up here.

"I've got something you can help me with," he said, "since you're at a loose end."

Isaac sniffed and looked down at his bare feet. There was mud smeared up to his ankles and stray strands of grass across his toes. He didn't even notice the numbing cold anymore.

"Special project for Joan," Eddie said. "Me and you."

"What kind of project?"

"The kind that gets you shoes." Eddie gave him a wink. It was like a convulsion, involving the whole right side of his face. "Come on, chance to do something useful."

Eddie's arm was getting heavier across his shoulders.

Slowly, reluctantly, Isaac bowed his head into a nod.

The minibus skidded to a stop with a sound like fabric tearing. Eddie hopped out of the driver-side door and it slammed shut behind him. Isaac sat in the juddering seat. It would be easy to slide across until his hands were on the steering wheel, his feet on the pedals. He could take off and leave behind whatever hare-brained scheme Eddie had planned. What was stopping him? Certainly not his mother – she'd miss her molar more than her son – and definitely not loyalty to the Sleepless. It was only Joan: the need to say goodbye to her, explain his reasons for leaving, and ask her if she wanted him to come back.

They were parked on the verge beside the Pier Shop. On the scrubland between the row of houses, facing the shore, and the shop itself. Eddie was raising a din from the back of the minibus. This was the moment. Isaac could take off and find a way of sending word to Joan, once he was back home. Back with his dad.

Eddie reappeared at the window with an expression that was partway between a grin and a sneer.

"Get out then," he said. "Fuck sake."

The moment was gone. Isaac scrabbled down from the minibus and around to where Eddie was standing. On the grass, spread out in front of them, were a couple of empty glass bottles, a jerry-can of petrol and a blue pinstripe shirt. Not just any shirt, Isaac realised, but the one he'd been wearing when he arrived at the commune. The one he'd worn to his college exhibition.

"We're not sitting on our hands," Eddie said. The grin was wider. "We're not sitting on our hands while these fuckers interfere with our business."

"Who?" Isaac asked.

Eddie raised a finger and tapped at the side of his nose. Then he grabbed a fistful of his robe and shook it, as if that explained everything.

"We're not planning on hurting anyone are we, Eddie?"

"Fuck me, heart of a lion in you, isn't there? No, we're not hurting anyone. We're sending a message, is all. A wee message before tonight's festivities…"

"And what's all this for?"

"Come on, Isaac, earn your Boy Scout badges – you can work it out."

Isaac looked at the objects on the grass and gave a shrug. But Eddie was right. It was the petrol that was the giveaway. And Isaac wished that he'd taken his opportunity to get out of there, with or without his final word with Joan; he cursed himself for letting that moment slip by.

Eddie set to work. He tore a strip from the shirt and sloshed petrol across it. The heady smell rose, obscuring the salty tang of seaweed and the peat smoke from a chimney further along. Next, Eddie lifted one of the bottles and handed it across. Isaac held it as far out from his body as he could, but Eddie wasn't careful with the pouring. Petrol got on Isaac's sleeves, on the toes of his plimsolls.

"What have they done?" Isaac asked, not knowing if he was talking about the folk in the houses behind or in the shop in front.

Eddie laughed. "They thought they could interfere. They thought they could corrupt the process and – well – they can't, can they? It's not for them to mess with our methods. We're in charge. We outnumber them."

"So, Joan ordered this?"

Eddie turned to him, eyes shining as if the flames were already reflected there. "Nothing happens without Joan. She's central to everything."

"Did she ask for this, though?"

It was all one movement: Eddie striding forward, lifting him the couple of metres to press him against the metal of the minibus, and whipping out a long-bladed knife. He held it to Isaac's throat. Isaac squinted down at the blade. It was thin, tapering to a point, and had a black handle. Where had it been? Up his sleeve? Tucked in at the side of his plimsoll?

"Listen to me." Eddie's voice was matter-of-fact now. "I don't like you. Your dad fucked us over and, far as I'm concerned, you will too. So, don't play the fucking golden-boy card with me, ok? This is your one and only chance to show me I'm wrong. One and only chance."

"Ok, ok. Easy."

"I'll leave you to bleed out somewhere between here and fuck-knows-where and I'll tell your mum and Joan that you took off. Neither of them will be heartbroken, lad, trust me on that."

Isaac tried to control his breathing. He was hyper-aware of his Adam's apple, of the fact that it moved closer to the blade when he swallowed.

"Is it the shop I'm th-throwing it at?" Isaac stumbled over his words.

Eddie nodded. He took a step back and smiled, the knife still clutched in his hand.

Isaac took a gulp of air. "What if there are people inside?"

"They'll get out."

"But, old people or…"

Shaking his head, Eddie leant over to the open window of the minibus. He reached his free hand in and pressed on the horn. He held it for a few seconds. In the silence that followed, the echo of it rang in Isaac's ears. At the window of the Pier Shop, the face of an elderly woman appeared.

"No more excuses," Eddie said. He took the bottle and pushed the fabric in at the neck. Then he handed it back to Isaac. He lifted a lighter, sparked a flame and held it below the fabric. "Once it's lit," he said, "I wouldn't fuck about."

Isaac watched as the blue flame took hold. It took only a split-second. He yanked at the sleeves of his robe, keeping them clear of the bottle. The flame darted up the pinstripe, was at the neck of the bottle. So, Isaac did the only thing he could – he lobbed the petrol bomb off in the direction of the shop. He let out a yell as he did it. Something torn from the sides of his throat. It tasted of petrol.

He watched as the bottle arced in the air. He'd thrown it deliberately short. It wouldn't reach the long, low white building.

The bottle split against the concourse. If there was a noise, then Isaac didn't hear it above the blood thumping in his ears. Flames rolled out from the broken bottle, but the fuel would soon burn out. There'd be no damage done beyond a scorched patch of concrete. Eddie would have sent his message to the folk in the shop and Isaac could find another way of getting back to Glasgow.

The first noise Isaac was aware of was a *peep, peep, peep*. Like a smoke alarm. He looked up to the sky, to a bird circling above them. An oystercatcher spurred to action.

"Perfect!" Eddie shouted. He was doing a wee hopping dance – foot to foot. "Some fucking aim."

"What?" Isaac turned to him, confused. He was aiming for the petrol-bomb to land short, but he wouldn't have expected Eddie to want that. Was there a bit of a conscience in the man, after all? Was he worried about the face in the window?

"You're a bloody genius."

It was then that Isaac saw the stock on the forecourt. A metre or so from where the bottle had landed, against the wall of the shop. Stacked plastic jugs of blue antifreeze, tins of engine oil, and netted bags of kindling and firewood. Worst of all, three large gas bottles, one of them with the hose still attached. The flames were spreading closer to it all, with the insistence of a lapping tide.

"Bastards!" The call came from the doorway. The elderly woman was out of the door and hobbling towards the flames. "We know your faces! The police will too!"

Eddie's grin got wider, his hopping dance more exaggerated. As he taunted the woman, the younger lad – her grandson – came out of the shop. He rushed forward with a fire extinguisher and, for a moment, Isaac thought that all would be well. The flames had caught, though, and the fire was rising up the wall and licking at the gas bottles. The grandson dropped the extinguisher and grasped for his gran instead: pulling her back from the flames, from the patch of concrete in front of the shop.

"Fucking kaboom," Eddie hissed, "the whole thing's going to go."

He turned and scrambled back up into the minibus. Isaac stood rooted. The gran and grandson pulled in different directions. The grandson was stronger. He was forcing her away from the door, away from the flames, over towards the shore. He would get her clear.

Peep, peep, peep. The oystercatcher again. And then the horn, Eddie leaning on it, his face as twisted as a soldier in the middle of a gunfight. Isaac backed away from the flames, felt behind for the cool metal of the minibus. He'd only got one leg up before Eddie jarred into reverse and sped back. The passenger door swung heavily against Isaac's other leg. There was a sharp jolt of pain and then he dragged it up. He wanted to cry out, but the noise that came out was a whimper.

The flash of light came a split-second before the boom of the explosion. There was a rolling flame out onto the road in front of the Pier Shop, which then furled back in on itself. Black smoke billowed up and, as it cleared, Isaac could see that all the windows of the shop had gone and that the fire was catching at the frames.

"Told you, told you, told you," Eddie sang. "Fucking kaboom."

He swung the steering wheel, turning in a semi-circle across the road, so that Isaac had to peer back over his shoulder to look for the owner and her grandson. There they were, over by the upturned boats on the other side. She was crouched over but, as he watched, she lifted herself upright and shook her fist in the direction of the minibus.

Eddie put the bus in gear and screeched off in the direction of the commune.

"Well done, grasshopper," he said, "finally got your hands dirty."

12

They stepped out onto an expanse of scrubby marshland. Liz's plimsolls squelched with every step and she felt the ooze of it between her toes. All around them, amid the brown, were flowers with long stems and bursts of pink at the top. From a distance they looked like puffs of cotton, but up close you could see the intricacy of the petals. Reaching down, Liz trailed a hand across the top of them as they moved towards the shallow dunes at the far end.

Joan had approached her after lunch. They had taken Liz's car because Eddie needed the minibus for commune business. With Joan directing from the passenger seat, Liz followed the road through Glenborrodale and then turned at Salen. With sunglasses on, Joan sat staring out of the windscreen.

The midges were out in force. Clouds of them drifted along at waist-height. Liz scratched at her bare arms but Joan, in her black puffer jacket, didn't seem too bothered by them.

At the end of the path was a small sign with 'Singing Sands – Danger – Unexploded Munitions' printed on it.

There was a spitter-spatter of rain. Not enough to disperse the midges. Liz looked across at Joan, who was gathering her hair up into a bun on top of her head. Her cheekbones jutted out against skin which looked mottled and grey, as though she was recovering from a virulent rash, a debilitating illness. Maybe there was no blood left for the midges to feast on.

As they reached the sand, Joan pressed the toes of one foot against the heel of the other to remove her plimsolls. Liz did the same and they carried their shoes in their hands. As their bare feet rubbed against the grains of sand, there was a slight hum, like the vibrations of a tuning fork. Liz pursed her lips into a gentle whistle, a counter-melody. She tried to ignore the itch at her ankles as the midges found fresh skin.

"You're used to his way of doing things," Joan said. She wasn't looking at Liz, but was facing forward to look out at the small islands on the horizon. She kept her hair pinned up on top of her head, with one hand, but couldn't stop strands of it flailing.

Liz decided not to answer, only nod.

"Manslaughter," Joan said, taking off her sunglasses, "attempted rape, false imprisonment, falsified tax returns, actual bodily harm, blackmail, possession of a firearm, money laundering, endangering the safety of an aircraft…"

Liz allowed herself a smile. "You've been reading the internet forums."

"He's a convicted criminal, Liz."

"Some of those charges can't even be filed in a European court."

"That's your defence, is it?"

You could see that Joan was trying to hold her anger in. Those grey eyes of hers were narrowed, her fingers closed into fists. An idealistic young girl railing against the world, asserting her independence from her mentor. No understanding of what had gone before, of what had been achieved. She stood on the shoulders of giants and thought it was sea-level.

"Without him," Liz spat, "you're just a child up past her bedtime."

Joan shook her head. "He's a man with good ideas and a great deal of hubris."

Liz smiled. She didn't know what 'hub-rice' meant, but what did this child know of the ins-and-out of the last decade? The backroom deals, the planted evidence, the honeytraps set up in Zurich hotel suites. She could be forgiven her naivety.

"We're trying to build something here," Joan almost hissed this. "Something that is pure and true and free from that grubbiness and controversy and constant conflict—"

"You're pure as the driven snow, Joan," Liz interrupted, taking a step towards her. "But that only means the powers-that-be will piss all over you. They'll piss holes in it all, they'll watch it melt. Don't eat the snow, they'll say, it's yellow."

Liz took hold of Joan's shoulder. A faint sigh of air escaped from the puffer jacket as she squeezed.

"You've done wonderful things here," Liz said, "you've managed well. But you have no idea how difficult this next step is. We've been through it, we've faltered –"

"You've faltered," Joan interrupted, "but I won't."

"With our help…"

"No, you don't understand. I've worked it out. Not as a concept – like Ravi did – not on the back of a bloody envelope. Theory is all well and good, Liz, but it needs someone with a practical mind to do the calculations."

Liz looked at Joan, at the grey eyes peering into her own.

"Ravi was always convinced he was ready," Liz said. "With each volunteer, every time, he was absolutely certain he'd cracked it."

Joan shook her head. Up beneath her chin was a patch of red-raw skin. Like a graze. Her fingers moved towards it but stopped short.

"He convinced himself because he wanted it to be time. But I put in the legwork, Liz. I worked it out. There's data out there. From the experiments in the Sixties. It shows the toxin build-up –"

"Ravi knows about that. He had it all prepared."

"If he was truly certain, Liz, if he was truly prepared and fully convinced, then he would have been the one to volunteer, no?"

Further along the beach, a golden labrador came bounding over the top of a grass-spiked dune. The dog was followed, a second or two later, by a man in a flat-cap, holding a folded leash in his hand. Liz watched as the dog careened down towards the waves.

When she looked back to Joan, the younger woman was gazing at her intently. And Liz found tears springing to her eyes, a sense of a weight lifting from her shoulders. What Joan said was true. Ravi had always performed his calculations with a manic energy, with an impatience for any delay or doubt. And there was none of that with Joan. She was confident and assured, quietly certain that her next step would fall on solid ground.

"You're sure...?" Liz breathed.

"Twelve days," Joan said, nodding, "from midnight on the first morning to midnight on the eleventh night. Ready to welcome the twelfth day. Two-hundred and sixty-four hours."

"I thought the twelve days was just showmanship..."

"It's that obsession with spectacle, with show, that's held Ravi back from actually achieving the next step. You know that. In your heart, you know that. But I've worked out how the toxins build up and I've calculated where – exactly where – the incision has to be made."

Liz looked away. Back down the beach to where the dog had stopped to worry at something he'd found among the seaweed. Water shimmered in the rockpools around him. He carried on towards the waves and then veered away. In the wet sand, he left a curve of pawprints as he doubled back towards his owner. She wondered if his paws were raising a tune from the sand.

"Midnight tonight?" Liz asked, softly.

"Midnight tonight."

13

Grafton parked beside the kirk. There was a charred smell to the air as he stepped out of the hire car. More acrid than chimney smoke. It caught at the back of his throat and he looked up to the trees on the hill, half expecting to see the forest on fire. All was calm and still.

He'd driven past the entrance to the commune, slowing as he passed the office. There was a new metal fence, perhaps eight-foot tall and jagged at the top, stretching from the first cabin along to the dry-stone wall which marked the next field. There was a corrugated-iron gate in the centre of it. Barbed wire was bundled in untidy rolls across the top. A spotlight shone across the patch of road outside the office and another was set up by the side wall. The sheep were using it like a sun-lamp.

The track up from the kirk was uneven and pitted. It wasn't yet fully dark, but the shadows were long enough that he had to shuffle forwards to avoid tripping. The sculpture made it harder. He carried it cradled in his arms, peering around the sides and over the top to keep an eye on where he was going.

He paused several times before he reached the back of the commune. He left the sculpted head on the gravel for a moment and crept forwards to scout out what kind of medieval battlements he'd have to clamber over, but there was only the single-wire fence.

The sculpted head went under the wire easily enough and Grafton climbed over. He tensed, for a second, because the thought suddenly hit him that they might have a series of booby-traps rigged up along the perimeter. No alarms sounded, though, no blinding light flicked on. He took a step forward and then another.

As he inched down the hill, he caught sight of a third light – in addition to the spotlights. This one wasn't the constant glow of the other two. It was a flickering, shifting light, on the patch of grass between the cabins. A bonfire. The silhouette of the A-frame obscured it and then, as Grafton walked on, stood out sharply against it. Small figures moved around in front of the flames, dozens of them. Some of them were dancing and the sound of voices carried on the breeze. They were chanting something, regular and in unison, but Grafton couldn't make out the words.

He took several deep breaths and walked more slowly. He was watching his footing, because he was conscious that a stumble could lead to a rolling fall and that he could end up drawing attention to himself. He was a good distance away, but he didn't want to give them any reason to look away from the bonfire.

The final stretch before the A-frame was steeply pitched. He could take a wider course – easier with the sculpted head – but then he'd be stepping out into the open. So, instead, he launched himself down that grassy slope. Stumble, stumble, one wheeling arm and – feet sliding on gravel – his free hand came up to brace himself against the slates. His wrist jarred and twisted. He hissed air in through his teeth, but kept himself from swearing.

He put the sculpture down and massaged at the wrist. And in that pause, that moment before he sneaked around the side of the building, he heard a faint noise: *click, click, click.* Then a second's silence. *Click, click.* What was that? He stopped rubbing at his wrist, slowed his breath. *Click.*

The noise was coming from the front of the A-frame. Grafton left the sculpture where it was and crept closer. With tiny, tentative footsteps, he moved to the corner. Then he craned himself forward and peered around the edge.

Click, click. It was a lighter, clicking but not catching. A huge shadowed figure held it up to his face, trying to light a cigarette. He shook it. *Click.* As the flame sparked, Grafton saw that it was Whippet. He wore a dark bomber jacket over his white robe and plimsolls on his feet. And he was smoking, which was forbidden. More than that, he had the unmistakeable shadowed shape of a shotgun slung over his shoulder.

Grafton rocked back on his heels. He had been so close to stepping out for that final slope, a split-second from calling out as his wrist slammed against the building. And there was Whippet standing a few yards away with a gun casually hooked over his shoulder.

What now? He couldn't try to get into the A-frame, not while Whippet was there, and he didn't fancy trying to clamber soundlessly back up the hill either. There was a gap between the gravel and the sloped roof, though. An overhang. Not a big one, but enough to tuck himself into. So, curling himself into the foetal position, Grafton shimmied in underneath. Then he reached out and rolled the sculpted head in as well.

He tried to control his breathing. Keep it shallow and regular, time it with the gusts of breeze and the voices from the bonfire. Now that he was closer, he could hear the words. "No more sleep!" they chanted. "No more sleep!"

Footsteps crunched on gravel. Grafton's body went rigid. Squeezed in that tiny space, his muscles ached, but he dared not stretch them. The footsteps got closer. *Crunch, crunch.* And the smell of cigarette smoke.

"Fuck," Whippet breathed. Soft as a sigh, but Grafton was close enough to hear it. Close enough to see the plastic sole of his plimsolls, to reach out and pluck at the hairs on Whippet's bare ankle.

Grafton inched his fingers down to his pocket and felt for the scalpel he'd used for the sculpture. He'd decided to bring it at the last minute. He eased it out, then slowly lifted the plastic guard. If it came to it, a scalpel against a shotgun wouldn't be a fair fight, but maybe Grafton would have the element of surprise.

But then the plimsolls moved away. *Crunch, crunch.* And up onto the grass. A grunt of effort from Whippet as he began to climb the hill. The cigarette end was flung behind. It came arcing back to land only a metre or so from Grafton. The tip glowed orange. Whippet carried on up the hill and, a few seconds later, he was gone.

Grafton shuffled out. He stretched his legs, eased out the crick in his back, then clicked the plastic guard back onto the scalpel and slid it into his sleeve. Lifting the sculpted head, he quickly moved around the corner and up onto the wooden porch of the A-frame. He listened at the front door, but all was silent. So he twisted the handle and stepped inside.

The light from the bonfire was cast into the room by the window at the far side. It caused the shadows to flicker, sending little scurries and scuttles of movement across the wooden floor. Grafton was reminded of lizards, then of rats. The room was empty though. It was only that echoing space and, from outside, a new, more insistent chant: "Wake up, wake up, wake up, wake up!" It was like a call-and-response, with some folk shouting the first part and the majority barking the 'up' back at them.

Grafton moved over to the shrine table. There were several new drawings and a small whittled wooden figurine. A couple of cards could concertina inside one another and he slipped some pictures underneath as well. When he had a space big enough, he set the sculpted head carefully down and lifted the clay scalp. The digital camera sat inside the hollow, lens against one of the eye-holes. He repositioned it until he was certain it was facing the stage and then he started it recording. It had enough storage to run until the battery gave out. It would record far into the twelfth day.

Grafton took a final survey of the shrine table. There was no doubt that the sculpture dominated it, but it didn't look out of place. He was thankful that he had been so cack-handed in making it, because anything less rustic would have stuck out like a showroom car in a scrapyard.

With that job done, Grafton could now focus all of his energies on finding his son and sneaking him out of there. The two of them could clamber quickly up the hill to the back of the commune, keeping a lookout for Whippet, and skirt around to the waiting car. Once they got safely back to Glasgow, he'd phone the police and tell them where to find the camera. All being well, it would have recorded something they could use as evidence or, if not, something he could use for his story.

But he needed to find Isaac first. And the search could only start in one place: at the bonfire, around which the disciples were still chanting, "Wake up, wake up, wake up!"

14

The building of the bonfire began only minutes after Isaac and Eddie returned from the Pier Shop. One bedframe was carried out of a cabin by the disciples and placed on the grass, then a mattress followed. Others lent a hand to take out bunk beds, before an airbed from a cabin further up the hill and a sofa with sunken cushions joined the pile. Soon the Sleepless were carrying out any scrap of fabric that could – at a stretch – be used for bedding. The bonfire of bedframes and mattresses grew and grew.

It was lit just as the colour began to bleed out of the sky. Billows of black smoke came from the base of it and rose to join the darkening clouds. Then the flames began to lick around the edges, began to catch at the wooden frames. And there was the heat. Isaac didn't realise, until that moment, how cold he was. For days, a deep chill had set in, like a layer of frost along his bones. A shiver and a shudder that you forgot about, chalked up to hunger or tiredness, but it was there as a constant. And now there was heat, glorious, sweat-inducing heat.

The Sleepless gathered in front of it. They swayed towards it, held their arms out, spun in circles and marvelled at the absence of midges in the smoky air. Two women began to dance a jig, hooked at the elbows, and it became a reel when others joined. There was no music, so Jed began to sing, deep and throaty Scottish ballads which didn't feel out of place. He sang of Mairi's wedding, of Caledonia, and the Dowie Dens of Yarrow. Then he sang Three Craws and Isaac, hearing an echo of his mother, whispered along.

Liz was nowhere to be seen, though. Isaac paced among the gathered disciples looking for her. And, as he walked, everyone he passed either laid a hand on his shoulder or smiled across at him. Faces lit by dancing flames, some he recognised and plenty he didn't. Many of them murmuring thanks and congratulations. For the burning of the shop, for the arson down by the shore which he was so deeply ashamed of.

There was no doubt in his mind now: he needed to leave. This was not what he'd envisaged when he told his mum to bring him along. Only, he couldn't think how to get clear of the commune. He was stranded. The plan had been to take his Euros to the Pier Shop, but that was no longer an option, and what could he do now? Call a taxi and hope that they'd accept foreign currency? Knock on doors in the village and throw himself at the mercy of the locals?

Behind him, the singing had faded and voices were shouting instead. Three words, over and over. Isaac couldn't make out what they were saying. He wandered into the cabin closest to the bonfire. The building would be in danger with the slightest shift in wind direction, but that didn't seem to concern those inside. Debbie was sitting at the table, intent on twisting at a wire coat hanger. She was using a butter knife to curl it around. She wielded it awkwardly because of the lumpy bandage on her finger.

"Ah, Isaac honey," she said, looking up, "this is your kind of thing – help me."

"What is it you're doing?"

"An eye, an eye."

As if that explained anything. Isaac let the silence settle for a moment, waiting to see if Debbie had anything to add. She swept her grey-red hair to the side.

"It's an emblem," she said, "like…like a tattoo."

Isaac stepped closer. The twisted wire had a doubled-over stretch as a handle and then an oval on the end. A tiny piece of wire continued into the centre and began a smaller circle inside. It did look like a staring eye, only without the pupil.

"How can it be a tattoo?" Isaac asked. "Do you mean tattoo…?"

"It's a type of tattoo." Debbie lifted the eye and showed it to him. "And we'll do the pupil with the point at the other end."

"Do you mean branding? Is that what you mean?"

Debbie shook her head and tutted with her tongue. As if Isaac was a schoolkid complaining that it was reheated cottage pie for dinner again. From outside, the chanting grew louder. Two words this time; the second shouted.

"It's a small thing," Debbie said, "to show loyalty."

"It's burning people's skin, Debbie. It's permanently disfiguring them."

"Deary me," Debbie muttered, "what a fuss to make."

"Where's Joan?" Isaac asked. "Where's my mum?"

Debbie tutted again. "If you don't want to take part, Isaac, no one's going to force you."

Then she stood and bustled past him, the improvised branding iron in her hand. Isaac hesitated for a moment, then turned to follow her.

As she walked up to the bonfire, Debbie gathered quite a trail of disciples. The queue formed on the move, like a conga line. Folk from closer in towards the bonfire skipped back to join, called out to others to hold them a place. By the time Debbie stopped a few yards away from the flames, she had about a dozen disciples lined up behind her.

Debbie didn't hold the wire out towards the fire. Instead she looked around. Isaac followed the direction of her gaze. Eddie was at the corner of the cabin, where the gravel path started. Nodding over to Debbie, he stepped out and raised his arms.

"Friends," he called, "we're approaching the moment of Joan's next step. This is the crux of it. At midnight she becomes truly wakeful and it will not be easy. Joan will need our support, will need us all to see her through these longest and darkest hours."

From the queue behind, Isaac heard a chant starting. It was an echo of what he'd heard inside. "Wake up," they called, "wake up, wake up, wake up!"

Eddie held up a hand for silence. "It is time," he said, "for us to show our dedication, for us to demonstrate that we are ready to stand with her and bear witness. It's time, friends, to proudly display your love for this family, your devotion to this cause.

"It is no more than a moment's pain, no more than a pinprick. But what a gesture, friends, what a way to show your appreciation for the sacrifice Joan is making for us all."

Isaac looked back over to Debbie. She held the wire hanger out towards the flames, as if toasting marshmallows. She kept the rest of her body back from the heat, her face turned away. The Sleepless, behind her, began to push and jostle. Those who had stepped out of line to listen to Eddie tried to force their way back in, those who found themselves near the front of the queue fought off any encroachment.

"This is our pact," Eddie called. "This is us saying that there will be no more half-measures. Following her example, we will all endeavour to take that next step…"

Isaac backed away from the pool of light cast by the bonfire. He moved slowly, keen not to attract the attention of Eddie, whose eyes were roving back-and-forth.

At the front, Debbie set the makeshift branding iron in at the base of the flames and took a step away. Eddie strode over towards her. Seizing his chance, Isaac darted around the side of the cabin to where the undergrowth was dense enough to hide. He leant there, his back against the wooden wall, and hunched over to catch his breath.

"Isaac," came a hiss from the bushes. "Isaac, over here."

15

There were a couple of walkers on the shore road, the reflective strips of their jackets catching in the headlights. They stepped onto the grass verge and Liz zipped past. One of them was carrying a torch. As the car passed, the beam lifted and shone into Liz's eyes. She screwed up her face and gripped the wheel.

Then she caught sight of the flickering flames up on the slope of the commune. Between the cabins. She looked across to Joan, waiting for her to notice. It only took a second or two, then her hand went up to her sunglasses and lifted them down from her face.

"Part of the plan for this evening?" Liz asked.

Joan nodded. "A bonfire, the tattooing, and then the next step."

"We'd better go join the celebrations then," Liz said, pushing down on the accelerator.

As she drove, she stole another glance at Joan. In the half-light of dusk, all the hollows and crevices of her face were shadowed. She was a beautiful young woman, beneath the veil of tiredness. And that veil would lift after the next step was taken. In the days to come, as word spread of their success, her photo would be on the front page of every paper, her name in every headline. There was no doubt it was exciting but, Liz realised, there was also a danger to it that she'd overlooked. She needed to get word to Ravi and make sure he felt included. Jealousy was not an emotion that Ravi was accustomed to dealing with.

They rounded the corner and the gritty grey light of evening was brightened by the spotlight at the commune entrance. Liz braked sharply. In front of the gates was a cluster of people, maybe thirty or so in total. They were milling around on the road. Several of them carried torches, but there were a couple with candles as well. The cardboard placards were out again.

Over on the far side, someone had left off a flare. Orange smoke – thick as sherbet – drifted up and hung in the air above the crowd.

As the car inched forwards, the villagers peeled off to the side or shifted into tighter-knit groups. Liz began to turn the wheel, though, and the protestors saw that the car was arcing in towards the commune. A shout went up. Not a word, but a yell of anger. Liz reached across and, calmly, clicked the lock. All the doors went thunk.

The nose of the car was at the closed gate now. And the smoke from the flare had risen to obscure the spotlight, an orange miasma. The faces around them were glowing with it. A hand slapped against the roof, another against the back window. The crowd was chanting: three words, over and over.

"Can you make out what they're saying?" Liz asked, looking over at Joan.

"Justice for Moira," Joan said, softly. "The woman from the Pier Shop."

The corrugated metal gate began to slide open in front of them. The car shook as hands pushed at the side of it, a fist battered against the passenger window. And, as the gap at the gate widened, there was a swell of movement. Like soldiers storming a castle, the locals moved forward and then, suddenly, they shrank back. There was a scream, a scattering, as people pushed and stumbled and fell away. Whippet had appeared at the gate, a shotgun held casually across his chest. He lifted a hand and beckoned the car inside. Liz revved and the rear wheels spun on the gravel. As the car lurched forward, a great globule of spit landed on the windscreen in front of her.

Once they were inside, Whippet pulled the gate back across and the shouts receded. Looking in the side mirror, Liz saw him give them a thumbs-up. He looked entirely unflustered. Joan, by contrast, was frowning deeply. She raised a hand to tuck a strand of hair behind her ear and Liz noticed the slightest tremble to her fingers.

"What if they ruin it all?" she said, quietly.

"They won't," Liz said, smiling. "You've done the calculations up to the procedure itself, yes? You've worked out how to proceed to the next step. But I'm the one who's been planning for the aftermath of that. Multiple times, over many years..."

Liz sat forward and pulled at the lever to send some washer fluid up onto the windscreen. The wipers swished – once, twice – and the phlegm was gone.

"You concentrate on what you need to do," she said, "and leave the rest to me. That's what I'm for, that's what the likes of Whippet and Eddie are for."

"I don't want the message to be tainted, though."

"Like I say, leave it to me. We've built up a network, we have an infrastructure...Eddie's been preparing for this for months and I've been prepared for years. Trust in him. Trust in me."

Joan looked across at her and they shared a smile.

"We'll protect you," Liz said. "Come what may."

16

"What the fuck is all this—?" Grafton said. "Looks like that scene from *The Wicker Man*."

Isaac shrugged. "What are you doing back here?"

"I've come to get you."

"About bloody time."

They both looked out at the bonfire. A group of the Sleepless had joined hands and were slowly turning in a circle with their heads tipped back.

Grafton was crouched in behind a tangle of weeds. He'd avoided the nettles, but thistles and sticky willow plucked at his clothing. He inched forwards to get a better view of Isaac. He looked thin, gaunt around the cheekbones.

"Have they brainwashed you?" Grafton asked.

Isaac looked down at him. "What?"

"You heard."

"No, Dad — I'm fine." Isaac paused, shook his head. "You know I'm only here because of you, right? Mum brought me, but it was you that started this whole thing. And it was you that left your son with twenty quid for a week's worth of groceries, with an empty fridge. You know that —"

"I'm sorry, I —"

"Let me fucking finish. Because I came here looking for you, didn't I? I came here because I thought you might have got yourself into some sort of trouble and, right enough, you'd been wandering through the commune waving a bloody recorder around like some spoof of a spy. Right?"

Grafton left a silence to make sure that his son had finished, that he'd got it all out of his system. For now, at least. They could have it out properly later, could deal with the recriminations of it when they were safely clear of this place.

"I'm sorry," Grafton repeated. "Mea culpa."

"Fuck, you're speaking Latin. It's not me they brainwashed then..."

Grafton grinned. "You ready to leave?"

A cheer went up from the Sleepless gathered around the fire. Isaac twisted around and Grafton followed the direction of his stare. Joan and Liz had appeared at the crest of the hill, walking up towards the others. Joan wore a black puffer jacket and jogging trousers. She had plimsolls on her feet.

It was odd to see Liz after all those years. You could still tell she was the same woman, of course, but she seemed broader in the shoulders and her hair – once so neatly tamed, pinned, and controlled – was like unpicked knitting.

"I don't think you can say goodbye, Isaac," Grafton whispered. "It's too tricky."

"I just want to see if she's alright."

"She'll be fine, she knows how to take care of herself."

Isaac shook his head. "She's got all this pressure – they all look to her."

Grafton frowned over at his son. And, in that moment, it occurred to him that Isaac probably wasn't talking about Liz, that his concern was for Joan. He rocked back. He'd been close to the edge of the bushes, close to reaching out from the cover to grasp at his son's robe. But he couldn't. He couldn't grapple and bear-hug him back to the car like you would with a toddler having a tantrum.

"Please, Isaac," he said, "come with me and we'll go to the police. People are getting hurt."

"The thing is, Dad, people are participating willingly..."

"Aye, like I was *willingly* doused in acid."

Isaac's eyes widened at that. Grafton held out his bandaged arm, but the A&E nurse had done such a neat job that it now looked no worse than a dressing on a playground scrape.

Out at the bonfire, Eddie had ducked into the middle of the circle of Sleepless. They had stopped spinning and were listening to him. Grafton and Isaac were too far away for the words to carry. The disciples in the line leading to the bonfire started to shift backwards to let Joan through.

"And you've been sleeping?" Grafton asked Isaac. "Even a little?"

No response. Isaac was too busy watching.

"Because you know it's all bullshit, right? You know that?"

Down at the bonfire, Joan slipped off her plimsolls, then reached down and rolled off her jogging trousers. The bottom of her robe flopped out from under the puffer jacket.

Isaac leant down towards the bushes. His face was inches from Grafton's now, his body hunched over at the side of the scrubland as if he were bramble-picking.

"She's going to do it," he hissed. "She's going to the front of the line."

Grafton had to get his legs out from under him. They were turning numb with little flurries of pins and needles. He levered himself backwards and sat on his arse. Something jagged into his thigh, but it wasn't worth shifting for. He could no longer see out to the bonfire, but he could still see his son.

"What does it matter?" he said. "It's not the first time that people have come to harm up here."

"It's not what she wants, though. It can't be."

Grafton looked up at his son, but Isaac was turned towards the bonfire. Down at this level, the smell of the burning wood was overpowered by the mulch of damp leaves.

"Leave it, son." Grafton squeezed his eyes shut, then open again. "You'll be off to Art School soon... And – my god, Isaac – you'll make a success of it. I can see the passion you have for it, that hunger and drive and...it reminds me of when I had that. And I threw that away. Not on you or your mother, but on the drink. I wasted that—"

Grafton came up onto his knees and peered out, beyond Isaac, to the group at the bonfire.

Reaching down, Joan held onto the bottom hem of her robe and, with one fluid movement, pulled it up and over her head. She threw it to the side and stood completely naked. Goose-flesh raised on Grafton's neck at even the thought of the cold. But she stood without a shiver.

"It's not what she wants," Isaac repeated, in a whisper.

Eddie moved forwards, then, to go and join her beside the bonfire. And the rest of the Sleepless stirred as well, spreading out across the grass in a wide semi-circle so that they all had a view of the scene in front of them.

Too late, Grafton realised that Isaac was following too. He was already several strides away from the bushes, already out in the open. Grafton rustled out to the edge of the weeds but didn't dare step out further.

"Isaac," he hissed after his son. "Where are you going?"

Isaac looked back over his shoulder. "Wait there."

17

Eddie turned as Isaac approached. The homemade branding iron was still in at the base of the flames. A couple of the Sleepless were crouched down — close enough to singe their eyebrows — strategizing about how to retrieve it.

"Ah, grasshopper," Eddie said, "just the man."

"Why?" Isaac stopped half-a-yard short of the group. "What?"

"It'd be a nice gesture to have the kid do it. Don't you think, Joan?"

Joan turned. There wasn't a trace of self-consciousness about her. She scratched at her hip, set her head on one side. Isaac tried to avoid looking at the wiry brush of hairs at her crotch, at the way her left breast hung a half-inch heavier than her right.

"On the shoulder," Eddie said, "as straight as you can manage."

Joan's eyes — those grey eyes — softened as she smiled across at Isaac, taking on the light of the fire. They sparkled and shimmered with it, like waves beneath sunlight. Isaac sucked in a breath. He looked at Eddie, who was staring back at him with the same intensity as outside the Pier Shop.

"You don't want this," Isaac said to Joan. "You don't really want to do all this, do you?"

He looked at her shoulder. The curve of it and the protruding clavicle, mirroring the smoothness of her naked hip and the jutting hipbone.

She held out a hand and cupped his cheek. Isaac felt as though his bare feet lifted from the grass, as if he was floating, suspended there between the warmth of the fire and the coolness of her fingers.

"Just a couple of hours until the next step," she said, softly.

Isaac shook his head. "You can leave. I'll take you."

From behind him, Eddie snorted derisively.

Joan smiled. "Everyone here will wear this mark to show that they are ready to bear witness, to demonstrate their commitment to taking the next step to true wakefulness."

"Jesus," Isaac breathed. He thought he understood her after those late-night chats, that afternoon up at the ruined village. These gestures, these gimmicks – the methods – were supposed to be for show, a form of theatricality that bound them all together and gave her the opportunity to demonstrate the possibility of a better life. A life of self-sufficiency and seclusion, protected from the harshness of the outside world. Not this brutality and paranoia, these acts of torture.

Far off, down in the village, a dog barked. It was answered, a second later, by a second bark from further off. Isaac wondered if the locals had seen the bonfire and phoned the police. Where was the nearest station, though? Probably miles away.

"Your body will go into shock, you know that, right?" he asked, not meeting Joan's eye.

"I'm prepared for it," she said.

Isaac took a breath. He could, perhaps, lay the wire gently against her skin. He might be able to keep it to first or second-degree burns. Maybe he could save her from the worst of it; so that she carried through with the gesture, but in a way that would heal over in a few days' time.

"How would I even do it?" Isaac asked. "The wire's red-hot."

"You lift it, youngster," Eddie sneered. "You reach in there and you lift it."

"I'll burn my hands, though."

"And…?"

Isaac felt that word travel up his spine. Not as a shiver, but as a jolt. With the slightest movement of his head, he checked that no one was close enough to grab him. He took a step back, away from Joan. He turned to his mum. She was standing watching, wide-eyed and smiling encouragingly. As if she was watching a school prize day or awards dinner.

"I'm going to Art School," he said, with his eyes on her. "I need my hands, you know that."

Liz didn't stop smiling, but her head tipped onto its side. As if he was a child saying something charmingly naïve, raising an endearing objection to having a bath or going off to bed.

"You're in or out, Isaac," she said, "there is no middle ground."

"Understand," Eddie added, "that this way of life is ending and we're preparing for a new order. It's a simpler way, son, and it's a way that requires us to commit to each other."

"But..." Isaac felt tears in his eyes, but he couldn't blink them away. He looked back to Joan. "In two hours, with the twelfth day, it will be over..."

She shook her head. "In two hours, it'll *begin*."

Isaac brought his hands up from his side. He looked at them in the firelight – at the delicate whorls and creases, at the fingerprints he'd left on a thousand clay pieces. He turned them over, thought of the paint he'd scrubbed from his nailbeds.

He looked back up at Joan. She needed to understand – even if his own mother didn't – that this was all he had, that these hands were his future. He was going to make things – he was going to continue to make things – which would change the world.

Isaac spun, on his heels, and sprinted, ignoring the shouts from behind. With his eyes on the bushes at the edge of the scrubland, Isaac ran as quickly as he could up the slope, away from the bonfire and his mother and the disciples and the girl he'd briefly thought was the messiah.

18

Liz watched him run with something close to the disappointment she'd felt at Ravi's sentencing hearing. As Isaac slipped and scrambled up the hill, Liz admitted to herself for the first time how much she'd been hoping he'd stay. She didn't think he was ready to bear witness to Joan's next step, hadn't thought he was strong enough to embrace life as a disciple, but somewhere, deep down, she had hoped that he would prove her wrong. That would have meant a great deal.

Still, if his decision was to go home, then Isaac should have left when Liz gave him the Euros or asked her again for the car keys. She could have driven him to the nearest bus stop or spoken to the local postie to see if he could hitch a lift. There were a hundred-and-one ways of getting off the peninsula, but running wasn't one of them.

Around her, the Sleepless all blinked at one another, then peered across to Joan. Her face had fallen and her arms had folded across her chest, covering her breasts.

Eddie stepped forward. "After him, then!"

A couple of the disciples took a half-pace.

"No!" Liz called, waving an arm back and forth. There was no anger in the word, it was scornful if anything. She frowned across to Eddie. "Where's he going to go? Someone – one person – go after him and tell him he's being foolish. Then we'll pack him up and get him in a taxi…"

Eddie didn't look convinced.

"He's not a danger," Liz reasoned, "and he's my son, remember…"

With a shrug, Eddie nodded. But there was a shout from one of the disciples behind him and his head snapped back around to look up the hill. Liz followed his gaze. As Isaac passed the log cabin, a second figure came out from the side of the building and joined him. The man was older, thicker around the middle. Together, they stumble-tripped up the slope. And, as the second figure peered back over his shoulder, Liz saw that it was him: Tom *bloody* Grafton.

This time the Sleepless didn't wait for instruction. Two of the younger men at the edges of the group set off immediately, one of them hollering at the top of his lungs. Liz looked across at Eddie. There was a practised ease to the way he reached into his sleeve and pulled out a knife. It had a long and thin blade, the type of knife a butcher might use for de-boning a carcass.

Liz swiftly checked for Whippet and his shotgun. He was nowhere to be seen. She needed to buy Isaac a few extra seconds.

Springing forwards, Liz joined the milling throng of disciples. Eddie was elbowing his way through, his knife held out in front like a bayonet. He was shouting, calling for others to follow. Liz focused on his bare ankles, the brown hairs of his legs meeting the green of the grass. She was close enough to take one skipping step forward and hook her foot in front.

He went flying, he went sprawling. The knife arced through the air and embedded itself in the soft ground. As he fell, he let out a great roar of anger and twisted his neck to look for the person who'd tripped him. But Liz was too quick. She'd already stepped aside, melted back into the crowd, with her eyes averted and her face blank.

She looked back to the hill, to where the two figures were disappearing into the copse of trees at the back of the commune. She'd done what she could. Or as much as she was willing to do. She'd bought them some time, but the rest was up to them.

19

As soon as Grafton saw Isaac coming, he broke cover and started to scramble up the hill. He needed the head-start. Isaac caught up as they passed the A-frame and Grafton was a couple of yards behind by the time they reached the trees. Behind them, several of the Sleepless were giving chase.

"Quick." Grafton fumbled the car keys from his pocket. "You go down to the kirk. The car's parked there. I'll lead them off the other way. Meet you down on the road."

"Why can't we both go—"

Isaac was interrupted by a shout from behind. Eddie was calling on Whippet, who was further down towards the gate with his shotgun in hand. Whippet turned and started towards them with a lumbering run.

"Go!" Grafton hissed, shoving the keys into Isaac's hand.

Isaac sped off and Grafton waited a second or two, to make sure that those coming up the hill could see him veering off to the left. The plan was to carry on as far as he could and then duck behind a tree, or crouch down in a ditch. He had no hope of out-running them – his lungs were already making a noise like the last squeezing from a bottle of washing-up liquid.

Still, Isaac would get clear. They could do what they liked to him, as long as Isaac got clear.

Grafton stumbled on, tripping on thick roots. The trees cleared suddenly. There was a gap with three or four stumps overgrown by weeds. And – *shit* – there were two white-robed figures. They had managed to head him off, had circled around to intercept him and he'd run straight out in front of them...

Except, no. They hadn't seen him. The two Sleepless huddled together on a tree stump weren't looking over in his direction. They were one on top of the other, moving rhythmically and grunting. The one underneath had acne scars on his neck and, straddling him, was a girl with her hair tied up with a yellow scarf. Ally and Morven.

Trying to keep to the shadows, Grafton took long, careful strides towards the trees at the far side. The grunts from Ally were picking up speed, Morven kept her head tipped back. You could hear the faint slap of flesh against flesh.

Grafton held his breath. As he reached the trees, there was a shout from the other side of the clearing and Eddie, Whippet and two others burst through.

"What the fuck!?" Eddie hollered.

Ally screeched.

Grafton didn't wait around. He made for the single-wire fence that led to the next field. It seemed doubtful that the shagging couple would distract Eddie for long, but maybe it would give him enough time to get himself down onto the shore road.

"Fucking traitors!" came the call from Eddie. Morven let out a scream that caused Grafton to check his stride, for a split-second. It was the kind of yelp a dog might let out if kicked by its owner.

Going back was pointless. He needed to get the police involved.

Ahead was the field, bathed in moonlight and dotted with resting sheep. Then, beyond that, down on the road, were the twin headlights of a car creeping along from the kirk.

It was only a few hundred yards. It might pop both his lungs, leave his heart hanging by one artery, but he could surely make it. One last dash. Taking a deep breath, he set off at a stumbling, tripping, arm-wheeling run. Out into the open, his footfalls clumsy but gathering speed, downhill momentum that would surely carry him down to Isaac and—

Bang. Something impacted with his right-hand side, catapulting him forward and then dragging him back. In the moment before the sound of the gunshot registered, Grafton looked down expecting to see a great beast hanging from his side. A dog with its jaws clamped beneath his ribcage, a wolf tearing at his flesh. He spun, twisting sideways, and fell to the grass. And the warmth of blood came before the flaring of pain, before the all-consuming agony.

He tried to turn his head, tried to look up to the line of trees, but his side was heavy now, was pinning him down to the ground. Even the slightest movement was searing.

"I've been shot," he said, aloud, although there was no one to hear it. The sheep in the field had scattered and Isaac was down on the main road—

Shit. Isaac.

"Stay away—" Grafton tried to lift his voice into a shout. "Keep going!"

He was answered by the sound of thudding footsteps, by panting breath. It didn't come from the bottom of the field, but from out of the trees...

20

Isaac heard the gunshot and saw his dad fall. In one movement, he pushed open the door of the car and tumbled out, but he hadn't even made it over the ditch at the side of the road by the time the white-robed figures ran out from the trees. Crouching down, Isaac watched as they ran up to Grafton.

Two of them leant over and lifted him and the screech – a banshee wail that echoed around the bay – told Isaac that he was still alive.

Drawing in a breath, Isaac looked at the hire car. It had rolled on a few metres, in an arc, so that the headlights were now pointing out to sea. He could get back behind the wheel and – what? Speed to the nearest phone-box? Or back to the protestors at the front gate? He'd already stopped there on the way along. Maybe it was that which had cost him precious seconds. He'd told them to call the police, raise the army – there was torture happening up there in the commune, there was likely to be dozens of casualties even from the branding and, come midnight, god alone knew what would happen...

Isaac peered back up into the field. The two Sleepless were carrying his dad between them, back up into the woods. Pushing himself up the bank and then through the wire fence, Isaac began to follow.

He had no trouble keeping up. In fact, at several points he had to hang back. It was Eddie and Whippet lugging Grafton. Another disciple carried the shotgun and was using it to lead two shuffling disciples, Morven and Ally, forward through the trees and back down the hill towards the A-frame. Isaac watched from the shadow of the woods until they all disappeared inside and then set off, at a sprint, down the slope.

At the back of the A-frame, Isaac looked up at the first-floor window. It was open a crack. That was the small room where

Joan prepared herself for the evening meetings.

Isaac took hold of the drainpipe and levered himself up. He thought it might come away from the wall, but it held. Getting his right-foot onto the cross-pipe, he pulled himself up onto the windowsill. He jammed a hand in at the window and tugged it fully open, then he swung his legs in.

The room was sparsely furnished – side table, dressing table, standard lamp in the corner – and there was a patch of darker carpet where the bed had been. Isaac moved over to the door and eased it open. He crept out onto the landing. He could hear music: trumpet-led jazz. There was a murmur of conversation beneath it. Dropping to his stomach, Isaac edged to the top of the stairs and looked down onto the room below.

The hall was packed. The disciples were swaying from side to side. Up on the platform, Morven whimpered as Eddie and Whippet tied her hands with rope. Beside her, Grafton was already strung up to the central rafter. He twisted slightly – as if in the breeze – and blood dripped from his side to the wood, where it glistened in the light from the strip-bulbs overhead.

After they'd finished binding Morven's hands, Whippet started on Ally. Eddie strode up to the edge of the stage and waved his hands for silence. Isaac inched forwards. He could see Joan standing at the front, huddled into her puffer jacket, but there was no sign of his mum.

"In this endgame," Eddie shouted, "every misstep is a weakness to be exposed by the enemy. And they are not just journalists – not anymore – they are MI5 agents and spies and the forces of corrupt capitalism and wealth. This final step is the most difficult, friends, because it is the one they do not want us to take…"

With the eyes of the disciples riveted to the stage, Isaac started to creep forwards. On his hands and knees, he moved slowly down the stairs and out onto the floor at the bottom. He looked around desperately for something – anything – he could use as a weapon.

"This is not correction," Eddie was saying, "this is not us saying that you have strayed. This is us demonstrating that we will protect Joan as she takes this next step, that we will ensure that nothing interferes with her plans for tonight and for the bright dawn of a new day."

Behind him, up on the stage, Grafton's feet were scuffing against the platform as he tried to stand up straight. His head was nodding then jerking upright, like a child trying to stay awake.

"This rat came scurrying back." Eddie held an arm out towards Grafton. "We had given him fair warning, had we not? We had shown him what would happen."

Isaac crawled forwards, aiming for the shrine at the side. He kept as close to the wall as he could, his elbow against the skirting board.

"The other two," Eddie was saying, "will be offered the chance to atone. Take them away, Whippet, and we'll deal with them later. But this fucking rat has been given his last chance…"

Isaac shimmied in underneath the shrine table and looked out, again, at the stage.

"…he distracted us from our moment at the bonfire when we were inscribing our support for our beloved Joan's next step, but in doing so he has also given us an *opportunity*…"

With shotgun slung over his shoulder, Whippet was leading Ally and Morven towards the exit. Where was Isaac's mum? Surely she wouldn't allow this to happen. In spite of all that had come between them, Grafton was still her ex-husband, still the father of her child.

Eddie held up the knife with a long, thin blade. "Everyone in this room will come up on the stage and contribute to his final moments. Everyone. This is the moment when we are all bound together, and that bond will lift us up in the days to come."

Isaac felt Eddie's words up the length of his spine. They were going to subject his dad to a death by a thousand cuts. Not content with him bleeding out from the shotgun wound, they were going to speed up the process. And with that realisation, came another – Isaac couldn't wait for the police, he was going to have to act himself.

"Who is going to volunteer?" Eddie asked, up on the stage.

All eyes scanned the crowd. There was a pause. And then, a few rows back, a hand was raised. A hand with a lumpy bandage wrapped around the index finger. Debbie stood and began to make her way forward.

21

"Please hold," the automated voice said. *"Bleiben Sie bitte in der Leitung."*

Liz was in the office. She had stretched the phone cable across from the desk to the window so that she could peer through the blinds. The locals still chanted on the other side of the gate and, as she watched, a stone was thrown and cracked against the spotlight to the side. The light flickered then died and a cheer went up from the crowd.

The automated voice on the phone clicked across to hold music. Something orchestral, classical.

Liz had watched the others scrambling up the hill until she was sure that they were going to chase Grafton rather than Isaac. Then she turned and made her way hurriedly to the office. Her conversation with Joan at the beach had brought two things into sharp focus. Firstly, Joan was likely to succeed where Ravi had failed. And, secondly, Ravi wouldn't necessarily take too kindly to that fact.

"Please hold. *Bleiben Sie bitte in der Leitung.*"

It was vital that she got word through to Ravi before Joan took the next step. That way he could share the credit, could take this young disciple under his wing. But she couldn't stay on hold with the Austrian Prison Service and miss the opportunity to witness history herself. She looked at the clock on the desk: 22.32.

Twisting the phone cord around her finger, Liz stepped away from the window and over to the only computer. The internet browser was slow to load. When it did, she opened up the account and quickly set up a private group message. She only included disciples she knew well. Only people she trusted.

Ardnamurchan, Scotland, she typed. *Promising disciple, Joan, ready for next step at midnight GMT. Tell Ravi before then if possible.*

Will update.

She listened to the hold music for a second, considering if there was anything else she should add. Then she pressed send and returned to the window. Through the blinds came an intermittent blue flash. It only seemed to come from one vehicle, but it showed they were circling. From somewhere, out in the bay, came the grumbling of an outboard motor.

"Please hold. *Bleiben Sie bitte —*"

Liz placed the phone back into the cradle. Then she reopened her private message and added another line: *May require reinforcements.* She pressed send and closed the browser. Then, calmly, she flicked through the papers on the desk until she found the security plans for the commune. Eddie had added to her original pencil drawings, had marked tiny crosses against all the buildings and pathways where he'd planted the plastic explosive from the pallets.

Liz reached into the bottom drawer and lifted out a tangle of electrical wire and a half-dozen blasting caps. Then, with a final glance at the rolling blue light coming through the slatted blind, she turned for the door.

22

Grafton had trouble focusing on Debbie as she approached the stage. His vision was blurred, his head spun and – with a pulse of blackness – he had to gulp away a wave of nausea. He watched her as though underwater, as if through an ever-shifting murky sea.

As she stepped up onto the platform, though, their eyes made contact and his mind surfaced. A sharpening of adrenaline. Maybe, just maybe, she was going to be his salvation. They had been close, after all, in his first days at the commune. She might take Eddie's knife and cut him loose.

Grafton tried to straighten, to ready himself. The movement spasmed at his side and he recoiled away, and then again, until he was twisted back into a slump with a pain so intense that he retched. With the taste of bile in his throat, he narrowed his eyes and looked again at Debbie. She bit at her lip as she took the knife, but she didn't falter.

He was aware of the cut on his thigh because he felt the wetness of blood against his skin, tacky against the material of his trousers, but the pain of it didn't register. He plunged down, again, into the swirl of dizziness. The wound at his side also seemed to be numbing at the edges, the agony of it receding. Dimly, Grafton registered that this probably wasn't a good thing, but he didn't care. At least Isaac had made his escape. That was all that mattered.

With an effort, Grafton lurched his head up and peered directly at the sculpture on the shrine table. The camera would still be recording, there would be a video of his murder. That was a comfort. There would be a reckoning, at some point, for what had been done to him.

But the sculpture was being lifted. By a figure in a white robe. Grafton tried to call out, but all that came out was a gargle from his throat. The figure looked familiar – his edges indistinct but something about the hair and the way that, after lifting the sculpture, he took a skipping step and then hurtled himself towards the stage. Like a wrestler making for the ring. *Isaac*.

"*Go the fuck to sleep!*" Isaac screamed, lifting the statue up beyond his shoulder and bringing it around to meet the side of Eddie's head. It connected with a wet crack. Right above the eye. Eddie swayed for a moment. Then the blood came and Eddie went down, face-first and with no attempt to break his own fall. He seemed to rebound off the platform, in a juddering bounce, and then he was still. He lay contorted in an unnatural shape; one arm twisted underneath, the other on top.

There was silence in the hall. Grafton swivelled his head to look at Debbie, standing holding the knife loosely at her side, and at Joan, who was clambering onto the stage to kneel down at Eddie's side. Then he felt fingers up at his wrists, untying the knots. He looked across to Isaac.

"What's the—" Grafton had to swallow away the taste of bile. "What's the plan?"

Isaac opened his mouth to reply. From out in the room, came another noise. One Grafton had heard often in films, but never in real-life. The sound of a cartridge moving into the chamber of a gun: *tch-tch*.

Grafton froze, his arms still stretched up to the rafter. The rope unravelled itself, though, and his hands were free.

"Like father, like son, eh?" came a voice from the back of the room. Whippet stood there, looking along the length of his gun at Isaac. With his hands in the air, Isaac backed away towards the edge of the stage. "Don't fucking move," Whippet hissed. And Isaac stopped.

There was a whisper of conversation now, as people turned to their neighbours and asked what to do next, how they should react. Grafton looked down at Joan. She was still crouched down beside the motionless Eddie. She was only a couple of feet from Grafton. Slowly, gradually, Grafton curled his fingers down towards his sleeve.

"Keep your hands in the air..." Whippet was saying to Isaac. "Walk slowly towards—"

A scream interrupted him. High-pitched and loud enough to rattle the glass in the windows. Grafton had launched himself at Joan and grappled her into a headlock, with the small red scalpel held against her throat. All eyes flicked across to them. And so did the barrel of Whippet's shotgun.

Joan was flailing in his arms, her elbows jerking backwards. Grafton felt each and every movement at his side, his wound tearing itself further open, but he clung on grimly. He would pass out before he let go. This was his one and only chance to save Isaac.

"Stay away!" he shouted. "She can't stay awake with a slit throat!"

Joan yelped. She clawed and scratched at Grafton's arm, but he kept his grip. Her eyes were widened in panic, her face flushing red. Several of the disciples closest to the stage rushed forward. Whippet moved forward too. Grafton took a step backwards, dragging Joan with him.

"Stay back," Joan spluttered. "Don't let him... I'm so close..."

Grafton took another step, this time sideways towards the stairs. Isaac quickly moved across to help and Whippet, although his gun swung around to follow, didn't intervene. There was no chance of him finding an angle to shoot them, not unless he was prepared to slice half of Joan's head away in the process.

They began to inch up the stairs. Grafton went first, his scalpel still held at Joan's throat, but Isaac was dragging most of her weight. Grafton had to grit his teeth, summon the last of his strength. First stair, then the second. The third creaked.

"Stay back," Joan repeated. "Stay back."

Whippet had moved up onto the stage. He kept his gun trained on them. And, all around him, the Sleepless started to hiss. It started off as a soft sound, like air escaping, but it began to build. By the time they'd climbed halfway up the staircase it sounded like static and, as they reached the top, it was like feral cats facing off in the nighttime.

Grafton twisted around the corner and into the small room at the top. He managed to, wincingly, keep a grip on the scalpel, keep an arm around Joan, while Isaac strode over to the window and slammed it shut. Then Isaac dragged over the side table and the dressing table to set against the door as a barricade. It wasn't much, but it would have to do.

There was a thumping on the door, first one hand and then many. Grafton waited to see if it would hold before he released Joan. Every ounce of energy drained from his muscles and he slid to the floor. Isaac stepped across quickly and took the scalpel from his hand.

Joan crawled on hands and knees, away from them. She had both hands to her throat. And when she turned to them, her face was near-purple across the patches of dry skin and her mouth was flecking with spittle.

"You selfish cunts," she spat. "You stupid, selfish cunts. You'll ruin everything."

23

The thumping at the door continued, a hissing underneath it as well. And then, suddenly, it stopped. There was complete silence. Isaac looked across at his dad. Neither of them smiled. At least when the disciples were hammering at the door, you knew where they were.

Stepping over to the window, Isaac twitched back the curtain and looked out. Could they shimmy down the drainpipe? Or jump for it? The landing seemed soft enough – moss and tangled ivy – but it was likely to break your ankle. And his dad was wincing even with the effort of sitting himself upright.

"What do we do?" Isaac asked, softly.

"There's a balcony on the other side of the landing...?"

"It's the same height. And we'd have to get past that lot."

Grafton nodded. Isaac watched his eyes flicker back and forth across the near-empty room. He held his hand against his side, the red of blood seeping through his fingers, and his face was grey and shadowed with pain.

Isaac's mind was blank of ways to get them out of there, but it kept fixing on possibilities for how the Sleepless might get in. They could get a ladder and come through the window, or take the door from its hinges, or try to smoke them out by setting fire to the building. The only thing that was stopping them was Joan. And, just like that, Isaac realised that they'd managed to get themselves into a hostage situation.

"Do we sit tight then?" he asked. "Wait for the police?"

Joan was silent now. She was sitting with her hands cupped on her crossed knees. As he spoke, though, Isaac could have sworn he saw a little shiver down the line of her spine. She didn't turn, but Isaac was sure there had been the smallest shudder. It gave him an idea.

"Aye, they can't be far away," he said, stepping over towards his dad. He gave him a nudge with his toe and nodded over to Joan. "Maybe only minutes away. They'll put a stop to this."

Grafton cleared his throat, hissed his words out. "No doubt about it."

"And they'll be well-trained in putting an end to sieges, wouldn't you say?"

"Aye." Grafton drew in a breath. "There are canisters they can throw in here: tear gas, knockout gas. That would be what they'd use. Send the lot of them to sleep."

There was a definite movement to Joan this time. She didn't turn, but her shoulders twitched and her breathing sped up a fraction. Isaac listened for noises from downstairs, but there was nothing. Whatever the disciples were up to, they surely didn't have long.

"Whatever happens," Isaac said, "the whole place will be swarming with police and the first thing they're going to do is find those who're injured or exhausted and they're going to take them to hospital."

Grafton had closed his eyes, but he still joined in. "They will," he said, "they'll sedate them."

"Course they will."

Joan brought her hands in from her knees and clasped them in front of herself. From somewhere, far-off in the distance, came a whirring sound. Isaac tried to place it — was it a lawnmower, or a chainsaw, or an outboard motor?

"That might be them," he said. "We don't know if they'll arrive by sea or land."

"Sounds like a helicopter," his dad said, his voice close to a whisper.

And, as the noise got closer, Isaac realised that it *did* sound like a helicopter. That was exactly what it was. The beat of it began to fill the room, vibrate against the wooden walls.

Joan stood and moved to the window. She pulled the curtain back. And there, against the darkness of the night, came the sweeping beam of a searchlight. It angled into the room, for the briefest second, and she flinched away from it and let the curtain fall.

The helicopter circled away from them, the noise receding slightly.

She shook her head. "They can't sedate me," she said, raising her voice over the din.

"Well," Isaac called back, "you can fight the effects of sleeping tablets, Joan, you trained yourself to. But the doctors have stronger stuff than that. The anaesthetists…"

She drew her arms across her puffer jacket, hugged herself tightly. And suddenly, she looked painfully young. Like a child dragged from bed. Shivering in spite of the extra layers, wide-eyed despite her tiredness.

"What's the time?" she said. "Is it close to midnight?"

She turned to Isaac. He was listening to the noises coming from outside. As the helicopter veered away, he could hear the sound of other engines out in front of the A-frame. Tyres against gravel. And was that a shout?

"Please, Isaac." Joan's grey eyes were pooled with tears. "What's the time?"

He shook his head. "How should I know? I don't have a watch, don't have my phone. But I know one thing, they're not going to wait around, Joan, they're not going to let you stay in here until you decide it's time to come out…"

"All I need is to be left until midnight. That's all I need. Then they'll see."

"No," Isaac called, "they'll take one look at you and decide you need to sleep. Wouldn't you say, Dad, they'll take one look at her and prepare the needle…?"

Isaac left a gap, a pause, for his dad to chime in. But there was no answer. Isaac jerked his gaze away from Joan and over to the corner where Grafton was slumped against the wall. His arms were splayed out to the side, his mouth hanging open.

"Dad!" he shouted, and moved quickly over to kneel beside him. Grafton's eyes stayed closed and his hand, when Isaac lifted it, was limp. But he was still breathing. Shallow and stuttering breaths.

"Well..." Joan's voice was at his shoulder. "Looks like it's you that needs out of here, looks like it's you that's running out of time..."

Isaac looked up at her. She was smiling thinly. "Fuck you," he said.

"Let me go downstairs," she said. "Let me go downstairs and you can walk out the front door."

"They'd never let you – Eddie and Whippet–"

"They'll do as I say."

From downstairs came the unmistakable sound of shattering glass. And then a thump and a shudder that carried up through the floorboards as the front door came in. There were some screams, and footsteps thudded across the downstairs. Then a shout – "armed police!" – and another – "armed police, stay where you are!"

"We're too late," Joan said, softly. She stepped away from Isaac, breathing slowly with long inhales. "They won't get to witness the next step..."

Isaac clasped his dad's hand in his own. "Hold in there," he whispered, "not long now."

"But you can," Joan's voice raised itself above the shouts and stampeding from downstairs. There was another thud and a voice shouted "clear!" Then came a screeching from one of the disciples, a bellowing cry from another. Isaac looked across to Joan. She gazed at him with steady, calm eyes. "You can be my witness, Isaac," she said, "you can have that privilege."

"It's over, Joan." Isaac shook his head. "You know that."

"You can witness history."

There was a banging on the door behind them. The barricade shuddered, but stood firm. The banging again and then more footsteps running up the stairs.

"They'll be in here any second," Isaac said.

"Exactly," Joan said, smiling, "what do you have to lose?"

And she walked towards him, holding out her hand.

"Give me the scalpel," she said.

Isaac looked down at the small, red scalpel he had clenched in his fingers. It was the one he used for his clay at home, only the size of a fountain pen. If it came to it, he was sure he could wrestle it back from Joan. And how much damage could she do, anyway, in the moments before the police broke through?

Behind them, at the door, came a deeper, more solid thud. Metal against wood. The door cracked, the dresser splintered, the side-table slid from the top and came crashing to the ground. And Isaac made up his mind.

Joan took the scalpel and nodded her thanks. She took a pace back into the centre of the room. The door shuddered again behind them, the dresser shifting a little further. Outside, the helicopter was circling round again, the noise of it drowning out the calls from downstairs.

Amid the chaos, Joan stood serene. With her free hand, she reached up and pulled her hair up into a knot, lifting it away from her neck. Then she took the scalpel and, with a short stabbing motion, jabbed it into the back of her head, at the hairline. Isaac watched her face, but there was barely a flicker as she began to dig and gouge, with all her strength, pressing the handle of the scalpel down as she tried to crowbar it deeper in.

"Armed police!" came the shout from outside the door. "We're coming in!" The spotlight from the helicopter trained itself on the window, sending angled beams of light through the curtains and into the small room. Again, the battering ram thudded against the door and the dresser slid towards them.

Joan's features began to contort with the effort, teeth set and eyes squeezed shut. She pressed and pushed, and Isaac could see the shudder to her arm, her neck twisting down towards her shoulder, as she used every ounce of strength she had.

And then, as the door came down, her hand seemed to punch forward slightly and her arm relaxed. Behind Isaac, bodies began to pile into the room, shouting commands. But Isaac kept his eyes on Joan, kept watching as her face cleared into a wide smile. She turned slightly, so that he could see:

The scalpel was lodged in at her hairline, down at the base of her skull, with the blade having completely disappeared and only an inch or so of the handle protruding. There was a rim of brown-red blood around it and then, trailing down the pale white skin of her neck, a single trickle of amber liquid, the colour and consistency of honey.

24

Liz watched from the bushes as the police, in their bullet-proof vests, swarmed around the A-frame like locusts. They kept darting in-and-out, bringing only instructions or shouted calls at first, but then beginning to lead out the white-robed disciples. The Sleepless had their hands secured behind their backs with cable-ties and they were being corralled onto the blue-strobed patch of grass beside the police vans.

Liz tried to measure the distance with her eyes, attempting to work out whether those disciples would be spared the worst of the blast. It didn't matter. She looked down at the small blasting machine clutched in her hand, her thumb poised over the button on the top. All she needed to look out for was Joan and the moment she was clear.

It was Grafton she caught sight of first. He was being stretchered out by two paramedics and at his side was some sort of thick padding which was rapidly turning pink. He obviously hadn't escaped Whippet then. Liz shook her head at his foolishness. What about Isaac, though? He was younger, faster. He'd have outrun them, surely...?

The paramedics moved quickly over to the ambulances parked further up the path. Those would almost certainly be out of the immediate radius of the explosion.

A few more disciples were ushered out and then one of the paramedics ducked back into the A-frame. He emerged moments later with Joan. She walked upright and her hands weren't tied. The paramedic kept a blue-gloved hand on the back of her neck. They moved slowly over to another ambulance and clambered up into the back of it.

That was perfect. Liz could take out the majority of the police by igniting the A-frame. Those who weren't killed or maimed would then go running to help the injured. Surely the paramedics would too. And Liz could run across to the ambulance and drive Joan away from the chaos. She could take her somewhere quiet, to conduct the next step in peace. It must be close to midnight by now.

Liz's eyes flicked back-and-forth from the ambulances to the A-frame. She didn't want to wait so long that the ambulance sped away but, by the same token, they were still leading disciples out. There was no point in losing followers if it could be avoided. There would be some collateral damage, of course, but there was no sense in those numbers being too high.

Moistening her lips, Liz closed her eyes and listened for Ravi's advice. If he had the blasting machine in his hand, it would have been pressed already, but if he was telling her what to do then he'd preach patience. Let another three or four out, he'd say. Liz decided on five. She opened her eyes and counted them as they came out, with their heads bowed. *One...two... three...four...*

The fourth one lifted his head. That familiar mop of hair, that flicker of a frown as he looked around himself. Her boy. He was supposed to be well-clear by now. Dropping the blasting machine, Liz sprang from the bushes. The policeman leading Isaac had an automatic rifle in his other hand. He was holding Isaac at his cuffed wrists and pushing him forwards. Liz sprinted towards them, her arms flailing.

"*Get off him!*" she screeched. "*Get your fucking filthy hands off my boy!*"

The policeman did what he was told. He released Isaac and raised his gun to level it at Liz. She was closing the distance between them. She didn't hesitate or slow.

"*He's done nothing wrong, you fucking —*"

She was only yards away from them when a blurred shadow hit her from the side. She twisted as she fell, trying to catch sight of what had brought her down. She squelched into the grass and felt her shoulder and arm jar beneath her. And then the weight fell on top of her. It was another policeman, in his bullet-proof vest, who'd rugby-tackled her before she'd had the chance to reach Isaac.

She tried to look out from under the bulk of him, tried to draw a wisp of breath into her lungs. His hand pressed her cheek down into the damp coolness of the earth. But she could still see Isaac, could still see her son, looking down at her.

"Are you ok?" she managed to hiss out.

And he smiled. With his arms behind his back, he leant down towards her. "I saw her do it, Mum," he said. "I saw her drain the toxin...I saw her take the next step."

25

When Grafton came around, Isaac was sitting by the hospital bed. He was wearing a jumper and jeans, rather than a white robe, and he had a small pizza box on his lap. As Grafton winced his way upright against the cushions, Isaac opened it.

"Tuna and cheese," he said, grinning.

Grafton smiled. "Jesus – give me the hospital food instead…"

"Ha. How you feeling, old man?"

Grafton considered. His side was agony when he moved, but pleasantly numb when he was still, and there was comfort in the tightness of the stitches underneath the dressing too. He was groggy after the surgery, after the transfusion, but he'd often felt worse after a night on the drink. Mostly he was relieved to see Isaac there, unharmed and in good spirits.

Before he could answer Isaac, there was a knock and one of the nurses popped her head around the door and smiled.

"Sorry to interrupt," she said, "but there's a call for you if you're up to it?"

"Oh, aye?" Grafton frowned. "Who's calling?"

"Someone called Danny. Says it's important."

Grafton looked across at Isaac, who raised his eyebrows.

"Go on then," Grafton said, reaching out and taking the handset from the nurse. He waited until the nurse had slipped back out of the room and then lifted the phone to his ear. "Hello, Danny?"

"I've just heard about you on the news…you ok?"

"I'll live, aye. They've patched me up."

"Quite the siege you got yourself involved in."

"Told you I could do more than traffic."

"Yes, well, seems you were right about the commune."

"Apology accepted."

There was silence on the line. Isaac lifted the TV remote and put his feet up on the bed. He peeled a slice of pizza free from the box.

"So," Danny said, on the phone, "we were wondering if you'd come in for an interview with Kathy. Once you're recovered, I mean. Not just for our show, but for the station as a whole… and other outlets might be interested too."

"Oh, aye." Grafton smiled. "Maybe it should be a regular segment, eh? Maybe a podcast?"

Danny didn't hesitate. "Good idea."

"I'll think about that, Danny."

"Of course…" Danny paused. "And, Grafton?"

"Yes?"

"Don't worry about the money for the taxi or the camera or…"

"Cheers, Danny."

Grafton hung up the phone. He turned to Isaac, ready to share his news. If they did some kind of mini-series at the station then that would leave him plenty of scope for written pieces too. He'd always fancied trying his hand at writing a book…

Isaac was holding his pizza slice halfway to his mouth, staring up at the TV. A camera was panning out on the familiar scene of the shore road leading along to the commune. Coming along the road was a slow-moving convoy of cars and camper vans. People were walking alongside, many of them bare-footed.

"A steady stream of new members," the reporter was saying, "since we first broke the story of Seattle and their twelfth day…"

"Fuck," Grafton hissed. Isaac looked across to him, with widened eyes.

"…several members in hospital with exhaustion and two with more serious injuries. Two arrests already and police investigating footage seized from the scene…"

"Pass me that remote," Grafton said.

Isaac handed him the remote and Grafton clicked the telly off.

"Don't worry about that garbage anymore, son," he said to Isaac, "you've got your summer to enjoy and then Art School to get started on."

"They're all there for Joan…" Isaac breathed, his eyes fixed on the blank screen.

"Don't worry about it. It's over."

Isaac blinked and looked across at him.

"Come on," Grafton said, "give me a slice of that stinking pizza."

26

Isaac waited until his dad fell asleep. It didn't take long. After a few bites of pizza, Grafton's head started to nod and he didn't protest when Isaac slid the crust out of his hand. Tipped back against the pillows, his breathing quickly grew shallow and his mouth slackened.

Placing the pizza box on the chair, Isaac left the room. He'd come back later.

He strode along the corridors of the hospital, bustling past nurses and a cleaner with a mop and bucket. The chemical smell of artificial lemon scoured his nostrils. He sniffed it away and carried on, through a set of double doors and towards the secure ward at the end with a policeman stationed at the door.

Further along the corridor, beyond the policeman, was a clutch of four doctors in white coats. One of them threw her hands up in the air and another gestured angrily with his clipboard. Beside them was a window into the secure room, with closed slatted blinds. Isaac wandered along the corridor towards them. The policeman eyeballed him, but didn't stir from his post.

The doctors broke apart as Isaac drew near. Turning to the wall, Isaac pretended to inspect a noticeboard. The doctor with the clipboard marched to the secure ward. The policeman opened the door for him and he stepped inside. As he did, Isaac realised that he could see a flash of his white coat through the very edge of the slatted blinds.

Isaac moved across to the window. Around the blinds was a half-inch gap. He crouched down to find an angle. And, sure enough, he could make out the doctor moving across to a small silver trolley and lifting a hypodermic needle. He began preparing it.

"Excuse me, son," the policeman called.

Ignoring him, Isaac pushed his forehead further in against the cold glass. He twisted his neck. Until he could see a slice of the bed. A long pale arm was stretched out across the covers. A handcuff hung from the thin wrist, attached to the rail along the side of the bed.

"Come away from that window," the policeman stepped along the corridor towards him.

Isaac watched as the needle went into the arm. Breathlessly, he waited. The plunger went down and the doctor pulled it out and stepped back.

He needed to see. He needed to find an angle. So that he could know whether she had finally succumbed to sleep or not. Because, if she hadn't and that moment they'd shared in the A-frame had been real, then Isaac knew that he'd spend the rest of his life searching for a way to capture the exact euphoria which spread across her face, mixing paints to precisely match the colour of the released toxin trail, forming sculptures to portray the future which had opened up for him.

The policeman grabbed at his sleeve. "Now, I'm warning you..."

Shaking him off, Isaac slammed his whole body, face-first, against the wall. His palms were flat, his stomach pressed against the paintwork. He squinted sideways through the window and, finally, saw her. Only a glimpse before the policeman pulled him away.

The glimpse had been enough. Joan was sitting up in bed, propped up against several pillows. Bandaging was wrapped around her head, with a spray of brown hair showing at the top. There was a drip attached to her other arm and a heart-rate monitor. The covers were tucked neatly across her legs.

And her eyes – those grey irises flecked with blue – were still fully open.

27

The bay at Kilchoan was certainly showing its best side for the cameras: sky of the purest blue with cotton-wool clouds. It was such a clear day that you could see a delivery van inching slowly along the shore road out on Mull. Cormorants flew above the water in a v-formation like an air-force display team, welcoming the new arrivals.

There was a group of protestors gathered, as before, at the gate to the commune. They'd been eased to the side by the news crews with their bulky camera equipment. The protestors held their placards resolutely in the air and glowered over at Liz as she stepped out onto the gravel, but they were mostly quiet, mostly respectful of the fact that – through the course of the morning – the scales had tipped and the Sleepless now outnumbered the locals.

Behind the commune, a chain of disciples were passing white tiles up to the hillside. Several of the wooden pallets at the side of the office contained no more than building materials. The tiles glinted in the sunlight as they were passed hand-to-hand. Those at the end of the chain were beginning to arrange them into their pattern. Debbie was in charge of that. There had been those who'd said that they should wait, that it was something only Joan could oversee, but Liz had overruled them: the television cameras were here now.

A woman in a beanie hat fussed and fiddled with a radio-microphone, looking for somewhere to clip it on Liz's robe. She eventually settled on taking a pinch of the fabric, up by the breast, and securing it there. Then she pressed the battery pack into Liz's hand and stepped back. The reporter was a young man with slicked hair. He was likely to be the only person for many miles wearing a tie.

"We're with Elizabeth Whelan," he said, into the camera, "a

spokesperson for the commune."

His accent was that curious mix of cut-glass and drawl you might find on the quad at Edinburgh University. He turned to Liz and the camera swivelled too.

"There were arrests here last night, of course, and several people were taken to hospital. Is there a culture of violence and bullying behaviour within the commune?"

Liz pursed her lips. "Of course not. One of the arrests you mention was of an ex-soldier with mental health problems. He doesn't represent the commune or our beliefs and we hope he gets the help he needs."

"As well as those in hospital, of course?"

"Of course."

"And your leader, Joan, is one of those hospitalised, is that right?"

Liz flinched, but kept her gaze steady. "Joan is one of our disciples," she said, evenly, "and she's proof-positive of the benefits of our teachings and our way of engaging with the world. She is the first to demonstrate that the next step can be taken and we are grateful to her."

"So, is it correct that she's stayed awake for twelve days?"

"She's not the important one."

"But…she's the one who's been staying awake, is that not true?"

Liz eased a breath out through her teeth. "She's a shining example of Swami Ravi's teaching," she said, "but it's our triumph as much as hers, it's our collective accomplishment."

"Whose teaching, sorry?"

"Swami Ravi."

The reporter paused. He was blinking rapidly at her, as if trying to communicate something through morse code. It was obvious that he'd done painfully little research, that he was all-at-sea here.

"Swami Ravi is our true leader," Liz said, "he's the one

who inspired Joan, yes, but he's also the one who gives us all a roadmap for our lives, a sense of direction and purpose. He is the one who prophesized the twelfth day and who will lead all of us into a new era for humankind."

She looked away from the reporter, directly down the barrel of the camera. She was imagining hundreds of people, thousands of people, searching the internet for Swami Ravi. They would find videos of his speeches, downloadable documents of his teachings. They would find the petition that had been set up against his incarceration, the accounts of his trail which laid bare the inconsistencies and inaccuracies in the case against him, the social media pages where they could donate money and aid the fight for justice. Where they could join the Sleepless and commit to taking the next step.

Liz moved to the side so that the camera had an uninhibited view of the hillside. The white tiles, against the green and brown scrub, had been arranged into the oval shape of an eye. Disciples moved within it, forming the iris. Later it would be planted with flowers and a spotlight would be placed in the centre as a pupil.

"And this proclamation," Liz said, "acts as a beacon, up on the hillside behind our commune, to show the way for anyone and everyone who wishes to join us. Anyone who wants to learn the methods of our dear Swami Ravi and follow in the footsteps of his most dedicated disciple, Joan."

Liz looked to the camera again and smiled broadly. She had no doubt that Ravi would see the clip, that someone would get it into his hands. And, when he did, he would know that she had come through for him, that she had succeeded in her task. Here, finally, was a secure home for him and his followers. When he was released he could come here to recuperate and rehabilitate, to teach and to write. They could keep him safe here, away from outside interference and prying eyes. This was where he could establish his legacy and ensure his place in history.

Joan could be part of that, if she wished, or she could stay away. It didn't matter, she had served her purpose.

"Yes," Liz said, making a sweeping gesture with her hand that took in the commune and the hillside behind, with its white-framed eye staring out towards the sea in the bay. "All of this is his."

Acknowledgements

I began developing this idea during a screenwriting development course, Write 4 Film, run by the Scottish Film Talent Network. My thanks to Holly Daniel and Anna Seifert Speck for support during that process and, especially, to my fellow writers on the programme: Alice Nelson, Laurie Motherwell, Russel McLean, Leyla Josephine, and Rachelle Atalla.

The first draft was finished just before the first Covid lockdown and the enthusiasm and support of Vicky Blunden and Joanna Swainson, along with the patience of my family, got me through multiple edits and submissions conducted alongside home-schooling chaos. Huge gratitude to Isabelle Kenyon, at Fly on the Wall Press, for taking on the manuscript and for being such a wonderfully attentive and engaged editor and cheerleader for my writing.

Thanks to Martin Stewart for early read-through and for running chats, and to my sister, Katy, for notes delivered over coffee. Thanks also to colleagues and students at University of Stirling, particularly Kevin MacNeil and Chris Powici. My parents, Ann and Charles, took us to Ardnamurchan for family holidays every summer when we were younger, so thanks to them for that experience – apologies for twisting those wonderful memories into a cult thriller!

As ever, there were a huge number of books and films which were useful for the writing process, but I'd like to mention two in dispatches: Fred D'Aguiar's wonderful Children of Paradise and Tim Guest's My Life in Orange. I also had a number of albums which I listened to during the writing of the novel, but the one which will forever be linked in my mind as the 'soundtrack' is Kamasi Washington's The Epic. Finally, thanks and love to my girls: Orla, Cora, Sarah, and Mango the cat xx

About the Author

Liam Bell is author of three previous novels, Man at Sea, So It Is and The Busker, as well as short stories and articles in publications including New Writing Scotland, Litro, and Northwords Now. He was born in Orkney and grew up in Glasgow. He has studied at Queen's University Belfast, the University of Glasgow, and the University of Surrey and now teaches at the University of Stirling. More information at www.liammurraybell.com or on twitter @liammurraybell.

About Fly on the Wall Press

A publisher with a conscience.
Political, Sustainable, Ethical.
Publishing politically-engaged, international fiction, poetry and cross-genre anthologies on pressing issues. Founded in 2018 by founding editor, Isabelle Kenyon.

Some other publications:

The Sound of the Earth Singing to Herself by Ricky Ray

We Saw It All Happen by Julian Bishop

Odd as F*ck by Anne Walsh Donnelly

Imperfect Beginnings by Viv Fogel

These Mothers of Gods by Rachel Bower

Sin Is Due To Open In A Room Above Kitty's by Morag Anderson

Fauna by David Hartley

How To Bring Him Back by Clare HM

Hassan's Zoo and A Village in Winter by Ruth Brandt

No One Has Any Intention of Building A Wall by Ruth Brandt

Snapshots of the Apocalypse by Katy Wimhurst

Demos Rising

Exposition Ladies by Helen Bowie

A Dedication to Drowning by Maeve McKenna

The House with Two Letterboxes by Janet H Swinney

Climacteric by Jo Bratten

The State of Us by Charlie Hill

The Unpicking by Donna Moore

Social Media:

@fly_press (Twitter) @flyonthewallpress (Instagram)

@flyonthewallpress (Facebook)

www.flyonthewallpress.co.uk